To remember what you've read, write your
initials in a square!

WOMEN OF A DANGEROUS AGE

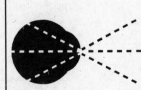

This Large Print Book carries the
Seal of Approval of N.A.V.H.

WOMEN OF A DANGEROUS AGE

FANNY BLAKE

THORNDIKE PRESS
A part of Gale, Cengage Learning

Detroit • New York • San Francisco • New Haven, Conn • Waterville, Maine • London

GALE
CENGAGE Learning®

LIBRARY OF CONGRESS CATALOGING-IN-PUBLICATION DATA

Blake, Fanny.
    Women of a dangerous age / by Fanny Blake. — Large print edition.
       pages ; cm. — (Thorndike Press large print women's fiction)
    ISBN-13: 978-1-4104-6522-1 (hardcover)
    ISBN-10: 1-4104-6522-5 (hardcover)
    1. Loss (Psychology)—Fiction. 2. Separated women—Fiction. 3. Large type books. I. Title.
PR6102.L3425W65 2013
823'.92—dc23   2013035511

Published in 2014 by arrangement with St. Martin's Press, LLC

Printed in the United States of America
1 2 3 4 5 6 7 18 17 16 15 14

To Robin, Matt, Nick and Spike

1

'You're going to India?' Fiona had sounded as if Lou was about to enter a dark labyrinth: fraught with danger and quite unsuitable.

'Yes, I am.' As she spoke, Lou had realised that was exactly what she was going to do. Going away would absolve her from all the problems of Christmas at home. She would escape from Hooker, their three children and her matchmaking friends who seemed to pursue their goal with an untimely and unwelcome fervour. Instead, she would separate the last thirty years of her life from the next thirty by getting out of the country — on her own.

Lou was enjoying for as long as possible the anticipation of the moment when she'd enter the Taj Mahal. Joining the scrum of tourists, she put the cloth overshoes provided for visitors over her functional but deeply unflattering walking sandals and climbed the steps towards the main entrance. Despite people crowding by her as she photographed the intricate inlaid marble-work, the interior was every bit as impressive as she had hoped. She skirted the tourists throwing coins down the steps to the tombs and followed the perimeter of the wall, admiring the detailed workmanship up close, looking up towards the solar motif in the dome. The noise made by schoolchildren experimenting with the echo was deafening. Twenty minutes later she emerged, squinting against the brightness and wishing for the umpteenth time that she hadn't left her wide-brimmed sun hat and sunglasses in their last hotel, in Jaipur.

The clear blue sky was only interrupted by the winged silhouettes of kites soaring high above the white dome. Lou walked behind the mausoleum to stare across the dried-up Yamuna river bed, imagining Shah Jahan, imprisoned by his own son in the Agra Fort not far along the bank with only a view of the Taj to console him. When Mumtaz, his favourite wife, died giving birth to their fourteenth child, he had embarked on the task of creating this exquisite memorial to her. Twenty-two years and twenty thousand workmen and specialists later . . . Lou tried to imagine what it must be like to feel that strongly about someone after so many years of marriage. Some of the shine must surely have worn off with all those children. Three had proved quite enough for her and Hooker.

She found a quiet spot in the ornamental garden where she could sit on the grass. After a moment, she delved into her string bag for a bottle of water and the guidebook that smelled of the suntan lotion that had leaked onto it the day before. She peeled apart the couple of pages devoted to the Taj, then shut them. She could read later. The thing was to experience the place to its full in the short time she had.

Feeling a little less frazzled now she was in the shade of a tree, she watched the chipmunks race through the bushes. The sound of tourist chatter was broken by screeches from electric green parrots that swooped over her head. A group of Indian students asked in broken English if they could have their photo taken with her. She smiled into their camera, conscious of how different she must look to them, her lime green linen outfit and red scarf standing out against their drab trousers and white shirts, her fair skin and wild reddish hair providing such a contrast to their dark complexions.

Once they'd finished asking her about London, she went to hunt for her travelling companions. The sun beat down on the queue of tourists jostling to be snapped on 'Diana's bench', with the Taj framed behind them. Demure Indian women in coloured saris rubbed shoulders with scruffy backpackers, neatly turned out schoolchildren and well-heeled Europeans and Americans on luxury tours. Lou was in two minds whether or not to join them. In exchange for a short wait, she'd have an ironically apt memento of her visit. Like Diana, alone in life. She was amused by the comparison, but only for a second. Come on, woman. Get over yourself. After all, whose choice is it that you're on your own? Certainly not Hooker's.

'I'll take yours,' said a voice behind her, 'if you'll take mine.'

Lou turned to find one of the other two single women on the trip standing behind her. She knew her name was Ali but that was about it. During the previous ten days, as they'd journeyed from Udaipur to Jodphur and Jaipur, Ali had kept herself at a discreet distance from her fellow travellers. Not that she had been unpleasant, joining in with whatever was going on, but, when the opportunity arose, she'd bury herself in a book or separate herself from the group, going off to explore on her own. Wandering around a gallery of exquisite Indian miniatures, exploring the Amber or Merenghar Forts, the piled-high fabric emporiums or cluttered jewellery shops, Ali was always the last to tear herself away, as if not wanting to miss the slightest detail, sometimes sketching in her notebook or taking a final photograph. After dinner, she almost immediately retired to bed. Lou, on the other hand, had thrown herself into the group, keen to find out more about the people she was travelling with, wanting to share and compare everything new she was experiencing. She had nicknamed Ali 'the cat who walked alone', yet couldn't help but be intrigued by her, the one person on the trip she'd failed to get to know. Ali was taller than Lou, younger, trimmer (not hard) and more elegant than her too. Not of course that any of these things could be held against her. Her oval face was framed by bobbed dark hair whose neat shiny finish gave away a small fortune spent on hairdressers and products. At that moment, she was looking at Lou, waiting for her answer.

Lou made up her mind. 'Yes. Why not?'

Together, they walked towards the Lotus Pool.

'Isn't this place incredible?' asked Ali. 'Beats every photo I've ever seen of it.'

They both gazed at the Taj.

'Those screens and the inlay-work in there are amazing, quite beautiful.'

'Bloody noisy though,' said Lou, and laughed.

So, as they began to talk about their reactions to the Taj, to the contrasting chaos of Agra and about the highlights of their trip, their friendship took its first steps.

By the time it was their turn to sit on the marble bench, Lou could feel the sweat running down her spine. Anxious about dropping Ali's professional-looking camera, she wiped her hands on her linen trousers. When she'd packed them in London, she'd imagined herself looking cool, stylish even, amid the heat and dust of India. Instead, they looked as if they'd been scrunched into a ball and put on without sight of an iron. She was aware of the sweat marks spreading under the arms of her not-quite-loose-enough, short-sleeved top as she waited for Ali to pose.

Wiping her brow, Ali took up Princess Diana's exact position: hands on her knees, clasped around her sunglasses, legs at a slight angle, head lowered to one side. She looked up coyly through her fringe. Afterwards, she laughed. 'That'll confuse my boyfriend. He's bound to wonder if there's a hidden message. Something about my wanting to be alone. As if.'

Lou returned Ali's camera, then fumbled in her bag for her modest compact bought especially for the holiday. As she passed it over, it slipped from her grip. Her attempt to catch it was about as successful as any she'd made on the rounders pitch at school. The camera bounced out of her hands and clattered to the ground. She could feel the crowd behind them growing mutinous at the delay so she snatched it up, saying tightly, 'I'm sure it'll be fine.' But when she pressed the On button, nothing happened.

'Let's use mine,' offered Ali. 'I can at least email you the picture.'

Lou took her place, annoyed by her clumsiness, and pushed her hair back, hoping her touch would tame the wayward frizz (much worse in the heat) into something as effortlessly chic as Ali's bob, and mustered a smile. As soon as the camera clicked, an American couple were already edging her off the seat, wanting their turn.

'What do you think?' Ali asked, tilting the camera so Lou could see.

In the sun, Lou's hair had transformed into a hectic halo that framed her face. Off the forehead was never a good look on her, but especially not when she was squinting and her forehead and nose were shiny with sweat. Her irritation with herself showed in her face. The way she had half turned from the camera made her look as if she had put on about a stone in weight. Not of course that she cared. Not really. But it was a look she'd rather wasn't captured for posterity. In the background, the Taj gleamed in the sunlight. She grimaced. 'Not exactly Princess Di, is it?'

Ali studied the image again. 'Mmm. But you're not exactly working with Mario Testino either.'

Laughing and, in Lou's case, resigned, both women stepped away from the bench and joined the crowds thronging the gardens.

'If you don't mind, I really want to have a last walk round alone,' said Ali, slinging her camera over her shoulder. 'Just to take it all in. I'll see you back at the gate.'

Lou nodded, happy at the chance of having a final wander herself. As the trip drew to an end, she was conscious of trying to drain every last sensation from the few days she had left. She wanted to be able to relive the holiday in detail during the winter months that lay ahead back home.

She thought back to that conversation with Fiona three months earlier, when she'd had no plans to go away over the Christmas break. Then, just as she thought she would explode if anyone else asked her how she was, or what she would be doing at Christmas now that she was single again, inspiration had come from nowhere. In reply to her close friend's invitation to her and her husband Charlie's remote Devon farmhouse bought only for its vast unrealised potential that, two years later, had still to be realised, Lou blurted, 'Actually, I've made plans. I'm going to India.'

The words were out before she'd even thought them. She still wasn't sure which of them had been more surprised by her answer.

To everyone's surprise, her own included, she had booked herself the last place on a 'Highlights of Rajasthan' tour. She had been told to expect the poverty and squalor, the streets teeming with people, the colours, the smells but nothing had prepared her for what she had experienced. Never had she been exposed to so many dizzying extremes at once. As exciting, after years of holidaying as a family or alone with Hooker, was the discovery that she enjoyed meeting new people, having responsibility for no one but herself. The holiday had done just what she'd hoped and drawn a thick line between her past and her future. When she returned home, everything would have changed. She would no longer be living with Hooker in their family home. She would be an independent woman with a life, a new business and a home of her own. She was resolved not to mess up this second chance.

As Ali walked away from Lou, she thought about their conversation. 'My boyfriend'. That's what she had called Ian. A word she had never used to describe him before, but it had emerged all by itself when they were waiting their turn for the photograph. She liked the description, the unexpected way the two words made her feel: secure, loved, part of a unit even though she and Ian had seen so little of one another since the evening he made his surprise announcement. He wanted 'to put the relationship on a more permanent footing', to have her not as a mistress but as a partner. That's what he had said. There was a lot to work out, not least of all his breaking the news to his wife, which he wouldn't do until after Christmas. 'It wouldn't be fair otherwise.' Even though his marriage had been over in all but name for years, he still had the decency to treat his wife with consideration and respect. That was just another aspect to his character that she loved and admired. Until he told his wife, Ali had to hug her secret to herself, enjoy its promise, and wait.

For the last couple of months before she came to India, work had taken them both in different directions. The lead-up to Christmas was always the busiest time of her year when people wanted to splurge their money on bespoke jewellery, so she had been busy designing and making to commission, as well as selling from her latest collection. At the same time, Ian had been called abroad to discuss some potential corporate merger. She hadn't taken in the details. They had at last managed to find time for each other the evening before she left. To her disappointment, he had to go home before midnight. He didn't go into details and she hadn't pressed him. She didn't want to know how he was spending Christmas with his wife while she was away. Next year, it would just be the two of them. Knowing that had been enough.

As Ali browsed through the rooms of the tiny museum, she thought how much Ian would have enjoyed being here with her. Well, as this was the last holiday she'd be taking on her own, she had decided to make the most of it. When she'd joined the group in Delhi, she'd been disappointed to find her travelling companions were a more sober bunch than she'd holidayed with in the past. Three smug couples, a middle-aged mother and her son, a widowed doctor and a man travelling alone since his wife had a fear of flying, and another slightly older woman she now knew to be Lou, whose idiosyncratic dress sense and wild hair made her look as if she at least might be fun. Ali had watched Lou with the others. At first Lou had been tentative, as if exploring her ability to make new friends but, as the days passed, she had become more confident. Soon her laugh was one of the things that marked her out, a loud earthy giggle, often at the centre of whatever was going on. Unlike her, Ali preferred to hold herself back so no one could make any demands on her, nor she on them.

She glanced over the architectural drawings, then stepped outside for a final look at the Taj, magnificent symbol for eternal love. With Ian in the forefront of her thoughts again, she crossed the garden to join the others near the huge arched main gateway, where she found Lou engaged in a vigorous discussion with Bharat, their guide.

'But I'd rather walk to the car park,' Lou

was saying, quite unaffected by the way those in the group already there were glaring at her, no doubt impatient to reach their hotel, a good wash and a gin and tonic.

'No, no, madam,' insisted Bharat. 'You must take bus.'

'But Bharat, it can't be more than half a kilometre at the most. I won't hold you up if I start now and I'll meet you there.' She was being quite calm, controlled but determined.

Ali walked over to the two of them. 'I'd like to walk too, Bharat. Nothing'll happen to us, if that's what you're worried about. There are too many people around.'

Surprised by her intervention, Lou smiled, clearly glad of the support. She flicked her scarf over her right shoulder.

Apart from the anxiety about deviating from the schedule by letting two of his charges out of his sight, Bharat seemed bemused that any right-minded visitor would want to walk when there was perfectly good transport. But he folded in the face of their joint determination. 'OK, madam. You go together. We'll meet you in the car park.'

Once beyond the gateway, past the entry queues — one for nationals, one for foreigners — waiting to get through security, they found themselves outside the sandstone walls. Immediately, they were besieged by postcard and souvenir sellers, mostly young children, who swarmed around them, thrusting their wares under their noses, shouting prices and persuasion alongside would-be guides.

'Where you from, madam? England? Very nice place. London, Manchester, Birmingham, Leicester . . . You want tour guide for Red Fort? Very important see everything.'

Dejected-looking horses and camels decorated with tinsel, their skin stretched tight over protruding bones, were hitched to carriages at the side of the road. Tuk-tuk and rickshaw drivers were touting for business too. 'You want rickshaw. Good price. Baby Taj then Agra Fort. Show you my magical India. Two hundred rupees.'

The two women had been in India long enough to know that the only way through was to say little, and keep on walking. Eventually, to their relief, everyone's attention switched to a large group of Americans emerging from the complex behind them and they were left alone.

'Thank God for that,' said Lou. 'I don't want to get Bharat into trouble but we spend so much time cooped up in the minibus. I had to experience some of this for myself.' As they waited in a herd of goats for the stragglers to climb onto the scrubby verge, a pair of ragged dark-eyed children approached them, hands out, begging, 'Dollar, dollar.' A man selling sugar cane juice turned his blue mangle and shouted something from the other side of the road. Lou shook her head and carried on walking, Ali running to catch up, the ragamuffins running behind her. The smells of horseshit, bad drains, woodsmoke and cooking drifted through the dusty air. They stood to one side as an electric bus whirred past. Ali took a couple of snaps of a moth-eaten camel pulling a cart, then another of the children who giggled when she showed them the image on her camera.

'I just wanted to escape the group for a bit longer. Not that there's anything wrong with them,' she hurried to add. For some reason, she didn't want Lou to think badly of her.

'They're not that bad.' Lou smiled. 'You just haven't got to know them.'

'I know, I haven't made much effort.' She sounded suddenly anxious.

'Don't worry,' Lou reassured her. 'You're down as a free spirit. I think everyone rather envies your independence.'

'Well, it's my last holiday alone, so I've been making the most of it.'

21

'Seems to me that travelling alone but in the company of strangers is about a million times less fraught and tantrum-filled than travelling with family — especially my husband.' Lou laughed at the thought. 'Show him an airport and I'll show you a man on the point of a coronary. And that's before we've even left the country.'

'You're married?' Ali noticed Lou wore no rings.

'Not any more.' Her face assumed a guarded expression. 'I guess you're not either?'

'No, but I'm moving in with my boyfriend when I get back.' Her cheeks were burning. Letting even a bit of her secret go made it feel less special, even though Lou didn't know her or Ian. She immediately wished she hadn't said anything. 'I'm not meant to talk about it really. At least, not until he's told his wife.'

'Oh! His wife,' Lou echoed.

Ali thought she heard disapproval, but when she looked, Lou simply smiled and gave the slightest shake of her head. They detoured round a white cow standing among a pile of rubbish and plastic bags. 'Odd the way sacred animals exist on such an unsacred diet.' And the subject was closed.

For the rest of the short way, they walked in a companionable silence, each lost in her own thoughts. Entering the busy car park filled with sudden exhaust and engine noise, they found their minibus and chose two seats side by side.

As they drove to the safari lodge on the Chambal river where they were spending their last two nights, Lou found herself enjoying Ali's company more and more. There was something about her that reminded Lou of her younger sister, Jenny, killed only eighteen months earlier in a motorway pile-up. Although Jenny had been a loner all her life, the two sisters had shared a particular bond. Since they were teenagers, they had confided only in one another, knowing that all their secrets were safe. Since Jenny's death no one had come near to filling her place in Lou's life, not even Fiona, her closest friend. Talking to Ali, Lou found a similar intensity to Jenny's. She heard something like Jenny's dry sense of humour, and sensed the same reserve. Lou had been given a glimpse into Ali's life but she didn't expect her to tell any more. Given her own unwillingness to bare her soul at this point in her life, Lou sympathised with the younger woman's reticence and didn't press her. She was relieved not to have to account for herself and explain the actions she'd taken only months before. There'd be plenty of time to examine the repercussions of those when she got home.

For those last two nights, Ali unexpectedly opened up. She followed Lou's lead and chatted with the others after supper around the dying embers of the bonfire, easily finding her place within the group. But this happened so late in the trip that there was no pressure for her to give anything of herself away. By the time they returned to Delhi for the flight home, Lou had arranged to meet Ali again on their home turf. She was intrigued by 'the cat who walked alone'.

2

Delhi airport was teeming with people.
Lou's suitcase felt heavy and unwieldy as
she concentrated on tipping it to one side
so that it could roll along on the one wheel
that hadn't jammed. She hated airports,
hated flying and was trying to drift into the
zone necessary for any air travel to be . . .
not pleasurable, never that, but endurable.
She was looking for that Zen-like calm
where anything problematic would just slip
by her. Key to that condition was maintain-
ing a cool indifference towards everything
going on around her. Otherwise, she would
be reduced to a gibbering state of impatience, then fear.

She and Ali stood together in the queue
that snaked away from the check-in desk.
They didn't talk, just observed the hordes:
families with children refusing to stay in
line; trolleys laden with belongings heading
with their owners towards a new start in

another country; couples entwined after the romantic holiday of a lifetime; others barely speaking.

Eventually, they reached the front. She hefted her case onto the scales, catching her breath as she felt an ominous twinge in the small of her back, and watched the number of kilograms clocking up. Please God, let the airline official turn a blind eye.

'It's four kilos overweight,' he announced, barely looking up.

Fuck. She should never have put in the fabric she'd bought in Udaipur. Instead, she should have had them shipped home like the rest of the fabric and the two bedspreads she hadn't been able to resist in Jodhpur. 'But you'll let it go?' she wheedled.

The official was unmoved. 'You'll have to pay the surcharge, I'm afraid. The desk's over there.' He could have been pointing anywhere. 'Or you'll have to remove some of the contents.'

And do what with them? Leave them on the terminal floor?

She could feel herself dithering, flustered, incapable of making a sensible decision. To pay a fortune for a few lengths of Indian silk, or not to pay? That was the question. Fortunately, Ali answered it. 'For God's sake, you mustn't pay on principle. You don't have to pay more for your seat because you're heavier than me.'

'Thanks for that,' Lou muttered.

'No, seriously, the same should apply to luggage. There's some room in my case. Let's just transfer a few things and I'll give them back when we land.'

Relieved to have her dilemma so easily resolved, Lou agreed and yanked her case off the weighing machine. As she slid it back towards the queue, the implications of this perhaps rash decision struck her. She was about to reveal her totally shoddy packing techniques to the entire airport. But too late now. Someone else had taken her place at the desk and Ali was already unzipping her case. She flipped the lid back to reveal her perfectly folded capsule wardrobe taking up two-thirds of the available space.

Reluctantly, remembering the haphazard approach she had taken to her own packing, Lou began to pull at the zip of her suitcase, eyeing the straining seams. It had only consented to fasten when she'd sat on the case and shifted her weight about on top so the zip could inch round. The only way forward was to repeat the process. She sat down heavily, then, holding onto the zip, her knuckles white with the effort of not letting go, she began to pull. Slowly at first, it then gave with a little rush before slowing again. With Ali holding the two open sides as close together as possible, the last corner was turned and eventually, to the amusement of everyone alleviating the boredom of their wait by watching her, the final side was coerced into unzipping.

Self-conscious, Lou clambered off the case, half falling as she did. Steadying herself with her hand on Ali's butt, she was aware that most of the queue could almost certainly see all the way down her cleavage as she bent forward. Mortified, she straightened up as fast as she could, adjusting her top at the same time.

Released from her weight, the case sprang open at the very moment that someone's uncontrolled child cannoned into it. The contents jack-in-the-boxed into the air. Her Zen-like calm still nowhere in the vicinity, Lou could only think of one thing as she watched her most intimate garments hit the terminal floor. Why had she packed the Indian silks at the bottom of the case, leaving all her more personal bits and pieces on top? Galvanised into action, she reached for the bra that was spread-eagled on the floor in front of the crowd and folded it in half, tucking the straps inside. She'd never thought of her breasts as especially large until this moment when the D-cups assumed an embarrassing enormity. Neither had she noticed how much the once pretty pink lace had faded and discoloured to a dusty greyish colour. If only she'd invested in the sexy new underwear she'd thought might help mark the start of her single life.

Just then a young boy made a dash for it, her other bra capping his head, the straps dangling over his ears. She watched in disbelieving horror as his mother yelled after him to stop, then gave chase across the terminal.

Ali was no help. She was bent double laughing. At least everyone else had the grace to pretend not to be.

As Lou shoved one bra down the side of Ali's case, the second was handed to her by the smirking child whose apologetic parent had a firm grip of his arm. She stuffed that one down the other side, her face burning with embarrassment. Still no one moved to help her. On her hands and knees, she reached out to grab the pairs of pants that littered the floor. Once they were stowed, she turned her attention to the contents of her washbag that had rolled towards the check-in.

As she snatched up the tweezers (the laser treatment to her chin was something else that had been too low on her priority list) and the bumper pack of ibuprofen, she became aware of a pair of unfamiliar male hands retrieving the pair of Bridget Jones knickers that she'd missed — the big cream M&S ones that only she knew she possessed. Until now. She'd brought them because they were perfect for the woman who only took her kit off when she was alone and who wanted to disguise her VPL without resorting to the bum-splitting discomfort of a thong. She certainly hadn't envisaged sharing them with anyone else. They had landed on his very shiny dark brown left brogue. She watched aghast as the hands folded them once, then twice, before holding out the neat parcel to her. She wasn't sure she could endure another moment of this.

Who would fold another person's knickers? Mortified, she glanced up to lock eyes with a smart, suited Indian man of a certain age who was squatting beside her. He smiled a sympathetic smile. She had watched the DVD of *Slumdog Millionaire* for the *nth* time before she left, and the only thought that crossed her mind was that he was a dead ringer for the quiz-show host played by Anil Kapoor. It couldn't be. Could it? Of course not. She took the knickers from his hand as briskly as she could without snatching.

'Thank you,' she mumbled, wishing the floor would rip apart to swallow her and her bloody case.

He nodded, straightened up and looked away. But Lou hadn't missed the glint of amusement in his eye.

Meanwhile, Ali had recovered herself and had squatted down beside her to help Lou retrieve the last few clothes and shove them into her own case. 'Let's get this sorted. Quick. A gin and tonic is definitely called for.'

'A large one!' Lou agreed.

An hour and a half later, they had reached the departure gate, the alcohol having aided the recovery of Lou's sense of humour. They were still laughing about what had happened as they walked down the tunnel onto the plane. Dodging elbows as hand luggage was stowed above heads and sidling past passengers preparing to sit down, they made their way through the nirvana of business class to the unholy limbo at the back of the plane. Lou was leading the way, checking the numbers of the seats, when she stopped dead. Ali bumped into her. 'Easy!' she said, taking a step back. 'What're you doing?'

'It's him!' said Lou, feeling her inner

temperature soar, the perspiration prickle. She gestured down the aisle to where, in the outside seat of three, sat her knicker-rescuer immersed in a magazine. 'Those are our seats! You'll have to sit in the middle. I can't small-talk with someone who's on such intimate terms with my underwear.'

'Sounds like a perfect match to me,' said Ali.

For once, Lou was unamused.

As they waited for him to stand up and let them into their seats, Lou tried but failed to avoid his eye. They acknowledged each other with the briefest of nods before Lou, feeling herself blush, looked away and slid into her seat by the window, followed by Ali.

Trying not to panic about having to spend the next eight hours cramped in the economy seat, Lou jammed the airline freebies into her seat-back pocket. Preparing for take-off and landing were the parts of the flight that scared her most. Shutting her eyes, she tried again to find the calm that had so far eluded her. She breathed in, closing her eyes and trying to direct her breath out through the centre of her forehead, her third eye. Wasn't that what the yoga teacher had said on the course she'd taken that summer, as he encouraged the class in the final relaxation exercise? She hadn't understood what he was on about as she lay freezing on the floor of the decaying church hall, wishing she'd remembered to bring a blanket, and she certainly didn't understand now. She tried again.

'What *are* you doing?' Ali's voice interrupted her concentration.

'Breathing. Not panicking. I'll be fine.' (Don't talk to me.)

'Tell me about your shop then.' Ali ignored the incipient hysteria in Lou's voice. 'Now we're on our way home, we might as well think about what we're going back to.'

'Give me a minute.' Lou took in another breath and tightened her grip on the armrests, closing her eyes again. She was better dealing with her fear on her own. She refocused her mind. What *would* be waiting for her at the end of the flight? Just the words 'Puttin' on the Ritz: vintage and vintage-inspired clothes' gave her a buzz of excitement. Her online business selling the vintage clothes that she'd acquired over years of working in the fashion biz, trawling vintage fairs, charity and junk shops, car boot sales and relatives' attics was going to expand into the here and now. Finding the premises would be her number one priority when she got home.

Home. Rather than open her eyes to her present surroundings, she let herself drift back to the day, a couple of months earlier, when she had moved into the small Victorian house that she had inherited from Jenny.

'Are you sure you'll be all right?' Hooker, her husband of nearly thirty-one years, had grasped her hand as tightly as if he was trying to pull her from a fast-flowing river. Then she remembered how, apparently satisfied that he'd succeeded, he leaned forward for a kiss.

She pulled back, ignoring the look of displeasure that crossed his face, reclaiming her hand and abandoning herself to the current that was already carrying her out of his reach. 'I'll be absolutely fine,' she said, firmly.

Until months earlier, that moment had only been wishful thinking, just like those times when she was drifting off to sleep and had fantasised about him leaving her or had even gone as far as imagining his funeral, what she'd wear and how she'd behave: respectful and grief-stricken on the outside, but gleeful about her new freedom on the inside. She was ashamed about those darker moments but he hadn't always been the most ideal husband, especially of late, and it wasn't as if she'd really believed anything bad would happen — or wanted it to. Not really. She had tightened her grip on the door as she began to shut him out of her life.

'You are sure you're doing the right thing?' He stood his ground. 'It's not too late to change your mind and come home, you know.'

Leaning against the door frame, she willed her apprehension not to show. She knew him too well. If he spotted any weakness in her, he'd be quick to exploit it. 'We've been through this a thousand and one times.' She spoke slowly, as if drumming the information through his skull and into his brain. 'We don't love each other any more. We've agreed on that. So I'm going to live here now. It's over.'

She remembered how she'd been reduced to romantic clichés. But they were true. She didn't love him any more. And she doubted that he'd loved her for years, not really. Her sadness came less from their parting and more from the fact that their separation marked the end of their family as they had all known it.

Cramped in her airline seat, she flexed her feet, lifted one leg and rotated her ankle, then the other. Ali said something, but she took no notice. To take her mind off the flight, she forced herself to return to *that* day, the day that marked the start of her new independence. From now on, she was going to be devoting some time to herself instead of to the hours demanded by being Hooker's chief wardrobe mistress, cook and bottle-washer: hours during which she had chosen to dismiss the occasional unfounded suspicion that Hooker might be playing away. That was a side to their recent life together that she'd never confronted. While the children were in their teens, she was determined to put them first. But they were grown up now and the need for that was finally over.

He'd run his hand over his thinning hair as if checking it was still there, clearly bewildered by her unfamiliar resolve but not convinced. 'All right,' he said, an edge of aggression entering his voice. 'I'll go. But don't expect me to wait for you forever. That's all. Let's hope my door hasn't closed by the time you change your mind.' He turned to leave, obviously pleased with his parting shot, and quite confident that she'd be back.

'Mmm. Let's.' She directed the words towards his back, not expecting him to turn this time. Insisting on having the last word was one of his shortcomings. One of his *many* shortcomings, she corrected herself, as she shut the door at last. She'd heard him rev his precious midlife-crisis of a sports car before he roared off, leaving her alone at last.

As if on cue, the roar of the jet engines intensified and the plane shook as it trundled towards take-off. Her white-knuckle grip on the arms of her seat tightened. Only another few minutes and she'd be able to relax — unless they crashed, of course. Everyone knew that take-off and landing were the most vulnerable moments of any flight. The shaking stopped, her ears filled as if she was underwater, then popped. Pushed back in her seat by the pressure, as the plane climbed to cruising height, she relaxed her hands.

'You've gone very pale.' Ali's voice came from a distance. 'Are you OK?'

Lou opened one eye, then the other. Everything was as it should be. The other passengers were strapped into their seats, adjusting the in-flight entertainment, chatting, reading magazines. The prevailing atmosphere was one of calm. How unnecessary to get so worked up — but necessity had nothing to do with it, her behaviour was instinctive. 'I am now.' She smiled as she let go the armrest. 'Still want to know about the shop?'

By the time the stewardesses were working the aisle, bringing drinks and dinner, Lou had finished explaining the plans for her business and had moved on to Nic, her daughter. 'She thinks I'm crazy, that I've no brain for business. She just doesn't get the market for "dead people's clothes" as she insists on calling them.'

'Then you'll just have to prove her wrong,' Ali said, as if it was the easiest thing in the world. 'What does she do?'

'She's a family lawyer. Took after her godmother Fiona who's always encouraged her. Look, it's not that we don't get on really, she just has strong views.' She paused with a short laugh, as always amazed to think how her almost edible, curly-haired toddler had grown up into such a touchy, opinionated young woman. Her father's daughter, she guessed. Or else her mothering skills had let them both down. 'My two boys, Jamie and Tom, are quite different,' she said, feeling she had to justify herself. 'They're much easier and more understanding.' She broke off as the trays were put in front of them, then changed the subject. 'What's waiting at home for you?'

'January's usually a bit of a hangover from

Christmas in my business, so I've got a few small jobs plus a ring to finish for a guy who was too late with his ordering. There's always someone.' Ali looked resigned. 'But, at the same time, I'll be thinking ahead and starting to dream up designs for a new collection. Business is much harder than usual thanks to the rocketing metal prices. But before I do anything, I'll have to go up north to visit my father and make up for missing Christmas with him.' She made it sound more of a chore than a pleasure. 'Not that we've spent it together for years.'

'Both my parents are dead,' Lou said wistfully, remembering the family trips they'd made to Scotland for Hogmanay when the kids were small. Log fires, long walks, icy cheeks and warm hands, skating on the frozen pond: annual pleasures that were all but ruined when her mother took to the bottle. Then, Lou would have to keep the children out of her way as her mother slipped from maudlin nostalgia into something more aggressive. When she was drunk, which she was more and more often after her husband's death, everyone was a disappointment to her and she became angry and vocal about it.

'Dad and I aren't very close. We've tried but it's been difficult.' Ali stopped as she peeled the foil lids off the containers in front of her, then replaced them and pushed the tray the full two inches away from her. 'God, the food never gets any better, does it?'

Realising Ali was not going to elaborate on her relationship with her father, Lou changed the subject. 'But aren't you moving in with your boyfriend? What's that?' Lou watched Ali pop a white pill.

'Imodium.' She grimaced and crossed her fingers. 'Let's hope it works. My boyfriend? Well, I'm going home to a new life, I guess.' A dreamy expression crossed her face. 'He's a fantastic man, a little bit older than me, who I've been seeing for the last three years. He's married but he's going to leave her. I've promised not to say anything to anyone until he's extricated himself, but by the time I'm back he should be there. Or near enough. Then we'll be together. I can't wait.'

Lou marvelled at Ali's apparent lack of concern. 'But aren't you worried about his wife? Or his family? Won't they make things difficult?' She couldn't imagine herself being in that position without having some concern about the hurt she must be inflicting.

'Why should I be?' Ali looked puzzled. 'That's their business, isn't it? But from what he's said, things have been pretty ropey between them for ages. Let's face it, he wouldn't have kept our affair going if they weren't. We've seen each other almost every week, gone out for meals, to the cinema. I've even been away with him when he's travelled on business. He couldn't have done any of that if either of them cared more about the other, could he?'

'But don't you talk about it?' Lou tried to sound interested rather than astonished, not wanting to point out the obvious: that plenty of men were happy to have their cake and eat it. Ali was too smart not to know that, but perhaps she was just salving her conscience.

'Never,' Ali said firmly. 'That's a rule I made and I've stuck with. Wife, children, pets and his domestic crises have always been right off the agenda. We have a great time together without them getting in the way. I never imagined he'd leave her, never wanted him to, so my being ignorant of all that stuff has meant that things have run happily alongside his marriage without nudging it off the rails.'

Lou almost choked on a mouthful of the rubber passing for chicken curry. 'Then how do you know he's the one for you? You can't know much about him at all.'

'I know enough. Really, I do. I know what

I'm doing, and I know why I'm doing it.'

But Lou hadn't been probing into Ali's motives. She was just intrigued at why anyone would see this as an ideal basis for a long-term partnership.

Ali went on. 'I know it's not a conventional view of a satisfactory or fulfilling relationship but until now I've always thought I was getting the best of both worlds: my freedom plus plenty of no-strings passion and entertainment.'

'Why change things? That sounds pretty damn perfect to me.' And the polar opposite to Lou's own marriage where, for the last few years, she'd sometimes felt as if she was being very slowly buried alive.

Ali looked uncertain of what to say for a moment. 'When he proposed it, I wasn't sure I wanted to. At the same time though, I knew that we couldn't keep things the same way forever. I'm not getting any younger. . . . Once I thought I'd get married, have children, but it never happened. Perhaps this is my chance. Perhaps it's time for me to make a commitment to someone else.'

She leaned back so the stewardess could take both their trays.

'Then you're lucky to have found him.' Lou remembered when she and Hooker had taken that same step together. So different, given that they had been more than twenty years younger than Ali was now, but how full of optimism they had been. And how disappointed now, so many years later.

While Ali disturbed her other neighbour so she could get out of her seat, Lou began to prepare herself for sleep. She didn't bother to check which films were playing. As soon as the cabin lights were dimmed, she slipped herself a sleeping pill donated by a doctor friend for the occasion, wrapped herself in her blanket, reclined her seat, put on her canary yellow eye mask and rested her head against the side of the plane. Sleep was the only thing that would make the flight go faster. She would catch up more with Ali in London. Ten minutes later, her mouth had fallen open enough to signify she was asleep but not quite enough to warrant total embarrassment.

3

The unearthly flickering light of the tiny TV screens set in the seat backs illuminated the blanket-wrapped huddles of passengers. Walking back down the darkened aisle, Ali thought how she could justify what she'd said about Ian and his marriage so that Lou would understand. Although she'd only known her a short time, theirs was already becoming a friendship she wanted to continue. She didn't want to derail it by not explaining herself properly. Besides that, she was intrigued by the fact that Lou obviously didn't want to talk about her own marriage and how it had ended. No, there was plenty more to find out about each other.

But by the time she returned to her seat, Lou was out for the count.

Ali's other neighbour was lying back, absorbed in a film, but let her pass with a polite nod before returning his attention to the screen. Denied conversation, she took out her travel pillow, blew it up and fitted it round her neck. She popped a second Imodium (probably a mistake) in response to a sudden cramping in her lower stomach, then closed her eyes and turned her mind to home, focusing on what she hadn't told Lou, what she hadn't told anyone: that setting up home with Ian was significant in more ways than one. It meant that her life as a serial mistress was almost over.

She hadn't considered her relationship with Ian in any way different from those she'd had with the string of married lovers who came before him, until six weeks earlier when he suggested they rethink their relationship. None of her previous lovers had come close to suggesting such a thing. Perhaps they had all believed she was one hundred per cent against one hundred per cent commitment. And they would have been right. Until now, she had been. She suspected Lou would say that it suited them to believe that. Lou's cynical take on life amused her, made her look at things in a new light.

Ian's suggestion that they live together was so unexpected that, when it came, she had been unable to reply immediately. They'd finished dinner quickly, Ian looking uncomfortable, obviously wishing he had put it another way, another time — or not at all. If she agreed, she didn't need Einstein to point out that her life and their relationship would change forever. What niggled her was how much that mattered to her. She couldn't abandon her way of life without some thought. Being his mistress had meant the relationship ran on her terms while she allowed him to believe that it ran on his. That's how she had preferred all her relationships with men to be since Don had left her over twenty years earlier. With him, she had enjoyed being half of the whole they made together. After they lost touch, she had remained single, unwilling to take the risk of committing herself to anyone else, scared of rejection.

Agreeing to Ian's proposal would mean a shift in their dynamic. But why not take that risk? The more she had thought about it, the more that shift appealed. Every evening they would come home to each other. Weekends would be spent together doing those things that couples do together: cooking, talking, going out with friends, sharing interests, and getting to know one another in a new way, discovering the truth. Now it had been offered, permanent companionship, something that had been so absent in her life for so long, something she had never thought would be hers again, was suddenly something she craved. She even dared allow herself to imagine that she and Ian might have a child together. She'd read about women giving birth in their mid-forties. It wasn't a total impossibility. She wondered what he'd say. After all, she was at an age where she could upend her life if she wanted to — as long as she held on to her independence.

Her memory of the morning following his proposal was quite clear. She had woken up beside him, her mind made up.

'Morning.' She'd kissed his left eye, then his right.

He'd groaned as he rolled to face her, squinting as he opened one and then the other eye. 'God! That brandy was a mistake.'

'But you're usually OK.' Their noses were almost touching and she could just smell his morning-after breath. She couldn't help noticing the few broken veins in his cheeks, the incipient wrinkles around his mouth, his greyish overnight stubble: all reminders that time was marching on. He slid his arm around her waist.

'Yeah, but last night was different.' He pulled back a little and looked at her. 'I'm sorry, I shouldn't have asked you the way I did. Stupid of me. I don't want to spoil what we've got either. I'm happy to leave things be, if that's what you want. In fact, perhaps that would be better for both of us.'

'Stop right there,' she said, not wanting him to retract anything, not now her own thoughts were changing so fast. 'I lay awake for half the night, thinking about what you said.'

'Did you? Poor baby. Forget it. We're fine just as we are. Really.' He kissed her, slow and lingering, the definite prelude for more. He slid his leg between hers.

She began to respond, then wriggled out of the embrace.

'Come on. Don't let a bloke down now. We haven't got much time.' He'd reached for her again. But she had something important to say.

'I know, I know, but . . .' She sat up, plumping the pillow behind her and adding a couple of the scatter cushions that had been relegated to the floor. 'We've got to talk.'

'About what?' He scratched his head so his hair stood on end. He leaned across her and flicked the *Today* programme over to Radio 3 as the presenter announced Debussy's *La Plus que Lente*. The notes of the piano swelled and fell in the quiet of the

48

room as he waited for Ali to speak.

'About last night. About what you said.'

He screwed up his right eye and with his right thumb on his cheekbone rubbed the bridge of his nose with two fingers. 'Yes?'

She heard how apprehensive he was, so hurried to put him out of his misery. 'I think it's a wonderful idea.' She watched his eyes open wide in surprise. 'I was shocked last night. But I've thought and thought about what it would mean and now I know that's what I want too.'

'You do?' He sat up too, his voice coloured with disbelief.

'I definitely do.'

He enveloped her in a bear hug, pulling her over so they lay face to face, but she hadn't finished. 'I love you and want to be with you. But . . . what about your wife? What will you do?'

'Forget about her,' he'd whispered. 'You didn't want to know about her before, so let's keep it that way for now. I don't want her to spoil anything.'

Remembering his words again now reminded her of how little she really knew about him. Lou was so right to have picked up on that. Aware of movement beside her, Ali opened her eyes, hoping to find her friend awake and in a mood to talk. But despite her change of position, Lou's head was slumped against the headrest, her distinctive eye mask still in place.

Disappointed, Ali shifted in her seat, slipping off her shoes, and returned to her thoughts. She had curled herself around their secret until she'd got used to it, squeezing every drop of private pleasure from it. She was dying to see the expression on her friends' faces when they heard she was going to settle down. Most of her women friends had become so wrapped up in their marriages and children, they didn't look outwards any more. That was one of the things she liked about Lou, her interest in the world around her. But Ali's friends saw her as a professional mistress — serially monogamous with other women's husbands. And not all (if any) of them approved or thought it as amusing as they might once have done, especially not after they'd got married themselves. Then their views on marriage underwent a sudden transformation. Ali had become a threat to all they held dear. To hell with them. How gloriously gobsmacked they would be at the change in her fortunes now Ian had come along.

Opening her eyes again, she was confronted by the on-screen flight information. The cartoon plane had barely moved since she last looked. She fiddled with the control pad, trying to switch off the image. What did she care about the temperature outside the plane right now? She wasn't intending to experience it for herself. She looked at Lou who had pulled her blanket right over her head, now dead to the world. Ali felt her stomach contract again. Cursing quietly, she excused herself from the row once again. 'I'm so sorry but I'm not too well.' To say she had Delhi belly seemed a somewhat insensitive euphemism to use to a native Indian. 'Rather than disturbing you through the night, I wonder if we could swap seats?' Lou would be horrified, but needs must.

'If you think that would be better for you. Of course,' he said, disentangling his headphones and gathering his possessions — a paperback, his airline toiletry bag and a bottle of water — and stood to let her past.

'I think it might.' Propelled by a certain degree of urgency, she transferred her belongings to the outside seat, then abandoned him to make his own arrangements.

When Ali returned, he was asleep in front of the thriller. She sat down, resigned to a long sleepless night ahead. She tuned in to an anodyne family comedy that required neither concentration nor intelligence but even so she could only think of Ian.

He had noticed how uncomfortable she was with the way he talked about his wife, and had hugged her tighter.

'I don't want her spoiling what we have. When I come here to your flat, I can forget everything else. I feel a different person. Do you understand that?'

'I suppose so,' she murmured, enjoying their closeness enough to drive away her concerns. 'But we can't exist in this weird little bubble forever.'

'We can try.' He began to kiss her again.

Once again, she pulled away, this time to his tsk of annoyance. 'Where will we live?' she asked.

'Where?' He let her go. 'What's wrong with here? I love this place.'

'So do I. But if we're going to have a new life together then I'd like to live somewhere that's ours. Yours and mine. A new start.' She snuggled up to him. He just hadn't thought this through. She had moved into her flat when she had accepted she was probably going to be single forever so this was *her* domain, *her* home. The place held too many memories that had nothing to do with him, and, if she was honest, were hardly appropriate to the life they were planning. No, if they were starting a life together, they needed a place of their own. She could tell from his silence that she had surprised him. One all, then.

Despite his apparent lack of enthusiasm, she'd made up her mind that was definitely what was going to happen. She'd already put out a few feelers before she came away but as soon as she got home she'd be combing the property pages and pestering the agents. He'd come round when he realised how a move made sense. Then she'd have to broach the idea of a baby. Too much too soon? But time was against them. If they didn't talk about these things now, it might be too late. And Ian loved her. He would understand.

Moments later, she had to leave her seat again. At the back of the plane, the cabin crew were in the galley, whiling away the hours until their more active duties resumed. The blonde I'm-Clare-fly-me one noticed Ali's coming and going, and asked if she could help. So it was that, provided with a beaker of water, Ali found herself lying full length on an empty row of seats, reasonably comfortable at last. By the time the stewardesses began the breakfast round, she was fast asleep.

Lou was woken by the sound of the trolley

and distant voices. Keeping the blanket over her head, she swallowed and ran her tongue around her mouth. The metallic taste was the side effect of her sleeping pill but her head was clear. Only a few hours and she'd be home, taking down the Christmas decorations. They'd looked so pretty all ready for her pre-Christmas Christmas dinner that she'd had with the kids before she left for India and Jamie and Rose his fiancée left for Tenerife to visit her family in their holiday villa.

Hooker had not been invited. Sitting the whole family round the table and pretending nothing had changed would have been inappropriate, not to say uncomfortable. As would a full-blown turkey extravaganza. Instead, she'd decided on the old family favourite — roast beef with all the trimmings. This was the first time they'd all be together at her new home, and she wanted everything to be right. This was the first time they'd celebrated Christmas without Hooker. She'd transformed her workroom with coloured fairy lights twinkling round the window. The chipped and scratched surface of her sewing table was hidden under a red tablecloth sprinkled with silver star confetti. No crackers this year. Instead, the table was elegant with Jenny's white china, the only decoration being the gauzy red ribbons that Lou had tied in bows around the bases of the glass candlesticks.

The meal was a triumph, even her Yorkshire puddings, and after they'd eaten, they moved into the living room for present opening. The fire blazed, glasses were charged, chocolates and mince pies passed around. The kids had clubbed together to buy Lou a Total Pampering Package that aimed to rejuvenate and re-energise. Oh, the optimism of youth! She had given Jamie and Tom cheques, socks and a shirt each — anything else ran the risk of rejection. For Rose, there was a book about Reiki healing. Then she took the last package and passed it to Nic.

'Honestly, Mum! You could have done better than brown paper.'

Aware of the effort that usually went into Nic's extravagant wrappings, she just said as brightly as she could, 'I'm saving the planet and anyway, it's what's inside that counts.'

As Nic tore away the paper, a loose deep green silk devoré velvet jacket slid into her hands. She shook it out and held it up to look at it, then against herself.

A pause as she examined it, then, 'Is it one of yours?'

Lou caught the faintest hint of criticism in the question.

'I'm afraid so,' admitted Lou, who still smarted from the time when Nic, as a young teenager, had begged her to stop making their clothes. She wanted to go shopping with her mates, and wear what they wore. And who could blame her? Uniformity was what mattered then — for the boys too. Ever since, Lou had restricted her dressmaking to herself and to friends. But she hadn't been able to resist this gorgeous fabric, which she had been so sure Nic would love.

Nic confined herself to shaking her head in a despairing sort of way. She slipped it on over her dress, then went upstairs to find a mirror. Despite Rose's quiet 'Wow!' and Lou's feeling of satisfaction in seeing a perfect fit, Nic's appreciation was less than impressive. When she returned to the room, she slung it over the back of her chair and kissed Lou's cheek. 'Thanks, Mum. It's lovely.' Her lack of enthusiasm had been barely hidden. 'It'll be great for that flappers and gangsters fancy dress party at New Year.'

Stuck in her airline seat, blanket over her head, Lou could still feel her disappointment. How she longed to have one of those close mother–daughter relationships instead of one that blew hot and cold with no warning. The jacket should have proved to Nic how beautiful vintage-inspired pieces could be, how successful Lou's business venture would be, but she should have known better. Nic had been as dismissive as Hooker sometimes was. They rarely thought of the effect their words might have. Well, she'd bloody well show them that she could make a go of this. If anything, Nic's scorn had only served to stoke the fire of Lou's determination. Who knew? Perhaps her success would bring them closer together. Success was something that Nic, like her father, respected.

The rattle of the trolley was getting nearer. She wondered what the time was, but was reluctant to brave the glare of the cabin to look at her watch.

'Excuse me.' An unknown voice sounded right by her ear. 'Would you like orange juice?'

Annoyed by the disturbance, she peeled the blanket from her head and took off her eye mask only to be confronted by a familiar face in the next seat. Her knicker rescuer. Beyond him, the third seat was empty. Where was Ali? He was passing her a plastic beaker from the stewardess. She took it and unfolded her table. 'Thanks. But that seat's taken.' Realising how rude she sounded, she apologised. 'I'm sorry, that sounded awful.'

'Not at all.' He inclined his head and gave a slight smile. 'Your friend was taken ill so she took the aisle seat, but I think she may now be sleeping at the back of the plane.'

Lou composed herself. She was a fifty-five-year-old woman, for God's sake. This man had only tried to help her, not stripped her naked in front of the whole airport. Even if that was what it had felt like to her at the time. The memory of his hand holding out her knickers came into her head and she fought a desire to laugh.

'I'm sorry about earlier on at the airport, too,' she said. Then, 'I'm Lou.'

He held out his hand, at least as far as the movement was possible in such a confined space. 'Sanjeev Gupta.'

They shook, elbows digging into their sides. Before they could continue their conversation, a stewardess was leaning across, offering trays of breakfast. Lou stared at the separated lumps of scrambled egg and the warm burned sausage that floated in a thin sea of tomato juice, before turning her tray around and picking up the yoghurt.

'Have you been on holiday?' her neighbour asked while cutting his sausage as if expecting something foul to crawl out. He gave up and turned his attention to the roll and butter.

Within minutes, Lou was detailing their route through Rajasthan, remembering the highlights, excited to be able to talk about what she'd seen without the rest of the group, who were scattered through the plane, interrupting. She only stopped to allow the breakfast to be removed. Sanjeev was an attentive listener, concentrating on what he was hearing, interrupting only to ask whether she had managed to visit certain places she didn't mention: Jaisalmer, Bikaner, Deogarh. By the time they'd finished their coffee, Lou was laughing.

'Two weeks obviously isn't anything like long enough. We've missed so much. I'll just have to come back.'

Responding to her laugh, Sanjeev smiled back. 'To Rajasthan? Or maybe somewhere else?'

'What do you think?' Lou wanted the opinion of someone who knew the country far better than her.

He began to tell her about the other very different parts of his country, from the unspoilt mountain state of Sikkim that lay in the Himalayan foothills in the shadow of Kanjenjunga, to the gentle white-sanded paradise of Kerala in the south. Lou listened, entranced by his descriptions and the stories of his visits there, at the same time making plans for countless future visits. Would her new business provide the necessary income? She would have to make sure it did. He took her journeying down the mighty Brahmaputra in the state of Assam, conjuring up the crowded ferries, the riverine island of Majuli, his visit during light-filled Divali, the ubiquitous tea plantations. He was describing the steep noisy street up to a Hindu temple outside Guwahati lined with stalls stuffed with devotional objects, crowded with holy men and pilgrims who had travelled there to have their wishes granted, when Ali returned to the outside seat.

Lou smiled a faint welcome but continued to let Sanjeev talk. So caught up was she in the places he was describing, she didn't want him to stop. However, seeing he'd lost her attention for a moment, he broke off and twisted round to see Ali. He immediately asked her if she wanted her seat back. 'Your friend has missed you. So, if you are better . . .' He let the sentence hang.

'Thank you.' She stood to let him out, so she could slide into the vacated middle seat.

Lou was disappointed to lose Sanjeev but

Ali wasn't to know how much she had been enjoying his company.

'What a bloody awful night,' announced Ali, who was looking pale despite the make-up that she'd obviously applied in preparation for landing.

'I'm sorry. I'd no idea. How are you feeling now?' Lou felt guilty that she hadn't even bothered to go to the back of the plane to find out. But Ali seemed not to mind.

'Much better. Once I was lying down and the Imodium kicked in, I was OK. But I had so much going around my head, I couldn't sleep for ages.'

'Once you see Ian, everything'll fall into place. You'll see.' Lou wasn't sure why she was speaking with such confidence when she knew so little about either of them. 'Is he meeting you?'

'I wish. No. I don't know when I'm going to see him. Depends on how things have gone with his wife, I guess.'

The pilot's voice broke into their conversation, announcing the start of their descent into Heathrow. Lou stretched her ankles back and forth, suddenly aware that she had barely moved on the flight and that a blood clot might be lurking in a stagnant vein, waiting to finish her off. Why hadn't she worn those awful white compression socks that had briefly graced the airport floor and were now buried somewhere in Ali's case? Confusion and vanity had combined to prevent her retrieving them. Her grip tightened on the armrest again as her hearing buzzed and blocked and she struggled to catch what Ali was saying. She gasped as a sharp pain drilled into her eye socket, then swallowed hard. Cutting loose from her neighbours, she focused on the pain in her head and on all the methods she knew that might relieve the pressure: holding her nose; swallowing; yawning; drinking the last of her water; trying and failing to find the chewing gum buried in her bag. Just when she thought she couldn't bear it another moment and her head would split in two, the plane hit the tarmac. As it bumped along the ground, the pain began to recede as they taxied towards the airport buildings.

4

Lou's eyes felt as if they'd been forcibly removed, sand-papered and returned to their sockets. Her limbs were leaden as she slid her suitcase through the melting snow along the path to her front door, vowing never to catch another overnight flight again. She stopped to look up at the windows, wound about with bare wisteria stems. Jenny's home was hers now, and waiting to welcome her back. Even so, it was strange not to be returning from holiday to the home she and Hooker had shared for so long. For a second, she felt more alone than she had since their split. As she rummaged in her bag for her key, she felt Sanjeev's business card. Would he make good his promise, hurriedly made as they walked towards Immigration, to invite her to dinner while he was in London? And if he did, how would she respond? Positively, she decided, given what she remembered of his manner, his way of conjuring up places, palaces, myths and Mughals, not of course forgetting his Bollywood good looks. And why not? There was no reason why she shouldn't indulge in a little post-marital entertainment.

As soon as she was inside, she swapped her too-thin mac for her voluminous knee-length leopard-print faux-fur coat that was scattered with Minnie Mouse faces. Walking through the house, inhaling the familiar scent of home, reacquainting herself with everything, she glanced out of the window into the garden. In contrast to the black slush covering the London streets, here was a frozen winter wonderland, only interrupted by the paw prints of local cats and foxes. Despite having put on the coat, she shivered and went to turn up the heating, exchanging her holiday shoes for her Uggs, before making herself a cup of tea, builder's strength.

Even though the house belonged to her now, she still felt Jenny's presence. After months spent grieving for her younger sister, wandering round the place, remembering, Lou had finally galvanised herself. Being practical was one of the things she did best. At first she had planned to rent the house until the property market improved. She'd sorted out all her sister's belongings before starting on a round of charity shop visits to get rid of the rest. Stuff — that's all her sister's possessions were now — just stuff that had little or no significance to anyone else, not even to Lou. She had found that terribly sad. Any tales about how Jenny came by certain things or why she kept them had died with her. Letters, old postcards from her friends, ancient bank statements and bills, diaries and notebooks: only fit for the bin. Lou had to go through them all first, despite hating the invasion of her sister's well-kept privacy. Apart from one or two personal mementoes, some gifts for the children and a few clothes, all that Lou kept were the basics necessary for a rental property. If it was to appeal to any potential tenant, her job was to neutralise Jenny's home, get rid of its character altogether.

But there wasn't going to be a tenant, after all. The moment of realisation had come three months ago, as she planned the redecoration of the main bedroom. She was poring over a paint chart with a couple of fabric swatches in her hand, undecided between shades — Raspberry Bellini, Roasted Red or the one she knew she should choose: safe, innocuous white —

when a blinding light dawned. Why do the place up for a stranger when it could be hers, done up exactly as she wanted? This could be her chance for a new start in life. How Jenny would have liked that: so infinitely preferable to the idea of a stranger taking over her home. Her sister had been the only one in the world who knew what Lou really felt about her husband in recent years, about her marriage. She would be so pleased to have helped her to an escape route. If her death was teaching Lou anything, it was to squeeze every drop out of life while you had it. There was no knowing when it would end. That same evening she had told Hooker she was leaving him.

To begin with he hadn't believed her. 'Don't be ridiculous,' he'd said. 'You don't mean it.' But she did, and over the following two weeks of protracted and painful rowing had finally got him to accept that her mind was made up. 'You'll be back,' he said. 'You won't like being on your own.' But the more he poured scorn on her plan, the more determined he made her. Any reservations she might have had were quashed.

In the living room, everything was as she'd left it. She tucked her knitting bag under the Eames chair that had been Jenny's pride and joy, then sat and opened her laptop on her knee. With tea and a small(ish) slice of home-made Christmas cake on the low table by her side, she lifted her feet onto the ottoman and began to download her photographs. Unpacking could wait. As the images materialised in front of her, she was ambushed by memories: Jaipur's Palace of the Winds; a Brahmin village chief preparing the opium ceremony; the swaying elephant ride up to the Amber Fort; groups of enchanting dark-eyed children; an old woman cooking chapattis over a fire in her front yard; and so they kept on coming.

At the same time as wishing herself back there, Lou also felt a deep pleasure at being back home. Now India was over, she was ready to concentrate on making a new life alone. The trip had given her a necessary shot of energy. Her current exhaustion aside, she felt stronger, empowered (though she hated the word), braced for whatever life would throw at her. Breaking up with Hooker had not been easy and she had an unpleasant sense that her problems might not be entirely over, but she felt ready to deal with whatever he threw at her next. The colours of Rajasthan had inspired her as much as the fabrics that she'd been shown in the large fabric emporiums where roll after roll of silk and cotton had been pulled out for her. She was itching to get on with her new summer designs for the shop. As she gazed at a photo of a sari stall in the Jodhpur market — all clashing colours, crowds and chatter — the phone rang.

'Mum?' Nic's voice sounded different.

'Darling! Did you have a good Christmas?' Lou felt the familiar fillip to her spirits that came whenever she heard from one of her children.

'I need to see you.'

Lou hit earth with a bump. Not even a Did-you-have-a-good-holiday? So this was how it was going to be. And just because she'd decided to absent herself for a fortnight to avoid any awkwardness over the Christmas break. She hadn't only been thinking of herself, but of the kids who would have been caught between their feuding parents. 'When were you thinking?' she asked. As the high that had accompanied her arrival home from the flight began to dissipate, Lou thought with some longing of her clean-sheeted bed that was waiting upstairs.

'Today? Now?' Was that urgency or was her daughter just being her usual demanding self?

'Has something happened, Nic?'

'I'll tell you when I see you. I'll be about an hour.'

'And I can show you —'

But Nic had hung up. Lou took a bite of leftover Christmas cake. Mmm, possibly the best she'd made yet. Outside, a train rattled by on the other side of the garden wall: a sound that made her feel at home.

An hour. Not long enough for that sleep which was becoming increasingly pressing. Instead Lou woke herself up with a shower, so that by the time the doorbell rang, she was feeling just about semi-human. She had discarded the coat, knowing the scorn it provoked in Nic. The thick burned orange sweater she wore over her jeans almost compensated for the fact that the water had been lukewarm and the heating had yet to make any noticeable impression on the house. Nic's disapproving glance at the jeans as she walked in didn't go unnoticed. And her 'Mmmm, very ashram' directed at the sweater was quite unnecessary. Why was it that her daughter felt she had to sanction — or otherwise — all her mother's life choices, including those in her wardrobe? However, once Nic had hung her overcoat on the end of the stairs Lou welcomed her with a hug, then took her into the kitchen, the warmest room.

'How was Christmas? Dad OK?' She pulled out a bag of coffee beans from the freezer.

'Quiet. Tom was with us. We missed you.' That reproving tone again, something Lou hadn't missed while away.

'Having someone to do all the cooking, you mean.'

They didn't speak while Lou ground the beans for the cafetière, then: 'That's so unfair.' Wounded now. 'I just think the two of you should be together.'

Lou decided to ignore her daughter's last remark. However uncomfortable Nic was with Lou's decision to move out of the family home, Lou was not going to let her be the arbiter in her parents' relationship. 'I'm only joking. Don't be so sensitive, Nic. Of course I missed you too, but going away was the right thing for me to do.'

Nic shook her head.

'No, really. India was amazing. You'd love it there.' Would she though? As well as everything that she had enjoyed, Lou remembered the dirt; the stink; the poverty; families living on the pavements, in the stations; child beggars tapping at car windows; Delhi belly; the drains; the reckless driving. None of that had been enough to negate her own thrill at experiencing the country

70

— but would her over-fastidious daughter react in the same way? 'Look. I've brought you a couple of things.' She pushed across the table a yellow and green drawstring jewellery purse, a paper bag containing a scarf she'd bought at a stall in a gateway at the Mehrangarh Fort, and a newspaper-wrapped statue of the elephant god, Ganesh, for luck.

Nic pulled open the purse and slid out the star sapphire ring that Lou had chosen with such care. 'It's lovely, Mum.'

Had she actually got a present right for once? Filled with disbelief and pleasure, Lou plunged the knife into the Christmas cake. Just another small slice.

As Nic slipped the ring onto her right hand, Lou thought she heard her sniff. When her daughter looked up, her face was a muddle of emotions, her eyes brimming with tears.

'Nic? Whatever's the matter? I just wanted to bring you back something special but if you don't like it . . . well, I can't change it, but . . .'

Seeing Nic so upset induced immediate and unwelcome guilt. She should never have fled the country. How selfish she'd been. Instead, she should have skipped Christmas by burying herself in Devon with Fiona and

71

Charlie after all. At least she'd have been in reach of home. However old her kids might be, they did still need her. She worried that this still mattered so much to her when she should be letting them go.

'It's not that, Mum. I do really love it.' There was a long pause during which Nic struggled to compose herself, twisting the ring around her finger, watching the six-pointed star move through the blue-grey stone. Lou stretched out a hand to cover her daughter's. Years ago, she might have been able to soothe any problem away but now, her maternal success rate was much lower. Nic was usually so strong, so self-contained. Since she'd been sixteen and had decided on a career in family law, following in the footsteps of her godmother, Fiona, she'd always given the impression that she'd rather lie bound to a railway track than seek advice from her parents.

Her daughter gave a final sniff and looked her straight in the eye. That familiar look of defiance was back. As Nic cleared her throat with a brusque cough, Lou had a sinking sensation, recognising that her daughter was about to say something momentous.

'It's just that . . .' Deep breath. Twist of the ring around her finger. 'I'm pregnant.' For a second, Nic looked just as she had fifteen-odd years ago when confessing to some childish prank, anticipating the appalled parental reaction, her justification at the ready.

Lou stared at her, her hand frozen mid-stroke. 'You're what?' Of all the things Nic might have said, this was the last she would have expected. Until now, her daughter's career had taken precedence over everything, including any boyfriends who were dispatched whenever they got too much.

Immediately Nic was on the defensive, moving her hand out of reach. 'I knew you'd be like that.'

'I'm not *like* anything. It's a bit of a shock, that's all.' Lou stood up to pour the coffee, as her mind raced through the implications. Having a baby would get in the way of Nic's life, her work, and she wouldn't like that. Presumably she'd come to ask for her mother's support for an abortion. 'Are you absolutely sure?' she asked, playing for time.

Nic tutted. 'Of course. One hundred per cent.'

'Who's the father? Max?'

'That's irrelevant.' She made a scything movement through the air with her hand, cutting off any further discussion about her on–off boyfriend of the last year or so. She pushed her cake away from her.

'Nic! How can you say that? Of course it isn't. You have to take him into consideration too.' But Lou could see that Nic was way ahead of her. She had made all her decisions and, as usual, Lou was going to have to try to catch up.

'He's made it plain that he wants nothing to do with this. He wants me to get rid of it.' She sounded both outraged and determined.

'And you? What do you want?'

'I'm going to keep it. This is what I've wanted for ages.'

Despite the relief she felt, Lou thought it wise not to point out that Nic had never suggested she'd wanted any such thing. A career, yes. A solid relationship, yes. But a baby? This was the first Lou had heard of it.

'What about your career?' she said, sounding like the sort of mother she didn't want to be.

'Mum, thousands of women have babies and return to work.' Nic was trying to control the note of impatience that had crept into her voice. 'You should know that better than anyone. That won't be a problem. I've thought it all through.'

'You have?' Lou took Nic's plate and transferred the cake back into the tin. Giving herself something to do meant she didn't have to look at her daughter while she tried to catch up with the conversation.

'Yes, I have. I'm going to take the statutory maternity leave and then find a nanny share. Like you did.'

This was not the moment to elaborate on the difficulties that could come with nannies however lifesaving they might be. Lou remembered how torn she'd been between her job as fashion editor at *Chic to Chic* and her young children. The job had been demanding and competitive, complete with the extra strain of feeling she didn't entirely fit the role with her sometimes off-beat sense of style. And when she'd been at home . . . How could she forget the soul-lacerating guilt when the smallest thing went wrong, the sense of abject despair when the children turned to the nanny rather than to her, the dull background feeling of inadequacy in both spheres of her life? They were only alleviated when she eventually became a full-time mother — even though that decision was forced on her. But there was no arguing with Nic once her mind was made up. If anything, any objection raised by Lou would only make her dig in her heels. Lou needed time to think through the ramifications of the news before discussing them with her daughter. Nothing had to be decided this second.

A baby! For a moment she envisaged the two of them, heads bent over this unexpected addition to the family, sharing the pleasure together. She felt a thrill of anticipation before she was brought back to the moment as Nic spoke.

'I just need you to help me with one thing.'

'Of course. I'll do whatever I can.'

Nic was fidgeting, tipping her mug back and forth, intent on her coffee, anything rather than catch her mother's eye. Obviously something else was troubling her and she was finding a way to say it.

Lou held her breath.

Without moving her head, Nic glanced up at her, then away again. 'Dad doesn't know.' There it was. The all-important missing detail lay between them like a ticking bomb.

'Why not?' As if Lou didn't know.

'He'll go ballistic, that's why.'

Light dawned. Nic hadn't come to share the news with her so much as to persuade her to be the messenger. 'And you want me to tell him?'

'You'll have to, Mum. The boys think so too.' Nic banged down her mug, as final as a judge's gavel. Decision made.

So she'd told her two brothers first. Even

though Lou had been away when Nic broke the news, that hurt, too. What had gone wrong with the adult mother–daughter relationship, which Lou had anticipated with such pleasure when Nic was little? She had imagined them sharing confidences, shopping together, even taking the occasional weekend break — everything Lou had missed out on with her own mother. But none of that had happened and it now looked as though it never would. Nic had always behaved like a cuckoo in the nest, making her presence loudly felt before taking to her wings as soon as she could.

'Shouldn't we talk this through properly first?'

'Mum, there's nothing to discuss. Not now anyway. I'm not asking you to be ecstatic for me, though that would be nice, but just to help with this one little thing. Please.' She drew the last word out into a childish entreaty. 'I'm nearly three months and I'll be showing soon.'

'But I haven't seen him for weeks.' Lou racked her brains for a better objection.

'Mu-um?' Nic knew there wasn't one.

Despite all her misgivings, it was hard to refuse her daughter. Lou remembered the excitement that had accompanied her own pregnancies, the absolute joy she had felt, the hopes for the future, the pure unfettered longing for a baby.

The news would travel among their old friends like a forest fire. Just as it probably had when they learned that Lou had moved out. How the more conventional among them would sympathise yet relish in the Sherwood family's misfortunes. How they would sigh with relief at having been spared a similar fate themselves. That thought gave Lou strength. Who gave a damn what they thought? She had summoned up the will to ignore their views when she left Hooker, and that's just what she would do again. Nic should be encouraged to take the path in life she chose for herself.

'All right.' Lou saw relief colour her daughter's face. 'I'll talk to him. And I'll give you all the support you need. Anything you need for this baby — you can rely on me. That's a promise.'

Perhaps Nic's motherhood would at last bring the two of them closer. Being a single grandmother had not been part of Lou's plans, in fact it wasn't a concept that had even crossed her mind. But at least Nic would understand what Lou had gone through trying to balance her work with the children's demands — and that she had done the best she could.

'Thank you, thank you,' said Nic, getting up and flinging her arms around her. 'I knew you would.'

Lou hugged back and for a moment all their differences melted away. Lou breathed in the smell of her daughter's hair, noticing how tense and bony her shoulders were. But she didn't comment or tell her to relax. Nic would tell her if anything else was troubling her in her own good time. If Lou couldn't have all of her daughter, she would take whatever part of her was on offer.

'Oh, and I'd keep off the cake if I were you,' Nic suggested as she shrugged on her coat and stepped out through the front door.

After her daughter had gone, Lou washed the coffee pot, thinking over their conversation. Communication between them had clearly broken down more than she had realised. Why did Nic want this baby so badly? Had Lou and Hooker unintentionally failed her somehow, so that she needed something more in her life to love and be loved by? But they hadn't been *such* bad parents, had they? Not when she compared them to all the dysfunctional families that were paraded through the pages of the daily tabloids. She couldn't believe that their growing distance from one another had been the cause. Now finally separated, they were about to become grandparents. Another tie that was bound to throw them together again.

Sighing, she picked up the phone and dialled Hooker's number.

5

Standing in her walk-in closet, Ali looked around her. Everything was as it should be. Her boxes of shoes were stacked one on top of another, illustrated labels outwards, so she could see which pair was where at a glance. Beside them were the drawers with transparent fronts. The order with which she'd organised her wardrobe would have amused her in someone else, but she hadn't been able to stop herself. Behind her was the hanging space, divided into sections: trousers, skirts, shirts, dresses and coats. No item remained unworn for longer than a year before it was thrown out. On the end wall was a well-lit mirror. She checked herself, stood sideways on, anxious to make the best possible impression on Ian, pulling at her black and cream striped asymmetric jersey dress so that it sat straight on the hips, then adjusting her hair. He'd once said how much he liked it short because it emphasised the length of her neck. A half-smile crossed her lips as she anticipated him running his finger along her naked right clavicle and up her throat to the point of her chin, before they kissed.

Satisfied she could do no more, she turned to walk through the bedroom, glancing round to make sure everything was ready. She touched the bedside table, checking that her few sex toys were out of sight. They were for later. Nothing too way out but she knew what he liked, and what she liked too. She ran her hand over the bedspread, making sure every wrinkle was smoothed out, before pulling the heavy curtains and arranging precisely the way they pooled on the floor. She straightened the pile of books by her side of the bed and moved the three red roses on the table to be just so, then moved to the door where she stood for a moment, surveying the scene she'd set for seduction, and dimmed the lights a little more.

As she went downstairs, Ali thought how lucky she was to have the apartment. Ten years earlier, one of her lovers, Peter Ellis, a wealthy middle-aged property developer, had been converting the Victorian school into a number of des res. A generous and kind man, he had thought nothing of offering her a place of her own in exchange for the several years of pleasure she had given him. Resistant at first, she had eventually been persuaded to accept.

She was as much in love with the place now as she had been then. She loved its quirkiness and the utilitarian elements of the design that featured exposed RSJs and cast-iron school radiators. Upstairs, the two bedrooms and bathrooms were designed to be more intimate but she never tired of the large dramatic space of the living area with its vast multi-paned windows and wide oak floorboards. She'd furnished it minimally but as comfortably as she could afford, concentrating on good lighting and statement rugs to separate the different living areas. A sofa sat in the centre with a coffee table in front of it, two smaller chairs opposite. Her dining table stood by the open-plan kitchen and in the opposite corner, under the low hanging light, was her jigsaw table, where Brueghel's *Allegory of Sight and Smell* lay scattered in six thousand pieces awaiting her attention. Enlarged photographs from her travels hung on the walls: rolling blue mountains of Mongolia from the Great Wall; Mount Fuji from the railway line; a farmer with horse and plough tilling a terraced hillside in Vietnam.

She poured herself a cranberry juice. Leaning against the divide between the kitchen area and the rest of the living space, she checked the time. Fifteen minutes and he would be here. He was never late. She switched on the wide-screen, wall-mounted TV and flicked through the channels unable to find anything that grabbed her interest. Instead, she went to the dining table, where her laptop lay open, her accounts file on-screen.

There was no escaping the truth. Her turnover was down on last year's. She'd hoped the three months before Christmas would make the difference as well as help cover the cost of her holiday. She ran her finger down the sales and stopped at the name 'Orlov', suddenly remembering that their order was still sitting in her safe, uncollected and unpaid for — a pair of emerald and diamond earrings with a matching necklace worth over three thousand pounds. She always asked clients to pay a fifty per cent deposit on commission so she was still owed the other fifty per cent. She made a note to contact the Orlovs as soon as she got to the studio in the morning. But for how long would that and her other commissions tide her over?

Perhaps she should call in the loan that,

in headier days, she'd made to Rick, her studio share and friend. When he was starting up his silversmithing business he was having trouble meeting his mortgage and alimony payments so Ali had agreed to let him use a space in her studio rent-free until he started making ends meet. Then, she could afford to be generous. Now, it was less easy. At the same time, she didn't want to jeopardise their friendship. Despite the odd reminder, he never seemed embarrassed by the debt. While she was debating how to persuade him to part with the few grand he owed her, the doorbell rang.

As she crossed the room, she felt she might burst with excitement. She was so looking forward to seeing Ian again, to making plans together. Three years of passionate but clandestine encounters, of secret overnight stays in hotels when he travelled on business, of meals in discreet restaurants and of entering and leaving theatres and cinemas separately — 'just in case' — were almost over. Soon their relationship would be in the open. She prayed that he had broken the news to his wife and that everything would be reasonably civilised between them. She didn't want anything to cloud their happiness.

But the minute Ian walked into the flat,

Ali knew something was wrong. Earlier, on the phone, he'd been unusually abrupt but she'd put that down to his being pre-occupied by something at work. Now she could see there was more to it than that. Although they hadn't seen each other for over two weeks, he barely reciprocated her welcoming kiss. She thought she detected alcohol beneath the strong smell of peppermint on his breath. By the time she'd hung up his coat, he was sitting on the sofa, staring into the middle distance, elbows on knees, hands steepled in front of his face, fingers tapping against one another. His shoulders rose and fell with each breath.

'How was Christmas?' she tried.

'Yeah. Fine.' He still didn't look at her. And he didn't mention his wife.

'Is something the matter? Difficult day?' This was hardly the reunion she'd envisaged.

'I'm sorry.' He snapped out of his reverie and turned to her. 'Something at work's bothering me. That's all. Give me a minute or two to come down. I want to hear about the holiday.'

Experience had taught Ali never to probe into whatever was troubling a lover. Her role was to distract, to provide an alternative to their other world. That was why they liked coming here. Her apartment was a retreat, not just for her, but for those men who had lives they wanted to forget for a few hours. Spending time with her was therapeutic although she was no therapist. She asked no awkward questions, never held them to any kind of emotional ransom. And in return, she got to run her life just as she wanted it.

She busied herself by bringing over two small bowls from the kitchen, one filled with the black olives he liked, and the other with cashews. After returning for the bottle of Medoc and two glasses, she turned her iPod to Pachelbel's Canon in D Major, one of the most soothing pieces of music she knew, and went over to him. She was practised in jogging a man out of his worries for a few hours. That was what she did. As she sat down, she thought she heard him sigh but she just tucked her feet under her and sat with her head resting on his shoulder. This was where she belonged now. This was how they would spend so many evenings in the future, just the two of them.

'I've missed you,' she murmured. 'Really missed you.'

'Have you?' he asked, sounding as if he was a million miles away.

'I think that was your cue to say how much you've missed me.' She gave a nervous laugh, sat up and looked at him, puzzled by what could be distracting him so much, feeling the first whisper of alarm.

But instead of turning to her, he stood up and went over to the window, staring out across the communal garden. His hands were in his pockets, jingling his loose change. 'Of course I did. You must know that.'

'But it would be nice to be told.' Annoyed with herself for sounding like the nagging wife she imagined he was escaping, she tried again. 'I'm sorry, but I've been so looking forward to seeing you.' Going over to stand behind him, she wrapped her arms around his waist. 'We could go upstairs. Or I've got champagne in the fridge.'

'Not yet.' He turned and kissed her nose. 'I've got a lot on my mind at the moment. I probably shouldn't have come.'

'But we haven't seen each other for weeks. We've got so much to talk about.' She took both his hands and kissed him back. Over the two years she had known him, Ali couldn't remember a time when he had refused an invitation to her bedroom. But, having trained herself not to question her lovers' moods but just to wait them out, she didn't object. She was confident he'd tell her what was bothering him when he was ready. Despite her growing unease, she was prepared to wait. Worming his troubles from him was a wife's job, not a mistress's. In a few weeks, when everyone knew they were together, things would be different. They would be able to talk and share so much more than they ever had before. She would get to know him so much better. She could afford to maintain a sympathetic silence now.

'Tell me about your holiday.' He held her hand and guided her back to the sofa.

'How long have you got?' Ali pretended she hadn't noticed how uninterested he sounded. But rather than bore him about what he didn't want to hear, she passed across the linen Nehru shirt she'd had specially made for him. In the Udaipur fabric emporium, she had been so sure it was the perfect present. But as he pulled it from the packet, there was something distinctly charity shop about it. The stitching, which had looked charmingly authentic in Udaipur, now looked embarrassingly amateur, the linen cheap, and, when he held it up, the sleeves were obviously way too long.

'It's not you at all, is it?' she said, disappointed.

'Not really.' As he put it over the arm of the sofa, they exchanged a smile that reassured her that he was coming back to her.

'OK, let's forget Christmas and India,' she said. 'Let's talk about now, about us.' Since it seemed the wrong moment to ask him if he'd told his wife about their plans, she went to the table where she'd put the particulars she'd collected from a couple of estate agents just before she went away. 'I love the look of this one. And I'm sure we could get the price down.' She picked up a brochure showing an end-of-terrace three-storey Georgian town house. 'Great kitchen and look at the roof terrace.' My God, I'm trying so hard, I even sound like an estate agent, she thought. Ease up or you'll never get him onside.

But Ian was pouring himself a glass of wine without even asking if she'd like one. 'I thought we'd decided to live here,' he said, his voice flat and matter-of-fact, the enthusiasm of a few weeks ago vanished.

'*You* decided to live here, but I thought that once you saw what was around, I might be able to change your mind.' She flicked over the photos in the brochure. 'I know we could be so happy somewhere else. A house of our own, with none of the history this place has.'

'You make it sound as if someone was murdered here,' he said, coming over to take

90

the details from her. He didn't look beyond the first page.

'Oh, you know,' she said, becoming more exasperated with his refusal to engage. 'There were other men before you.'

His face tensed as he put the brochure down. 'I thought we'd agreed not to talk about them.'

'But of course there were,' she protested. 'I thought you'd be happy that I want to leave behind the life I had before you.' She could feel herself beginning to gabble, so reined herself back. It would be a wrench to leave the apartment but she felt sure it was the right thing to do. 'Anyway, we need somewhere a bit bigger than this.'

Ian placed his hand on top of hers, heavy and warm. 'I honestly don't think we do.' His grip tightened. 'I can live with your past if you can.' Her relief at the sudden improvement of his mood was muddled by the growing realisation that they didn't see their future in the same way at all. During her holiday, she had used the time she spent on her own to think of little else, planning and plotting their life together. How disappointing to realise that he obviously hadn't done the same. There was so much ahead of them that he hadn't even considered.

'And if I get pregnant?' The words slipped

out without her having time to stop and think. Watching his face darken, she would have given anything in the world to be able to retract them.

'Pregnant!' He sat down as if he'd been winded, the wine tipping in his glass. He saved it just in time. 'Are you serious?'

'Why not? Why are you looking at me like that? Wouldn't it be wonderful? We'd be a family.' She wished she could erase the need from her voice.

'Family,' he echoed, so quietly that Ali could barely hear him. But she didn't need to, to know that she had just made a huge mistake. She began to backtrack as fast as she could.

'Not that I mind if we don't, of course. I can understand that you might not want any more.' She stopped, not knowing what else she could say, at the same time feeling sadness engulf her as her dream foundered.

'But you've never mentioned anything about wanting children.' He seemed perplexed. 'That was never part of the deal.'

'Because they were never an option. But when you asked me to live with you, I couldn't help thinking. I want more out of my life now than I've ever dared to admit to myself. You've presented me with a chance . . .' She wanted to explain, to persuade, for him to take her in his arms and assure her everything would be all right. But that was not going to happen.

He'd put down his drink and crossed his arms over his chest, wearing an expression that was new to her: distant, calculating.

'But of course, I was being stupid,' she went on, desperate to rewind the whole conversation and start again. 'It was a silly fantasy. I shouldn't have said anything.'

'I would've thought I'd done my bit towards populating the world. I'd never imagined us . . .' Words failed him as he tried to imagine. 'And, well, aren't you a bit . . .' He paused, searching for a kinder way of putting it and failing. '. . . too old?'

He had no idea how hearing him say that hurt. Fired up by his insensitivity, she retorted, 'Women can have babies any time before the menopause. It just gets more difficult.' To her fury, she felt her chin wobble, and her voice began to crack. 'Just forget it. Please. I shouldn't have said anything.' She went to pour herself a glass of wine. She took a big gulp before turning to look at him. He had emptied his own glass and returned to stare out of the window. Something had happened to make this evening go way off track. He'd arrived in the wrong mood and she had only made it worse. Much worse. But why should she make it easy for him? A few weeks ago, he had been desperate for them to be together. What had changed? Perhaps she had gone a bit too far, but she didn't deserve to be knocked back so cruelly. She sat down again, and waited, dreading whatever he was building up to say.

Eventually he turned, but his face was hidden as he concentrated on his right thumb, pushing at the cuticle of his left. 'I'm sorry,' he said. 'So sorry.'

'So am I.' A sigh of relief escaped her. They would sort out their differences and things would be all right after all. 'I got far too carried away. Of course we can live here — to start with, anyway. Whatever you like.' She plumped up the deep red cushion beside her and rested it against the back of the sofa, making a space for him, but he made no move to join her.

Instead, he murmured, almost as if he was talking to himself, 'It's too late.'

Nervousness churned in the pit of her stomach. 'For what? We've got plenty of time.'

He seemed to summon all his energy, lifting his shoulders and closing his eyes. 'I didn't mean to tell you this today, but . . .'

'But what?'

'I've met someone else.' His shoulders dropped with the evident relief at having got it off his chest.

'Someone else? I don't understand.' The shock took her breath away for a moment. 'But I've only been away for two weeks. How can you have?'

At least he had the grace to look shame-faced before he spoke again. 'She's someone at work who I've known for months. Then, at one of the Christmas parties . . .'

'At one of the Christmas parties,' she repeated. 'But that can only have been weeks, days after we agreed we were going to live together.'

'I know. But you've been so busy we've hardly seen each other over the last month or two.' He shifted from one foot to the other, his thumb worrying at the cuticle.

'And you couldn't wait?' Her outrage was mixed with a profound sense of injustice. She had trusted him. 'For God's sake, Ian. You sprang the idea of living together on me. I had to work every hour God sent to complete my Christmas orders. It's my busiest time of the year. We agreed. I offered to cancel India, but you said I should go while you sorted everything out.'

There was a long pause. An unpleasant thought wormed its way into her head.

'Have you just come here from her?'

An even longer pause.

His thumbs were still as he stared at his feet and nodded.

She shook her head. 'I loved you.' The three words were laced with recrimination, regret and sorrow as she realised how little she knew him.

'I know.' He crossed the room to stroke her head with a gesture that, only hours ago, would have made her shiver with pleasure.

'Don't,' she said, shrugging him off, as he went on.

'Surely you understand that I can't provide the sort of commitment you're asking. I'd no idea that's what you wanted. Yes, my wife and I are separating but we've still a lot to work through. I can't take on the responsibility of a new house and I certainly don't want a baby.'

'So, what exactly were you planning?' she spat, knowing the answer. 'You were going to live with me and have another mistress on the side. Same pattern all over again?'

'I hadn't planned anything. It's just the way . . .'

'I thought so much more of you. You should go.'

There was nothing else to be said. She went to get his coat, her eyes blurring with tears that she refused to shed until he had gone. Suddenly, all she wanted was Ian out of her home with the minimum fuss and with her dignity intact. Then she would allow herself to absorb what had happened between them.

He pulled on his coat. 'Thank you for being so understanding.' He leaned forward to kiss her but she jerked out of reach. 'Perhaps in a week or two, we could have a drink or something.'

She looked at him, astonished by his nerve. Eyes burning, she opened the door and stood back to let him pass. 'I don't think that would be a good idea.'

'Ali, you can't . . .'

She silenced him with a look as he edged by her, then shut him out of her life for good.

For the next half-hour, she moved around the flat taking down her Christmas decorations. She wrenched off the balls hanging from the twisted arrangement of willow, breaking their threads and stuffing them disorganised into their box. Cards with new addresses were saved while the others were ripped and thrown away, the lid of the recycling bin snapping loudly every time. Her shock and hurt alternated with fury. She had let down her guard, fallen in love, and been completely screwed over as a result. Other relationships had broken up and she'd recovered, but none of them had been with a man who had led her to expect so much. Most of them went home to their wives, their marriages sometimes reinvigorated by the liaison with Ali. Others drifted away, found someone else. She had believed Ian was different. How could she have been so stupid?

Ali had resolved a long time ago never to let herself be cast in the role of victim. As a result, whenever one of her lovers decided to move on, she always picked herself up and got on with her life, however painful. That was part of the deal. And she would survive this too, despite the intense hurt that she felt right now. She slammed the box of decorations into the cupboard with a bang.

When the flat was back to normal, she went upstairs and ran herself a deep bath where she lay for ages, thinking, every now and again topping it up with hot water.

Still pink from its heat, she wrapped herself in her kimono, her hair in a towel, and came downstairs to pour herself a glass of the champagne she'd bought specially for them to toast their new life. She picked up the Nehru shirt that he'd left behind, draped over the arm of the sofa. Taking the kitchen scissors, she cut and ripped it into the smallest possible pieces. Then, and only then, did she allow herself to cry.

6

Arriving at the studio the following morning, Ali immediately saw that Rick wasn't far away. The kettle was hot, and the beginnings of a bridesmaid's tiara lay across his soldering brick, beside a half-drunk cup of coffee. Beneath the large window, their long, shared workbench was the usual organised jumble of pliers, hammers, files, cutters, tweezers and soldering equipment crowded round the two semicircular cut-outs, each underhung with a leather skin to catch precious cut-offs and filings. Every time she walked into this room, Ali felt this was the place she belonged, the place where she could lose herself in creating beautiful pieces of jewellery, where the world could be kept at bay.

However much she wanted to bury herself under the duvet for the rest of the week, she had dragged herself out of bed. Whatever it had done to her, she wasn't going to allow

Ian's bombshell to blow away her business. Cleo Fellowes was due at eleven thirty to see the sketches for the pendant necklace that Ali had designed using the diamonds from a brooch belonging to Cleo's grandmother. After that, if the design was approved, Ali would spend the rest of the day untangling a chain that had got mixed up in the tumble polisher before polishing a couple of rings. She switched on her laptop for the first chore of the day: dreary admin. Her heart sank as she went to her mailbox and saw the number of incoming emails. She ran her eye down them, deleting any junk or spam that had found its way through the firewall. What was left was mostly bills.

She pulled up her accounts on the laptop again and grimaced. She remembered Mrs Orlov coming to her a couple of years ago, ordering an elaborate floral brooch using pink tourmalines and tiny round diamonds. For pieces that valuable, she rarely took on a customer without a personal recommendation and Mrs Orlov had been introduced by a previous client. That sort of word-of-mouth business had been crucial to her livelihood so far. However, in her excitement over Ian's proposal followed by her rush to get away to India, Mrs Orlov's failure to collect the new pieces had slipped her mind. As a result, over three thousand pounds' worth of jewellery was languishing in her safe, contributing to the hole in her finances. A customer's failure to collect an order was unusual but it did happen. Ali was uneasy, furious with herself for allowing her eye off the ball for the first time that she could remember. Bloody, bloody Ian.

She tried ringing the Orlovs. An automated voice picked up the call, informing her that the number she was calling was no longer recognised. She swiftly fired off an email. Within minutes, it pinged back into her in-box marked *Delivery Status Notification (Failure).* The gentle pealing of alarm bells went crazy. Was Mrs Orlov going to be one of those rare customers who didn't collect? It never failed to amaze Ali that anyone could pay a hefty deposit for a piece of beautiful bespoke jewellery and then go away for weeks on end without a word or even never turn up again. She looked up at the sound of the door slamming.

'Happy New Year.' Rick walked over to his end of the bench, touching Ali's shoulder as he passed her, simultaneously slipping on his overall over his checked shirt and jeans. 'Good time away?' He sat down and slugged his lukewarm coffee before picking up the tiara.

'Happy New Year. Yes, wonderful, thanks.' On her way to the studio, she had resolved not to discuss her personal life with Rick. Saying aloud what had happened would only drive home what she already knew: how stupid she had been to believe in Ian. Not talking about herself meant she could focus on something else. However crushed she was feeling, she was not going to risk her business any more than she had to. Life had to go on. So, sharpened by grief, she addressed her most pressing problem. 'One of my customers hasn't collected, so I'm going to have to ask you for that money you owe me. I'm sorry. Things are a bit tight.'

He ground some borax into a bowl and, with a drop of water, mixed it into a paste. As he brushed it onto the tiara, he said, 'They're probably on holiday — skiing or something. And I'm really sorry but I can't pay you back at the moment. I don't have the spare cash. Simple as that.'

His laissez-faire attitude to life usually amused her, but not today. She watched him cut the solder into tiny squares that he placed on the joints with precision, then she back-pedalled. 'You don't have to pay me the full whack immediately. What about two grand? That should tide me over. If I had another big client on the horizon, it wouldn't matter so much.'

'Haven't you got any exhibitions coming up?' He swiveled his stool to face her, picking at a stray bit of borax on his jeans.

'Not until the spring and anyway, that's not the point,' she insisted, irritated by his attitude. 'We agreed when I lent you the money that it was a loan, not a gift.'

'Al, be reasonable.' He switched on his blowtorch, focusing as the solder flooded the joints of the tiara. 'It's hardly my fault if your business is going through a bad patch. You can't expect me to repay you without giving me any notice.' His look challenged her to an argument but Ali was stunned into silence. She had always considered Rick a friend. They spent hours in the studio together, working, gossiping or discussing their respective designs. They had shared so much heartache and heartbreak — his mostly as he flitted from one woman to another in the wake of his divorce. His indifference was shocking.

His face relaxed as he switched off the torch. 'I'm sorry. Really. But I don't *have* the money. I paid off my credit cards and I'm just about on course with my overdraft, but Anna's still bleeding me dry. Christmas was expensive. I'm only just keeping on top of things. Can't you give me a little bit longer?'

How many times had she heard that? She was sympathetic to the drains on his pocket, especially from his ex-wife and young daughter, but, given the circumstances, she couldn't let this go. 'OK, let's say in two months you start paying me back. Fair? And if you can't, I'm going to have to get someone else in to share this place. I can't go on supporting both of us.'

'That's fair. That gives me time to find the money. Thanks.' Although his voice was cheery, his eyes betrayed his anxiety. But, Ali reminded herself, she couldn't let that concern her. For the rest of the day, they worked in silence apart from when Cleo Fellowes turned up to go over Ali's sketches for the pendant design. Otherwise the studio was filled with music from Radio 3. Ali relaxed, concentrated on polishing the first of her rings and put her finances and Ian to the back of her mind.

On her way home, she decided to call at the Belgravia address Mrs Orlov had given her. In her bag was the uncollected jewellery. From across the street, the imposing six-storey Georgian terraced house looked uninhabited. The upper windows were uncurtained, the ground floor and basement were shuttered up. Two plant pots chained to the railings on either side of the porch were empty. Thinking she saw a faint light in the basement, Ali crossed the road and rang the bell. While she waited in vain, a diminutive Filipino maid in a navy uniform came out of the neighbouring house. She blinked quizzically over the fence at Ali.

'I'm looking for Mrs Orlov,' Ali explained.

The maid looked uncertain. 'Mrs Orlov?' She shook her head. 'Mrs Orlov not here. They gone.'

'What do you mean "gone"? Gone where?' Ali thought of the gems in her handbag. 'They can't have.'

'I'm not sure. They don't live here no more. Maybe home — Russia. Sorry.' With no more to say, she ran down the steps, leaving Ali staring after her.

Perhaps giving her fortunes a couple of months to turn about was way too optimistic after all.

The four-hour drive north to visit her father in Preston was no more nightmarish than usual. Long queues of traffic crawled by stretches of unmanned roadworks. As Ali drove, her thoughts turned repeatedly to Ian. Eighteen hours had passed since she'd asked him to leave and she was still reeling.

What had he been thinking? Had he really been trying to leave his wife to live with her when, all the time, he had another woman waiting in the wings? Had he been hedging his bets all along just in case this mystery woman turned him down? Ali couldn't believe that anyone, least of all a man she believed she had loved, would be so calculating, so careless of the lives of people he professed to care for. How she had misjudged him. How she had misjudged herself.

As the miles passed, her mind flitted between what had happened and what she was going to do with her life now, one possibility fading out as quickly as another came into focus: move to another country, change career, find a man, adopt a child, run away, become a recluse, retire under the duvet for good. Time for a change. But a change was impossible without a cash injection to pay her bills. Her father was unlikely to help her. She knew exactly what he'd say. 'It's your mess. You get out of it.' She couldn't count the number of times she'd heard that as she grew up. He believed in the school of hard knocks and, thanks to that, she'd learned her independence.

She eventually turned in between the two brick gateposts and parked beside her father's old silver Honda. Her heart sank a little as she envisaged the twenty-four hours that lay ahead, but at least she would have to think about something other than herself. Grabbing her overnight bag from the boot, she walked through the side gate and round the corner of the house to enter it by the back door. Her father would be in his study, tuned out from any interference including the doorbell.

'Dad!' Ali yelled.

She was greeted by the muffled sound of barking: Sergeant, the ageing but still sprightly Border terrier who was her father's fierce and constant companion.

She tried again. 'Dad! I'm here.'

'Be down in a minute.' His voice travelled from the study where Ali knew he would be at his battered but trusty Corona typewriter, the laptop she'd given him ignored, surrounded by what mattered most to him: shelves containing his library of history books, including those he'd written himself; maps stuck about with pins marking out military campaigns hung beside pictures of the historical figures who fascinated him; a huge noticeboard littered with hundreds of yellow Post-it notes tracing the structure of his latest book. By his desk was a table covered in toy soldiers that he manoeuvred as if he was in the Cabinet War Rooms.

Ali went into the kitchen where she poured herself a gin and tonic — no ice, no lemon. Her father hated his drink diluted. The tonic was the only concession he made to his few guests.

When her mother had walked out, Ali had been thirteen. From that day, everything in this house had changed. She leaned against the sink, looking around the room. Without her mother to put a bunch of flowers at the centre of the table, to weigh in against the nasty aluminium Venetian blinds that replaced the floral curtains, or object to the removal of the dining chair cushions, the room had taken on the shipshape air of an officer's mess. There was no feminine touch here. The welcoming smells of baking and stewing, washing and ironing belonged to the time when they had been a family. Her father had done his best and so had Ali, but this kitchen had stopped being the heart of the family home long ago. Anything not put away was neatly aligned on the pristine worktop. Without thinking, she pulled open a drawer to discover his cooking utensils regimented, all handles to the right. Knowing the contents of the other drawers would all be similarly arranged almost made her laugh. The stainless-steel sink shone. Dishcloths were draped on the Aga bar, all folded and hung in exactly the same way, their edges level. The pans hung above it in descending sizes. Order. That was what stopped you from going under. Like father, like daughter.

'Al! There you are.' He entered the room just as she shut the drawer. 'Having a good poke around? Don't blame you. Checking up, I suppose. No need.' He laughed grimly as he grasped the whisky bottle and a tumbler, and poured himself a generous slug. 'See you've helped yourself. Cheers.'

'How are you, Dad?' Ali ignored his accusation. No point in getting her visit off on the wrong foot. Plenty of time for that. He looked well. Despite the hours he spent at his desk, writing and researching, he still held himself ramrod straight. The legs of his trousers were sharply creased, the brass buttons on his blue jacket bright. His moustache was neatly trimmed although there was a piece of tissue stuck with dried blood just beside his nose.

'Can't complain. Deep in research over a little-known aspect of the Wars of the Roses. Made some fascinating discoveries. Won't bore you with them though.' He tipped back his head and sucked his whisky through his teeth with a noisy hiss.

Ali gritted hers in dislike of a drinking

habit that had something unnervingly Hannibal Lecterish about it.

'I wouldn't be bored,' she protested, despite knowing that within minutes of him detailing whatever historical minutiae he was studying, she would be yawning. She longed to be able to sit down and share his enthusiasm and had often thought how being thrown together should have made them closer. Instead, her mother's departure thirty-two years ago had driven a wedge between them. A bitter cocktail of blame and guilt had driven each of them into their respective shells as they struggled to cope with the loss. As a teenager, Ali had blamed herself for not being a good enough daughter. As an adult, she learned that nothing was ever that clear-cut. Always, at first in the forefront of her mind and then, as time passed, fading to an infrequent fantasy, was the idea that her mother might come back for her. But they never heard from her again. Ali came to understand how devastated her father must have been, how humiliated when his wife left. His reaction had been to clam up, retiring to his study as frequently as he could, refusing even to mention her mother's name. Moira Macintyre. Ali wondered whether he ever thought that he might have behaved differently towards her, his daughter, by trying to explain what had happened to her mother so that she would understand. She had long wanted to bridge the gap that had existed between them since her mother left, but he'd always rebuffed her.

'Of course you would.' He chuckled. 'Tell you what, though. I've got a little surprise for you.'

'You have?' She pretended to think for a moment, knowing what was coming. 'We're going to the pub for dinner?' He nodded, clearly looking forward to the evening out. So no surprise there, then. Whenever she came to stay, they always had their first meal in the Swan, and the next morning she went to the supermarket and stocked up for him before making lunch, then going home.

'We are.' He began to do up the buttons of his jacket. 'But that's not it.'

'What then?'

'Don called me, asking for you.' His faded blue eyes shone with pleasure at the startling effect of his news.

'Don?' She repeated the name she hadn't heard for years. 'Don Sterling?'

He nodded.

'Are you sure?' He must have made a mistake. Don was a chapter in her life that had been closed for many years. Yet just the mention of his name was enough to unsettle her. She checked herself. Why was that surprising? They had been sweethearts since they met in the sixth form, both determined to escape their roots and make a new start. She remembered their disbelief when they'd both been offered places to study in London, she at the Cass and he at the London School of Economics. They had shared a rundown flat in Hackney from the start. The years during which they had lived together there had meant everything. Back then, she had believed that Don was her saviour and her soulmate, each of them useless without the other. To think that she had ever been so sentimental. Her friends had loved him. Her father had loved him — as much as he'd loved anyone since the disappearance of Ali's mother. She'd loved him.

'Are you sure?' she repeated.

'Oh, one hundred per cent,' he said, satisfied with the effect his news was having. 'He wanted to contact you so I gave him your email address. That was the right thing to do, wasn't it?'

'Well, yes, I guess. But why didn't you tell me before?'

'Because he only called a couple of days ago and I knew I'd be seeing you today.' He spoke deliberately slowly, always impatient if he thought she wasn't immediately cottoning on, never more so than when he was primed to do something else. Right now, get down to the Swan.

'Don! I can't believe it. I haven't heard from him for years.' When he left to join the Greenpeace ship — the dream job that nothing, not even Ali, could stop him accepting — his letters, at first frequent, excited and newsy, dried up to a trickle and then nothing as he abandoned himself to his new circumstances. In return, Ali's had been frequent and sad, abandoned as she was by the second person she'd truly loved. She'd given herself to him so completely that she didn't have any close friends to help her through.

'Well, maybe you won't hear from him now.' Her father was heading for the door. 'Maybe he'll think better of it. Come on, table's waiting.'

'Maybe he will.'

Ali followed him out into the rain-slicked street, disconcerted by the long-buried memories that were beginning to surface. ' 'Tis better to have loved and lost, than never to have loved at all.' But was it really? And to have lost twice over when she had been so young: her mother, then Don. And now, again. Despite her resolve, she couldn't stop her thoughts returning to Ian. She wouldn't talk about him to her father, but she couldn't get him out of her mind. Wrapping her coat around her, bowing her head into the wind, she followed her father, imagining that the evening would now follow its familiar pattern. As indeed it almost did.

The pub was its usual humming Saturday night — at least four people at the bar and one table out of seven taken. Eric nodded at the other regulars, took his usual table and ordered a bottle of wine. He read the menu through, eventually ordering the steak and kidney pie that he always had, allowing her to order scampi, before he spoke to her again.

'He sounded well, you know. Phoning from Australia, he was. Must have done well for himself. Always liked the boy.' He stroked his moustache with little up-and-down movements of his finger.

'I know you did, Dad. So did I.' She remembered with a jolt just how much and added as an afterthought, 'He saved me, you know.'

His finger stopped moving as he looked puzzled. 'Saved you?'

'After Mum left, don't you remember?'

'I don't know what on earth you mean.'

His face closed up, just as it always did whenever her mother was mentioned. Thirty-two years of unasked and unanswered questions lay between them. Characteristically, he changed the subject. 'How's the business?'

'Tough. Money's tight at the moment,' she answered automatically, then the frustration she had controlled for so long surfaced without warning, not giving him a chance to deliver his stock answer to her business problems. 'Dad, why won't you talk to me about her? She left so long ago and I still don't know why.'

Across the table, he unrolled the napkin containing his knife and fork, then placed them very deliberately, first one, then the other, on either side of his mat. He didn't look up as he aligned the salt and pepper exactly in the middle of the table. He was still expecting Ali to return to the matter of her business. All he had to do was wait long enough. He was oblivious to the recklessness that all of a sudden possessed her.

'What I meant was that I used to blame myself for Mum leaving until Don made me understand that there could have been any number of reasons. That's what I mean by "saving" me. He showed me a way through when you wouldn't — or couldn't.'

She surprised herself. That was more than she'd ever admitted to her father about what had happened. But it was true. To this day, she had no idea why her mother left or where she had gone. Divorce and death were words never mentioned in her hearing. She had only been thirteen, stretching her wings, testing the boundaries by bunking off school to smoke and snog boys down in the bushes by the public playground, by lying about going shopping when she and her friend Laura went to their first X-rated film or, when she was grounded, squeezing herself through the tiny bathroom window, shinning down the drainpipe and racing off to meet Mick Kirby and his mates in the car park of the local hotel. Life was hers for the taking. Or so she'd thought. Then, one day, she came home for tea to find the table laid and her mother gone. 'You didn't even tell me where she went.'

'I didn't know. That's why.' He sighed as if all the life had been punched out of him. 'I didn't know.' He kept his eyes on his table mat, chipping with his fingernail at a scrap of food that was stuck to it.

'But . . .' Ali had so many questions that had been bottled up since that time. Now the moment to ask them had finally presented itself, she didn't know where to start.

'Perhaps I should have talked to you, but I didn't know what to say.' He looked in the direction of the pub kitchen, as if willing his dinner to materialise and give him an excuse to stop the conversation. 'Not talking made it easier. Still does.'

Now *that,* she understood completely. That was another trait she had inherited from him: batten down the hatches and pretend nothing has happened. Keep going. Show no emotion. And the truth was that now she had breached his defences and could see his anguish, even after all these years, she didn't want to make it worse. 'Dad, I know that. I've always known and I learned from you to do the same thing. But sometimes, I do still wonder where she went. How could I not? Some of the girls at school joked about her running away, and I remember telling them she'd be coming back for me. Eventually everyone lost interest. But I didn't.' She didn't want to remember the alienation she'd felt throughout the rest of her schooldays until she could reinvent herself at art college.

She shifted to one side as her scampi and chips was put in front of her and watched as her father tucked into his pie, his relief at having a distraction plain. She played with her food, waiting for him to continue.

However, he ate as if his life depended on it, not pausing to talk. As soon as he had cleared his plate, he asked for and paid the bill, then stood up. 'Finished? Let's go home. We'll talk there. Not here.'

Back at the house, he led her into the living room, a faded memory of what it once had been. The musty unaired smell gave away how infrequently the room was used. While her father lit the ancient sputtering gas fire, Ali drew the curtains against the increasingly wild night outside before sitting on the spring-bound sofa. Her father took the chair opposite, perching on its edge, his body stiff and angular: knees bent, elbows on them, hands clasped, staring at the floor.

'Perhaps I should have spoken to you but I thought you'd come to terms with the loss of your mother in your own way.' He raised his eyes to her, then looked away as he smoothed his hair with one hand. 'I didn't want to open old wounds and make it worse for you.'

Ali's frustration got the better of her. 'For God's sake, Dad!' How, after so many years, could he not understand her better than that? 'She was my mother. You owed it to me to tell me what you knew. You still owe me.'

He got up and crossed to the bureau at the back of the room, pulling open a desktop drawer to remove an envelope before closing it again. 'It's complicated, Al. Too complicated for me.' His voice was so low that she had to lean forward to catch what he was saying. 'Moira had such a miserable upbringing herself, constantly undermined by her father and older brother. She wanted to do everything she could to make yours the perfect childhood. But, because of that upbringing, she grew up with no faith in herself. In the end, she left because she thought she was doing the best by us. There. Now you know.'

'But how could she possibly have believed that?' This went against everything she remembered about her mother. 'Why couldn't you make her see she was wrong?' Her agonised plea came from the young girl she'd once been. Her eyes stung with tears.

Her father was looking ill at ease. He wouldn't look at Ali, wouldn't comfort her. So much so that Ali had the distinct impression that there was something he wasn't telling her. This was as hard for her as it was for him. Now they'd finally come this far, she had to know — if only to put the subject to rest at last.

'I tried, believe me. But she left with no

warning. All I had from her was this.' He passed across the envelope that contained something solid. 'I never wanted to tell you this, because I thought it would hurt you as much as it did me. You didn't deserve that. But maybe I was wrong.'

From the envelope, she took out a piece of lined paper. Two rings fell out: a plain wedding band and a ring with a simple solitaire diamond. Ali turned them in her hand, then opened the paper, recognising the handwriting immediately.

Eric. Don't come after me this time. You won't find me. I'm giving you back my rings. Alison will have a better life without me. I love her so much but I'm not the mother I wanted to be to her, nor am I the wife I wanted to be to you. It's better this way. I'm sorry.

Moira

' "This time"? She'd done this before?' The assumptions that had supported Ali throughout the adult part of her life had been whipped away without warning. She felt as if she was in free fall.

He nodded his head, unable to speak.

'But didn't you look for her?'

He looked so weary, so defensive. 'Of

121

course I looked, Al. Of course I did. What do you think I am? I was no more confident of being a good father to you on my own than she had been about being your mother. And I wanted her back.' He paused. 'For me as much as for you.'

For a shocking moment, Ali thought he was going to cry. But he coughed, averting his head so she couldn't see his eyes. That was the first time Ali could remember hearing or seeing him express any feelings for her mother. She had imagined arguments, other men, affairs, fallings out of love, but never this.

'But why couldn't you find her?'

'Because when someone doesn't want to be found, they can make it almost impossible for you. That's what she did. That note's the last thing I had from her.'

What sort of mother could desert her only child? The shadowy figure that her mother had become over the years was taking a step towards the light. Where could she have gone? Perhaps Ali should look for her. Perhaps she was waiting to be found.

Her parents must have been in their late forties then, a little older than she was now: a dangerous age, a time when you look at what you have and what you want. Life is getting shorter. Either you act and effect a change or you settle for what you know. She understood as well as anyone what was involved and how difficult it could be. Most of all, she identified with the person she imagined her mother to be: restless, questing, searching to be the best she could. The woman wasn't quite such a stranger any more.

Later, lying in her old childhood bed, comforted by its familiar sag, Ali thought about their conversation. Fleetwood Mac, the Rolling Stones and Queen looked down on her from the faded posters tacked to the wall, their edges curling: the few things in the house that her father hadn't submitted to his desire for order. Perhaps there was a sentimental old fool in there trying to find a way out after all? Otherwise any other signs of Ali's childhood had been stashed away in the chest of drawers and wardrobe or in the attic. In all these years she had never once dreamed that her mother might have left in the misguided belief that she was acting in her daughter's best interests.

She twisted her mother's two rings around her right ring finger. How would she have supported herself? Had Eric given her any money? Did she have some of her own? Where could she have gone? There must be more to the story than Ali's father was giving away. But why? Who was he protecting? Her mother? Himself? Or Ali? Had she been such a terrible child? Was she the reason that her mother left? Then she remembered how Don had taught her that no one's actions were governed by a single reason. Life was far more complicated than that.

Imagining her father through the wall, lonely in the room he had once shared with his wife, Ali wondered whether he was lying awake, staring into the dark, like her. She wondered briefly if she was destined for a life alone. After what Ian had done, she couldn't imagine trusting herself to anyone again. When they had finally turned in, Eric was still visibly distressed, having been unable to tell her any more. After giving her a glimpse of the truth, the shutters had come down again. She would not prise any more out of him this weekend. Ali had never tried to imagine the life her parents had together. As soon as her mother disappeared, she was encouraged to forget her and, eventually, that's what she had almost managed to do. Until now.

7

The pub was busy with early-evening drinkers as Lou pushed her way down the long Victorian bar, all dark wood and brass real-ale pumps. Behind it a couple of frazzled bar staff tried to keep up with the customers who were waiting, shouting orders, brandishing cash and turning away with their drinks held high so as not to spill them. The noise was way up the decibel scale and Lou was wondering why on earth she had agreed to meet Hooker here, a place where she'd have to strain to hear a word. Perhaps that was indeed the answer. She was protecting herself against his expected anger.

She had been surprised by how pleased her ex had seemed at hearing from her although, like Nic, he'd been uninterested in her holiday beyond the fact that she'd come back in one piece. She had hoped her family might like to know what she'd got up

125

to without them. Equally, she hoped he hadn't interpreted the call, so soon after her return, as a sign that she had been missing him. She thought she'd detected a warmth in his voice that had been absent towards her for years. For a moment, her feelings towards him softened before she told herself to get a grip. Old habits, she warned herself. That's all it was.

As soon as he realised that she wanted to meet him, he had suggested the Maryatt Arms, a pub she hadn't visited for more years than she could count. Long ago, she came here with her brother Sam and his teammates after those dreaded university rugby matches. She used to stand with Jenny, shivering on the sidelines, united in their incomprehension at what was happening on the pitch, freezing to death, yelling their hearts out when Sam scored a try. The Maryatt Arms was where she'd first met her future husband. His keen sportsmanship was of course how he'd got his name. To everyone, including his family, he was 'Hooker'. He'd caught her eye both on and off the pitch so when he offered her a drink and to educate her in the finer points of the game, she accepted. Wirier than some of his teammates, he had a certain twinkle in his eye that translated into a come-and-get-me charm. So she had gone and got him.

Lou couldn't begin to count the number of nights she'd whiled away in this place, first with Sam and the team, and later with Hooker when they'd continued to come here, long after the matches had stopped and the players had moved on to life after university. Convenient to the house that he was then sharing with three other would-be lawyers, the pub was warm compared to the unheated chill of home, and convivial since someone or other they knew would usually turn up of an evening. Since then, the place had changed. The old boys and locals who propped up the bar were long gone, turfed out in favour of gastro-pub splendour.

She knew exactly where he'd be sitting. At the table by the fire, where thirty-something years ago (no, she couldn't remember exactly: always a small bone of contention between them), he'd leaned across and asked her to marry him. Moments after accepting, she'd watched him get dragged off to a game of pool. Given the flak from his mother's appalled reaction to the unromantic nature of his proposal, he'd taken Lou out to dinner and repeated it, organising the diamond engagement ring to be found in the bottom of her champagne glass. She accepted delightedly to a bored round of applause from three Turkish waiters.

Now she thought about it, the romance that was so absent from his original proposal had been absent from most of their married life. They had loved one another, of that she was sure, but those early years devoted to their careers and babies made it hard to carve out pockets of time for themselves. Their separate jobs — hers as a fashion journalist, his as a corporate lawyer — took them travelling to opposite ends of the country and sometimes of the world, leaving a succession of overpaid nannies to hold the fort. The money she earned salved Lou's conscience — at least she was paying for the best childcare possible when she was away. By the time she began working from home, when Jamie was fifteen, Nic thirteen and Tom ten, the original driving force had disappeared from their marriage altogether. Almost without them noticing, Lou and Hooker's paths began to cross less frequently until they had started to live their lives almost entirely in parallel.

There he was, just as she expected, nursing the remains of a pint, an untouched glass of white wine opposite him. He looked up, spotted her and raised a hand. Measuring in at just over six feet (with a heel on his shoe), he was still a handsome man, distinguished-looking some might say, with deep-set eyes, a vertical furrow running up from the bridge of his slightly skewed nose (rugby-playing break), smooth skin that, when he was feeling particularly smug, reminded Lou of a frying sausage about to split its skin. Imagining the speed with which this bonhomie would be transformed into something far less pleasant as soon as he heard her news, made her want to turn and go home. Then she remembered Nic and her resolve stiffened.

'Excuse me?' A young woman touched her arm. 'Excuse me, but aren't you Lou Sherwood?'

'Mmm?' Half turning, Lou took a closer look. Shiny fifties-styled hair, heavily lashed brown eyes intent on her, lipsticked lips, neat black suit, glass of champagne in hand. A distant bell of recognition clanged somewhere in the back of Lou's mind but she couldn't place her.

'It's Tess. Tess Granger. It's been years. How are you?'

Tess Granger? Lou racked what she laughingly called her brain for something that would give her a clue to the younger woman's identity.

'Tess, of course.' She was still trying to identify her while she bluffed. 'What are you doing now?'

'After you left, I was made assistant to Belle Flanders. If it weren't for you, I'd never have got this far.'

Aha! So they'd worked together over ten years ago at *Chic to Chic.* Belle had been one of the hungry young things snapping at Lou's fashionable heels, but who the hell was Tess? She must have been there when she'd left, forced to give up her exhausting career partially thanks to redundancy but also by the equally exhausting demands made on her by Nic who was setting out on her teenage years with alarming abandon, and the two boys — so much easier. Nic was running wild, refusing to curb her will to any au pair. That and the redundancy had come at a time when Lou had begun to wonder what she was doing in the magazine world. She had become tired of the travelling and the endless demands made on her time. Her face didn't fit any more, but she'd had enough. She'd even thought she might start her own dress shop then but Hooker had insisted the children needed their mother at home. He didn't trust the sequence of au pairs looking after them not to fill their heads with rubbish and foreign swear words. He said only a parent could be trusted to teach their children what they

130

needed to know. But Lou sometimes wondered whether she'd managed to teach them anything at all. However, she had begun to notice the way he had been looking at the young women they'd employed in the name of childcare, and caved in, partly for that reason and partly because she was too exhausted to resist.

'I'm so glad it's all worked out for you.' Her powers of recall had totally deserted her.

'It certainly has! I left six months after you and went to the States. Now I'm back as the new editor of *Stylish*. We're celebrating.' She gestured towards a young man and a couple who were talking and laughing at a table by the window. 'Where are you now?'

Stylish? The glossy young rival to *Vogue* and this young woman was the editor. Suddenly Lou felt about a hundred years old. She looked down at — oh, no — her fleece, the convenient style bypass for the middle-aged woman. Shit! She deliberately hadn't followed her resolve to stick to statement dressing that would advertise her business, because she hadn't wanted Hooker to think she was making a special effort just for him. She hadn't given a thought to the fact that she might bump into someone she knew. If only she'd changed into the pomegranate velvet coat she finished just before she went away. It had taken ages to make but the cut was so flattering, it had been worth every minute.

Hideously aware that the make-up she'd put on that morning was no longer a refuge for her almost certainly shiny nose, and praying her lipstick hadn't leaked into the tiny vertical wrinkles that had recently been making a bid for domination around her mouth, she thanked God that her recent haircut had temporarily tamed things so at least in that department she looked accept-able. Perhaps Tess wouldn't notice the rest.

Of course she would. Just move on, swiftly.

'That's fantastic news. I'm so sorry I can't stop to chat, but I'm late meeting someone.'

'Well, great to see you. We should catch up. Lunch or something.' She held out a small embossed card.

Knowing Tess had absolutely no intention of following up this suggestion, Lou took the card, at the same time registering how useful the other woman might be to her. But it wasn't too late to say something. 'In fact, I'm setting up a new business that might interest you.'

Tess cocked an eyebrow. 'Really? Then we should definitely stay in touch. Call me.'

But she sounded as if anything initiated by Lou would be of little interest to her.

'Thanks. I will.'

They both turned back towards their respective engagements, Lou aware that Hooker was watching her, his glass now almost empty. He gestured a request for a replacement since she was by the bar. Irritated by the way he assumed she would do his bidding and even more by the fact that she was doing it, she shouldered her way through and ordered a pint of Adnams, Hooker's long-time preferred real ale, and a large vodka and tonic for herself as the need for a shot of Dutch courage more powerful than the waiting glass of wine overcame her.

Hooker half stood as she approached, hobbled by the chair seat digging into the backs of his knees. By the time she'd put down the drinks, divested herself of her coat and sat down, his welcoming smile had changed into a grimace of pain. He sat down with evident relief. Unlike so many men his age, he still looked good in jeans — not bagging round the arse and knees or disappearing under a beer gut — teamed that day with a deep blue shirt. This was a man whose looks still counted — to him at least. Which was more than they did to Lou any longer. She controlled the urge to point out the two rogue eyebrow hairs that curled over the frames of his specs. No. No longer her concern.

'The holiday's obviously done you good,' he commented. Now she'd arrived, he could relax.

They clinked glasses, more out of habit than good cheer.

'How was it? Christmas, I mean,' she asked.

'Quiet. I took Nic and Tom to dinner at the Mermaid's Heart, that new fusion restaurant in Shoreditch. I thought being at home might make things a bit difficult, with you not being there and Jamie and Rose in Canada. Besides, can you imagine if I'd tried my hand at a turkey . . . ashes is the only word that leaps to mind.'

Surprised by this unusual sensitivity towards their children, she laughed nonetheless.

'Where were you?' he asked. So he was interested after all.

'At a tented camp, sitting around a blazing fire under the stars. Not a turkey or a Christmas tree in sight.' To be teleported there right now would be a prayer answered.

'Camping?! That's not like you. The Lou I know likes her creature comforts: good food and wine, sprung mattresses, hot water on tap, light to read by.'

'Oh, we had all that. I didn't know tents like those existed, or I'd have gone long ago. And there wasn't a boy scout to be seen.' She was about to wax lyrical about the luxury they'd enjoyed — the comfortable beds, the electric light, the home-cooked meals, the showers — when she noticed that he'd adopted that look she knew so well. Indulge her for a while and then, with a bit of luck, she'll shut up and we can get onto the main agenda so I can get off to do the next thing on mine. Well, if that's the way you want to play it, bring it on, she thought, draining her vodka. Feeling suitably fortified, she summoned up all her sangfroid and leaned forward. Then I'll begin.

'Actually, I called you for a reason.'

Hooker looked gratifyingly alarmed by her earnest expression, then snuck a look at his watch. 'Come on, then. Spit it out. Whatever it is, can't be that bad.'

'There's no easy way of putting this. I've got some news for you that you may be less than happy with.' She hesitated and took a sip of the white wine, then taking a breath, she braced herself.

'We're going to be grandparents!' There.

'What? Jamie and Rose?' He banged his glass on the table, looking more pleased than she could remember seeing him in a long time. 'That's terrific news. But why didn't they tell me themselves? Perhaps they thought I'd prefer it if they'd waited till after they'd got married. Well, I would of course. The timing's not perfect. But when's the baby due? Are they bringing the marriage forward? My God!' He crashed his fist onto the table, so his beer almost slopped over the edge of his glass. 'A grandfather. That's not something I ever expected to be so soon. What about you? Grandparents, eh? This calls for something stronger.'

Lou sat silent, unable to interrupt. Then, as he sat back, beaming with pleasure, she prepared herself to prick his balloon.

'No, not Jamie and Rose.' She took another sip.

'Not Jamie and Rose.' He repeated her words slowly as he absorbed their meaning. 'Who then? Tom?' He shook his head. 'The little idiot. How many times have I warned him about not using condoms.' He gave a little snort of laughter.

I bet you have, she thought. One of your specialist subjects, no doubt. There was an underlying pride in his voice at having a son who sowed his wild oats with abandon and virility. Every feminist bone in her body objected to his tone but she bit back any comment. This was not the time for personal recrimination. This was a moment when they should be pulling together. Let's get this over with.

'No,' she said, her fingers stroking the stem of her glass. 'Not Tom. Nic.'

As he stared at her, she thought his head might explode. His face grew a deeper and deeper shade of red until he let all his breath out in one convulsive rush. 'Nic? No. She must have made a mistake.'

'There's no mistake.' Keep calm, breathe deeply. If anyone's going to make a scene, it's not going to be you.

Hooker seemed genuinely flabbergasted at first, as if unable to believe such a thing of his beloved daughter. Watching his face, Lou saw his thought process: from shock, to confusion, to denial, to acceptance, to fury. With his anger came the return of his power of speech.

'Who's responsible?'

Pointing out that Nic inevitably bore fifty per cent of the responsibility would not help. Instead, Lou said, 'Max, I think.'

'You think? Why aren't you sure? When I see him, I'll . . .' He stopped, unable to think of a sufficiently terrible threat.

The people on the next two tables had paused in the conversation and turned to see what was going on.

'Shhh,' Lou cautioned. 'There's no point getting worked up.'

'Worked up? What the hell do you mean? I've every right to be worked up. You walk in here and tell me that my daughter's having a baby and expect me to be calm.' He lowered his head into his hands. 'Oh, my God. A grandfather.' His earlier pride had given way to despair. He angled his head so that he could see her. 'I definitely need something stronger. A whisky.'

'And you want me to get it?' Lou bridled at being asked to go to the bar for him a second time. Nor did she relish the idea of a repeat encounter with Tess and her fashionista companions who she'd noticed looking in their direction.

'No, no. I'll get them. Same again?' He picked up her empty wine glass as he edged out of the narrow space, his other hand already foraging for the change in his pocket.

She nodded, relieved to be left on her own for a moment.

By the time he returned, his expression was something approaching normal. Having finally accepted that a man had defiled his precious only daughter without his consent but with hers, he had moved on to a new tack.

'Presumably you've persuaded her that the sensible way to deal with this is for her to have an abortion?'

Here we go.

'No, I haven't.' She registered the taut straight line of his mouth. 'This is Nic's life and Nic's decision. She wants to keep the baby and I only want to support her.'

'For God's sake, Lou. She's far too young. Surely even you can see that.' He was speaking to her as if she was irredeemably stupid. 'A single mother. My daughter. No.' He gave a heartfelt groan. If what they were talking about weren't so serious, Lou would have laughed at the theatricality of his response.

'Hooker, get a grip. Yes, she's your daughter but she's not the toddler you built sandcastles with every year any more. She's not the thirteen-year-old whose pocket money you stopped when she threw her Bacardi Breezer bottles into the neighbours' garden. She's got her own life now and she doesn't have to account to us for what she does any more. Whether you like it or not. Our job's to give her all the help we can. That's all we can do.'

'But her career . . .' His voice was muffled,

139

as he nursed his whisky glass in front of his mouth.

'Thousands of women have babies and return to work. That won't be a problem because she's already thought everything through.' Echoing Nic's words made Lou share her daughter's confidence that everything would work out.

'You say that . . .'

'I know that,' Lou said firmly. 'She's always loved looking after things so perhaps having a baby . . . Let's see.'

'Do you remember when she rescued that pigeon with a broken wing? She was always such a softie.' Hooker smiled at the memory. Lou's recollection was less of the softie and more of the pigeon shit that had covered the living room when the bird had escaped its cardboard box. Nor had she forgotten the hours that it had taken to clear up the room to Hooker's satisfaction, but without his help. Oddly, Nic too had found something urgent to do. But she was glad that Hooker's mood was changing as the whisky took hold. 'And Ripper, her hamster whose hair fell out.' She smiled too, remembering how Nic had lavished affection and mite dust on the poor little wrinkled, bald creature until it had finally died.

As they began to swap reminiscences, their

differences were put to one side. Whatever happened between them in the future, these memories would always be theirs alone. Their shared family experiences interested no one else in the world but them.

Once she leaned over and touched his arm. Still talking, he covered her hand with his just before she swiftly removed it. But one memory led on to the next and, as they travelled back in time, Lou began to recognise the Hooker she had once fallen for, the man who could make her laugh. She checked herself. Perhaps she should go home. But, memories and tongues loosened by alcohol, the two of them stayed where they were in the warmth of the fire, drinking and reminiscing, till the chairs were being put on the tables around them. By then she was aware of how pleasantly hazy the world seemed.

Reluctantly they dragged themselves out into the night air. Feeling definitely the worse for wear although triumphant that Hooker had eventually taken on board and almost accepted Nic's news, Lou stepped forward to give her ex an affectionate peck farewell. Slightly surprised at herself, she overbalanced, righting herself with one foot in the gutter, her hand on his chest. 'Whoops. Shouldn't have mixed my drinks.

Sorry.' She giggled and removed her hand as if it was burned.

He smiled. 'I've missed the sound of your laugh, you know.'

What? She struggled to get a grip of herself but she was at least one glass of wine too late. If only she'd had more than a packet of peanuts to soak it all up. But she hadn't thought.

'Let me see you to a taxi, Lou. I'm sure we'll find one if we go this way.' Always the gent, and always the one in control. But the combination of drink and the cold air had done for her defences. Instead of sobering up, she was giddy with forgotten affection.

'My knight in shining armour.' She stifled another laugh as she concentrated on walking in a straight line beside him, trying and failing to use the breaks in the paving stones as a guide.

'Take my arm. Go on.' Hooker angled his elbow outwards so she could slip her arm through, just as she would have done years before. Old habits. Hard to resist.

As they made their uneven way along the pavement, Fred Astaire's and Judy Garland's couple of swells unaccountably danced into her mind. She began to sing under her breath.

For once, Hooker didn't comment on her

questionable musical ability. In fact she thought she heard him hum a note or two himself, before he said, 'Grandparents, Lou. Just think of it. Us!'

As they walked and talked and sang, they hardly noticed that not one single taxi made an appearance in the empty streets as they drew closer and closer to Jenny's house.

8

When she woke the next morning, Lou's head seemed to be gripped in a vice that tightened with each new waking moment, the focus of the pain drilling into her skull just above her right eyebrow, then rippling outwards through her brain. She rolled slowly onto her left side, then paused until her head stopped swimming. Propping herself up on one elbow, wincing at the slight sensation of nausea, she reached for the glass of water. Almost empty! When had that happened? She had no memory of drinking it. The little that was left trickled onto her tongue with as much effect as a couple of raindrops in the Sahara. She ran her tongue around her mouth in a vain attempt to improve the bottom-of-a-birdcage taste. Someone had fur-lined her teeth during the night. She must have brushed them before she came to bed. Surely? That was routine. Looking down, she saw that she was naked. Her pyjamas were in a ball that just edged out from under the pillow. She spotted her bra at the end of the bed. She groaned.

Oh, God, please no! I didn't.

From behind her came confirmation in the form of a gentle rumble like the sound of a gathering storm.

Oh, God. I did.

We did.

She inched herself into a sitting position, swung her legs out of the bed and reached for her purple velveteen dressing gown, a gift from the boys two Christmases ago, that was hanging on the back of the door. In the dim light that leaked into the room through the narrow gap between the curtains, she could make out the silhouettes of their discarded clothes on the carpet. Cue another groan. Wrapping her robe round her, unable to steady her spinning head completely, she collapsed back onto the duvet, welcoming the comfort of the pillow. Vodka, wine, then brandy when they'd arrived indoors — a cocktail mixed in hell. What had she been thinking?

She turned her head. Beside her Hooker lay beached on his side, his back to her, naked as the day he was born, reeking like a brewery. As he farted and moved backwards a smidgeon, she spotted a couple of old scratches between his shoulder blades. Not recent enough to have been put there by her, thank God. Her eyes closed as she tried to piece together how she had got herself into this situation.

Fuelled by alcohol, all that talk of the children's childhood, all those shared memories, had made Lou feel a warmth towards her ex that she hadn't felt for years. She couldn't remember the last time they'd run over so much shared ground together: ground that was uniquely theirs. Or, indeed, when they'd had so much to say to each other. What on earth had happened?

They'd emerged into the winter night and she remembered linking her arm through his, leaning against him, enjoying the unfamiliar sense of mutual support. 'Imagine. Us as grandparents,' he said as she stumbled against him. 'I'm not sure that I'm ready for this.'

'Of course you are.' She concentrated on walking in a straighter line. 'It had to come sometime. We just weren't expecting Nic to be first.' At least she thought that's roughly what she had said given that, oddly, she couldn't remember every word. With her coaxing, Hooker had come round to the idea that they should support their daughter whatever he felt. She at least recalled the result of their conversation, if not the exact means of achieving it. He had finally accepted that, with or without his blessing, the baby would be born.

Once they'd reached her gate . . . what had happened? In an unwelcome flash of clarity, she remembered asking him in to call for a minicab. After he had walked her back, it had seemed churlish to send him out into the empty streets to find a taxi. If only they had come across one en route, they wouldn't be here now. Hooker would have dropped her off and continued on his way. Instead, she had suggested coffee. Seeing the bottle in her store cupboard, he suggested cognac. Her protests that it was only there for the Christmas cake were short-lived. By then they'd had enough to drink not to care and the phone call was never made.

She opened her eyes. There on the bedside table, beside her water glass, was the evidence — an incriminating tumbler that had once contained her brandy. She didn't want to remember any more. Instead, she got up and went into the bathroom where she stood, eyes half shut, under the shower, waiting for the jets of water to batter her into some semblance of life. But however much she might not want to recollect what had happened the previous night, random disconnected images floated into her consciousness. Hooker coming up behind her in the kitchen and slipping his arm around her waist. Her laughing him off. Spilling the ground coffee all over the worktop. The brandy. A second glass. Fumbling for the living-room lights. Stumbling towards the sofa. Laughing at a joke. His touch. His whispered endearments. The unexpected comfort of a pair of arms around her. His quiet insistence on taking her up to bed. Her quiet assent. His undressing her. Sex. Oh, God!

Whenever they'd last made any kind of love was lost in the mists of time. She rifled through her memory bank and came up with Fiona and Charlie's anniversary party. That was well over a year ago and memorable for being the last time she'd been drunk, thanks to the imaginative cocktails that had packed a punch as hefty as any from Muhammad Ali. So alcohol had proved her downfall yet again. Note to self: do not ever, ever, drink with Hooker under any circumstances again. Newly resolved, she hopped out of the shower. Yes, definitely feeling better. Rather than return to the scene of the crime, she decided that she'd be better off with a strong black coffee to help her assess her next move and anticipate his.

What must *he* be thinking? At the moment, nothing much judging from the snore that trumpeted from the bedroom. She felt her way down the stairs, pulling open the blind halfway down, allowing a bleak wintry light to illuminate the staircase. A train rumbled past, making the windows rattle.

In the kitchen, she wiped up the coffee, relieved that she'd still got enough for a jug left in the packet. As the smell of it brewing took over the kitchen, she slumped at the table, lost in thought. Succumbing to Hooker's dubious charms was a worrying, not to say decidedly retrogressive, development in her bid for independence from him. Apart from the drink, and the relief at having broken Nic's news, something else had definitely made her respond to him. She couldn't even pretend to herself that she hadn't enjoyed what followed. And just when she had all but accepted that her interest in sex had galloped off to the dying grass of middle age. Obviously not yet.

She made space for their mugs on the table by arranging the newspaper supplements and two days' worth of opened post into an uneven pile among the half-burned candles, the vase of tulips and assorted table mats. Out of the corner of her eye, she caught sight of the calendar pinned on the wall by the phone, reminding her that she had an appointment to meet the lettings agent at eleven to look at possible premises for her shop. She contemplated postponing until a time when she'd feel less mothy and in more of a decision-making mode. But no, that would be too pathetic. She couldn't allow one evening that veered off the rails to scupper her future.

From upstairs came the sound of Hooker moving around. She heard the shower being turned on, a door shut, opened, more footsteps. At the sound of his tread on the stairs, Lou braced herself.

'Morning!' Breezy was the word to describe his entrance. As he pulled out a chair and poured himself some coffee, he looked as if he hadn't a hangover in the world. 'Anything to eat?'

' 'Fraid not. I could kill for a piece of toast, but no bread.' She didn't mention her extremely shaky resolution to keep off bread for January. And now alcohol. He'd only sneer at its familiarity and her annual failure.

'Well!' he said with some satisfaction. 'Who'd have thought it? It may have been a long time, but you certainly haven't lost your touch.' He stretched a hand towards her knee but she swiftly uncrossed her legs and tucked them out of reach under the table, pulling her dressing gown across them.

Patronising her had always come as second nature to him, just one of so many reasons for her leaving him, all of which were sneaking back into her mind just now. But too late to undo the previous night and besides, despite herself, she couldn't help feeling a little glow of satisfaction at his remark. Good to know that she was still in acceptable working order, even if the compliment came from the one man she'd rather not hear it from.

'Look, Hooker.' She concentrated on what she wanted to say. 'What happened last night was a mistake. I was drunk. So were you. It doesn't make any difference to the way things are between us.'

'Doesn't it?' His grin was wider than the Cheshire cat's.

'No. Absolutely not.' Yes, that was the tone she wanted: firm, decisive.

'You're being a bit harsh, aren't you? Perhaps having a break from one another was all we needed.' He tried to meet her eye, but she looked away.

'No, no, no.' She tried to string together a few coherent thoughts. 'You've forgotten, that's all. We had separate lives. We don't want to be together.'

'Come on. It wasn't that bad. Last night proved that.' That hand reached out towards her again, the signet ring glinting on his little finger.

'Yes, it was.' Indignant, she stood up and backed away as coherency returned. 'Over the last few years, you've led your life exactly the way you wanted. Sometimes we barely spoke for days on end. I was lonely and felt taken for granted. I couldn't go on like that. Now it's my turn. I'm sorry.' She turned to go upstairs.

'Where are you going?' His hand was on the coffee pot, ready to pour himself another cup. His ring chinked against the china.

Panicked by the idea of him settling in, she replied without thinking. 'I'm looking at a shop at eleven, so I need to get myself together.'

'What shop?' He shook his head in disbelief. 'You're not seriously going to go through with that idea?'

One of the kids must have told him. Annoyed with herself for not swearing them to secrecy before she went away and not wanting to hear his opinion, which was obviously going to be negative, she tried to dismiss the subject. 'It probably won't come to anything.'

'How are you going to afford it?' Money. That's what so much came down to with him.

'I'll manage.' At least the kids hadn't spilled the beans by reminding him of the savings she'd stashed away after her parents' deaths. Sam and Jenny had burned through their share — he by taking himself to a new start in Canada, she by buying her house — but Lou had saved most of hers for the rainy day that had finally arrived.

'Anyway, isn't running a shop a bit, well . . . I don't know . . . beneath you?'

'For God's sake, Hooker! Unlike you, I don't care what other people think.' That, she realised, was almost true. What a great position in life to have reached at last. 'And I'm not going to be coming to you for a sub, if that's what you're worried about. *If* I go ahead with it, I'll let you know. But don't hold your breath. Now, I must get on.'

'But don't we need to talk about Nic and what's going to happen?' He adopted that little-boy-lost look. But its once seductive charm cut no ice with her any more. Or, almost none.

'We did that last night. She's having the

baby in about six months and we're going to help her with whatever she needs. There's no more to say for now.' She'd done what had been asked of her — and much, much more besides. Now, all she wanted Hooker to do was walk out of the door and leave her to get on with her life. 'Anyway, haven't you got anything to do this morning?'

At last, he got the message and rose to his feet. 'Perhaps you're right. Perhaps we did get a bit carried away.'

'A bit!'

'Too soon, I suppose.'

She thought she heard a measure of regret somewhere.

'Hooker . . .' Spoken with as much of a threat in her voice as she could muster. 'It's not too soon — it's too late.'

He waved his hand in the air as if brushing away an insistent wasp. 'OK, OK. I'm off. I'll find myself a cab home.' He picked up his overcoat from the back of the kitchen chair. 'Thanks for the coffee.' Then he winked, before leaning forward to kiss her cheek. She tried not to flinch at the contact. How could she have slept with him? Like an idiot, she had only succeeded in complicating matters between them. Vowing never to let another drop of alcohol pass her lips ever again, she went upstairs to get ready, leaving him to make his own way out.

As soon as they walked through the door of the empty shop, Lou fell in love with the place. Just off the High Street, in the middle of a row of four shops and a café, the premises were small but ideal for what she wanted. Between a boutique and a small art gallery, with a deli, two furniture shops, another couple of high-street clothes shops and a paint supplier lower down the hill, she'd be assured of enough passing trade. The large plate-glass window was big enough for imaginative displays of her clothes. Behind it was a light-filled L-shaped space. Immediately Lou could see its potential. If she put a counter across the arm of the L, there'd be enough room behind it for shelves where she could store fabric and stock on the left, and for a central cutting and sewing table on the right. At the very back was a tiny kitchenette and toilet, separated by a window and glass door leading into a tiny courtyard. On the back wall of the main shop, beside her imagined counter, were two changing rooms that had been installed by the previous owner. The body of the shop was wide enough for hanging rails and shelves on both sides. Perhaps she would put a low chair and table in the corner by the changing rooms. All the place needed was a good clean and a bit of imagination on the decorating front.

'What do you think?' she asked Jamie who conveniently had the day off from the film set where he was working. He'd been so excited when he'd landed the job of production assistant but the long hours and night shoots were taking their toll. He had seemed happy to come along to give his opinion on the shop instead. At that moment, he was poking his head round the toilet door. He turned to her, pulling a face.

'Looks OK. Smells a bit.'

'Honestly, Jamie. Don't go overboard. You might die from the enthusiasm.'

'It's hard to get really worked up over a shop, Mum.' He opened the door into the back yard and stepped back as a torrent of water sluiced out of a broken gutter. 'Are you absolutely sure this is what you want to do with your money? You could lose the lot.'

'I could. But if I don't do this, then I won't know. You know what they say: Better to have tried and all that.' She wanted him to understand but he only mustered a half-hearted 'Yeah, yeah' as he paused in front of a mirror fixed to the wall. Jeans straight — check. Shoes, trendily unpolished — check. Jumper just skimming the belt so a band of branded pants elastic could be seen — check. Navy single-breasted wool coat, collar up — check. Hair waxed, just so — check. Looking cool.

How world-weary the young could be, when everything was still at their feet. Unlike Jamie, she knew how fast life and its possibilities could slip away. The thought was followed by a prickle of excitement.

'Look, this is a real ambition of mine that I've never had the time or opportunity for. So you know what? I'm going to go for it. And you never know, I might just succeed.' She let the words, or I'll die trying, remain unsaid.

'Right, Mum! You gotta do what you gotta do.' He turned back to her with a broad smile that touched her heart.

'You really think so?' She still wanted his reassurance.

'Yeah. I really do. What are you going to call it?'

As he put his arm around her, she sank back against him. Not so long ago, she had been the one who comforted, consoled and supported the children. She couldn't have told him how much pleasure she gained from this unexpected reversal of roles.

She'd had the answer to his question at her fingertips for years now. ' "Puttin' on the Ritz".'

As she said it, he squeezed her shoulder. 'That's cool. I like it.'

At that moment, the young sharp-suited lettings agent walked through the door, having been arguing the toss with a traffic warden since he'd let them in. His flushed complexion suggested their discussion had not gone the way he would have liked, but he had a job to do, a commission to earn. 'What do you think?'

'It's terrific. Just what I was looking for. Now what do we do?' She held out her hand for him to shake.

'Whoa! Mum! Don't you think we should go home and double-check the finances first?' Jamie looked anxious as she propelled herself headfirst into an agreement, probably worried about the flak he'd get from his brother and sister for not keeping their wayward mother in check.

'Don't worry. I won't blame you if it's the wrong decision. But this place feels so right. And it's not as if I haven't done enough research on the area. Imagine that wall a smoky pink, dark grey curtains in front of the cubicles, bleached floorboards, off-white shelving . . .' She could see that she'd lost him as he responded to the chirrup of his mobile.

'Mm. Still think you shouldn't make a decision on the spot. Shouldn't you think it all through one last time?' he insisted as he turned his attention to texting someone.

'He's probably right,' added the agent. As he fingered his tie, loosening the knot and unbuttoning the top of his shirt, she noticed the acne scars along his jawline. 'You don't want to make a mistake. Perhaps talk to your husband first?'

That did it. Jumped-up little git.

'I've been through everything with my financial advisor [Fiona] and my guarantor [Fiona]. I know the area, I know what I want, what I want it for and what I can afford. This is it. End of. And, for your information, I don't have a husband.'

The young man looked nervously at Jamie who tore his attention from the tiny screen for a moment to shrug his shoulders. 'I'd agree if I were you, mate.'

'Do we have a deal, then?' asked Lou, hand outstretched, already envisaging herself behind the counter, sewing her latest orders while customers browsed through the stock. She refused to entertain the idea of failure. She would introduce a range of vintage and modern accessories . . . and then a brainwave struck her — she would ask Ali if she'd be interested in creating a range of jewellery unique to the shop, or if she knew someone who might. She had loved hearing Ali's enthusiasm for her own business and had admired the pieces of jewellery she had with her on holiday. When she'd got home, she'd visited Ali's website to see more. The idea of them collaborating was genius.

'I'll get the paperwork ready for you then,' said the agent as he shook her hand.

Out on the street, Lou kissed Jamie goodbye, and agreed to turn up at the lettings office the next day to complete the necessary forms. Left alone, she turned to look at her shop, imagining the name 'Puttin' on the Ritz' in black on a deep pink fascia. Or should that be green? She crossed the road and stood on the other side of the street, gazing at her future, relishing her nervous excitement and resisting the temptation to do a triumphant jig. This really was the start to a new chapter. She was not going to be at home, invisible any more. She dug into her mock-croc bag for her mobile. The number calling wasn't one she recognised, but the caller's voice was.

'Lou? It's Sanjeev. Sanjeev Gupta. Remember me? We met on the plane from Delhi.'

'Of course I remember you. I'm not *that* senile!'

The sound of his laughter reminded her how much she had enjoyed his company.

'I'm in London for a few more days and wondered if you might like to meet for dinner. Are you free at all?'

And now it looked as though she might enjoy it again. She didn't have to think about her reply. 'Yes, I'd love to.'

'That's good. I'd like to introduce you to my favourite London curry house. On Thursday, perhaps?'

'Actually I'm meeting Ali then. You remember my friend from the plane? Why don't you come along?' Good idea. Safety in numbers. After last night, she wasn't sure how much she trusted herself any more — even with a stranger. She and Ali could talk business over the phone before then.

'No, that wouldn't be right at all. I don't want to spoil your evening together. I'm leaving for Birmingham the next day. But the IT company I work for is keeping me over here for some time. I'll be back in London in a couple of weeks. So what about the Friday or Saturday then instead?'

Lou was about to insist that he joined them, then realised that perhaps his invitation wasn't intended for two. And so what if she didn't trust herself? He wasn't her ex-husband and she did like him. That frisson, the one that she'd almost forgotten about, was definitely there. Instead she said, 'Friday would be perfect.'

'Good. Could you get to Burma Street, just off the London Road, for eight o'clock? A little restaurant called Indian Spice.'

'I'll be there.' As she hung up and turned down the street, she gave a little skip. A day that had begun so badly had turned out so well. How much she would have to talk to Ali about when they met. How little did Lou know.

9

The Tube was jammed. People pressed up against one another, the smell of wet clothes filling what little air there was in the carriage, jabbing umbrellas and bags, windows misted with condensation. As the train came to a standstill in a tunnel, Ali shut her eyes. She preferred travelling by bus whenever she could, but when the weather was as wet and windy as it was today, with traffic snarled up in every street, the Tube was the only way to get anywhere fast.

She became aware of a foot crushing hers. Her eyes snapped open and she glared at the middle-aged man in front of her whose hand was much nearer than necessary to hers on the handrail. He murmured an apology and moved it a few inches along, moving the offending foot at the same time. Ali returned to her thoughts, taking her mind off however many minutes the train was likely to be stationary.

For the last few nights, she hadn't had much sleep as her thoughts propelled themselves round her brain at an ever more confusing speed: mother; father; Ian; Don; mistress; marriage; work. So many of the assumptions that had kept her grounded for so long had been put in doubt and now an email from Don was sitting unanswered in her in-box. She knew the words off by heart.

Dear Ali,
I know this will come as a surprise. I've started and scrapped so many emails to you that I'm going to keep this short in the hope you'll reply. I'm coming to the UK, and contacted your father who gave me your email address. To ask how you are seems absurd after so long. But — how are you? I'd like us to be in touch again.

Don

She had done nothing about replying. She had enough on her mind, trying to reconcile herself with all that had happened to her since she had returned from India. As the shock of Ian's rejection wore off, she had been left feeling utterly empty, wondering if she was fated to be left by everyone she loved. Each morning, she'd wake late, exhausted, her eyes sore, her head aching and nothing resolved. She didn't want to talk to anyone, preferring to remain alone until she was ready. Even the studio didn't provide its usual consolation. She had found it easier to avoid Rick by going in late, when she knew that he would have left for the evening.

When the coast was clear, she'd stay long into the night attempting a new collection inspired by some of the Mughal floral and leaf motifs she'd seen in India but in need of some clever contemporary twist that she had yet to find. Distracted by her problems, she'd return home in the small hours, exhausted and frustrated by having achieved so little. She knew she couldn't continue like this if she was to keep her customers satisfied. Or keep her customers at all.

On the one hand, she was bruised and devastated by Ian. She blamed herself for having been so stupid as to believe that a man like him would change. Once a lover, always a lover. And now she was the older jilted woman. Yet, strangely, as long as she went over what had happened, she couldn't stop a tiny splinter of relief working its way into her heart. She had begun to realise that she wasn't grieving the loss of Ian so much as the loss of the dreams that she had pinned on him. As the days went by, anger began to take over from grief. For three days now, she had been in a continuing conversation with herself as she attempted to clear her head, to give her space to think about how to react to the news both about her mother and Don.

A younger woman was tapping her arm, offering Ali her seat. She shook her head, managed a smile and mouthed, 'No, it's all right, thanks,' and shut her eyes again, thinking, I'm only forty-fucking-five not sixty! I must look truly awful. Note to self: step up the concealer.

At last she was able to push herself through the crush of bodies and out onto the platform at Green Park. She emerged into the ticket area, careful not to slip on the grimy rainwater washing across the floor. As she walked down the wet street, head bent against the sheeting rain, poorly protected by her red spotted umbrella, she wished she had postponed their first get-together since India until she felt livelier, more interesting. Originally, she had been going to meet Lou in the evening but she had suggested tea instead. Feeling as she did, she wanted to keep the meeting short, so she could go on to the studio from there. Lou had sounded surprised — 'afternoon

tea' didn't seem to be a familiar concept —
but had agreed to switch her day around
and sew in the evening. She had said she
had something to ask Ali, but wouldn't hint
at what it was.

Ali jumped back as a bus swished through
a huge puddle, sluicing water across the
pavement, then she turned the corner
towards the Regis. She'd picked the hotel
because she occasionally met clients there,
more convenient for them than having to
traipse out to the studio. Sitting in hushed
five-star luxury added a bit of pizzazz to a
meeting, and an aura of success to her. She
made her way through the lobby to the
lounge where she sat herself at a low table,
protected by a pillar but with a good view
of who was entering and leaving the hotel.
Arranged around the room, low tables were
placed at a discreet distance from one
another, surrounded by taupe and beige
faux-suede bucket chairs. She looked
around the couple of murmured business
meetings, an elderly mother being entertained, what must be an illicit afternoon
liaison, a couple keeping their small daughter in check. No sign of Lou.

Sitting by the marble fireplace, her back
to the oak-panelled wall, Ali got out her
BlackBerry and began to answer one of her

recently ignored emails, then clicked it off. She reckoned she could squeeze in a couple more days of self-pity before having to knuckle down to her usual routine. She was about halfway through her in-tray when a clock chiming made her look up and she spotted Lou. She barely recognised the woman who stepped in from the lobby. A tailored maroon coat and a pair of wet mauve suede ankle boots had replaced the loose gaudy linen and walking sandals; the hair was as uncontrolled as before but discreetly applied make-up made her look younger. As Ali waved, Lou's face lit up in recognition and she came over. She unwound her richly coloured paisley pashmina. Worn in India it shrieked tourist, but here it said expensive, elegant and warm. Removing her coat and hanging it over the back of the chair, she sat down, pulling her skirt straight as she did so.

'Great coat.'

'Do you think so? Thanks. I made it.' She turned to hand it to the waiter.

'You did? I'm impressed.' Ali could see that the quality of the workmanship was not far short of couture standard. And although the overall look was too incoherent, too gaudy for Ali's own taste, somehow Lou carried it off with panache. Ali glanced

168

down at her own neat black trouser suit and white shirt.

'Well, be even more impressed.' Lou was obviously bursting with her news. 'Since we got back I've found the shop that is going to be the making of me — and you too, maybe.' She took the menu from the di-minutive brown-uniformed waiter who was hovering over them. 'My Lord! Forty-six pounds for a champagne tea's a bit steep, isn't it? I'd thought we were just going to have a cuppa and a biscuit.'

'Let's share one then and have another glass of champagne.' Ali placed their order. 'Now tell me. What's happened?' She was surprised to find that just being in Lou's company was making her feel better already.

While they waited for their tea, Lou began to explain, her excitement infectious as she described the premises and her plans for them.

'So,' Lou concluded, 'I want the shop to have a touch of class, an added something. I thought a unique range of jewellery would do it and, of course, I thought of you. I'm going to add vintage and modern bags and accessories as well. Destination shopping. What do you think?'

Ali fingered her necklace as she noticed Lou looking at it. She doubted Lou's customers would run to quite such expense, but perhaps this was an unlooked-for opportunity, and with what superlative timing. 'You want me to design a range for the shop?' she asked, tentatively. She had often considered designing some more modest lines, using semi-precious stones that would stretch her in a new and more commercial direction, but had never found the impetus to get anything under way. A new challenge and a new source of revenue were exactly what she needed.

Lou nodded. 'Why not? We'd discuss ideas but you'd have completely free rein otherwise. I've looked at your website and I love your designs.'

Ali felt instantly enthused. 'Tell you what. Why don't I come and see the shop and why don't you come to the studio where we can look through my ideas? If we both think it will work, then we'll find a way to go forward. But in principle, I love the idea.'

'Deal,' said Lou, holding out her hand to be shaken. Ali took it, already confident the two of them would make a sound working partnership.

As they let go, the waiter returned with two silver pots of Earl Grey, fine bone china cups and saucers, two flutes of pink champagne and a cake stand carrying minute sandwiches, two tiny scones each and some minuscule fancy cakes on top.

'Goodbye, resolutions,' said Lou, taking an egg-and-cress sandwich. 'You'd think they'd use something other than sliced bread at that price. Look at it! Still, at least the crusts are off. My God, I almost forgot,' she said suddenly. 'Another thing to tell you. That guy from the plane, Sanjeev, called me. I'm going for a superior curry with him when he's next in town.'

'Really?!' This was the last thing Ali would have expected given the way they'd met. Besides, Lou barely knew the man. Ali cut her sandwich into three neat pieces, remembering the tall, distinguished Indian with such impeccable manners.

'I know.' Lou chortled. 'But he's an interesting guy and no strings. A delightful change from the man I once called my husband. Who, incidentally, got me drunk and blagged his way into my bed. What was I thinking?' She screwed up her face as she reached for a scone and started slathering it with cream. By the time she'd finished telling the story, Ali was weak with laughing.

'That's better,' said Lou. 'When I came in, you looked miserable. Whatever's happened?'

Having been so sure she didn't want to

talk to anyone, Ali needed no more encouragement. Perhaps because she hardly knew Lou, perhaps because she felt she was a friend, or perhaps because they knew no one in common to whom Lou could betray her confidence, the words came easily. Lou sat quietly, intent on what she was hearing, only interrupting with the odd question to clarify, helping herself to a tiny fruit scone as she listened. Out it all came: Don, the string of lovers, Ian, hopes for the future, broken promises, unrealistic and disappointed dreams, the email from Don as yet unanswered. All she left out was what she had recently found out about her mother. That belonged to another conversation altogether and could wait. As she unburdened herself, something she rarely allowed herself to do with anyone, Ali felt an unfamiliar sense of release. Talking to a sympathetic listener who understood without judging her was giving her a new perspective. 'My God,' she said when she'd finished. 'You're the first person I've told about all that.'

'Sounds to me like you've had a tough time but a bloody lucky escape,' was Lou's conclusion. 'Ian sounds like a Grade A bastard with a midlife crisis. I've no time for those men who are prepared to kill their relationship with a good woman just to prove they're still irresistible to someone younger. And someone from the office too. Pathetic. And what about his wife?' She picked up the teapot, only to have it taken from her hand by the over-attentive waiter who poured for them.

Ali waited until he'd moved to the next table before continuing. 'You're probably right. It's just that I thought I was happy with things as they were, but since he suggested us living together and I saw another kind of life was possible, I know that I'm not. I don't want to be that person any more.'

'Be careful what you wish for. Wasn't it Katharine Hepburn who said, "If you want to sacrifice the admiration of many men for the criticism of one, go ahead, get married"? She had a point, you know.'

'But you've just come out of your marriage. You're bound to see it like that.' Ali scraped an almost invisible layer of cream onto her scone followed by an equally meagre dab of jam.

'Of course. But from where I'm standing, life as a mistress sounds pretty good in some ways. All the good bits of a relationship and none of the bad.' Lou spooned empty a shot glass full of raspberry mousse. 'Mm. I could get used to this.'

'I know how it sounds. Romantic week-ends away, decent meals out, good sex, none of those male issues, a life of your own. But . . .'

'But no boredom factor, no irritating habits, no being taken for granted.'

'And no children, no commitment, no companionship, no love,' added Ali, twisting her mother's rings round her finger. 'When I thought he was offering that to me, or at least some of it, I was shocked at first. Then I realised those were the things that I wanted, what was missing. And now they've been taken away, I feel awful, bereft. I don't want a future of being alone.'

At that moment, the little girl detached herself from the next table where her two parents were arguing in too-loud whispers. Lou caught the wife's angry 'You said you'd arrange it' just as their daughter wandered off in the direction of the cake trolley. They didn't see her trip over and fall, hitting her face on a chair leg. A loud wail carried around the room. All the tea drinkers looked up from their conversations, startled. The mother leaped to her feet, throwing a 'Why weren't you watching her?' at her partner who called for the bill, then rushed out after them.

'That's what you want instead?' Lou asked.

'I know the chances of me having any of that are worse than slim now and the risks huge.' Ali sounded regretful. 'But yes, I do at least want a partnership, someone to grow old with.'

'Easy,' said Lou. 'You're not even fifty. Plenty of time yet. The later you leave it, the more likely it is to last.'

'It's all very well for you, you cynic,' objected Ali with a smile. 'You've tried it and made the decision to move on. I'd like the option before it's too late.' She wondered what Lou's husband was like. What sort of man would fall for a woman who had such an idiosyncratic sense of style and who seemed so sure of her own mind? Someone who must have an equally robust self-confidence not to feel overpowered by a partner with a personality as strong as Lou's.

'I understand that, I really do,' said Lou, flicking the lime green crumbs of her second macaroon from her skirt. 'God! This stuff's like nuclear dandruff. . . . And if you really feel like that, then there's an answer staring you in the face.'

'What?'

'Don, of course. Reply to his email and

meet up. You obviously still haven't got over him. You went all moony when you were talking about him.'

'I didn't!' Ali protested, at the same time experiencing a tiny fillip at the mention of his name. Too much time had passed to have any expectations again. She was curious to know what had happened to him but it was absurd to expect any more than that. That particular door had closed or, at the very least, someone else would have walked through it.

'Don't look so bloody miserable,' Lou commiserated. 'What's the worst that could happen?'

'A) He's become an Australian and B) he'll almost certainly be married.' As Ali spoke, she realised how much she wanted to see him again if for no other reason than to tie up loose ends and find out what kind of life he'd made for himself without her.

A movement in the lobby caught Ali's eye and she looked up in time to see a middle-aged man emerge from the lift with a much younger woman. She was looking up at him, adoring, hanging onto his arm and his every last word. Not more than thirty-five, a tumble of dark curly hair, leggy, giggly and gamine. The two of them were totally caught up with one another, oblivious to the world around them. Ali felt a brief pang of envy, looked away, then looked again. She couldn't see his face as he turned to look down at his companion, but wasn't that slight strut familiar? It couldn't be! She caught her breath as the couple turned towards the desk and for a split second she saw his complete profile. The nose, the slicked grey hair, the physique she knew so intimately.

She watched as he ran his hand down over the woman's hip to cup her enviably rounded arse, while the receptionist handed him what must be a bill. No guesses needed for what. Squeezing herself back behind the pillar so there was no chance of him seeing her, should they come into the lounge, she couldn't take her eyes off the pair of them. He was helping the woman on with her coat, kissing her, holding her hand. Astonishment drove the breath from Ali's lungs.

'What's the matter?' Lou looked alarmed. 'Have you seen someone you know?'

'It's . . .' Ali closed her eyes. 'It's Ian,' she managed to whisper. 'I can't believe he'd do this. He knows I sometimes bring clients here.'

Lou turned, following Ali's gaze. She didn't say anything for a long moment, but she stiffened. At last she said slowly, 'Not the man in the grey suit? That's your Ian?'

Ali nodded, a lump sticking in her throat. She was only a whisker away from crying.

'But I know him.' Lou's voice was little more than a murmur.

'I mean the one who's leaving with his arm round the young woman in that pelmet of a skirt.' Ali could hardly get the words out but wanted to clarify Lou's mistake.

'Yes, him.' Lou turned again and together they watched the couple leave the hotel, the man shaking out a large stripy umbrella, the woman snuggled in close to him. 'I know him very well indeed.'

Ali was struggling to control her tears, but managed a choked 'How?'

Lou wheeled round, her face white with repressed emotion. 'That's Hooker. That's my husband.'

10

'How could you have ended up on the same holiday together?' Fiona was sitting sideways in Jenny's chair, her shoes abandoned on the floor, her arms wrapped round her legs with her chin resting on her knees as she listened to Lou's account. This was the first time they'd seen each other since Lou had passed up on Fiona and Charlie's offer of Christmas in Devon. Despite frequent phone updates, there was still plenty for Fiona to catch up on. Her eyes had widened in disbelief as she heard what had happened in the Regis. 'The chances of that happening must be one in a million.'

'Not really.' Lou was kneeling on the floor beside her, laying a fire in the tiled fireplace. She put a match to the paper and watched the kindling take light. 'I wondered about that for ages, then realised we must both have booked through the same travel agent, Taylormade. They were recommended to

Hooker a couple of years ago when we booked that disastrous week in southern Spain.' She groaned at the memory. 'No sun, no sex and a gorgeous villa that would have been great if the kids had come as planned but they found other better things to do. Why was I so surprised?' She had lost count of the number of times she had tried to arrange a jolly family holiday that had come to nothing once the children had their own lives. Even a long weekend had been impossible to organise. 'I never asked how he heard about them but I can only guess that the recommendation came from Ali.'

'So once you'd both realised your exes were one and the same — then what? God, I wish I'd been a fly on the wall.' Fiona grinned, letting go of her legs and stretching them out.

Lou felt Fiona could have tailored her obvious enjoyment of events with a dash more sympathy. 'If you mean, did we leap to our feet and confront him? Or did we slug it out? No, we didn't.' Then, it hadn't occurred to her: now, she was tickled by the vision — her, irate; Ali, upset; Hooker, caught red-handed. 'I think we were both too shocked to react. I dashed off to the Ladies for a moment on my own and, by the time I got back, Ali had paid the bill and was ready to go. She was almost in tears, said how sorry she was and dashed off. It was all over in minutes, by which time Hooker and his teenage companion . . .' she said the words with all the disdain she could muster, '. . . had disappeared into the afternoon.' She paused, aware that Fiona was watching her, hanging on for whatever she was going to say next. 'What I can't work out is why he told Ali that he was about to leave his wife, when I had already left *him* three months before. Doesn't make sense.'

'I suppose he looked as if he was the one calling the shots. Can you imagine Hooker letting himself appear out of control? God! If I were you, I'd have been livid.' At last the empathy Lou had been hoping for.

'Weirdly, I wasn't,' she replied. 'Not right then, anyway. It wasn't till I got home that it hit me. The bastard's been having an affair with Ali for the last three years. Three years! I'm sure she's not the first, but although I had the odd inkling over the years, I always chose not to investigate. Didn't care enough, I guess. Didn't want to rock the boat while the children were still at home. Or it was just easier not to.'

'But how ironic that, only minutes earlier, you'd been commiserating with her for being dumped by the lover she believed was going to change her life. And it was Hooker all along!' Fiona rubbed her hands together.

Lou had told Fiona everything now, except for one detail. She hadn't been able to confess that, only days earlier, she had succumbed to Hooker's charms herself. She knew her friend would be far from understanding, having a much more robust grip on life and affairs of the heart, thanks to the number of marital bust-ups that passed across her desk every week. Lou was still puzzling over what on earth Hooker had been playing at, the night he stayed with her. She'd never thought of him as having a particularly romantic or nostalgic bent, but perhaps he had been as touched as she had been by those shared family memories. That, the drink and the comfort of what you know. In the light of what she now knew, however, his suggestion that they might still have a future together seemed so perverse.

'What's this Ali like?' Fiona asked, picking up Lou's knitting and holding it up for a moment before trying to stuff it into the bag. She didn't share her friend's addiction to the home-made or second-hand that Lou had embraced so enthusiastically once she had left the magazine business. Like Nic, she preferred fashion that came straight from the designer. 'Younger version of you, I suppose.'

'You've got such a jaundiced view of life sometimes.' Lou shook her head in mock despair, grabbing her knitting before the stitches slipped off the needles. 'Actually, no. At least I don't think so. She's a tallish gym-bunny type with dark hair, cheekbones and a Minnie-Driver jawline, and with the appetite of a bird.'

'No similarities there, then.' Fiona passed her the packet of dark chocolate ginger biscuits. Lou stretched out for one as she settled herself on the floor, with her back against the sofa, feet to the fire, knitting bag beside her, then hesitated as she remembered the control she used to be able to exert over her eating habits when she was in the fashion biz. How much more relaxed she was now. She wrestled one out of the wrapping.

'Thanks! And there's something a bit controlled about her, as if she doesn't want to let anyone in. Yet, for the last couple of days of the holiday, we got on really well. She told me about the boyfriend she was going to move in with and I mentioned that I'd left my husband, but I don't think we ever named them. Back here, we've chatted a couple of times and then she told me all the rest when we met. Until Hooker, she's been a commitment-phobe after some guy broke her heart when she was in her early twenties. Since then, she's had one married lover after another — no ties, lots of fun.'

Fiona looked disparaging. 'So she's a home wrecker. I see tons of them in my business.'

'I don't think so,' Lou corrected her, as she untangled the four coloured balls of wool she was using in the next few rows of the Fair Isle vest she was making. She began the next row, concentrating on following the pattern, counting the stitches before she changed colour. 'She told me that she's never put any pressure on any of her lovers to leave their husbands. That wasn't part of the deal.'

'Yeah, right.'

'I believe her. Honestly, Fi, you'd like her. I did. In fact, I still do.' She paused, and unpicked a few stitches before adding in a new colour.

'It's not her fault that she was having an affair with your husband, I guess. How was she to know?' said grudgingly, but as if she might be convinced.

'Exactly. That's the conclusion I've come to. It's not as if she was my best friend and knowingly deceived me. That would be unforgivable. I suppose I could take a moral stance over a woman who chooses to be a mistress, betraying the married sisterhood or threatening the status quo, but that's not what I feel. Not in her case, anyway.'

'Don't you think you should? Women like her are responsible for endless broken homes across the country.' The divorce lawyer in Fiona had emerged and was drumming her fingers, businesslike, on the arm of her chair.

'And you have to pick up the pieces, I know, but she's not like that. Circumstances dictated the way she's led her life. Like the rest of us.' She ignored Fiona's indignant splutter. 'I understand that. She wasn't looking for a man to marry, just to have fun with. And don't forget I'd left Hooker before I knew any of this for a fact. We were over a long time ago. If I feel angry with anyone, it's with him, not her. How can I have spent over a quarter of a century with a man and understand him less now than I did when we first got together?'

She wasn't expecting an answer and only just heard the one she got. 'You're not the first to feel that, you know.'

'I thought I understood him and our relationship,' Lou went on. 'But I'm not so sure that I do any longer.' She still wasn't going to own up to her drunken slip-up. She jabbed the poker into the fire, making the flames dance. 'And . . . here's another reason not to tell her to get stuffed. Ali's a wonderful goldsmith whose designs would add that extra touch of class to the shop. And do you know what? The idea of teaming up with Hooker's ex-mistress without him knowing gives me a certain satisfaction.'

'You must be out of your mind,' spluttered Fiona, almost choking on her biscuit. 'No one else would even consider it.'

'I know. But how often at this age do we make new friends? What's more, I've an instinct that her jewellery would work with my clothes. I'll show you her website. And imagine . . . when Hooker finds out!' A glow of satisfaction spread through her. She had no idea when that time would come, but come it would. She would make sure of it.

'That is definitely not a reason to involve her in your business.' Fiona looked stern.

'I'm not giving her a financial stake in the business. Nothing like that. She'll just supply the jewellery and I'll take a commission from sales. If it doesn't work, we can always go our separate ways, but I've a feeling that it will. And if it does, then I'll have a colleague too. What matters is that the Ritz takes off.' As she spoke, Lou was increasingly persuaded of the rightness of her plan. 'And if you're still worried, why don't you meet her?'

'Have you gone completely mad?' Fiona was looking at her as if she'd landed from outer space.

'Not at all. I swore that from the day I moved here, I would lead my life the way I wanted. I feel oddly responsible for what Hooker's done to her.' She ignored another grunt of disbelief from the sofa. 'Hooker's made her see she wants something else out of life and now it may be too late for her to get it. I'm going to call her.'

Ali was hammering a strip of white gold round the mandrel, Radio 3 in the background. She had almost got the ring to the size and shape she wanted when her phone rang. She ignored the call, caught up in the rhythm of her work. If important, they'd phone back. The commission of two rings and matching earrings couldn't have come at a better moment for her. Rick's repayment of his debt had become a little less urgent as a result. The couple were in a hurry, determined to be married before the imminent birth of their child, so she was working against the clock. The simple design of a tapered band and a baguette-cut aquamarine in a rub-over setting would sit easily with the plain wedding ring they'd chosen and promised not to be too time-consuming to make. The couple had picked a matching setting for the earrings. The stones came from her Hatton Garden supplier: pretty pale blue gems from Brazil.

She barely looked up until she had perfected the setting for the stone. Satisfied with what she'd achieved, she put the two pieces away, ready to be soldered together in the morning. She began tidying up, turning off her laptop, straightening up her tools and switching off the radio. Picking up her mobile, the voicemail alert reminded her of the earlier call. With her notebook and diary at the ready, she waited for the message. Expecting to hear a customer, she was brought up sharp by Lou's voice.

'Ali? Hi. It's Lou. I haven't called because I needed time to think. I'm sure you did too. Obviously, we should talk about what's happened, about Hooker — er, Ian — but it doesn't have to change things. I'd still like you to go ahead with a range of jewellery for the shop. Maybe you won't want to now, but I hope you will. Call me.'

A click and she'd gone. Ali sat back in her chair, unsure how to react, then bent forward to put on her trainers. A week ago, she had left the Regis, furious, humiliated and ashamed. Lou's face, tight with emotion, was still etched on her memory. However much she might have suspected her husband of having an affair, being presented with the evidence must have been devastating. Ali screwed up her face as she remembered how much she had told Lou about her affair with Ian. None of that could be taken back.

She remembered their last meeting. After leaving the hotel, she had walked the streets for almost an hour, not noticing the time passing or the direction she was taking. Eventually, as the rain grew heavier, she found herself outside the National Gallery and had walked in for shelter. Over the years, she had often come here to visit some of her favourite paintings. Losing herself in them always brought some calm into her day. Walking through the echoing, mostly empty rooms, she finally sat down in the room containing Veronese's *Four Allegories of Love*.

Since then, she hadn't been able to stop thinking of what had just happened at the Regis. Lou might not have realised the full extent of what Ian got up to behind her back, but she must have had an idea. Why else would she have left him? But what Ali

189

didn't understand was why Ian had lied to her about leaving Lou. How much more straightforward he could have been by telling the truth. She had no choice but to accept that, whatever his reasons, her relationship with him was over as, regrettably, was any friendship with his wife. With plenty else to think about, she had resolved to forget the Sherwood family altogether. She had thrown herself back into her business, restoring a familiar framework within which she could think about her father's confession, and about Don.

But now this message. She locked the door of the studio and turned into the darkening street. If Lou was generous enough to forgive and forget, then perhaps she should respond. She shivered and upped her pace, swinging her arms as unobtrusively as she could, dodging the other pedestrians, wishing she hadn't taken the resolution to walk as far as the fourth bus stop every night. A potential business involvement with her ex-lover's wife was madness and yet . . . and yet, why not? They liked each other. She wanted the new challenge. She needed the money. And the idea of a new like-minded colleague appealed to her. Standing at the bus stop at last, she wondered what Lou was thinking. There was only one way to find out.

At the sports club, she changed and folded her clothes neatly into the locker. First she completed a set of stretches and a punishing ten sets of ab curls, then, getting into her stride on the treadmill, she was able finally to exorcise the outside world and concentrate on pushing herself to the limit. As she moved round the gym to the cross trainer, the rowing machine, then the weights machines, she could feel her heart pounding, her muscles straining, the sweat running off her. After forty minutes, she changed into her swimming costume and stepped under the shower before doing twenty minutes' brisk crawl in the empty pool. Eventually she emerged into the street, hair washed, eyes shining, feeling alive and resolved. As soon as she got home, she would text Lou and suggest they meet as originally planned.

Three days later, Lou arrived at Ali's studio at five thirty sharp. Ali answered her knock. They looked at each other. Lou stepped forward. Ali stepped back. Then she stepped forward to greet Lou with a tentative hug that was returned more enthusiastically as Lou clasped her to her Minnie Mouse fur. Neither mentioned Ian (or Hooker) at first.

Instead, they skirted the subject by focusing attention on Ali's work. She showed Lou the paraphernalia of her trade, answering her questions, explaining which tool was used for what. Neither of them wanted to address the one subject that they knew, in the end, they must.

When they arrived at the safe, Ali keyed in the numbers and swung open the heavy door, pulling out a tray carrying pieces from her autumn and winter collections in one half and, in the other, the antique brooch being refashioned into a pendant, a single pearl earring that she had been asked to copy plus the unpaid-for Orlov commission, and the aquamarine earrings, engagement and wedding rings that were ready as ordered.

Lou dug out a pair of green-framed glasses from her bag, gave them a wipe on the hem of her green jacket, then picked up pieces from the collections, one after another. She turned them in her hand, looking at them closely, holding a necklace to her throat, an earring to her ear. 'These are beautiful. I love what you've done here.' She picked up a pendant gold earring that hung like an elongated teardrop with a tiny amethyst in its base.

'The thing is, my customers come to me

for a certain kind of classic look so I've got a bit stuck in my ways. That's why your idea for the shop really appeals — it gives me the opportunity to try something a bit different.' Ali reached over to her sketch-book. 'Since we spoke, I've been trying out some ideas.'

Lou pushed her specs back on her nose and flicked through the pages. 'These ones with the art deco feel are perfect and the bee and butterfly designs should definitely go well with the newer clothes. And the keys. Very Tiffany.' She put down the book with an appreciative smile towards Ali as she noticed the second tray in the safe. 'May I?' At Ali's nod, she pulled out the one below that contained several tiny plastic bags and labelled microwave boxes contain-ing precious and semi-precious stones. She gave a gasp of surprise. 'I'd no idea you'd keep so much here.'

'I know, but I can't resist. It's an illness,' Ali smiled. 'Going to the trade shows is like being taken to a sweet shop — I get seduced by something every time, then pray I'm go-ing to be able to use them.' She tipped four pink sapphires onto her palm. 'Aren't these beautiful? I'm going to use them in a beaten gold pendant, circling a small diamond.'

Lou peered more closely, nodding in

agreement. 'If only we could sell stuff like this.'

'Don't worry. I think I've got a pretty good idea of what you want. I'm dying to get going, but what will Ian say when he finds out?'

Lou removed the glasses and fitted them into their case. 'I told you on the phone. He has nothing to do with my business — financially or otherwise. We don't need to bother him!'

Her smile assured Ali she meant it.

A couple of glasses of wine and a packet of Twiglets later and they were both relaxed on the studio sofas talking freely, quickly agreeing that neither of them could be blamed for the way Hooker had behaved. Lou had made herself at home, her coat and bag thrown over half of one sofa, while she comfortably took up the rest. Ali was nothing but pleased that their friendship seemed back on track.

'So what *do* we do about him?' she asked, as the possibility of Ian getting his comeuppance crossed her mind for the first time.

'Hooker?' Lou looked thoughtful. 'Nothing. Not at the moment, anyway. I want to get the shop up and running, then think about that. To be honest, I'm still wondering how to play it. Of course, I'm angry and hurt by everything he's done but, despite all that, like it or not, he is still the children's father.'

Ali glanced up, surprised to hear her friend's voice crack but the moment had passed.

Lou recovered herself as she reached for the last Twiglet when the packet was nudged in her direction.

'That's just hokey nostalgia getting in my way. I don't want you or anyone to think that our marriage was rotten all the way through, that's all. Time, habit and my flagging libido simply got the better of us.'

'I don't think anything except that he's a chunk of my life best forgotten. I'm moving right along. I've decided to reply to Don's email,' Ali added, reading Lou's pleased expression. 'But only because he and I are unfinished business, even after so long. Besides, I'm off men right now. This is just a long overdue tying-up of loose ends.' If she kept saying it, she'd come to believe it.

But Lou looked doubtful as she raised her glass. 'Well, may it work out, one way or another.'

'For both of us,' corrected Ali, taking over the toast. 'And to Puttin' on the Ritz.'

'I'll drink to that,' said Lou.

11

By the time Lou arrived, the three rooms in the students' union devoted to the vintage fair were buzzing with expectant buyers. She had got up at five o'clock to get there on time but roadworks on the M4 had held her up by at least an hour. If there were any finds to be made, they'd have been snapped up by now, picked off by any cognoscenti and dealers who would have been there as soon as the doors opened. However, all was not lost. Fortunately, she wasn't exhibiting, having decided to hold the stock she had until the shop was up and running. The likelihood of finding anything here to add to it was remote, the dealers would have marked up the prices too high for her, but nonetheless she loved the hunt. There was always the possibility that something might have been overlooked. Having paid her entry, she walked in, savouring the distinctive smell of a vintage fair. However well the clothes had been cleaned, there was always the whiff of mothball in the air.

She fingered her way down a rail of colourful day dresses, none of them what she was after, except in the way of inspiration for patterns and fabric. She paused at a fifties floral and candy-pink striped cotton prom dress with straps, a seamed waist and full skirt. She could use exactly this shape in the shop. Looking closer, she noticed that the left side seam and a long tear in the skirt had been badly repaired and the fabric under the arms was faded. In five minutes, she had bargained the stallholder down to a few pounds and the dress was hers. When she got home, she'd take it to pieces and use them to make her own pattern.

Edging round a couple of young women trying on hats in front of a long mirror, she halted in front of a jewellery stall. Black velvet cushions pinned with deliciously gaudy paste brooches and earrings were angled behind rows of beaded necklaces. Bracelets and more necklaces dripped from stands. She turned over a pair of terracotta cameo earrings, tempted for a moment, then returned them, moving on to the next stall. Seeing them convinced her that she was right to get Ali to provide something more contemporary for the shop.

Slowly she worked her way round the fair, pausing to look at more dresses, watching to see what people were most interested in, listening to the prices they were prepared to pay, chatting to a couple of the stallholders whom she knew. Eventually she found a chair in the café where she treated herself to a heavily iced cupcake. Coming here had provided the therapy she'd known it would.

Sipping her coffee, she went over in her head what more she needed to do before the shop finally opened. The Puttin' on the Ritz website was almost ready. Over one long Saturday, Jamie had photographed all the clothes with Rose and Lou dressing first one dressmaker's dummy, then the other, while a mate of Tom's had been drafted in to update and rebrand her existing website. Lou had sat up late into the night, writing copy for the various pages, explaining what the shop would offer — fifties to eighties vintage designer and vintage-inspired clothes — giving potted fashion histories of the four decades, setting up her blog. That had been the most difficult bit. To begin with she'd been self-conscious, unsure what to say, until she got into the swing. Writing on a subject about which she felt so passionately was a pleasure.

Her regular online business had been slow

so far this year but, once the shop formally opened with the publicity she hoped to generate, she was confident everything would pick up. The builder–decorators were due to move out next week, having taken an age to fix the toilet and the tiling at the back, but the main space was already looking good. She and Ali had agreed that she would open without fanfare and then, once Ali's designs were ready, they'd have a formal opening. Lou had already dusted off her old contacts book in preparation. The invitations were due from the printer by the end of the week.

She hadn't seen Hooker since that afternoon in the Regis. She didn't want to, knowing any kind of confrontation she might initiate would go the way of most confrontations: Hooker — one, Lou — nil, disabled as usual by his verbal dexterity. He was always able to justify himself. And in truth, what would she say? He was entitled to spend time with whoever he liked, whenever he liked. Even if they were half his age. She really didn't want to tackle with him his affair with Ali or indeed any other infidelities during their marriage. They belonged to the past and shouldn't matter to her any more. Nor did she want his disapproval of what he would regard as a risk rather than an investment in the shop. Lou had already had enough of that from Nic.

'Why don't you get Jamie and Tom to paint the place for you?' her daughter had asked. 'Much cheaper and it's not as if you need it to be perfect. It would be different if you were selling contemporary designers, but these are just old clothes. Someone else's at that.' Nic wrinkled her nose in disgust, smoothing her dove-grey wool skirt and crossing her legs to show off her shiny plum leather pumps. There was just the merest swish of nylon.

Lou laughed. 'Honestly! I give up. They may not be brand new but some of them are gorgeous. Did I show you that very fitted purple Zandra Rhodes dress in slubbed cotton? It's so you.'

'I don't think so, Mum,' she disagreed, with a small movement of her head. 'Retro isn't me at all. Anyway, I'm about to be more of a Mamas and Papas girl.'

Lou touched her daughter's stomach, the bump barely visible. 'I know. I'll have to keep my eye out for vintage maternity. Perhaps I could start a whole new line.' She pretended to make a note.

'Not on my account!' Nic's pregnancy had obviously been issued with a stern sense-of-humour bypass. 'I don't want you to go bust before you've begun.'

'Give me some credit, darling. I've worked out my budget extremely carefully. You mustn't forget that I really want this to work. I'm not going to do anything that might jeopardise it.' She passed her the draft of the invitation to the opening, hoping she'd be impressed.

Nic read it, then passed it back. 'Actually, this looks great!'

'Don't sound so surprised.' Lou took it and once again admired the design, as funky and interesting as she'd hoped.

'I'll come if I can. Do you think anyone else will?' And no sign of a smile. Trust Nic.

But Lou refused to be deterred. In fact, she'd been surprised and touched by the response she'd received from the few fashion journalists she'd spoken to so far, to mark their diaries. Many of them knew Lou from her magazine days and trusted her knowledge and idiosyncratic good taste — and those were what she was relying on.

Ever since she had conceived the idea of the shop, she'd been increasing her stock, using the mornings to trawl anything from charity shops and eBay to jumble sales or auction rooms, visiting the mother of another friend of Fiona's who had a couple of old trunks she wanted to empty — anywhere she might find the perfect pieces. Most afternoons and evenings, she sewed like a fiend, both for the shop and for the various friends and friends of friends who had commissioned her to alter or make something for them. She had never been so busy.

She finished her coffee and spent another half-hour rummaging through more stalls. The only things she found were indulgences to add to her own collections: an art nouveau hatpin with a twisty gold finial and a blue stone, and a sixties French evening bag decorated with jet and gold glass beads.

Driving back to London, she slid Billy Joel's *Piano Man* into the CD player at top volume, shrieking out an almost-in-tune accompaniment as she drove. Cocooned in the relative comfort of her Ford Focus with a large packet of Maltesers well within her reach, for the next couple of hours alone in Billy's, then Mark Knopfler's, first-rate company, she felt happy, secure in the feeling that all would be well with the world.

Having arrived home, she spent the remainder of the afternoon with Fred Astaire setting the mood while she made a start on her initial stocktake. Two laden clothes rails were set up in the sitting room and every item had to be logged onto the laptop, priced and labelled. As she worked, she mentally catalogued her wardrobe upstairs, wondering what she had that would be suitable for her evening's date with Sanjeev.

India had receded in her memory, overtaken by recent events; their meeting on the aeroplane, likewise. She was already anxious that she might not recognise him again, or that they wouldn't get on. Agreeing to a date had seemed such a good plan when she was just back; hearing his voice conjured up all sorts of possibilities but now the reality was more nerve-wracking as she imagined the conversation flagging, him making a pass and her not recognising it *was* one, getting her kit off in front of him . . . She refused to think any further, having already gone way too far. This was going to be a friendly meeting. That was all.

Her 'brush' with Hooker and subsequent discoveries about what he'd been up to had put any kind of liaison with someone new on the back burner. She was with Ali on this. All things considered, another man in her life would be way too much trouble and anyway she was better off on her own, particularly when she had so much to keep her busy. Ali had visited the shop and had been impressed and boosted Lou's confidence in the project. The two of them talked and emailed often, Ali talking through her ideas and Lou telling her about any new purchases and how the shop was shaping up. They had barely discussed Hooker since they met at the studio.

Ali's lack of self-pity and the way she had picked herself up and got on with her life was impressive. Lou wanted to follow her example. But, relieved as she was to have made a break from Hooker, there was still a tiny bit of her that missed him, that thought of him as hers. She had tried to suppress that feeling but, despite herself, it still could make itself felt when least expected. She was determined this wouldn't happen to-night and prevent her from enjoying the evening with Sanjeev.

She went back to considering her ward-robe and decided on the fifties-style coral-coloured cocktail dress that she'd designed with a sweetheart neckline not too low (cover the crêpey cleavage), elbow-length sleeves (flatter the flabby upper arms) and a pencil skirt (make the most of those pins) — an understated statement of a dress for a woman of a certain age: tighter than it once had been, but flattering for all that. Cap-ping the look were her new shoes bought despite being a half-size too small. She had wanted to be persuaded by the sales assistant that the divine pale grey suede would stretch easily, and so she had been.

In the end, she recognised Sanjeev immediately, the tall lean physique, the black hair with flecks of grey over the ears, the thick eyebrows over long-lashed dark eyes, the moustache that looked more dashing than she remembered. She'd never been much of a one for facial hair, but somehow on him, it didn't look so bad. He was muffled up, standing on the street corner, waiting for her. To her surprise, she felt a definite tingle of anticipation as she approached him. She'd quite forgotten that feeling and how pleasant it could be.

But then, as she walked towards him, she felt two bands of pain wrapping themselves more tightly around the first joints of all her toes, building to a crescendo in both her incipient bunions; she cursed under her breath and tried not to limp. They exchanged chaste kisses on the pavement and she inhaled sandalwood and citrus from him. She heard his slight intake of breath when he helped her out of her coat in the restaurant lobby, and sent up a prayer for her already straining side zip to last the night. For some reason her body seemed to have expanded on the way there. As a precaution, she had prepared for the worst, but unlikely, eventuality by pinning safety pins at strategic points to reinforce things.

'Follow me,' he said. 'The food here's more authentic than any anywhere else in this city.' Realising he must know London better than she'd thought, she followed him up the workaday staircase, gaffer tape over the worn bits of carpet, faded Bollywood film posters lining the walls. They arrived in a large room with a long central row of crowded noisy tables flanked on either side by booths for four. Large ceiling fans circulated the air, despite the season, rocking slightly as they turned. The mirror running down the left wall gave the impression that the place was double the size. Waiters in red jackets darted up and down the room, balancing plates, sweating. Lou had expected a smart London restaurant: instead she felt as though she'd been beamed back to India. Here, her dress and shoes felt all wrong, overdressed, English.

Sanjeev was welcomed like a prodigal son by the old man sitting at the top of the stairs. Embraces over, he showed them to a booth where a waiter flapped a white tablecloth into place, then returned with cutlery and the menu. Sanjeev ordered a couple of Kingfisher beers, thus depriving Lou of the glass of red wine that she was longing for.

Black mark number one. Ordering for her without asking, as if she couldn't read the menu and choose for herself, was one of Hooker's maddening habits. And the new Lou was not going to revert to being that invisible woman.

'Beer is better with this food,' Sanjeev explained, as if reading her mind. 'Trust me. I want you to experience the real thing all the way from north-west India.' He picked up both menus and passed one to her.

'Even so, if you don't mind, I'd like a glass of red wine while we order. I can always change to beer later.' She wouldn't, of course, but equally she didn't want him to think she was completely impossible. Better to start the way she intended to carry on: if not in the driving seat, at least as the co-driver.

Despite the raised eyebrow, she recognised that glint of amusement in his eyes as he called the waiter back so she could order a glass of French Merlot. That was the look that went with his return of her knickers. Half regretting her bolshiness, she considered the list of dishes, then put the menu down. 'I honestly don't know where to start. Would you choose?'

'Very well.' His voice was reserved but not

unfriendly. 'The *murgh makhani* is very good here or, if you like prawns, perhaps the *tandoori jhinga,* and the black lentil dhal is excellent.' With each suggestion, he pointed at the list of dishes with a lean, well-manicured finger.

For a split second, Lou imagined the finger touching her. Surprising herself, she swiftly redirected her attention to the menu.

'Or . . .' He hesitated, pondering the choice. As his hand hovered over the table, she noticed the silver band around his wrist. Lou dragged her eyes from it to his face, her anxiety about having kicked the meal off to a bad start turning into appreciation of the way he offered her a choice without taking over the meal in the way she'd dreaded. Without her saying anything, he seemed to have understood her.

They chose quickly, Lou deciding for herself within his recommendations, and finally they could talk. They roamed through each other's lives, recapping what they had found out about each other on the plane, moving on to what had happened since they'd met. Lou concentrated on the shop and Ali's role in it, leaving out the details of her marriage. She wasn't ready to offer up her and Hooker's relationship as conversation to a near stranger. They returned to his life. He talked easily about his middle-class childhood in Delhi, his doctor father and German mother, his married twin sisters who were a paediatrician and a housewife, and his brother, a biochemist. Lou listened, liking the affection and respect he showed for them all, fascinated by hearing about such a different background from her own where achievement had been regarded far less highly. Especially if you were female. She reciprocated by telling about her children, their achievements and Nic's pregnancy. Her own backstory could wait until another time. If there was one.

By the time the main courses arrived, they were in full flow. Another glass of red wine had just been brought to the table when, with an emphatic gesture, Sanjay knocked it with his hand. Just when everything was going so well. There was nowhere for Lou to escape. She shrank back against the wall of the booth and watched as a mini tsunami of wine rushed towards her, drenching the front of her dress. How could so little spread so far, she wondered as she stared downwards, aghast.

Sanjay was half on his feet, grabbing the glass but too late. 'I'm so, so sorry. What can I do?'

'It'll be fine,' she said, exerting more self-control than she knew she possessed.

The waiter was already beside them, armed with paper towels, lifting the table-cloth and sliding them underneath. Since they soaked up nothing from her dress, Lou excused herself to go to the Ladies. As she stood, she felt as if someone had plunged a knife into both her feet. They must have swollen while she'd been sitting and the shoes weren't giving an inch. Why hadn't she stuck to her flat pumps instead of going for such high heels? Being seduced by appearance over comfort had proved a major mistake.

Aware of the eyes of the other diners, she concentrated on pulling herself up tall, on not going over on an ankle and on looking quite unruffled by having red wine spreading down her skirt — all the time seething inside. The dress was ruined. The waiter followed her, fussing. He showed her to a tiny but brightly lit room that contained a wash-basin and hand dryer as well as a toilet. He touched the dryer. 'You wash out the stain, then dry it here,' he insisted. 'Better to do quickly.'

She shooed him out and locked the door, sitting down on the loo seat, levering off her shoes and wiggling her toes until the feeling returned to them, glad to be on her own.

Knowing she hadn't got long, she stripped off her dress, infuriated with the safety pins that made the whole exercise such a palaver. She ran the tap and held the stain under it, only succeeding in drenching a much larger area than she'd intended. As she squeezed out most of the water, she became conscious of standing in her elastically challenged underwear and tights under the photographic gaze of a bunch of novice saffron-clad Buddhists on one wall; of wild-haired, half-naked Indian holy men on another: and of dewy-eyed village children on the last. She had an overwhelming urge to laugh at her predicament just as someone tried to open the door.

'Won't be a minute,' she yelled, moving across to the hand dryer, holding in her stomach — then letting go. Her audience was only made up of photos, for Christ's sake. The dryer exhaled a feeble gush of warm air that made next to no impression on the dress. Lou gave it four or five goes, punching the chrome start button each time. By then, whoever was outside was growing more frantic, twisting the door handle and jiggling the door.

'I said hang on,' she shouted, frustrated that, in the one patch where the water had dried, the wine stain was about as visible as when she'd started. She gave the dryer one last chance before doing the only other thing left open to her. She put the dress back on, slipping the discarded safety pins into her bag and hoping for the best. Feeling as if she'd just put on a wet swimsuit, she glanced in the mirror, appalled by what she saw. She coaxed at her hair with her fingers to produce a look that was more wash-and-gone than wash-and-go, slicked on her favourite new carmine lipstick, coerced her feet into the shoes and smoothed down her dress as best she could. Then, putting on her bravest face, she unlocked the door, nodded an apology to the woman who was huffing and puffing outside and returned to the table.

In her absence, the food had been removed, the table relaid and her glass of wine replaced. The only thing that hadn't changed was Sanjeev who, when he saw her coming, got to his feet, his eyes widening as he took in the enormous damp stain over the front of her dress. Her bag, even strategically placed, did little to hide it. The other diners weren't bothering to conceal their stares or their amusement.

'I know. I've made it much worse,' she said, suddenly unable to stop herself smiling. 'I should have had the beer. You were right.' She edged herself back into her seat and raised her glass. 'Cheers!'

Uncertain how to react, he looked at her and picked up his own glass, slowly returning her smile. So he did see the funny side too. Then, as the waiter returned with their food, they started to laugh.

As they eventually left the restaurant, Sanjeev held the door for her. 'I really am sorry about your dress,' he murmured.

'Don't be. I've had a lovely evening.' That was the truth. She'd long ago forgotten what it was like to enjoy the company of a man who wasn't Hooker, who was in fact a lot more charming than Hooker, and the discovery was more pleasurable than she'd expected. Much more.

'I want to ask how I can make it up to you.' They stepped out into the street, and turned towards the crossroads, looking out for a taxi.

As Sanjeev hailed the first that appeared, Lou made up her mind. No, she wouldn't ask him to cover the dry-cleaning cost. How chintzy would that be? Instead she said, 'By letting me take you next time.' She interrupted his protest. 'No. You've shown me quintessential Indian cooking. I'm going to show you something just as quintessentially English.'

'What will that be?' His eyes glittered in the street light as he looked down at her.

'Wait and see,' she said, having not the slightest idea. 'A surprise for when you're next here.'

'That would be delightful. Then I accept.' He put his hands on her shoulders and kissed her, this time a good deal less chastely than when he'd greeted her.

Two minutes later, she was in her taxi travelling home, shoes off, thoroughly discombobulated by the fact that not only had she enjoyed the kiss, she had also responded in kind. She hugged herself. Things were looking up.

12

Beyond the shutters, the night was dark. Reflected back in the large window was the interior of the shop, currently busy with activity. The decorators had moved out ten days earlier and the official opening of Puttin' on the Ritz was only hours away. The brown paper covering the window had been ripped down. Inside were bleached white floorboards, white walls except for the one on the right which was painted a cool Scandinavian green — Lou had ditched the bright pink as too predictable — with changing-room curtains in just the grey she'd originally imagined. The rail along the left wall was now hung with dresses that she was rearranging for the umpteenth time. 'Do you think they're better hung by length, style or colour? I think length, don't you?'

Ali looked up from the glass cabinet where she was arranging her jewellery. 'Well, length pretty much governs style, doesn't it?

So, yes — sounds good to me.'

'But by colour's easier on the eye and might be better for browsing. I think I'll leave them like this and put these two in the window. Yes?' She held up a floaty three-tier Jean Varon dress in a green floral print muslin and the dark blue moss-crêpe Ossie Clark.

'Why not one of your own dresses?'

'Not for tomorrow. I want to show the quality and the timelessness of the vintage and then swap it all round next week. I thought I'd hang a couple of mine on the wall, though, and perhaps one behind the counter.' She went across to inspect Ali's handiwork. 'Ali, these really are beautiful.' She picked up a simple gold key that hung on a gold chain, weighing it in her hand before holding it up against her in front of the mirror. 'These will give the clothes a contemporary feel. I love them.'

Ali never tired of the pleasure she experienced when someone complimented her work. There was nothing better than the feeling of a job well done and of knowing that someone appreciated the effort and imagination that she poured into what she did. For the next half-hour, they worked together to get the place looking exactly as they wanted.

'So are we ready?' Lou straightened the pile of press releases on the counter and then one of the postcards showing a cocktail dress and one of Ali's delicate insect necklaces — a bee in flight suspended on a delicate chain. 'We've asked everyone who might be useful to come . . .' She stopped, a look of panic crossing her face. 'Suppose they didn't get their invitations?'

'Of course they did.' For the last two weeks, Ali's role, apart from official goldsmith, had been to soothe and reassure. She was astonished how much she'd had to prop up Lou's anxiety. This was a side to her she hadn't seen before.

'And if they haven't?'

'Then we'll drink the drink and have another official opening day when we can afford some more.' Brave words but inside, Ali was as nervous as a kitten. If no one turned up, the business would be much more of a challenge to get under way. Originally the plan had been for her not to be there. Lou had been too anxious that Hooker might turn up unannounced and neither of them wanted him to find them together, tomorrow of all days. Then, at the last minute, Lou had discovered that he was going to be safely holidaying on the other side of the world. The way was clear for them to host the opening together.

'The kids are coming to take me out for dinner afterwards. I'd ask you along but . . .' Lou hesitated.

'Don't worry. I know the score. We don't want any chance of them mentioning me to Hooker.' She found that using Ian's nickname put a pleasing distance between them. 'Anyway, I'm going home to put my feet up. And Don may be calling me,' she added suddenly, looking to see the effect her announcement would have on Lou.

'Really? I thought he was in Australia,' said Lou, surprised. 'Not that he can't call from there, of course, but . . .'

'But he's not. He's back here, involved in setting up an NGO dealing with international human rights. Still saving the world.' She sat in the reupholstered junk-shop chair that they'd put outside the changing rooms, picked up one of the fashion magazines from the small table and started flicking the pages, as if his being in the country barely affected her.

'You never said.' Lou sounded suspicious.

'I forgot.' Not quite true. She just hadn't been ready to say anything.

'Any wife, partner, girlfriend?'

'Marriage on the rocks, apparently.' She tried to sound nonchalant, as if nothing could be less significant.

'Well, Miss Macintyre. Looks like your ship might be about to come in.'

'I don't think so,' she protested. 'I've sworn off men, remember? We're just old friends.' She wasn't going to admit to the flicker of excitement she'd felt on hearing his voice.

'Yeah, yeah. We'll see.'

'Enough!' Ali slapped down the magazine and stood up to change the subject. 'Come over here and look at what we've done. The place looks terrific.'

'You really think so?' Lou stepped out from behind the counter and joined her at the back of the shop. Together they took in the two rails of clothes, the shelf of bags, belts and gloves above the left-hand vintage rail, all meticulously arranged. Above the opposite vintage-inspired rail, two dresses hung on the wall, one a green and blue striped *Mad Men* style day dress, the other a cocktail dress in deep green shot silk designed by Lou along the lines of the one Sanjeev had so ably drenched in wine. By the counter stood the gleaming cabinet containing Ali's jewellery that winked under the ceiling spotlights.

'Have more confidence, woman! We're going to be busy.'

Lou hugged her. 'I hope you're right.'

The next day Lou woke at 4.30 a.m. as the first train of the day rattled past, so hot that she had to throw off her duvet. She turned her pillow over, waiting for the flush to pass so she could cover herself up again. But even when she'd cooled down, she couldn't sleep. She lay on her back, breathing deeply, trying to persuade herself that whatever happened today wouldn't matter. But it would. Desperately. Preoccupied by fulfilling her ambition, she hadn't given a thought to how exposed she'd feel when the dream became reality. She had put so much of herself into her own designs and the choice of fabrics, as well as into the choice of her stock, that she felt as if she was about to stand up stark naked in front of the world. And if everyone looked away or took no notice? As much as she told herself she didn't care, deep down she wanted her choices validated by the approval of her ex-colleagues and friends. She wanted success. Just thinking about what, she was increasingly sure, would be a disaster, made her heart pump quicker.

At least Hooker wasn't here to gloat over her failure. Nic had dropped his visit to

Thailand into the conversation a week earlier.

'Alone?' Lou had asked pointedly.

Nic looked sheepish. 'Well, there might be someone. But what does it matter? He needs the break after everything he's been through.'

Lou said nothing. Thailand indeed! The most exotic they'd ever got to was Europe. But she knew Hooker too well. Holidaying on his own was not his thing. His companion from the Regis would no doubt be glued to his side. If Nic knew about her, then it must be more serious than she'd thought. But it couldn't be. The woman had looked half his age. All these thoughts went round and round. Then her alarm went off. It was seven o'clock.

As she was sitting down to a bowl of muesli, telling herself that calories from the dried fruit and nuts didn't count, there was a knock on the door. Gathering her dressing gown round her, she padded across the hall, expecting to see the postman.

'Tom!' She hugged her youngest to her, pretending not to notice the acrid smell of stale cigarette smoke. His life, not hers, she reminded herself. 'Isn't this a bit early for you? Is something wrong?'

He pulled out of her embrace and went to

the kitchen. 'Mmm. Coffee. Actually, believe it or not, I came by specially to wish you luck for today. Cassie on the fashion pages said she was going to drop in on you, so I thought I'd swing by on the way to work.'

'That's so sweet of you. But I'm miles out of your way.' She started making a fresh pot of coffee.

He winked. 'But not out of Sarah's.'

'Who?' She didn't remember the name.

'Someone I met last week. She likes to get to her office at eight so kicked me out at seven fifteen!' Like a magician producing a rabbit out of a hat, he conjured two warm croissants from his bag. 'So I thought of you.'

Lou knew better than to ask for details. Tom buzzed from one woman to another like a bee in a wildflower meadow. She had long ago got used to the fact that by the time she'd cottoned on to the latest girl's name, he'd already moved to the next. Although his behaviour offended every feminist bone in her body, there was nothing she could do to stop him. He'd learned at the knee of a master, she thought with regret.

'Well, sit down then and tell me what else is happening in your life.' She produced two plates and joined him in the much bigger breakfast than she'd intended to have. Over the next half-hour, she was updated on his football team's place in the league, his friend Sam's decision to take a foreign reporter's job in Saigon, his frustrations with the way he was treated at work. Why was it that he, like Jamie, behaved as if the world owed him a living? She was sure she and Hooker hadn't led them to expect success on a plate. Nic and Rose, Jamie's fiancée, both worked without complaint. Oh, well, she loved his chat all the same. Eventually and reluctantly she stood up.

'I'm going to have to kick you out now. If I don't get ready, the shop won't open.'

'Shit!' He looked at his watch. 'And I've got to run. The news editor will give me such a bollocking if I'm late again.' A brief kiss and he was gone, leaving Lou to run her bath, taking a coffee with her, touched by his visit.

As she stripped off, she dropped her clothes on the floor as she went, still delighting in the new freedom of not having to set an example or to keep the place as ordered as Hooker liked. She wished she'd been bolder about removing Jenny's floor-to-ceiling mirror but she'd been worried about the state of the wall behind it. Some things were better left hidden. A view amply confirmed as she caught sight of her own reflection. Her sister had been convinced that a daily reminder of the shape of things would help her stick to all her dietary resolves. But Lou had never stuck to such a thing in her life. Besides, she told herself, their family gene pool predicated that the women shouldn't look absolutely perfect. Not for them the bodies she'd seen paraded every other day in her former incarnation on *Chic to Chic.* When she left the magazine, she had vowed not to make her waistline a priority in her life, nor to conform to anyone's fashion dictates but her own. She braced herself as she turned back to confront her image. Remember, she told herself. The new me is someone who celebrates what they've got and makes the most of it.

She stared at her mirror image. Not bad, but when *did* that happen? She was genuinely mystified. It wasn't even a question of having let her body go — it was more a case of her body having walked off in another direction without her noticing. Starting at the lowest point, neat ankles that hinted at her former size and legs that were still in good(ish) shape, apart from the hint of cellulite and the slight sag of the inner thigh. From the front what struck her most was not the slightly protruding stomach or the less than perky breasts (she'd had three children, for Christ's sake) but the beginnings of a spare tyre that had settled just above her hip bones, or at least where she remembered them being when they'd last been visible. Where had that come from? She turned sideways on. There it was again, at home around her back, protecting her kidneys and obliterating the waist she thought she didn't care about. Celebrate, she warned herself as she dragged her eyes upwards. Her arms were still slim at least.

She looked at herself in the eyes, a direct appraising stare. Not such a bad old face. Others might have gone for an eye-, neck- or face-lift — but not her. She lifted the sag of her jawline with her fingers. Even if she had the money and the encouragement of her family, she'd rather stick with what nature gave her: a friendly face, she liked to think, with wide eyes surrounded by a tracery of fine wrinkles, cheeks a little too apple-like for her liking, a mouth that had lost its plumpness but still turned up at the corners.

Before she stepped into the bath she sloshed some Moroccan rose otto bath oil into the water. She half shut her eyes and inhaled. Can a girl ever have too much of such a good thing? She remembered Hooker's yell as he once saved himself from slipping on the bottom of the bath when he climbed in to take a shower, only moments after she'd exited the room steaming and perfumed with lime blossom bath oil — his birthday present to her, chosen no doubt by Sally, his compliant PA. Unfortunately the only casualty had been the shower curtain.

After a good soak, she dared the mirror again, staring despondently at her hair that looked more like Medusa's snakes. However many years passed, however much she tried to accept the rest of her, she would never be happy with the hair God gave her, especially now that it took the equivalent of the national debt to keep the once natural Titian red up to the mark. And no amount of 'product', as her hairdresser insisted on calling it, would make it conform to the unruffled businesslike look she was hoping to project through the day. She had no choice but to accept the wild woman of Borneo look. She gazed at her face, leaning forward as she noticed a couple of new wrinkles appear in her right cheek if she tilted her head a certain way. She removed her specs. That was better. How wonderful nature is, she mused: as your looks begin to fail so does your eyesight. If God had meant us to see how decrepit we were growing, he'd have provided us with a lifetime of 20/20 vision. She brushed on her illuminating concealer. An expensive con surely, but no, it did seem to help. Cheered, she continued her preparations to face the world: not too much blusher, lipstick or mascara but not so little that she looked as if she'd just exited an intensive care unit.

By the time she left the house she had drunk so many cups of coffee that she felt as though she might take flight. She had chosen to wear one of her crêpe silk tea dresses in a vivid floral print on a navy background, smocked on the shoulder and under the bust, cut to skim the body. One of Ali's key pendants glittered in the V-neck. She hoped that she was demonstrating that a woman of any size could wear the style and look good. Or good enough. Teamed with a dark cashmere cardigan and dark tights, the outfit gave her a certain confidence.

When she arrived at the shop, Ali was already waiting. Lou admired her elegant eighties black wool Azzedine Alaia that clung in all the right places, accessorised with drop earrings and a glittering wide gold cuff. She looked stunning.

'Are you planning to wear those shoes all day?' She couldn't help comparing her own kitten-heeled pumps with Ali's towering gladiator sandals that looked as challenging as a pair of stilts.

'Mmm. Jury's out, but I thought I'd better look the part. I can always take them off when the place is empty. I couldn't resist them though.'

'Give me comfort over corns every time,' said Lou, remembering the intensity of the pain induced by the grey suede numbers that now lay abandoned in the recycling. 'I'm thinking about giving up on heels altogether. Going flat — that's the way forward.'

'You can't! Give up on heels and you give up on life. I won't let you.'

'But I'll never be able to run away, never mind for a bus. And who'll push the wheelchair when they finally cripple me?' Lou laughed. 'You remind me of Jenny, you know. She was always on at me to make the best of myself. But once I was out of the magazine, it was such a relief to be able to relax on that front.'

'But the evidence says she was right. That dress looks a-may-zing. Have you lost weight?' Ali tilted her head and stared.

Despite her vows not to care, Lou enjoyed the compliment. 'Sadly, no. I've squeezed myself into these bloody control knicker things that come right up to here.' She yanked the top of them back up to where it was meant to sit, just under her bust. 'I can barely breathe and can't eat but the dress looks a billion times better.'

'I wish I could say it doesn't, but . . .' She dodged Lou's hand that mimed a quick slap to one cheek then the other. 'Right, let's do it!' Ali finished raising the security shutters, then crossed the road where she stood hands on hips, appraising what she saw and ignoring the wolf whistle from a builder on some scaffolding a couple of buildings down. Lou gave a last check that everything was where she wanted it, then went outside to join her. The shop looked just as she had hoped it would: inviting. The signwriter had painted the fascia the same green that she'd chosen for the inside wall and the name stood out in shiny black.

'Ladies,' came a voice. 'This is your shop?'

'It is,' replied Lou, turning to face a short, heavily moustached elderly man in a white overall who had just emerged from the deli a few doors down.

'I'm your neighbour, Stefano. I've been in Italia for the last weeks. But now I congratulate you and I offer you my best espresso on the house as a well-wish.'

Lou's heart sank at the thought of more

coffee, but it would be rude to refuse. At that moment, two women walking down the street stopped outside the shop window. 'Thank you. But business calls — I hope.'

'No problem. I bring them over.'

Lou and Ali both thanked him and crossed back into the shop where one of the women Lou thought she recognised as Stephanie Baker from *Flashion,* the definitive monthly style bible, was already scrutinising the stock, touching the vintage dresses as if she might catch something from them, despite not having removed her aubergine leather gloves. Her companion had taken out a notebook and pen from her shoulder bag.

'Can I help you? Or give you a press release?'

'I don't think so.' Ms Baker moved across the shop to Lou's own rail. She sniffed as she examined the cocktail dresses, saying something in an undertone to her companion who kept a careful half-step behind her as she scribbled something down. Lou wanted to rush over and talk them through what was behind her choice of fabrics and styles but a second sense told her that these two didn't need a hard sell. They would form their own opinion without her help.

'Did *you* make these?'

The question came just as Lou had sipped

the hot coffee brought in by Stefano. She swallowed, burning the back of her throat. 'Yes,' she whispered in momentary agony, reaching for the accompanying glass of water. 'Yes, I did.'

With the self-satisfaction accompanying the assumption that one's revered wherever one goes, Ms Baker's face cracked into the slightest smile. 'They're very good. Not original, of course . . .' Lou's bubble burst. 'But very well made.' She looked Lou over, sizing up her dress.

'Thank you. I'm hoping one or two of the magazines might give us a mention or even feature the dresses.' Don't sell too hard, she warned herself, wishing the woman would turn her attention to Ali.

'They're not really our sort of thing, are they, Flora?' Flora shook her head, her eyes never leaving her mentor. 'But I like to consider new talent for myself. Tess Granger from *Stylish* mentioned you.' She moved over to the jewellery. 'This is impressive. I'd like to look more closely at some of these.'

Ali stepped forward to take out the pieces Ms Baker was interested in. Eventually she swept out, ultimately noncommittal, Flora in tow. Lou and Ali looked at each other as they heaved a joint sigh of relief.

'Are they all going to be like that?' Ali col-

231

lapsed into the chair.

'I bloody hope not. I'm hoping a few familiar faces will show who'll be a bit more supportive or we're in trouble.' Lou pulled a face.

At that moment, two new women looked through the door. 'Are you open?' said one of them. 'Can we look around?'

Ali and Lou looked at one another, then Lou turned to welcome them. 'Of course. Come in.'

While Ali whispered, 'Let battle commence.'

13

As the day drew to a close, the two women were exhausted. After a slow and not particularly promising start, things had picked up around lunchtime and since then, a steady stream of journalists or friends had visited, picking their way though the rails, examining what was on the shelves. During the last couple of hours, the post-work crowd had arrived with a thirst for champagne and a party. The prosecco was opened and poured. Press releases were taken and encouraging noises made. A couple of orders were taken for Lou's dresses and three of the vintage items were sold. Ali's jewellery received a similarly positive response. The day was everything Lou had hoped for. The shop was now formally open.

By eight o'clock, numbers were thinning as people drifted on to their next party or off home. Eventually Ali and Lou yanked down the security shutter, leaving enough space for them to creep underneath, and put the Closed sign on the door.

They shook hands. 'After la Baker, I thought we were doomed but I think that counts as a success,' said Lou, diving behind the counter and into the loo, only to emerge with her unevenly overstretched and under-achieving control pants in her hand. 'Thank Christ for that! I've been dying to rip them off all day. Now I can start to enjoy myself. Nic should be here to pick me up soon.' She fished in her handbag for her ringing mobile. 'That'll be her running late.' She checked the caller's identity. 'It's Hooker!'

'Don't answer it. Don't let him spoil the day.' Ali made a face as she regretted what she'd said. 'Sorry. None of my business.' She began to swap her sandals for the trainers she'd hidden behind the counter.

'I don't want to, but I'd better.' Lou was puzzled. 'He hasn't called me for weeks. He wouldn't from Thailand unless there was a reason.' She put the phone to her ear. 'Hooker?'

The line buzzed, then she could hear his voice over the crackle. 'Lou? I need your help.'

'What's happened?' She was immediately reminded of the numerous times he'd called to ask her to do something for him.

'We've been mugged . . .'

She caught her breath, making Ali look up. 'Are you all right?'

'Yes, fine, thank God. Just a snatch-and-grab in a busy street, nothing life threatening. But I've lost my passport. I need you to go to my desk at home and dig out the photocopies I meant to bring with me, scan them and email them to me. Can you do that?'

Why didn't he ask one of the children, she wondered. Or Sally, his doormat of a PA? Why Lou? After everything she'd said to him about being taken for granted, she was still his first port of call. But, in the circumstances, she could hardly refuse. 'Give me your hotel email and I'll do it this evening.' She scribbled down the details and hung up. 'Bloody man! Why didn't he scan them himself before he went? He still treats me like the little wife. When will he realise that we've all moved on?' She spoke under her breath in an angry mutter.

'When we tell him?' Ali made it sound like a question, as she titivated her make-up in the mirror, concentrating on her careful application of Russian Red gloss before smoothing her lips together.

'We will.' Lou put on her coat. 'You get

off home. I'll shut up shop when Nic comes.'

'OK. Tomorrow I'll be back at the coalface, working on a few more pieces of stock — more butterflies, bees and keys — and thinking about my Mughal collection. I'll call you.' With that, she squeezed herself under the shutter and disappeared into the night.

Within minutes, Nic arrived, apologising for her lateness. 'A colleague called me into his office to discuss a child access case and I couldn't get away. How did it go?' She began to inspect the vintage rail, touching various hangers so she could see what was there.

Lou waited for the inevitable riff on second-hand clothes. Instead, she was surprised when Nic pulled out the second Ossie Clark and held it against herself so that it obscured her dark suit.

'This is gorgeous.' The astonishment in her voice made Lou smile. 'If only I wasn't about to be the size of a house, I might even . . .'

'You'll never be that big. But I could save it for after the baby — a present from me.'

'Mum, no!' She held it front of her, twisting and turning in front of the cheval mirror. 'Actually, you know what? I think I'd prefer something new. The idea of it having hung in someone else's wardrobe gives me the creeps.' She screwed up her face at the thought and put it back, moving over to the jewellery cabinet. 'I like these, though.' She pointed at a set of stacking rings in which Ali had contrasted smoky quartz with pale citrine and bluey indicolite. 'Can I try them?'

Lou unlocked the cabinet and passed the rings to Nic who slid them onto a finger and held out her hand, turning it to see the effect, obviously pleased with what she saw.

'I wasn't expecting you to have such class stuff.' She stripped them off, swapping them for one with a toffee-orange coloured stone. 'This is gorgeous.'

'That's a spessartite garnet,' Lou informed her.

Nic looked surprised. 'Get you! I didn't know you knew about jewellery.'

'I don't,' Lou admitted. 'But these make me want to find out. They all sound so beautiful — rubellite, tourmaline, peridot,' She picked up one with a greenish stone and held it under the light before putting it back. 'And they are.'

Nic replaced hers in the cabinet. 'I might take a rain check in a week or two.'

Lou basked in Nic's approval, then said, 'We'd better go. We've got to stop off at

Dad's first. I'll explain on the way.'

Pulling into the driveway, Lou shivered at the familiarity of the place as the security light came on, its glare illuminating the decorative tiling between the upper and lower bay windows. She hadn't returned here since the day she moved out, not wanting to be reminded of all the history she had left behind. Nothing seemed to have changed. The three storeys of the large semi-detached Victorian villa loomed above her, dark windows like eyes watching as she made her way to the porch on the right of the building. Nic stayed in the car while Lou slipped the key into the lock and went inside. Immediately she was struck by the smell of empty house: stale, cold and uninviting. She disabled the burglar alarm, the numbers automatically at her fingertips. Standing in the wide hall, she was overcome with nostalgia and had to fight back the memories: Jamie pushing Tom downstairs by mistake; the football that broke the hall window; Nic's little face staring down through the banisters to see guests arriving for dinner before she was packed off to bed.

To her left was the sitting room. Lou couldn't resist putting her head round the door, half expecting to find the children sprawled in front of the television, as they would have been years earlier. Flicking on the light, she saw the familiar deep brown sofa and chairs, the gingersnap Wilton, the crowded bookcases, the seascapes that Hooker and she had collected on holidays over the years against the gardenia walls. Her eyes travelled to the windows where, to her surprise, hung swags of heavy cream damask instead of her favourite floral Designers Guild curtains. She felt the change like a blow to her solar plexus, then recovered herself. Almost. Of course Hooker was allowed to change what he liked, just not her favourite curtains! She would have taken them, if she'd known, cut them down to fit her spare-room windows. Then she noticed that the glorious light-filled painting of figures standing at the sea's edge in Dingle had been removed from pride of place over the mantelpiece and replaced by an ugly modern mirror. Whatever he liked, she repeated to herself. But that picture had been so perfect there for so long: a reminder of their many happy family holidays in Ireland when the kids were small. Hooker had bought it for her. 'Because I love you,' he'd said all those years ago.

No, no. She stopped herself again. This was his house now and he was right to put his stamp on it. Just go to his office and ignore the rest, she told herself. Nic was waiting. She went upstairs, trailing a finger along the banister. Their bedroom was straight in front of her. She found herself standing in its doorway, her hand on the switch. Light flooded the room, showing the neatly made bed that had been turned side-on to the window. She was saddened, remembering how the view of her garden from the bed had been one of her favourite things about the room. On the bedside table, she noticed a Jackie Collins novel, not hers and not Hooker's. On the blanket chest, newly positioned at the end of the bed, was a red lacy bra. Not hers and certainly not Hooker's. Bile rose in her throat as she made a dash for the bathroom. She retched into the toilet, then put the lid down and sat on it, gathering her swirling thoughts. What had she expected? That Hooker would embrace a monastic existence once she'd gone? Stupid even to think it, given what she now knew. As she took a few steadying breaths, she looked around her, noting the fluorescent pink toothbrush in the holder beside Hooker's, a pot of vanilla and anise body cream. On an impulse, she picked up the cream and stuffed it into the bathroom cabinet, snapping shut the door. Imagining another woman was one thing, being presented with the hard evidence in what had been Lou's home for so long was a violation.

She made her way into Hooker's office. Nothing had changed here: blind pulled down, labelled box files regimented on wide shelves, legal textbooks on others — not one at an angle, pictures straight, desktop clear, leather executive chair half turned towards the door as if he'd just got out of it. Anxious to get away from the house as quickly as possible, she went straight to the desk and concentrated on what she had come for. The top drawer contained nothing but elastic bands, paper clips, propelling pencil leads and a few chewed Bics. The one below contained various papers. She pulled them out and leafed through what was there. Halfway down the pile, she could hardly miss the words 'WILL OF IAN JAMES SHERWOOD' printed large on the front sheet of some stapled pages.

Years ago, they had spent hours with the lawyer drawing up their wills, entertaining themselves for months afterwards over their letters of wishes as, whenever someone annoyed them, they joked about how they would gift them something wholly undesirable. They'd enjoyed imagining the look on their relatives' faces when they found themselves empty-handed, or gifted something no one in their right mind would want. Unable to stop herself, she turned to the letter at the back, to remind herself how his had been left. As she did so, she registered the date on the will. This wasn't the one he had drawn up at the same time as her. This was 25 September 2006. He had revised this five years ago, without mentioning to her that's what he was doing, or suggesting she do the same. She flicked back to the front of the will. 25 September 2006. But why would he have made a new will? It didn't make sense.

Lou had long ago been taught not to read other people's private papers. She once got stuck into her best friend's diary, to find that Emma's tortured thoughts about her, and their other friends, did not make edifying reading. That was the end of what until then had been a solid friendship. Postcards were private too. But if they were left lying around, how could one be blamed for reading them? Same goes for your husband's will, she reasoned. That it hadn't exactly been left lying around was neither here nor there. She needed to know what Hooker had been up to behind her back. For the children's sake, as well as for her own.

She skipped over the legalese until she got to the part she was looking for. She read it once, twice, put the papers down, picked them up and read them again. Her hand was shaking, her mouth dry. There was no doubt. She had not misunderstood. Hooker had changed his will. Instead of leaving his entire estate to her should he die first, as before, he had willed her the house, leaving his other assets to be divided immediately between his children. His four children.

She shook her head as if the number four would transform by some miracle into a three. The names of her children were there: James, Nicola and Thomas Sherwood but followed by another: Rory Sherwood Burgess. A name completely unknown to her. There must be a mistake. But this was Hooker's will. What was there, in black and white, had to be true. This boy must exist.

She collapsed, winded, into the chair. It rocked backwards with her weight. Hooker had another child somewhere? A child she knew nothing about? Her initial shock gave way to fury as the implications of her discovery piled in on her. How old was this boy? Who was his mother? What did they look like? Would he look like Tom or Jamie? Where did they live? What was Hooker's relationship with them? Did the boy know Hooker? As she waited for her head to stop spinning, the car horn sounding outside brought her back to the moment, to the reason why she was here. His passport. Sod him. She was tempted to let him stew in Thailand. But he was no good to her there. If he was back in the country, she could at least confront him and get answers to her questions. So she replaced the papers in the drawer and banged it shut. Then she let out a sob. Don't, she reprimanded herself. Stop that, now. She reapplied herself to the drawers and opened the one below. In a file marked 'Travel Documents' were the photocopied pages of his passport. Instead of switching on his scanner and computer and sending them immediately as she'd originally planned, she folded them and tucked them into her bag.

Enough surprises for one night. She didn't want to think what more she might find on his computer. In the six months since she'd left him, she'd already discovered that he had been leading a second life, quite separate from the one they'd had together. But now there was this. The odd short-lived affair, she had suspected, but not one that had lasted for three years and certainly not the existence of a child from another. His deceit staggered her.

How old was this child? How old?

She switched off the lights, reset the alarm

and slammed the front door, before double-locking it. That, at least, made her feel a little better. Nic's startled face was visible through the windscreen of the car.

'Easy, Mum. You don't need to bring the whole house down.'

'Sorry, wasn't thinking.' It was true. She had plenty of other things on her mind.

'Are you OK? Going back into the house must have been a bit difficult.'

She brushed Nic's unusual concern away with, 'No, not at all. It's his house now, he can do what he wants with it.'

Nic turned towards her as she reached for the ignition. 'What's wrong? Did something happen in there?'

'Really not,' she insisted, not wanting to share her discovery just yet. 'The boys'll be waiting. Let's go.'

Nic tutted, annoyed that her mother wasn't going to say more, but reversed out into the road. Relieved she didn't have to drive, Lou leaned back against the headrest and shut her eyes. What a day. All sorts of questions jostled for answers but, if she was going to enjoy the celebratory meal that her three were giving her, she had to push them out of her mind until later. The one thing she would not do was tell the children what she had found. Hooker could bloody well explain himself to all of them when he returned. She would make sure of that.

For the rest of the evening, being with her children acted as a panacea. Even Nic rose to the occasion, dismounting from her high horse and joining in. Perhaps those hormones would be the making of her after all, thought Lou, as she watched her daughter convulsed with laughter over one of Jamie's tales from the film set where he was working. As the two boys joshed each other along, Lou relaxed, happy in their company. When they were like this, sparking off each other, there was nothing to beat their company. They ordered pasta dishes before raising toasts to the shop's success and her future, to the baby, to Jamie and Rose's wedding and to Tom's hoped-for promotion. No one was left out. Except Hooker. His name was neatly avoided. The meal was over all too soon and Jamie drove her home, Nic protesting that she had to get a reasonably early night because she was in court the next day.

With Eric Clapton's 'Tears in Heaven' — always good for a bit of late-night self-indulgence — making her own tears well, Lou sprawled on the sofa, dress zip undone, mug of hot chocolate at her side. The mystery of Hooker's fourth child worried at her. What upset her most was not so much this unknown's existence but the fact that Hooker had concealed him from her and more importantly from his brothers and sister, denying the child part of his natural family. What made Hooker believe he had the right to do that? Had he thought he was saving her and the children? That the knowledge of this child would somehow derail them? Or was he saving his own skin by keeping this Rory secret? She was pretty sure she knew the answer. She removed the CD and sat in silence.

Still only half past ten. She wasn't in the mood to go through to her workroom. Not tonight. But she wouldn't be able to concentrate long enough to watch anything on TV. She kept thinking about the boy, going over and over the same ground. She couldn't remember Hooker ever having spent great stretches of time away from London, so she didn't think he could be running another family out of town. The child must be the product of an affair she had pretended wasn't happening. But who was this woman, somebody Burgess? The more she tried to fend off the questions, the more insistent they became. At the same time she felt sorrow about what this would mean to her family. Unlike her moving out of the family home, this would surely cause a seismic shift in the children's relationship with their father.

She took out her patchwork bag and dug her hand into the bits of familiar fabric that belonged to clothes and other items that had punctuated their family history. Hexagons of colour from her mother's dressmaking days, from Jamie's muslin nappy that he took everywhere as a toddler, from the shirt Hooker wore to the first day of his first job at Jeffries and Shunt, a small firm of commercial lawyers, various Babygros and children's clothing, bits of curtain and cushion fabric, dolls' dresses, the kids' and her own clothes. 'Project Quilt' had become such a family joke that she hadn't got it out for years, tired of the jeers that greeted it, but she still squirrelled away pieces of fabric, inwardly vowing to complete it one day. Instead, her knitting had taken precedence. However, since she'd moved out, in her few wobbly moments she'd gained comfort from the quilt and from the repetitive mindless work it involved. She picked out the latest fabric octagons she'd cut as well as a number of smaller ones made of card. She took one of each and turned the red silk around the card, pinning and then tacking it. Usually an activity that was guaranteed to induce a mindless relaxation, this time it failed to distract her at all.

She put the lot back in the bag and stuffed it under her chair beside her knitting. Although she had grown used to her own company, for once she wished someone else was with her. She wanted nothing more than to talk, to externalise the problem. As long as everything was circling round inside her head, she couldn't think straight.

She picked up her phone, called up Fiona's number, then aborted the call. Fiona's strong opinions were not what she wanted at this moment. She was already adamant Lou should pin Hooker down on their finances. Lou had resisted, not believing that Hooker would do her out of anything not her due. But now this. Fiona would have a field day. The last time they'd spoken she had made her views clear. 'I know the form. At the beginning, everything's civilised. Nobody's going to do anybody out of anything, all the assets are going be split right down the middle. Then when the mists clear and lawyers are brought in, the husband becomes ferociously protective of what's his and that's when the fighting starts. Trust me. I've seen it a thousand times. For God's sake, get something in writing while he's still feeling benevolent.'

She was probably right, but the money wasn't what was upsetting Lou. She needed someone who would listen and who would let her come to her own conclusions without bludgeoning her with theirs. This was exactly the sort of moment when Jenny would have known what to say and what to do. Lou lay staring at the ceiling, thinking about her sister. She had learned to lodge the pain of her loss safely in the background until times like this when no one but Jenny would do. She allowed the tears to come for a while, then she sat up straight and blew her nose. This was getting her nowhere. She would go mad if she didn't talk to someone. She made a snap decision and called the one person who knew Hooker and what he was capable of, as well as she did. She listened as the number rang, then Ali answered. At the sound of her voice, Lou immediately knew it had been right to call.

14

Ali tugged harder. The retractable ladder didn't move. Another even more forceful yank and it creaked towards her, the spring rusty with disuse.

'I'll go up first and see what's what. OK?' she said, grabbing a roll of bin bags and a dustpan and brush and tucking them under her arm.

Lou nodded, looking apprehensive about what she had let herself in for.

They were standing on the landing of Ali's father's house, and the sound of his voice carried under the door of his study followed by the click of the receiver being replaced. He coughed. Then silence. Engrossed in his latest piece of research, he wouldn't emerge until seven o'clock at least, whatever was going on in the world outside. He had shown little interest when Ali had said she wanted to turn out the attic. Nor had he objected when she'd asked if he minded

Lou coming to help. If anything, he'd seemed pleased by the idea that they might impose some order on the accumulated family junk.

As far as Ali could see, the arrangement was win-win all round: she would have the support of a friend as she combed through the family detritus, hardly daring to hope that she would find something that might tell her more about her mother; her father would get the order he so valued; and Lou would get twenty-four hours of distraction from the latest of Hooker's revelations. Gripping her torch in one hand, she climbed the ladder, steadying herself as it bounced under her weight. At the top, she stopped, letting her eyes adjust to the darkness as she swung the feeble beam of light from side to side. 'My God!' She took a few more steps upwards until she could hoist herself into the loft.

'What is it?' Lou was already on the bottom rung, impatient for Ali to make way for her.

'No one's been here for years.' Ali peered down. 'But I've found a light switch at least. Come on up.' A short neon strip attached to the central joist flickered into life, lighting up the central part of the boarded-out loft. Drifts of spider's webs hung from the

trusses and a film of dust covered everything. She wiped a finger along the top of a
child's blackboard and checked it. 'No
wonder the house downstairs is so tidy. He's
just chucked everything he didn't want up
here. I'd no idea.' Apart from a narrow
central pathway running from one end to
the other, every inch of floor space was
covered with tea chests, cardboard boxes,
cases, trunks, old toys and games, mirrors,
pictures, an old mattress, and stacks of
newspapers and books.

Lou clambered up the ladder to join her,
looking around. 'Blimey! There's no way we
can empty this lot out in an afternoon.
Where do we start?'

'I'm not sure. Everything's filthy. Are you
sure you're up for this?'

'Of course. That's why I'm squeezed into
these old jeans. Let's do it!'

Encouraged by her enthusiasm, Ali took a
step forward. 'Look! That's the toy pram I
was given when I was about six and . . . oh,
Harriet's still in it.' Ali crossed the floor,
bending her head to fit under the slanting
roof, and picked up a baby doll with a bald
plastic head, a pouting pink mouth and a
grubby fabric body. Holding Harriet out in
front of her, as if she were real, Ali smiled,
returning her to the pram as if she didn't

want to hurt her. 'How I loved her. And here's my doll's house. See how perfect it is inside. I remember Mum spending hours sticking on the wallpaper and fixing up the electric lighting.' She knelt down so her face was on a level with the rooms and as she began straightening the sitting room furniture, she sang quietly, 'Ally, bally, ally bally bee, Sittin' on yer mammy's knee . . .'

Lou looked up from a box of children's books. 'What's that?'

'Oh, just something my mum used to sing to me. It suddenly came back to me.' Her voice tailed off.

Lou approached a pile of cases mounded behind a dismantled baby's cot, touching Ali on the shoulder as she inched past her. 'What about this pile of cases? Shouldn't we be looking in them? Maybe there's something there that will tell you something about her. After all, that's really why we're here, isn't it?'

Ali looked at the chaos around her. 'But I wasn't expecting it to be quite this bad. I don't think they can ever have thrown anything away.'

'Wouldn't it be easier just to pump Eric for a bit more info?'

'I've tried.' Ali felt the burden of her and her father's shared past but it was hard to explain, even to Lou. 'If I press too hard, he just clams up. Between us, we've buried stuff so long that now we're both too frightened to disturb the surface in case things we don't want to remember come flying out. He's made a new life for himself and I don't want to overturn that. I can't. Cantankerous old sod though he may sometimes be, I guess he did his best for me.'

'But if you don't, it could be too late,' Lou warned.

'Too late for what?' Ali wanted this conversation to stop. She wanted to kill the curiosity that she'd begun to feel since her father's revelation, to stop its insistent nagging. She didn't want to be disappointed or let down again. 'Mum left us. That's the bottom line. Whatever her reasons, she didn't want us then and there's nothing to make us think that she ever changed her mind. I'm really clearing this for Dad.' She stood up, backing into the centre of the attic where she could stand straight, knowing Lou was as conscious as she was that she was lying.

At least Lou was sensitive enough not to say anything more.

'Come on, then. Let's move the cot. Oh!' Ali stopped, switched on the torch again and aimed the beam towards the back of the cases where a meringue-like object the size of a football was suspended from one of the roof trusses. She turned to Lou. 'What the hell's that?'

Lou edged past her. 'Looks like a wasp's nest.' She took the torch and shone it closer, illuminating the papery exterior wall. 'Isn't it beautiful? Look at the colours.'

'Be careful.' Ali took a step back. 'Shouldn't we get Rentokil or someone?'

'No rush. The wasps are all dead. The queen might be in there but she won't come out till it's a bit warmer. Then she'll abandon this nest and start all over again. New home, new life, new worker wasps. They won't come back here.'

'How can you be so sure?' Ali took a step towards the way out.

'We had one in the garage once. They never go back home. Once the evil little buggers were exterminated, Hooker took the nest down to show the kids. It was amazingly intricate, all made of woodchip and spit. The boys kept it in their room for years.'

Ali heard the catch in her voice, and put her arm around Lou's shoulders. 'You're meant to be having a day off from thinking about him.'

Lou inclined her head so it rested against Ali's. 'I know I'm meant to be, but I can't forget what he's done. I can't believe he thought he'd get away with it. He must think so little of me, must have for years. I'd no idea.'

'Not necessarily.' Grateful for a change of subject from her mother, Ali moved away to pull down the top case, careful to avoid the nest just in case Lou was wrong. 'Take this one. Think about it from his point of view.'

'I'm trying to. Christ, this is heavy.' Lou let the old blue case fall to the floor with a bang. They smiled at each other when they heard a muffled angry shout from downstairs. 'Look, I know all the clichés about being driven into another woman's arms once the wife's too exhausted for anything other than the quickest of shags on a Friday night while her attention's all on the kids. But, if that was the case, I don't really understand why he didn't leave us years ago.'

'Why would he?' Ali knew she was treading on sensitive ground. 'I've met several men who, despite being completely happy with their wives, needed something else to fulfil them as well. I don't think there's anything wrong with that, is there? At least provided it doesn't hurt anyone else. A mistress can oblige without necessarily being a threat to the marriage.'

'You would say that.' Lou flicked open the catches of the case.

'Of course I would,' Ali agreed. 'But I believe it. Look, it's crazy having this conversation with you, given my history with Hooker. But I can promise you that he never, not once, mentioned being unhappy.'

'But what's the point of making those vows if you're not going to bother to make at least an effort to keep them? Not that I'm such a shining example any more, I admit. But I did try.' Lou picked up a battered-looking book and opened it. 'Look at these. Stamp albums. The case's full of them.'

'They're Dad's. He'd spend hours poring over them. It drove Mum mad.' A picture of the three of them flew into her mind. She was by the door in a favourite blue and white cotton dress, her hair pinned to the side with a floral slide; her father sat, shirt open at the neck, sleeves rolled up, exhaling smoke from his pipe. Through the haze, she could see her aproned mother standing at the stove, stirring something. 'Mum would be listening to *The Archers,* making supper and getting impatient that his collection was scattered over the kitchen table.'

Lou didn't respond immediately, then as she replaced the album in the box, she said,

'What about the boy — Rory?' She seemed to have difficulty saying his name. 'Has Hooker ever said anything to you about him?'

Ali continued picking up the albums, flicking the pages, careful not to disturb the stamps. A couple of loose paper hinges fluttered to the floor. 'Nothing. I promise.' The last thing she wanted was to give away the fury she'd felt when Lou had phoned her late that night and told her what she'd discovered. She didn't want to admit to the quite irrational resentment she felt about Hooker having a baby with another woman, even if it was years before they'd met. This knowledge reinforced her own sadness at missing out on motherhood but had also confirmed how much she despised him. She slipped the hinges between the pages. 'I told you that I never wanted to know about that side of his life. And that's true. It would have made everything too difficult. My way, he could spend a few hours in a bubble that had nothing to do with the real world, and I knew he'd want to come back.' She put the last album down without looking at Lou, regretting her final words.

'I hate hearing you say that.' Lou shut the case. 'I know you didn't know me then and it's not your fault but it makes me feel so bloody inadequate. And sad.'

'I know and I'm sorry, but it shouldn't. Meeting you and Hooker has completely changed the way I see things. I'm so done with married men.' She slammed shut the lid of the case.

'Yeah, yeah.' Disbelief was scored through Lou's voice, as she helped drag it back to the pile.

'No, really. I was so blinkered, never thinking, never wanting to think, of the effect of what I was doing on anyone else. I'm ashamed by how selfish I've been. Honestly.'

'Oh, ease up, for heaven's sake. You were only protecting yourself — that's understandable too. You know, you've never really told me how you got into this serial mistress thing, except that it happened after Don. Perhaps I should take it up now I'm a free woman.' Lou put her thumbs into the belt loops of her jeans and hoicked them up. 'Suppose there weren't any takers though. How humiliating would that be?'

Ali was too busy retrieving another of the cases to reply. She concentrated on prising open its locks as she began to explain. Talking about herself was easier than talking about her mother or her affair with Hooker. 'After Don left I carried on working as a store assistant at Makepiece and Strutt.

Jewellers by Royal Appointment,' she said, imitating the cut-glass accent of a typical customer. 'But at night, I'd design and make my own stuff at the kitchen table. I started to sell a few things but, at the same time, I was restoring jewellery for Makepiece's customers. Things took off as one or two of them began to commission original pieces from me and then passed on my name to their friends. But all that time, I stayed single, focused on the business. I couldn't commit to anyone else after Don. I didn't want to be hurt like that again and besides, I didn't think I'd meet anyone else like him.'

Lou seized a case, blew the dust off it, and snapped it open. 'This one's empty apart from a few bits of newspaper. Shall we try another?' She stood up. 'Go on, don't stop. I'm listening.'

Ali wiped her hands on her jeans and went for another case. 'OK. Eventually, after a short-lived affair with Aaron Sotheby, devoted husband and father of four who I met when he commissioned a necklace for his wife, I cottoned on to the idea that married men weren't necessarily looking for commitment either. No emotional ties and mutually convenient and fun. That suited me down to a T. After him, I took another married lover, then another, until it became a sort of way of life.'

'Didn't you ever think about what you might be missing?'

'Not really. At the beginning, I suppose I thought that one day I'd find the one, but I never did and life was good in other ways. It was Hooker's proposal — if that's what it was — that made all those feelings bubble up again. Years and years later. And then I met you.'

'But now you're going to meet Don again.' Lou placed the next case on the pile for removal.

'I wish you wouldn't sound so hopeful.' But she couldn't ignore the burst of pleasure she experienced whenever she thought about their imminent meeting, despite not wanting to be disappointed. 'In fact, I'm beginning to wonder whether meeting him is such a good idea.'

Lou responded with a raised eyebrow.

'Why? What harm can it do? You said you wanted to tie up loose ends, and that's what you will do. If nothing else.'

'Maybe. But I'm not sure I can cope with that as well as finding out what happened to my mother. I can't believe that after so long they've both come back into my life at the same time.'

'Of course you can cope. You must.' Lou

was dragging over a trunk that she'd found at the end of the attic. 'I have a good feeling about this one. Help me with these knots.'

Between them they undid the washing line that held the trunk shut. They knelt in front of it and opened it together. The sharp scent of mothballs rose up to meet them. Lou was first to speak.

'Bingo.'

There was the same little blue and white dress that Ali had remembered earlier. It lay folded on top of a Laura Ashley print dress, sage green with tiny white flowers that she recognised as the one her mother wore at the last school sports day they went to together, the one where she won five red ribbons. One of them was still pinned to her mother's collar where Ali had insisted it went so they could share her success. She struggled to catch her breath, as Lou put her hand on her arm.

Ali took out a folded fox fur stole and swung it about her neck. As she felt the softness against her face and smelled its faint perfume, she remembered her mother and father standing by the front door, dressed up, ready to go out for the evening. She almost could smell her father's hair cream mixed with pipe smoke, her mother's *L'Air du Temps*. She heard the rumble of his voice, the ring of her laughter. Two of the paws and a bit of mothball fell into her lap.

Lou picked up the animal parts. 'Easy enough to repair.' She watched Ali lift up the clothes in the trunk, one after another.

'But I don't understand. Why would she leave her clothes behind? That doesn't make sense.'

'Perhaps she only took what she needed. Perhaps your dad trained her not to throw anything away, so they've just stayed here ever since. Gosh, this Jaeger camel coat's in mint condition.' She shook it out and passed it to Ali. 'Very on trend, my dear!'

Ali slid her arms into the three-quarter-length sleeves. 'I can't resist.' She gave as much of a twirl as the space would allow.

'Looks great on you. Those wide lapels are just the thing these days.'

Lou turned back to the trunk but Ali closed her eyes and let her mind go blank. She felt a piece of paper in the pocket, took it out and unfolded it: a brief shopping list written in her mother's hand; on the reverse, a child's painstaking writing. 'I LOVE YOU MUM LOVE FROM ALI.' She stuffed the paper back where it came from. 'I think I'll keep this.'

Lou wasn't listening. Instead she was holding up a deep yellow beaded evening gown, with front and back V-necks, the fabric overlapping from left to right with a small bow covering the zip fastening at the back. 'This is fantastic. Your Mum had great taste.'

'I don't remember her ever wearing that.' As she took the dress, Ali wondered when her mother might have worn it. Something she could never ask her father. Never.

How little she knew about her parents beyond her life with them, and even her memories of that were sketchy. Too painful. Nonetheless, her father's version of events didn't ring entirely true. How would her mother have survived without some sort of financial help? She hadn't worked for years, as far as Ali knew. He must know more than he claimed about where she went, otherwise nothing made sense.

'You didn't say she was a dressmaker.' Lou laid the top drawer of the trunk beside her.

'I don't think she was.'

'Then who did all these belong to?'

Ali snapped to and knelt beside Lou to see what she was talking about. There, on the bottom of the trunk were neatly piled packets of dressmaking patterns — Butterick's, McCall's, Simplicity — each printed with coloured illustrations of the garments to be made.

'They must have been my nan's. Look at the styles.' She folded the dress and put it on the pile beside her. 'But Mum obviously kept them.'

Lou was examining them. 'Fitted jacket blouse with notched collar . . . buttoned shoulder tabs . . . centre front inverted pleat.' She picked up another. 'These Audrey Hepburn-inspired blouses and these halter-necked sun tops — perfect summer stock.'

'Then you must have them. All of them,' said Ali, beginning to pile them beside the trunk.

'But they're vintage,' Lou protested. 'I'm sure you could sell them to collectors.'

'Then you do that if you don't want them. No one else is going to use them. Certainly not me or Dad.' She smiled at the idea of them sitting totally bemused in front of a sewing machine. 'In fact, I think you should take some of these clothes if they're the sort of thing you can sell.'

'I couldn't,' said Lou firmly, replacing the drawer and shutting the lid of the trunk. 'Not your mum's stuff.'

'But what good's it doing up here? Of course, I'll talk to Dad but I'm sure he'll agree. He wants the place emptied.'

'I can't take them, Ali. They've got way

too much sentimental value. What would you feel like seeing them hanging in the shop or being tried on by someone? These patterns are enough for me.'

'Rubbish. I've had my moment with them. That's plenty. Besides, I've got these.' She held out her right hand where her mother's rings shone under the light. 'They're enough for me. Them and the coat.'

For the rest of the afternoon, the two women got on with clearing one small area of the attic at a time. As they made their way through one case after another, one box then another, they limited their conversation to debate over whether the contents were destined for the tip or for recycling. Bin bags were filled, tied and labelled, before being lugged down the stairs and into the front room. For Ali, the ruthless approach was the only way. If she allowed herself to get emotional over what they found, she knew she'd never get out of there. Besides, it wasn't her mother's clothes she was looking for, it was answers to the questions that she'd used so much effort to suppress for so many years. And it was obvious she wasn't going to find them there.

15

Ali was already fifteen minutes late. She pushed through the one of the glass doors into the bright hotel foyer, her face smarting from the cold. She walked across a large patterned Persian rug towards the oak-panelled concierge's desk on the left. Having dealt with a fur-wrapped matron quizzing him about local restaurants, the concierge turned to Ali. 'Can I help?'

'I'm meeting a Don Sterling.' Saying his name out loud made her even more nervous. She rested her hand on the desk, then focused on taking off her gloves as she willed her composure to return.

'Oh, yes. Mr Sterling asked me to direct you to the bar.' He pointed through a door opposite the desk. 'Through the dining room.'

In that split second, Ali saw her choice. She could turn and walk out of the hotel alone into her future or she could enter the bar and risk reconnecting with her past. She thought of the Don she had once known, charismatic and wayward. How would he have changed? She looked out into the street, slipped her gloves back on and, grasping the lapels of her coat with one hand in anticipation of the icy wind outside, took a step towards the front door. As she did so, she caught sight of her reflection in a large gilt-framed mirror. What she saw was a woman in her prime, looking good if a little tired, in charge. That was enough to tip the pendulum in the other direction. She was the one in control here and she was being ridiculous. Meeting Don would have as much or as little effect on her life as she allowed. She was struck by the realisation that not only did she want to see him, she wanted him to see her. She wanted him to know that she had changed too, that his leaving her hadn't destroyed her. She remembered with shame the final letter she had sent him, pleading with him to come back, to which he never replied. She had arranged to have supper with Lou in a couple of hours' time, forestalling any possibility of staying with him too long. Before she had time to change her mind again, she crossed to the door of the restaurant–bar and walked through.

Since agreeing to meet him, she'd kept thinking of their last days together. She had lost him the moment Greenpeace offered him a place on one of their boats. It was the career break he'd been waiting for. During the weeks that followed, she pleaded, begged, shouted, but he insisted on going it alone. He loved her but he was too young to be tied down. They walked in silence out of their dilapidated one-bedroom flat to catch the bus to Heathrow. Don was bright eyed with excitement while Ali concentrated every effort into not letting him see how much his decision was tearing her apart. That was not the way to make him come back. Instead, she added another layer to the veneer of self-control she'd first developed when coping with her mangled emotions following her mother's disappearance.

They'd queued at the check-in, her hand in his for the last time. They'd made small talk in a café surrounded by other travellers, noisy and unforgiving, promising to keep in touch, neither able to say what needed to be said. He'd be back, he said. One day. Eventually, he'd stood up and led the way to the departure gate. She felt as if her heart was being ripped out of her as he kissed her goodbye, then watched as he presented his boarding card and passport.

He turned to wave once, giving a last smile in her direction before he disappeared behind the screens. Still she held back the tears.

And now, he had come back.

She entered the restaurant, passing through the busy tables towards the brilliantly lit bar at the back. Who would have thought the country was in the grip of a recession? There were plenty of young men and women here desperate to be seen, spending the cash that allowed them to be. She scanned the crowd sitting on the bar stools, pushing round them, drinking cocktails, chattering. Not a familiar face among them, all about half Ali's age, she guessed. This was the sort of place that Don would have run a million miles to avoid when she'd known him. How incongruous to be meeting here now. As she approached the bar, she saw that to its left, the room extended to where low-slung leather sofas and chairs were arranged in a much more intimate, dimly lit space.

In a quiet corner sat a tall, slim, middle-aged man. There was no mistaking Donovan Sterling. His wild black curls had been snipped into submission and had turned a steely grey, instead of jeans and a T-shirt he wore a dark suit, but she'd have known him anywhere. As he looked up towards the bar, he saw her and immediately his face lit up. As he began to smile that all-too-familiar smile, the years rolled away and Ali felt herself smiling back.

'Ali! You came. I was beginning to think . . .' He left the sentence unfinished as he stood to greet her. He touched her arm as he kissed both her cheeks.

'Of course I came.' She thanked God for the discreet lighting that hid her blush. Suddenly she felt as wound up as she had on their first date. Then, he had taken her to the local Odeon. They'd sat in the back row, smoked and kissed. She had been so nervous that she'd emptied his packet of Rothmans onto the floor as she tried to take one. Result: they'd missed a crucial chunk of the film as they scrabbled to find the fallen cigarettes.

'Sit down, sit down. A drink?'

She asked for a Sea Breeze, praying the vodka would steady her. While he signalled the waiter, she removed her coat and gloves and sat down opposite him.

Don turned back to her. 'Well! You haven't changed a bit.'

Caught in the full beam of his attention, she was uncomfortable, disconcerted by the unsettling effect he was having on her. She laughed off his remark. 'Don't be silly. Of course I have.'

'Well, we're both older, of course. But that's not what I meant.'

Close up, she couldn't but notice his eyes were a paler hazel brown than she remembered, now edged by crow's feet and shadowed underneath. The nose was the same straight line, but the lips were thinner and the slight cleft in the chin less pronounced. Frown lines crossed his forehead. His old features were all there, but gently blurred by age. She fidgeted, looking round for the waiter, as Don gazed at her without offering any other words of explanation. His silence was unnerving her, so she broke it.

'So what brought you back to England? I thought I'd never see you again.' That's better. Steer the conversation on to more neutral ground.

'Long story.' He smiled again, a smile that took her back more than twenty years. 'But as soon as Susie and I split up, I couldn't get back fast enough.'

Susie? Of course he must have had other relationships since they parted but, despite being aware of that, she felt peculiarly let down.

'What about your children?' she asked, trying to blot out the happy sensation of having found something that she had lost. She reminded herself why she was here. Tying up loose ends. That was all.

'Didn't I say? No, I didn't have kids. In fact, Susie's my second wife. She walked out a year ago to be with someone else. My closest buddy, to be precise.'

'That's awful! How long were you married?' Asking the question was like the twist of a knife in her gut. Once, a long time ago, she had been the one who was going to be his wife, for better or for worse.

'The first time? Ten years. She never wanted children. Thought there were enough in the world who needed help without us adding to them. Then Susie already had a son from her first marriage and she was adamant she didn't want any more. We lasted eight years together.'

He sounded quite matter-of-fact as he described the two women. So life hadn't necessarily been kinder to him than to her. They had both had to make their own accommodations.

'What about work? The last I knew, you were on one of the Greenpeace ships. What happened then?'

'I needed to get a proper land-locked job and settle down.' He laughed.

'Settle down! I never thought I'd hear you

say that.' The Don she knew had always been charged with energy, wanting to explore and experiment. Deep down, perhaps she had always known she'd never be able to keep him but his enthusiasm and his wanderlust, with his desire to make a difference, were among the qualities that made her love him.

'Nor me. I didn't want to leave the organisation but it was time. I've stuck to some of my principles though. I've worked for various NGOs ever since. Susie's father underwrote the last lot I was with. He's a big fish out there. Very wealthy. His involvement made it harder for me to get away. But in the end I finagled things and now I'm involved in setting up an organisation dedicated to defending human rights all over the world. I think I told you. I'll be travelling a good deal but the head office is in London. Besides, I wanted to come home.'

Based here? She hadn't expected that. 'Where will you be living?' She concentrated on the way the light fell from the wall sconces, illuminating the prints of Hogarth's *Marriage à la Mode* below them as she tried not to imagine them together in her flat. What was she thinking?

'Not sure yet. I'm still finding my way

around again. I'll probably rent, then buy. But enough about me. I really want to know what's happened to you.'

Finding it less unnerving to be the one doing the talking, Ali embarked on the story of her career, just as she'd told it to Lou, at one point removing the white gold chain from her neck to show him the pendant in the shape of a single wildflower that she'd designed in pavé-set diamonds.

'Ali, this is exquisite.' He held it in his hand, turning it so that it flashed despite the dim light.

'My most extravagant present to myself. I made it after I'd completed a commission for one of my Russian clients. Some of them have money to burn.' Their conversation ran on, with Ali remaining careful to stay on neutral territory as she brought him up to date with what had happened to those few mutual friends with whom she had kept in occasional touch. She didn't talk about the personal side of her life and nor did he press her to. She was relieved at not having to justify herself and the way she had chosen to live after he'd left her. Eventually she glanced at her watch. 'My God, look at the time. I'm going to have to go.'

He stared at her so she turned away, busying herself by gathering up her things. Then he spoke in a whisper, almost as if he was talking to himself. 'I should never have left.'

She froze. 'Don't say that. It was all a long time ago and we've both moved on.' She didn't want to admit to him how long it had taken her to do just that. She dreaded his sympathy, his guilt or, even worse, his disinterest.

She thought she could read regret on his face. But what, she wondered, had he expected? That she was going to walk in and pick up exactly where they'd left off? How Lou would have loved that. Or had she imagined the expression because that was what she wanted to see? Whatever it had been, within a second, he had recovered himself. 'Well, I wish you all the luck in the world.'

'Thanks.' She leaned over to kiss him goodbye. Their lips met briefly and, just for that moment, she was transported back to the last, very different, kiss she had given him at the airport. She felt the pressure of his hands on her arms and withdrew herself. Lou would be waiting.

'Take this.' He passed her a card. 'It's got my details. I'll be staying here until I've sorted myself out. Perhaps we could get together again, maybe dinner. There's so much we haven't talked about.'

'I'm not sure it's really such a good idea. Not now.'

'Come on, Ali. Old friends, that's all.' He smiled. 'Call me. Please. I'll be waiting.'

Old friends. Was that really what they had become? As she stood up, she relented. 'Well, maybe.' She turned to go, anxious to get away before anything was said that she might regret. In her heart, she knew as well as he did that this wasn't just old business they were dealing with. She should never have come.

In the taxi, she sagged against the seat as she tried to impose some sort of order on her emotions. She had anticipated all sorts of reactions to seeing him — anger, sadness, even regret — but what she hadn't expected was to feel the pull, that sense of belonging she had all but forgotten. She had believed she was in love with Ian, but the feelings she had for him were very different from what she was experiencing now. It brought their relationship into sharp focus. She had thought she wanted Ian but she'd been wrong.

'Well?' Lou flung open her front door and rushed Ali through to the sitting room where she poured her a large glass of white wine. 'What happened?'

'Nothing, really.' Ali didn't want to talk. If she hadn't arranged to be here, she would have gone straight home to think about the implications of their meeting. Instead, she was going to be forced to share her reactions to Don before she was ready.

'Nothing? Good God, woman. You meet the first and only real love of your life after twenty years in the wilderness — all thanks to him — and nothing happened! I don't believe you.'

'Despite all the talk, you're still such an old romantic deep down,' said Ali, sitting down and taking a restorative swig of wine, her headiness making her take it slow.

'Less of the deep! Just because I don't particularly want it for myself any more, doesn't mean I can't want it for you. So, tell me . . .'

Ali had not been to Lou's house before and, although the room was different from any of the minimalist white-walled interiors she favoured, she felt unexpectedly relaxed here. One of the dusty pink walls was almost covered with framed antique samplers, small and large. Turn a corner and there were two rows of vintage fashion prints running above the fireplace. On the wall between the windows hung a floral dress framed in Perspex.

'My mother's,' Lou explained, seeing Ali staring at it.

Ali looked around her at the rails of clothes pushed back against the wall, the jug of gaudy alstroemeria on a table by the window, the magazines and a couple of paperback novels on the floor. She envied Lou her relaxed patchwork approach to living. But she knew it would never be hers. Losing control: she couldn't even imagine what that might be like. Except when it came to sex, but even then she made sure she was the one in charge whatever her current lover might think. That was the trick of it. She could count on the fingers of both hands the number of times she had been completely spontaneous, at least since Don had left.

Ali sat back in the sofa, moving Lou's knitting out of the way. 'I didn't know you knitted. Is there no end to your talents?'

'Nope, none.' Lou grinned. 'Anyway knitting's the new sex. Didn't you know?' She picked up the front of the Fair Isle vest, winding it round the needles before putting it away. 'Just as well, since I'm not getting any of the old one.'

'So you want me to instead?'

'Well, one of us might as well, while we've still got the chance.' The knitting bag was shoved under the Eames chair, alongside her neglected patchwork, before Lou picked up the wine bottle.

'You've got the chance. What about Sanjeev?'

'I don't think I'm quite ready for that. Early days. And even if the spirit was willing, the flesh isn't all it might be.' She topped up her glass, then squeezed her waistline. 'Pinch an inch? More like six.'

'But you look great. And besides, body fascism is for the young. We're at an age when other things matter. I thought we agreed on that.'

'I do. Just sometimes I forget.' She stretched out in her chair, crossing her ankles. 'Come on, how did you get on?'

Ali was not going to escape without giving some kind of answer. She could see that. But although her instinct was to keep the affairs of her heart private, perhaps talking through her muddled feelings with Lou might help her understand them better. She hesitated. 'I don't know. It was so weird seeing him after so long. So much has changed and yet so little has. It's hard to explain.'

'Well, try.' Lou leaned forward in her chair, encouraging her. 'Is he married?'

'Was. Twice.'

'And?'

'No children and he's moving here for good.'

'No!' Said loud and with such glee that, if she'd been twenty, it would have been accompanied by a scream of pleasure. 'You're in there, girl.'

Ali wished Lou could be a bit less keen to see her hooked up with Don and a bit more attentive to her state of mind. 'God, ease up on the excitement. Even if anything were to happen, which it's not, we've got a long way to go.' Then she remembered their parting kiss.

'Yeah, right,' said Lou, disbelieving. 'If you could see your face, you'd know that's not true.'

They moved through to the kitchen where the tea lights were lit, the lights dimmed, the table laid. Lou made the last additions to a steaming Provençal fish stew while Ali tried to persuade them both of her casual indifference towards Don. However hard she tried to convince herself and Lou otherwise, something had happened this evening to revive so many feelings she'd all but forgotten.

At last, Lou sat down and looked at Ali. Finally, she observed, 'You're nuts. It's blindingly obvious that you've still got the hots for him after all this time, but you're just scared. I can see it in your face. I'm not going to let you throw this chance away. Do yourself a favour and phone him. I know you're still a bit raw after Hooker, but Don isn't Hooker.'

'I don't know,' groaned Ali. 'He left me too. There must be something wrong with me. To lose one is bad luck, but to lose two — and all those in between . . .' She stopped, despairing of her own carelessness.

'There probably is.' Lou dished up, ladling the aromatic stew into two bowls. 'But probably not more than there is with any of the rest of us. Trust me. Call him. Just once. Go on.'

Ali held up her hands.

'OK. OK. I will, just to shut you up. Happy?'

Lou grinned and banged her fist on the table. 'Result! Well done.'

Making the decision was like removing a stone in her shoe. With it came instant relief. Ali did want to see Don again but was nervous, despite having nothing to lose. She wasn't the same person he had left behind. She had years of experience under her belt now that would stand her in good stead for whatever happened. She could cope with this. Decision made, she moved the conversation on to Hooker, to how Lou was going to confront him about the contents of his new will. Suddenly his discovery of their friendship had paled into the background. She was as concerned as Lou that he should be made to pay for his duplicity.

'He got back today and I'm going round to the house to confront him, tomorrow morning,' Lou announced with the confidence born of a couple of glasses of wine.

'Not neutral territory?' Ali poured them both another as Lou removed their bowls, replacing the stew with green salad and a choice of cheese.

'Nope. My whole argument is about family and I've decided where better to have it than in the place where our family lived for so long. If we're there, I might be able to get him to understand what an idiot he's been. Not with me but with his other *three . . .*' she stressed the word, 'children. I've said nothing to them about this at all but I'm going to make sure *he* does.'

Although Lou sounded so strong and so certain of her next move, Ali heard the sadness in her voice. Having Hooker renege on his promise to her was one thing, but he had taken away much, much more from Lou. One of the foundation stones of the last ten to fifteen years of Lou's life had been removed the moment she read his will.

Worse than betraying his wife with Ali or anyone else was the fact that Hooker had betrayed their children. For their sake, Lou was going to put matters straight once and for all. Ali had every faith that's just what she would do.

16

Under a washed-out blue sky, a gust of wind lifted a Tesco bag and sent it tumbling along the gutter. Standing at the end of the road, alone on the pavement, Lou was unaccountably reminded of all those spaghetti westerns that had gripped her and her brother in their teens. Nothing beat a night at the movies when the Man with No Name rode into town. She looked down to the end of the empty street, a stranger in this neck of the woods herself now, only returning because she was possessed with a sense of justice so strong, she was determined to put right Hooker's wrongs. She and Clint were as one. His worn Mexican poncho thrown back meaningfully over the shoulders of her chocolate shearling sheepskin gilet, freeing her gun hand; her straight-legged black trousers, his jeans; her shiny brogues, his dusty boots; her rakishly angled fedora, his battered stetson. Her imagination stopped short at his cheroot.

As she began to walk, she noticed the hush in the street. She stopped for a moment. Not even the sound of a bird. Not a car engine. Whistling Morricone's score under her breath, she hitched her bag onto her shoulder, and took another step forward. Almost expecting the jingle of her spurs, she heard instead her Take That ringtone jangling in her bag. Her imaginings disintegrated as she fished out her mobile. Hooker.

'Where are you?' His zero tolerance for unpunctuality obviously hadn't been modified by his holiday. 'I'm going out and I'd like to leave before nightfall if possible.'

His tetchiness conjured up his face as he spoke: brow furrowed with annoyance that his plans were having to be changed, right eye narrowed in the way it always was when he was crossed. Lou bet he'd be chipping his left little fingernail against his front teeth.

'Don't be absurd, Hooker. It's not even one o'clock. I'm in the street and I'll be with you in a minute or two.'

'Is this really so important that it can't wait? Not something to do with one of the children, is it?' He didn't wait for her to answer. 'No. You'd have said.'

'Actually, in a way, yes, it is,' she replied,

grimly satisfied by the knowledge that he had no idea of the trouble heading his way.

He huffed and puffed something about how she could have chosen a better time but she ignored him, cutting the phone off as she turned into the drive. She stood in the porch, taking a few yogic-type breaths to calm herself. The composure of the Man with No Name had almost totally deserted her now.

She had prepared what she wanted to say, going over and over it to the whirr of her sewing machine, and she was prepared for his reaction. This would not be easy. She pressed the bell. The chimes sounded distantly on the other side of the door. Footsteps came closer, the bolt slid back, the key turned and the door opened.

Hooker looked unseasonal but relaxed in a hibiscus-printed short-sleeved shirt and summer trousers, as if he hadn't got round to unpacking. Around his neck was a hippyish-looking necklace of small brown beads. Rubbing his arms against the chill wind, he stepped back to let Lou pass.

'Come in.'

'You look well.' In fact about ten years younger, but she wasn't going to give him the pleasure of hearing her say that. The holiday had obviously done him good.

'Mmm. Good holiday on the whole. Coffee?' He led the way into the kitchen. Lou stood in the doorway as he took two coffee cups and saucers that she'd never seen before and started fiddling with a brushed chrome state-of-the-art espresso maker. She guessed he hadn't had it long, judging by the tuts and muttered curses that accompanied proceedings. The whoosh from the steam nozzle was a signal for milk to spurt across the granite counter to the accompaniment of more sounds of frustration. Eventually, he turned to offer her a cup, his face flushed with exertion and triumph. As she took it, he grabbed a shaker and dusted chocolate powder over her coffee, her hand, her trousers and a sizeable patch of the floor. Rather than clear it up or apologise, he just suggested they move through to the sitting room.

Following him, Lou said to his back, 'You're really OK after the mugging?'

'Oh, yes, fine,' he replied without turning around. 'It was just bloody inconvenient. Thanks for sending over that bumph, by the way.'

'No problem.' If only you knew. She noticed the way his hair just overlapped his collar, remembering how she would have reminded him to get a haircut. Not her job now. Did he think it made him look more dashing?

They sat facing each other in the two chairs on either side of the fireplace, their coffee on the low table that provided a convenient barrier between them. On the mantelpiece was something new — a recumbent brass Buddha smiling benevolently down at them. Not a souvenir she would have chosen. Lou took a tissue out of her bag to wipe the chocolate from her hand. She looked up to see him staring at her. She stuffed the tissue back in her bag, leaving a smear behind.

'Well? What's so urgent that can't wait till I've got over my jet lag?' Not aggressive exactly, but not particularly friendly either.

But what did she expect? Hooker liked to be the one in charge, and for once she had him on the back foot. She sat up straight, refusing to let herself be intimidated. It was now or never. 'Who's Rory?'

He didn't miss a beat. 'Who? Sorry, Lou, you've lost me.'

But she saw his right eye contract just a touch.

'Rory. Rory Sherwood Burgess.'

He stared at her, his cup raised to his mouth then, very slowly, he put it down, his eyes never leaving her face. 'Who?'

She willed herself not to look away. She was not, absolutely not, going to be psyched out by any of his bullyboy tactics. She clasped her hands together in her lap so neither she nor Hooker would see them shaking. 'You know exactly who I'm talking about. I found your will when I was looking for the passport photocopies you wanted.' She could see his jaw tense, small movements as he ground his teeth together: another tic in times of stress. Otherwise his expression remained immobile. 'Yes, I read it,' she went on, gaining confidence. 'I shouldn't have, I know, but I did and now I know. You owe me an explanation, Hooker, not to mention your other three children.'

'You had no right,' he protested, as his right fist tightened and relaxed. 'No bloody right.'

Lou refused to be intimidated. 'What I want to know is why you weren't brave enough to tell us. Were you really going to keep him a secret? Can't you imagine what effect springing that on the kids after your death would have?'

'Who said anything about keeping him a secret till I was dead?' His voice lacked some of its earlier strength.

'How old is he? Where does he live?'

'Eleven. Edinburgh.'

'When were you going to tell us about him?' Her gaze moved to the framed family photographs that he'd kept on the console table. Beside the children's graduation portraits was one of their wedding, her veil blown across Hooker's face, her hair everywhere, them laughing together. At the back were posed and faded photos of both their parents and, in front, were the children in a paddling pool; another of them on a felled tree trunk, Hooker making sure Nic didn't fall; another of them screaming blue murder on a Chessington roller coaster, Hooker in the middle. Occasions as clear in her mind as if they'd happened yesterday.

'Oh, God!' he sighed, and leaned forward, elbows on his knees, head in his hands. 'All right. I always meant to, you know, but it was so hard at first, never quite the right time, and then it became impossible.'

His capitulation was so swift and so complete that she almost felt sorry for him. She couldn't help noticing the hair standing on end among the goosebumps on his bare arms.

'What could I have said to you, that you would have accepted?' He rubbed his arms, reached for the apple green cashmere jumper that was thrown across the back of the chair and wrestled it on.

'That *I* would have accepted?' Suddenly she was to blame for his silence. This was typical of the way Hooker always manipulated a conversation to give himself the upper hand. But this time she wasn't going to let him. 'I would have had to accept the fact that you'd fathered a child with someone else, whether I liked it or not. The children would have had to accept that too. And at least you would have given them and him a chance to know each other. They do have that right, you know. Like it or not, he is part of their family.'

'Family!' he snapped. 'You're hardly one to talk about family. The woman who walked out on hers.'

'Oh, Hooker.' Lou shook her head sadly. 'What we had was over years ago.'

For a moment, he had the grace to look ashamed, but then he assumed the wily look of a child who's been caught with his hand in the biscuit tin. 'OK. Hands up. But what do you expect me to do? The affair was over long ago.' His words betrayed his confidence that there was nothing she could insist he did to change the situation. A cocky half-smile played on his lips.

Having thought long and hard about the answer to this, she knew exactly what she expected. 'I expect you to tell me about him and his mother and I expect you to tell Jamie, Tom and Nic. Then I want you to invite him to stay so that they can meet him.'

The look of horror on Hooker's face was pure gold. 'You're insane.'

'Not at all. If anything, I've never felt more sane. I'm not having my children's lives upset some time in the future when a stranger marches through the door announcing he's their brother.'

'They'll hate me.' He got up and went over to the fireplace where he stood, looking down on her. Up on his toes and down.

But Lou was not giving up the psychological advantage. 'They're adults, for God's sake. Surely you see that they've got a right to know and a right to react in their own way. You may be surprised.'

'And if I won't?' he challenged, defiant again.

'I'll tell them myself. Don't look like that. I will. It's their right to know.' She separated her hands and reached for her cup to take a much-needed shot of coffee, relieved that he had obviously registered the determination in her voice. There was a silence as he took in her threat.

'My God, Lou. What's happened to you? You never used to be like this.' He picked up a small bronze dancing hare, the only other ornament there was room for on the end of the mantelpiece. 'Remember when I gave you this?'

She nodded. They'd been on holiday before Jamie was born and he had given it to her on her birthday. 'A mad March hare that reminds me of you,' he'd said. Remembering that made her soften but only for a moment. That was exactly what he was hoping for.

'I've realised life's short and I know what I want from it at last, that's all. And one of the things I want is to hear the whole story from you. Now.' Leaning back in her chair, she waited for him to begin, feeling relief but knowing she could not relax yet. There was still time for him to hit back.

By the fireplace, any last vestige of holiday bonhomie had abandoned Hooker. 'All right.' That combative note had returned to his voice.

'So he's eleven years old, and he lives in Edinburgh?' she began.

'Yes.'

Her first thought was how relieved she was that the boy wasn't in London. Even after leaving Hooker, she would have hated the thought that this child and his mother might have been around the corner for the last eleven years. Yes, distance was good.

'With his mother?'

'Yes. Shona Burgess. She's a lawyer too. Younger than us. I met her when she was on a secondment in London about thirteen years ago.'

'How long did it go on?'

'For about eighteen months.' He sounded clipped, matter-of-fact, as if he was challenging her to cross-examine him. But she had no questions. Instead she was thinking back thirteen years to when Jamie, Tom and Nic were in their teens and she had been made redundant. New editor, new look, new staff. Simple. She remembered that as one of the toughest times in her life as she struggled to keep herself going, half persuaded that she was to blame for losing her job, forgetting how disillusioned she'd become. She knew better now, but at the time her self-confidence had been at its lowest ebb, perhaps not the best time to have found herself at home alone looking after the children. Nic had been in the throes of establishing her very own spiky personality, and throwing her weight around at the least opportunity. When Lou had needed Hooker's support most, he'd been unable to give it. Worse than his physical absences that he explained (and she believed) were essential to his career was his inexplicable emotional absence. If ever she tried to talk about the way he seemed to have withdrawn from her, he'd protest and blame her 'ridiculous insecurities'. Of course, that was when they began their drift apart. And now she knew why.

'When she went back north, Shona didn't tell me she was pregnant so I'd no idea. A couple of months after she left, she phoned me, told me, and insisted that I go up there to see her and discuss what we were going to do.'

Lou closed her eyes at the word 'we', knowing it excluded her, but let him go on.

'I didn't want to go, but she went on and on until I had to agree. That's when I had to miss Nic in that school play. Remember? But I thought I was doing the honourable thing.' He spoke as if eliciting her sympathy with his predicament.

She remembered the hours of hysteria and blame she endured when Nic found out that her father wasn't going to be there to see her in her year's production of *The Crucible*. Her first starring role. Nothing Lou could say or do would console her. In retrospect perhaps not such a terrible thing, but at the time it had blown into a huge family drama that lived on for months of childish recrimination that none of them had completely forgotten.

'Explain to me exactly which part of what you did is honourable?' she said, controlling her temper. 'I'm sorry but I'm finding it hard to quite get that.'

'I was in a terrible state. You must be able to understand. If not . . .' He shook his head as if baffled by her lack of support. 'Do you want me to go on?'

A lump had risen in her throat and she was having difficulty keeping her tears at bay but he was not going to see how upset she was. All that time, she had still been under the illusion that she was in an, if not idyllic, at least a good working marriage. Then, she'd still held the faith that they would weather whatever storms lay ahead. She nodded.

'Like Nic, she didn't want to have an abortion . . .'

Lou gasped at his bracketing Nic with this woman, presumably to enlist her understanding. Well, he could forget that.

'So I agreed to pay towards Rory's maintenance and to have a small role in his life. I mean, surely you agree that every child should know their father?'

'Know him?' He might as well have punched her in the stomach. 'You mean you still see him?'

He kept his eyes fixed on the patterned Indian rug as he spoke again. 'Not often. But three or four times a year.'

'Three or four times a year?' She fought to control the rising pitch of her voice.

This time Hooker looked up at her, his face conveying his guilt. 'I know I haven't been the most perfect of husbands . . .'

'Tell me about it.' She spoke under her breath but could see that he'd heard.

'But I've at least tried to be a good father. To *all* my children.'

She felt a sudden overwhelming desire to puncture his self-righteousness. 'As far as most of the world is concerned, being a good father and being a good husband go hand in hand. Us not knowing what you were up to doesn't make what you did all right.'

His surprise at her answering back renewed her confidence. For years, he had accused her of being 'ridiculous' when he wanted to end an argument. By asserting his claim to the superior intellect or the moral high ground, he unfailingly made her wither. Almost without exception, she would cede whatever point she was trying to make. But this time was different. She wasn't that person any more and would stop talking when she wanted to, not when he bullied her into silence.

'Don't be ridiculous, Lou.' He resorted to the usual belittlement to dismiss what she had just said. 'I probably haven't done anything my father didn't do and my mother stuck it out for the long haul. She loved him and was happy for him to live the way he wanted to.'

'What? Like father, like son and that makes it all right? They were another generation with a different moral code and different expectations. Don't you understand that? And I certainly don't remember any illegitimate half-brother popping out of your family woodwork.' Lou realised she was in danger of shouting and took a second to compose herself. 'Welcome to the twenty-first century, Hooker. Women expect to be treated like equals.'

'That's just feminist tosh.'

Hooker's sneer made Lou want to hit him. But she didn't. 'I'm going to ignore that. I know you're not stupid enough to believe it.'

At that moment a sound came from upstairs. Lou looked up. Hooker ignored both the noise and the fact that she'd noticed it. She remembered the red bra and the body lotion. However, if that was how he was going to play it, she would follow suit. To his evident surprise, she continued: 'Well, you're not getting away with anything any more. I meant what I said about inviting Rory here. I want to meet him too.'

'That's a terrible plan. How would you cope?'

Was that a suspicion of consideration for her that she heard? She made herself remain firm. 'I'd prefer it if you didn't patronise me. I'm the best judge of what I can cope with. Don't think I haven't thought about this.'

'Darling! Have you nearly finished?' The voice shrilled from upstairs. 'We'll be late.'

Lou remembered the young woman from the Regis. 'Nothing changes with you, does it?' She stood up and made her way to the front door. 'I won't keep you.'

'That's not fair. The only reason she's here is because you're not.'

Thinking she must have misheard him, she turned towards him. 'I'm sorry?'

'You heard me and you know that it's true. I didn't ask you to leave. I didn't want you to go.' His gaze was still fixed on the carpet.

'Oh, Hooker! What did you expect? We've been here before. You took me for granted for too long. Your mother mightn't have had the means to start afresh, but I do. And I do still care about the children — more than anything. So make a date to see them this week and explain. Or I will.'

They both turned at a sound on the stairs where, sure enough, the girl from the Regis stood. This close, Lou could see that she must be in her thirties at most, still able to carry off the leggings and jacket look. Not much older than Jamie.

'Enjoy yourselves,' she said. 'I'll look forward to hearing that you've spoken to them.' She exited with all the grace she could muster.

17

Ten o'clock in the morning and Don and Ali were still in bed. After a long, leisurely and extremely pleasurable period of coming to, during which they'd confirmed and then reconfirmed the utter rightness of their being together, he swung his legs out of the bed, grabbed his dressing gown and left her up to her neck in duvet, cocooned in the warmth, with no plans to relinquish this state of affairs until she absolutely had to. Ali was revelling in the sensation of being in a new bed in a room that didn't belong to her. Despite the passing thought that she'd have changed the bed linen days ago had it been hers, she felt quite happy where she was, secure even. Then she felt panic. Should she have put on the brakes a bit? Normally, she would have held herself in reserve until she was sure of what she was letting herself in for. But this time had been different. She had held nothing back with the result that they'd spent almost the whole weekend in bed, first hers and now his. What would he be thinking of her? After all, despite everything, she hardly knew him at all.

Before Don left the room, he dropped a kiss on her cheek, producing another of those pinch-me moments when she had to double-take on what had happened to her, to them. And happened with such speed.

After her supper with Lou, she had eventually persuaded herself to phone him. She spent the whole of the following day taking out her mobile, beginning to dial, then thinking better of it. Finally, she overcame her nerves. She could hear the pleasure in his voice when he realised who was calling. Immediately, he'd suggested dinner on the following Friday evening. She accepted.

They met in an unpretentious yet fashionable Italian restaurant on Ali's side of town. Ali arrived first wearing a blue jersey dress: understated but elegant. After five minutes, her anxiety translated into certainty that he wasn't coming. By the time he rushed towards her, blurting apologies about public transport, she was looking at her watch wondering whether she should leave. He gave his coat and scarf to the waiter and sat opposite her, looking amused by the bread sticks that she had crumbled over the tabletop. She tried to brush the crumbs into her hand, but the ones that didn't stick to the cloth, flew onto her dress. After an awkward few minutes during which the conversation stopped and started, both of them being careful not to say the wrong thing, they began to relax. Within an hour of being together again, it was as if they had never been apart. Ali stopped noticing the silent couple on the next table, barely tasted the five-star food, was oblivious to the time passing as they filled in the details of what had happened in their lives since they last wrote to each another. Don talked readily about his first wife but passed over his second marriage swiftly before concentrating on his work, the NGO he'd worked for that helped the indigenous population in Australia, before moving into the field of international human rights.

Eventually, he stopped.

'Nothing's changed, has it?' He had eventually voiced what she was feeling, as they waited for the bill.

'I don't think so.' She didn't want to agree too enthusiastically in case she jinxed what she felt was happening. If nothing else, her experience with Hooker had confirmed her tendency not to rush at things. How odd it

305

was that she rarely thought of him as 'Ian' any more. Using his family nickname had definitely helped distance her from their involvement.

'To think we've let all these years go by.' He sounded so wistful. 'We might have got married, had children.'

She struggled to shake off a sudden unbearable feeling of sadness. 'Don, don't. Please. What happened, happened. There's no point.'

'True.' He lay his hands on hers, fixing her with his gaze. 'But perhaps it's not too late?'

'Let's take it a step at a time.' Her natural caution took over.

'If that's what you want.'

'I think I do.' But that's not what she thought at all. Far from thinking anything, she was suddenly feeling giddy with desire.

Afterwards, they had shared a cab despite not living in the same direction. Neither of them mentioned the fact although they both knew exactly what was happening. Don accepted her offer of a coffee without comment. As they continued to talk, Ali could only think of one thing: which of them would make the first move? As he told her about the joys of life in Australia, his enthusiasm and success at surfing, not to

306

mention the swimming, the sailing, the kite surfing, they were both aware of holding back, nervous of rejection, commitment, misunderstanding. Then, he had got up to leave and they had kissed goodnight. And kissed again. And sent the cab away. After that, there had been no going back. The next day she went briefly to the studio before meeting him for lunch, and now here she was the morning after that, waking up in his flat.

She wondered lazily what the weather was like, whether it would affect what they would do that day. Ali was not religious but she was fervent about Sunday being a day of rest. Without a break, her head wouldn't find the space for new creative ideas that only came when they were given room to ferment and surface. This was the day when the germs of some of her best ideas had arrived. She would never have been inspired to make her pavé-diamond daisy pendant if she hadn't spent a lazy summer Sunday afternoon picnicking on Hampstead Heath.

Lying on her side, facing the space Don had just vacated, she reluctantly opened her eyes. Outside, the sky was cloudy above the Thames-side apartment buildings that lined the other side of the river. Looking back to the room, Don's laundry basket, which he seemed to treat like a basketball hoop, was the first thing to catch her eye. Clothes had been tossed in its direction but the socks and pair of Calvin Kleins that had missed lay abandoned on the floor beside it while a shirt was draped over its edge, half in, half out. The mirrored door of the pine wardrobe facing the end of the bed was slightly ajar, a couple of ties hanging from its handle. On the chest of drawers were a hairbrush and comb, cufflinks and a mess of his pocket emptyings — loose change, receipts, Oyster card, a couple of pens. She realised that she didn't mind untidiness so much as long as it was not in her domain. On the wall beyond his side of the bed, the Ron Arad bookshelf curled like a large snail to hold a few broken-spined paperbacks. She lifted her head to make out the lower titles: Dawkins' *The God Delusion;* Jonathan Franzen's *Freedom;* a biography of Morrissey; a guidebook to Paris; a fading copy of *Zen and the Art of Motorcycle Maintenance* and *The Dice Man.* She smiled. That really dated him. On the walls was one forlorn indistinct watercolour that was crying out for company.

She lay back again, feeling utterly content. Then a thought struck her — this was the first of her lovers' bedrooms that she had ever seen, let alone slept the night in. Inevitably, those men, now almost ghosts in her imagination, had usually stayed at her place. Otherwise, in the years since Don had left, she had been entertained in countless anodyne hotel bedrooms where every creature comfort was provided but any personality excised. She had never visited one of her lovers' homes, had never seen the side of their personality that they kept there.

As she revelled in the pleasure of being here, of being able to share this place with Don, of being on the brink of a relationship where there were no 'other halves' — the euphemism amused her — to complicate things, the door opened and he edged round it, carrying two mugs of tea. He placed one of them on the empty bedside table beside her before returning to his side. There, he balanced his own mug on a couple of books and climbed back into bed.

'Brr.' He shivered, then settled on his side and placed his hand on her stomach, tucking his feet between her legs.

She lurched into a sitting position, clinging to the duvet, half laughing. 'Christ! Get off! You're freezing.'

'I thought you could warm me up.' He adopted that Australian inflection that turned the end of every sentence into a question.

'You're insatiable!' She hopped out of bed and took the second dressing gown on the back of the door. 'I've got to have a pee and then I want to drink that tea. And then . . . well, we'll see.'

Don returned to his own side of the bed with mock reluctance. 'Spoilsport,' he grumbled, but with a smile. 'But I guess I can wait.'

Three-quarters of an hour later, the tea was drunk and they had begun to compare the possibilities that the day held in store with the merits of just staying put. However tempting the latter, Don had work to do. They agreed to meet later to see a movie.

They showered together in the large black-and-white tiled wet room dominated by a massive power showerhead in the centre of the ceiling. Ali closed her eyes to the few grey hairs she spotted in the plughole and the mildewed grouting in one of the corners. After they'd dressed, Don went to book their cinema tickets online so she made a start on breakfast. Pottering happily in the kitchen, she found the cereal and the sliced bread. She removed the slice with the corner of greenish mould and binned it. In the fridge, she discovered an inch of skimmed milk in a plastic bottle beside a couple of Bud Lights. An elderly lettuce that looked more liquid than leaf was contained in a plastic bag that lay by a couple of wizened carrots in the grubby salad drawer.

'All done,' he said, returning to the kitchen area. 'Oh, no, don't go there. I didn't think . . . I haven't really got myself organised yet.'

'I could give it a quick clean.' Ali was almost ashamed by the frisson of pleasure she got from the idea of restoring the fridge to pristine condition.

'Absolutely not. In fact, let's go out for breakfast. I could murder a decent cappuccino.'

She shut the fridge door. 'If you're sure . . .'

'Completely. Let's go.' He held out his hand. She took it.

Twenty minutes later, they were sitting in Manda's Bakery, mugs of cappuccino and half-eaten croissants in front of them. Don was already deep in *The Sunday Times*' sports pages, while Ali was leafing through the news, her mind only half on what she was reading.

'Have you *got* to work?' she asked, hoping he'd have a change of heart and they could go back to the flat to pick up where they'd left off.

'What? Today?'

As he looked up, Ali studied his eyes, dark and steady, his smile bracketed by deep laughter lines, the Sunday morning stubble shading his jaw, and felt a blaze of happiness. She nodded. 'Mmm.'

He groaned. 'You know I don't want to but I've got so much paperwork to get through before I start in earnest next week.'

'Must you?' she almost pleaded, stretching across the table for his hand. She gazed down as she traced her finger up and down between the bones, over the raised blue veins.

'I'll be done by six. Promise. Don't tell me you haven't got anything to do.'

'Well, maybe I'll call in on Lou and see how the shop's doing. She's open till five.' Instead of her usual reticence, she was bursting to tell Lou about what had just happened, never mind catching up on what had happened between Hooker and the children. Everything was changing. That was the second-best way she could think of spending her free afternoon.

'You don't think I've dived in too quickly, do you?' Ali wanted to be reassured. 'You don't think he'll be put off?'

'Good God, woman. He's probably de-

lighted. I thought you said he felt the same.'
Lou took one of the sleeves she had cut
from a damaged charity-shop find and
began to pin it onto the contrasting bodice
of a similarly patterned dress.

'But he might not have meant it . . . Weird,
really,' Ali said, thoughtful as she rearranged
the jewellery in the cabinet for something to
do, putting the bees and butterflies and
beetles at eye level and the more popular
keys below, mixing the rings among them.
'For the first time, for almost as long as I
can remember, I don't feel in charge of this
relationship. For the first time, I know what
it's like to want someone so totally it hurts.'

Lou raised her eyebrows. 'Haven't you
ever had that feeling before? Not once?'

'Never allowed myself to.' Not even with
Hooker, she thought. Ali saw Lou's resigned
expression. 'It's true,' she insisted. 'Whatever they said, there was always a wife in
the background preventing me. If you know
what I mean.' She could have kicked herself
for her tactlessness.

'I can imagine.' Lou's attention was focused on the fabrics she held as she fitted
one exactly to the other, pinning them in
place. She held up the bodice. 'What do you
think?'

Ali was relieved by the change of subject.

'I like it. Clever idea to mix the fabrics like that.'

'Recycling gone mad. Thought I'd do a few of these off-the-peg mix-and-matches and put them on the website. Don't suppose *Chic to Chic* or *Stylish* will like them but I don't care, since . . .' Lou paused to concentrate on her sewing, squinting as she stabbed the thread in the direction of the needle's eye, then giving up and casting about for her specs. '. . . *Stylish* called in two of my sundresses for a possible summer shoot and we've been promised a mention in *Chic to Chic*'s diary section.' Her face was triumphant.

'No way! You never said. But that's brilliant.'

'I only heard late on Friday. I did try to call you but couldn't get through and to be honest, most of the time my head's been taken up with this whole business of Rory. And as for this afternoon, you've only just let me get a word in. One more thing . . .' She silenced Ali's protest, then paused for effect. 'That glossy freebie, *City Life*, wants a solo interview with you.'

'No!' Until now Ali had shunned overt publicity, preferring her reputation to be built by word of mouth. This could mean a completely new direction for her.

314

'Mmm.' Lou put in the last pin. 'Looks like our grand opening is starting to pay off already. All I need is for the customer count to pick up as the spring comes. Anyway, I've given them your number.' She stopped as a couple of women entered the shop. They looked through the stock, then stood loudly debating the merits of a short-sleeved Horrockses cotton day dress, blue with large stylised flowers in grey and white, and in mint condition. Eventually, one of them was persuaded to try it on. Ali sat back and watched as Lou's inner salesperson took over, suggesting one of her own designs that might work as an alternative. The customer had no hope of getting away scot-free. Half an hour was spent in front of the mirror, trying one, then the other, then a vintage grey crêpe shift dress with capped sleeves. Just as Ali was on the point of screaming, the woman plumped for Lou's creation, paid up and left the shop with her companion.

They were alone again. Lou entered the sale on her laptop and took up her place at her sewing table. 'And now . . .' She glanced at Ali over the top of her specs, re-threaded her needle, picked up the dress, then put it down again. 'My turn to tell you about how the kids took the news of Rory.'

'I'm sorry. I should have asked straight away instead of droning on about me. They know then?' She was dying to ask about their feelings towards Hooker, but knew the children took priority and she would have to wait.

'Oh, boy, do they know.' Lou came out from behind the counter and sat in the chair. 'Hooker finally invited them to his place on Friday night and broke the news. I wasn't there, obviously, so that they could concentrate on him and what he was saying, not on their betrayed mother.'

'And how did they take it?' Ali sat on the floor, back against the counter.

Lou shook her head, sad despite the smile. 'In fact, the boys took it far better than I'd thought they would. They both called me once they'd got home. Jamie thought the affair was basically our business, although he's up for meeting Rory. As for Tom, if anything, he seemed more amused than anything by the idea of his father playing away. Why doesn't that surprise me? Why is it that men can think so clearly sometimes yet totally bypass their feelings?' She added the last as an afterthought.

Shrugging her shoulders to show she had no answer but agreed with the sentiment, Ali asked, 'And Nic?'

Lou's expression changed. 'Devastated. Overwhelmed that her dad isn't the man she thought he was. Says it skews her whole childhood and makes her relationship with him into something else, something she doesn't recognise.'

'Isn't that a bit overdramatic?'

Lou looked up from her work. 'You haven't met our Nic, yet. If you had . . .' She shook her head. 'I knew she'd be the one who would hurt the most, or at least be the one who would express it. We talked for ages but she's coming over tonight to give me the unexpurgated version. She swears she's never going to talk to Hooker again.' She looked weary, then brightened a little. 'She'll probably come round in the end.'

For the remaining hour of the afternoon, they were only interrupted by a couple of customers who browsed but left without buying. They ran through the possibilities of what was likely to happen when Rory came to visit. Despite Ali's doubts over Lou's insistence on welcoming the boy into her family, Lou was adamant that his getting to know his brothers and sister was the right thing for them all, so long as his mother was in agreement.

Eventually, the clock struck five. Sunday closing time. Ali got to her feet. 'You cash

317

up and I'll tidy.' Lou left her sewing where it was, ready for the next working day, cashed up and tucked the money in the safe while Ali straightened the stock, leaving the gaps between the hangers that she knew Lou liked. Then they locked the shutter and left the shop, walking to the top of the road, easy in each other's company. At the corner, they embraced before going their separate ways.

18

The fire was lit, the salad made and the smell of supper permeated the house but, the moment Nic came in, she pulled a face.

'Oh, Mum, tell me you haven't done baked potatoes! I'm being really strict till I've had the baby.' She removed her black mac and tossed it over the end of the banisters. 'Otherwise I'll be the size of a house. Look at me already.' Her bump was definitely noticeable now.

'One potato won't do you any harm.' Lou hugged her resistant daughter to her, careful not to squeeze too hard. Releasing her, she admired her anthracite wool jacket, her neat black skirt and heeled boots. She smiled to herself. Nic wouldn't be seen dead going into labour in anything other than her designer schmutter — appearances mattered to her, always had. 'You look absolutely fine, gorgeous as always. Come and sit down.'

With a large wine for her and a cranberry juice for her daughter, Lou readied herself for what Nic had to say. After she'd piled her plate high with salad, Nic scooped out her potato, leaving the barest amount of flesh on the skins and discarding the rest on a side plate. 'All the vitamins in a potato lie right underneath the skin. Did you know that?'

Lou shook her head, not trusting herself to say a word. Instead she took a generous slug of wine, then transferred the offending potato to her own plate where she mashed in a generous chunk of butter.

'Honestly, Mum! Have some potato with your butter. Don't you think you ought to be a bit careful at your age?' Nic carved off a tiny piece of dry-looking potato skin and popped it into her mouth.

Deep breath. Keep calm. Ignore. 'Why don't we talk about last night?'

Nic stopped toying with her salad leaves and looked at Lou, tears welling. 'Well, I've told you really but . . .' She sniffed, and fumbled in her bag for Kleenex.

'I want to hear it all again,' reassured Lou, reaching for the kitchen roll.

'I'm so furious.' Nic blew her nose. Lou was struck by her likeness to Jenny, the same slightly jutting chin: not conventionally pretty but striking. 'I knew something was up when he asked us all over like that. He never has before, but I just assumed he must be going to tell us Emma was moving in.' She said her name as if an unpleasant smell had just drifted under her nose.

'So soon?' Lou was stunned to hear how speedily Hooker's new relationship had developed. 'Really?'

'No, I suppose not. But I couldn't think what else it could be that would affect all three of us. As soon as I got there, I knew I was wrong. He looked terrible — as he bloody well should.'

Lou felt a little spark of pleasure at that bit of information but, again, she tried not to show what she was feeling. Whatever her differences with Hooker, she refused to ally herself with the children against him, however tempting. 'So tell me again what he said.'

Sitting back in her chair, Nic studied her mother's face, gauging her reaction. 'He poured us all a drink, sat us down in the living room and told us. He said how difficult it was for him, that he'd rather it hadn't come to this, but that you were insisting that he tell us. I was so angry that he said that, as if the whole thing was your fault.'

Lou could envisage the scene as well as if she'd been there. Hooker would be standing in his favourite spot, warming his arse at the fire, hands turned towards the flames, preventing the heat from reaching the others in the room. Up on his toes and down. Gaze fixed on a spot on the carpet.

'He said he wasn't proud of what he'd done but he'd screwed someone twelve years ago. He didn't put it like that of course . . .' She paused, as Lou failed to hide her surprise at this new abbreviated version of events. 'And that she'd had a baby. He couldn't bring himself to look at us. Then he said you were the one insisting that we met this boy and, unless we objected, he'd arrange it. That was it. He didn't even sit down.'

How typical of him to spin the truth so he emerged as saint and her as sinner. Her decision not to be present had been a mistake. Somehow her insisting that he told them about the existence of his son had been transformed into a worse offence than the eighteen-month affair itself, now miraculously reduced to a one-off, one-night aberration. He was vindicating himself of responsibility by lying. He knew that Lou would never undermine him by telling the children the truth. If only she could enlighten Nic and the boys about their father's behaviour throughout their long marriage. But sharing her suspicions and knowledge with their children meant she'd be using them as pawns in this tiresome game that was going on between her and Hooker, something she'd vowed never to do. Her motives would be coloured by wanting them on her side, and that was wrong.

'Is that why you left him, Mum? If it is, I don't blame you. I wish you'd told me. I'd have understood.'

Nic's face was set, torn between anger and distress at being let down by the one person she had always relied on. There was no point in making things worse by telling her what she knew. Perhaps it was better for Nic to believe that Hooker's affair with Shona was a one-off. Why damage father–daughter relations any more than they already had been?

'Sweetheart, I told you why I left. Once you guys had gone, there wasn't anything holding Dad and me together any more. Our relationship had run out of steam and I felt the time had come to start again on my own.' That at least was the truth. 'I didn't know about Rory, no. But when I found out and that Dad has had regular contact with him, I thought it was important you all know each other.'

'But I don't want another brother. Two's more than enough, thanks.' Nic managed a smile despite the tear that slid down her cheek. 'Why are you so keen for us to meet him? I wish he didn't exist.'

'Don't be silly, Nic. Like it or not, he's part of your family. It's better to get this over with,' Lou coaxed. 'Because he *is* your brother.'

'No, he's not!' Nic's voice rose. 'He's Dad's mistake and Dad's problem and nothing to do with us.'

'Nic, listen to me.' Lou was going to stick to her guns, despite her increasing concern that she'd handled the matter all wrong. 'Like it or not, he is to do with us. Because of Dad, we're his family too.' She noted the taut mouth, the raised eyebrow: Nic's frosty expression spoke volumes. 'Isn't this better than finding out in years to come?'

'But *we're* not a family any more, are we? It's all very well your taking the moral high ground. But you should stop to think how your decisions affect other people. Us.' She pushed her plate to the centre of the table. 'We don't live together, you and Dad are separated because you have some weird idea of there being another life out there for you, and now we're expected to cosy up to the kid that's the result of some soulless fuck somewhere.'

'That's not fair.' Lou was shocked by her daughter's vehemence. 'And not how it is, at all.'

'No, Mum. You're the one who's unfair. How is it *fair,*' Nic gave the word new emphasis, 'to expect us to fit in with some idealised image you have of a happy family especially when you've done your best to smash the existing one to pieces?' She stopped as if to rearm herself.

'I know you're upset . . .' Lou didn't know how to reach out to her daughter, how to find the right words. How could she make her understand that she'd done what she'd thought was best for everyone? Just as her relationship with Nic seemed to be improving, she'd managed to put it into reverse.

'I'm not upset. I'm angry.' But then, to Lou's relief, Nic appeared to run out of anything more to say. Instead of fighting on, she pushed back her chair with a scraping sound and began to clear the table.

'Nic, you haven't eaten anything,' Lou protested feebly. Even in the most hostile circumstances, feeding one's brood came first, as if the provision of food could smooth over any fissures and make them disappear.

'I'm not hungry any more.' Said with such finality that Lou despaired of ever bridging the gap between them. She sat with her head in her hands, wishing for a solution to this unholy mess.

But when Nic turned from the sink, her voice had softened. 'I'm sorry.' She stood behind her mother, put her hands on her shoulders and bent to kiss her on the top of her head, unaware that beneath her Lou was stunned by this unexpected switch of mood. 'It *is* me that's being unfair. I know you're right, really. You were only doing what you thought was best in the circs. I don't know why I was so sympathetic towards Dad when you left home. He's a typical bloke, led by his prick — I see them all the time at work.'

'Nic! Please!' Despite everything, Nic's offhanded dismissal of her father upset Lou.

Nic grimaced. 'I know I shouldn't talk about him like that but I can't believe what he's done. I feel like everything I believed about my childhood was lies. I thought we were all happy together.'

'We were. You were. This didn't happen until you were in your teens, remember?'

Nic ignored her, obviously determined to think the worst of Hooker. 'I suppose I do see why you want us to meet this kid but even you can't make me warm to the idea. But all the same . . . this has made me think about my baby . . .' She stroked her stomach proprietorially. 'About the relationship she or he should have with Max. He hasn't exactly come round to the idea of being a father, but at least we're speaking again. However difficult it's going to be, I think I'd want him or her to at least know Max's family too. You're right.'

For a moment, Lou had to double-check that she hadn't entered an alternative universe. No, this was her daughter speaking in the here and now. The unpredictability of Nic's mood was like the weather. One moment, storms and rain, the next the sun was emerging from behind a cloud, the sky clearing and the day as fine as any you could wish for. 'So what's the plan? Is there one?' She felt safe asking now.

'He's going to arrange for Rory to visit within the next couple of months, tying in with school holidays and when he can have a week off. I think he was hoping that we'd tell him not to bother, but the boys are curious. Idiots. And the truth is I was so taken aback, I didn't think to object.'

'I suppose his mother'll come too?' Lou went over to the fridge and pulled out the fresh lemon tart that she'd made. 'You won't want any of this, will you?'

'Well, maybe a slither.' Nic's resolves reliably went west in the face of her favourite pudding. Triumphant, Lou tried not to smile as she cut the tart. Nic went on: 'God knows what she'll do. That's up to Dad and her, I suppose. I'm certainly not going to meet her.' She paused. 'Do you know what she's like?'

'No. At least she's nobody I know. I'm not really as interested in her as I am in her son. Her involvement with Dad was over years ago.' Nic didn't need to know that Hooker had gone on seeing her.

'He's not going to be able to handle this alone. I can't imagine him looking after a child on his own. He'll be hopeless.' Said with all the scorn Nic could muster.

However good a father Hooker had been, the family joke had always been how he drew the line when it came to the domestic nitty-gritty, leaving that exclusively to Lou.

'If he has a problem then no doubt he'll let me know when my presence is required.' She put Nic's plate in front of her.

'Don't be so sarky, Mum. It doesn't suit you.' But she reached out to touch Lou's arm to show she was joking.

'Sorry, darling. Defence mechanism, I guess. This is as difficult for me as for you,

you know.' Lou sat down again, plates on the table, and opened the wooden drawer in front of her to give them both a couple of slightly tarnished spoons.

Nic took hers, turned it round in the light, but refrained from comment. Her pursed lips said it all, however. 'I know. I do, really. I can't imagine how much stuff this has thrown up for you. I should shut up, shouldn't I?' She acknowledged Lou's slight nod with a rueful grin. 'But we will get through this, won't we?'

Lou was about to reassure her when there was a knock at the front door. She went to answer it. Tom and Jamie stepped in, hugged their mother, then unwrapped their scarves and slung their coats over the banister.

'It's brass monkeys out there,' said Tom, leading the way to the kitchen. 'Anything to eat?'

'You're such a pig,' said Nic, disapproving. 'Mum and I are having a serious chat about Dad and the boy.'

'Got to eat to live, you know, Nic.' Tom hugged her until she shook him off, then headed to the fridge. 'But there's nothing worth eating in here,' he protested in disbelief. 'And I'm starving.'

'If you'd said you were coming, I might have been prepared,' said Lou, unperturbed by the immediate raid on her food supplies. This was what happened whenever the boys came over. 'How about defrosting some sausages?'

Tom's face said exactly what he thought of that idea.

'Shut up, Tom.' Jamie took over. 'We haven't come over so you can stuff your face. We knew Nic was going to be here, Mum, so we've come to give you a bit of support too.'

'That's very sweet of you, boys.' Lou was touched. 'But I'm fine now I've had time to get used to the idea. Honestly. I've been much more worried about how you'd take it.'

'Don't be. We're taking the news on the chin, aren't we, bruv?' Spoken to his brother's back as Tom burrowed in the cupboard and came out, triumphant, with a bag of crisps.

'Of course. Dad's an idiot not to have told us all years ago. My guess is that this isn't the only one — the affair I mean, not the child.' Tom's last words were muffled in the sound of crunching crisps but he looked embarrassed. 'Sorry, Mum.'

'Honestly, Tom.' Nic's disapproval was glaring. 'Why don't you just sit down and have a slice of tart.'

'How apt!'

Both the boys grinned. Lou felt it inappropriate to show her amusement as they pulled out chairs and started helping themselves. 'Wine anyone?'

'Yes, please.' Jamie moved the heap of letters and newspapers from the side of the tabletop to the floor so there was room for his glass. 'The next thing we know, Emma'll be expecting.'

'Jamie, don't!' Nic looked horrified.

'Well, think about it. How else is he going to keep her? A woman her age is almost bound to want children sometime. And if he won't give them to her, she'll find someone else who will. The maternal urge is strong, isn't it? You should know, Nic.' He batted away the tea towel that she flicked in his direction.

'If that happened, his kid would be the same age as his grandkid,' Tom said thoughtfully, staring at Nic's micro-bump. 'How embarrassing would that be? For him, I mean.'

'I suppose you think it would be cool. You're pathetic.' Nic rested her hand on her stomach again. 'I'm just embarrassed to have a father who's turned out to be such a filthy old lech.'

'That's enough,' interrupted Lou, seeing

331

things were sliding out of control. 'Whatever Hooker's done and, I agree, some of it leaves a bit to be desired, he's been a great dad to you all —'

She pretended not to hear Nic's outraged 'A bit!'

'— and a good husband to me.' Perhaps that was going too far.

'Mum! How can you say that?' Jamie banged his glass on the table. 'He must have been playing away for years.'

'You don't know that.' Despite herself, despite everything, she still felt a residual loyalty to Hooker. And she was right to. It hadn't all been bad. Whatever else he'd done, he had never let anything disrupt the children's lives. He could have left them to fend for themselves. None of them should complain.

'No, but I can make an educated guess.'

'Educated? You? Some hope.' Nic poured herself some more cranberry juice.

Why did Nic sideswipe at her brothers whenever she could, Lou wondered. When they were growing up, she'd always thought Nic was well placed with a brother on either side of her. But instead, Nic had always felt that life never played her fair and one or other of the boys was always being favoured over her. Being a middle child was never easy, as Lou knew from her own experience. Her older brother, Sam, was the one praised for his achievements, sporting and academic, while no one noticed hers. Jenny was the baby of the family and had all the attention that went with that. Now she understood how her parents tried to favour her, but how she had rejected them in the same way Nic rejected her and Hooker's attempts to show how much they loved and supported her. Nothing was ever enough.

'Have you lot just come round to have a row? If so, I'm leaving you to it.' Lou refilled her glass and went through to the sitting room where she flumped into the Eames chair and put her feet up.

'Sorry, Mum,' Nic called through, making her second apology of the night — a higher strike rate than usual. 'We'll be right through.'

She could hear the sounds of tidying up and muttered voices, closed her eyes and tried to let her mind go blank. Impossible. Tomorrow's tasks immediately invaded the space, chasing through her mind: finish jacket commissioned by Fiona's friend, order fabric, pay outstanding bills, chase up journalist who'd left her contact details on the email, check website orders and write new blog.

'You know what,' said Jamie, coming into the room. 'I think it'll be quite cool to have a little brother. You don't mind my saying that?'

She opened her eyes. 'Of course not. I'd rather you did. I know it'll be awkward at first but —'

'Mum, don't worry. We'll make sure it's all right.' He threw himself into the arm-chair, stretching out his legs in front of him. 'How hard can it be to get on with an eleven-year-old kid? None of this is his fault. And it's up to us to work out how to deal with Dad. I know Nic's taken it badly, but that's Nic. She'll get over it. She just needs a bit more time to get used to the idea. I'll talk to her. Promise.'

Lou relaxed. She could always rely on Jamie eventually taking the lead and, what-ever the objections, on the other two falling in line. 'I know you will.' She reached out a hand and caught his for a moment. He returned her squeeze.

'So what's going on in the great world of retail?'

She began to answer as the other two came in. 'Going OK, I think. So far I've sold enough to cover my overheads but I'm going to have to step it up a bit. The web-site should generate more summer sales once the weather warms up. I've got some great styles I've made up for commission and I've renewed contact with various bods I used to know who are still in the business. So fingers crossed.'

As she talked, Tom came to sit on the floor by Lou's legs, his back against her chair. She reached down and started stroking his hair. Nic lay on the sofa, looking more content than she had only minutes ago. Jamie leaned forward to poke the fire and throw on another log. Sparks shot up the chimney. Flames began to lick around its base.

Despite the occasional tears and tantrums, what more could she want than the company of her three children? She didn't need anyone else. For now, knowing that her family was intact, or as intact as it could be, gave her the strength to deal with whatever other surprises Hooker might have up his sleeve. What was important was that she and the children should stand firm under the weight of the revelations of his personal life so they moved forwards without giving way to recrimination and resentment.

She couldn't help wondering whether, if she'd behaved differently within the marriage, putting him to the front of the queue for her attention, he would have behaved differently too? She'd never know. As it was, she had spent too many evenings waiting for him to come home, wondering where she had gone wrong. The time for blaming herself was well and truly over.

19

They had almost completed their first lap
of the park when a young Staffordshire bull
terrier came barrelling up behind Ali, chasing and nipping at her ankles. Running on
the spot, watching Don disappear into the
distance, she looked for the animal's owner
as the dog dashed about in excited circles
making it impossible for her to continue.
There, halfway across the football pitches,
ambling towards her, was a young lad, his
tracksuit bottoms indecently low on his
hips, the jacket of his hoodie flapping open,
the hood covering a black baseball cap, his
phone to his ear.

'He yours?' Ali shouted, still jogging on
the spot, the dog in a frenzy around her legs.

Whether the lad heard her or not was
unclear. He didn't acknowledge her, just
yelled, 'Lash! C'm'ere.'

The dog took no notice and his owner
made no attempt to hurry as he finished his

call. His nonchalance infuriated Ali.

'For God's sake, control your dog.' She was risking a scene, but there were other people around to rescue her if she provoked anything serious.

'Or what?' The lad was standing in front of her, staring her down, his sallow complexion brilliant with acne, his eyes insolent.

'Or I'll . . .' she flailed about for a suitable threat, 'I'll report you.'

'Oh, yeah!' he replied, grinning, as he eyed her up and down and attached a leather lead to the dog's heavy studded collar. 'To who and whose army?'

Without a ready answer and feeling suddenly vulnerable in her skimpy running kit, Ali didn't stop to discuss this detail, but ran off, pumping her arms, pounding the earth path that had been worn down by countless runners before her. She overtook a lonely anorexic struggling to shed more calories, feet barely leaving the ground, before a muscle-bound hunk doing fartleks in the opposite direction almost knocked her flying. As he raced by her, she imagined that, above the rasp of his breath, she could hear the chafing of one massive muscular thigh against the other. She followed the curve of the park and entered the avenue of plane trees, their branches silhouetted against the flat Tupperware-coloured sky. Music blared out from one or two windows of the estate on the other side of the park railings. A tabby cat was curled on a post, eyes half shut, observing the world go by. A knot of rudeboys huddled together gave Ali a passing glance, then returned to their business.

She had thought of Lou and Hooker frequently since that late-night call after Lou had discovered the existence of Hooker's love child. What a bastard! When he'd protested to her that he'd done his bit towards populating the world, he hadn't been joking. The knowledge only confirmed her desire to have nothing more to do with him. What she didn't really understand was the way that Lou's feelings still seemed to blow hot and cold about her ex. In her position, Ali would have just cut all contact with Hooker, but Lou seemed unable to sever completely the ties between them. Was that what having children did to a couple?

Although her friendship with Lou was young, it had quickly taken root, surprising Ali by how much it already meant to her. Being taken into another woman's confidence was something that she hadn't experienced before. Just the last few months had already shown what she had been missing. She loved being able to chat openly with

Lou, being asked for advice, being trusted and, even more, being able to expect the same in return. For the first time in years, she had begun to let someone in and the feeling was good. She was excited by the thought that Hooker would eventually find out about her friendship and business involvement with Lou. It wouldn't be long now but the fact of Rory's existence had put everything else on the back burner. Yes, she thought, revenge would be definitely a dish best served cold.

In the distance, by the gate to the main road, Ali could see Don running on the spot looking round in her direction. His physique, now resplendent in shorts over Lycra, a faded Led Zeppelin tour T-shirt and state-of-the-art trainers, was that of a man who looked after himself. She liked that. When he saw her, he jogged over.

'What kept you, slowcoach?'

'A savage dog, is all. Where were you when I needed you?'

Their breath clouded in the cold air.

'I'm sorry. I'd no idea. I was so determined to beat last week's time that I didn't notice.'

She laughed. 'You're hopeless. I thought we were meant to be doing this together. A gentle Sunday run, you said.'

'We are.' He took her hand as they stepped aside to let the same muscled hunk race past them. 'We are. I just got a bit carried away. We'll take it easy for this lap and I'll stick by you whatever happens.'

'You'll have to catch me first!' Ali sprinted off, taking Don by surprise. Within a couple of hundred metres, she slowed her pace, hearing his footsteps coming up behind her.

'I meant that, you know.'

'What?' She looked sideways. They were running exactly in step now, at a speed that was stretching but not too uncomfortable. Sweat ran down the groove of her spine.

'The bit about sticking by you whatever happens.' His expression said everything she needed to know about how serious he was. 'I'm not going to let you go again.'

'What a moment to tell me that!' She tried to lighten the mood. 'If I wasn't running, I'd hug you.'

'You do feel the same, then?' Sweat was making his T-shirt stick to his chest and between his shoulder blades, his hair to his forehead.

She glanced at his face, as familiar as if it were her own: the thin white scar under his right eyebrow, the mole by his left ear, the changing planes depending on his mood.

'Indubitably, Holmes.'

They ran together without talking more until Don broke the silence.

'You know what? I'd like to see Eric again. What if we go up for a weekend?'

His question came so far from left field that Ali almost stopped, then speeded up again. 'Why?' she asked.

'I want to help you clear up what happened to your mum. I know how much her disappearance has been nagging at you since you last talked to him.'

She touched her mother's ring with her thumb. 'There's nothing more to say. I've tried and he's told me all he's going to.'

'But you said you were sure he wasn't telling you everything. I thought I might be able to help.'

'What? Man to man?' She heard how scornful she sounded and hated herself for it. 'Sorry. But there's nothing left to say. Shit happens. I've come to terms with her taking off like that. If she'd wanted to know me, she'd have been in touch.'

He looked unconvinced but, instead of protracting the conversation, he tapped his watch to signal that their pace was flagging. Keeping in step, they picked it up until they were running just too fast for easy conversation. As Ali focused on pushing herself forwards out of her comfort zone, Don's words echoed around her head. Of course, he was right. After all these years, she did want to know what happened to her mother, and whether she herself was in any way to blame for her leaving. She did want her relationship with Don to last. She did want her life to change.

Then, as the effort required to keep up with him took over, she lost track of all thought, giving herself up to the physical demands of their run. As she closed out her surroundings, she felt her body respond to what she asked of it. The sweat pricked, her lungs burned, legs ached and, as eventually the park gates came into view, the familiar and satisfying sense of achievement kicked in.

Later, back at her flat, Don returned to his subject as he watched Ali carefully bite the curve of chocolate off a Tunnock's Teacake until a perfect dome of white foam was left. She was contemplating the pieces of her latest jigsaw, Velázquez's *Las Meninas,* having separated out all the edge pieces. Now, she joined a couple together.

'Seriously, Al. Why don't we go up to see Eric together?'

She put the biscuit on her plate and licked chocolate from her fingers before moving all the pieces belonging to the back of the artist's canvas to the left of the table. 'Because it won't achieve anything.'

'How do you know that? He and I got on well before.'

An image came to her of the two men building a bonfire at the bottom of the garden while, with very bad grace, she made ham sandwiches in the kitchen. 'That was years ago. So much blood's gone under the bridge since then, and he's got very set in his ways.' The words 'like me' remained unspoken but very present.

'Up to you.' He picked up one of the newspapers that he'd spread over the sofa and surrounding floor just as she identified a couple of pieces belonging to the dog's paw and fitted them together. 'But he might listen to me. Just saying.'

The thought echoed in her head. If Don could change her then maybe he could change her father. Perhaps she should at least let him try. 'OK, I give in. At the worst, I guess you could help where Lou and I left off with the attic, and I could sort out some of Mum's clothes for the shop. Lou wouldn't take them last time.'

'She could always come with us?' The suggestion sounded rather half-hearted.

'Nice thought, but no. She's too pre-occupied with the arrival of Rory and what that'll mean to her kids, especially her daughter.' She began to look for dog-coloured pieces of puzzle.

'The father sounds an idiot.' Don's attention was half on the article he was reading on a major oil spill in the Pacific.

'Think so?' Ali didn't trust herself to say more, disturbed by the unintentional turn in the conversation. Hooker was not a subject on which she wanted to linger. As she moved the pieces around the table, she wondered if Don was hiding anything from her, and whether he'd mind if he ever found out what she was hiding from him. All she had told him was that her last boyfriend had dumped her without ceremony after having asked her to live with him. She hadn't needed to name him. He didn't need to know everything that bound her and Lou together, particularly not the more intimate details of her relationship with her friend's ex-husband. She had also decided not to tell him about all her past lovers' marital arrangements. She was nervous about how he would react. Not that she was ashamed of the path her personal life had taken but she wanted him to understand, not judge, her. The way Lou had. For the time being, her silence was best kept.

Distracted from the jigsaw, she gazed out

of the window. Outside, a toddler had just fallen over on the pathway and was being comforted by its mother. If only, she thought: fruit cake in front of a roaring fire and a mother to soothe the pain and sort the ills of the day. Hers might have provided that once upon a time but for almost as long as she could remember, Ali had relied on herself to get through. She smoothed out a wrinkle in the rug with her foot. 'I think I'll just go upstairs and change.'

'Sounds like a plan. I might make a start on something to eat. No!' He stopped her from interrupting. 'My treat. I bought some stuff for lunch when I got the papers.'

She shut her eyes, took a deep breath in and out. 'I'm not sure I deserve you.'

'Nor am I. But I'm willing to hang on until you reach such a state of grace when you do.'

She smacked his arm. 'Twit! I'll be down in a minute.'

'Sure you don't want company . . . help with a zip or a hook or something?'

He sounded so hopeful, she felt bad refusing — but not quite bad enough. 'Tempting, but no. Give me a few minutes to get myself together.'

He nodded and went back to the paper. She appreciated how he understood her need to have her own space from time to time. Upstairs, her bedroom usually provided her with a reliable safe haven where she could lie down and think. Less so that day, however. She picked up Don's socks and pants where he'd left them on the floor. She hung up his jacket that lay on the bed and folded his jumper before putting it into one of the drawers that she'd allocated to him. Although he still had his rented flat, he spent so much time here, his clothes needed their own space too. She stripped off, putting her clothes in the laundry basket as she went.

In the bathroom, she swilled water round the basin to wash away the little black hairs left from Don's shaving and lifted the dissolving soap from the pool of water where he had left it. Having lived alone for so long, she was used to things being just so. Her other men friends had rarely stayed long enough to rattle her. She didn't want to admit it, even to herself, but with Don she was finding it hard to adjust to having someone in her flat on quite such a regular basis. But what was a bit of disorder compared to the feeling of completion that she felt in his company, the sense that everything was right with the world? The experience was completely new to her.

So now life was going to be different. She dropped Don's running shorts into the laundry basket, then picked up a towel from the floor, folded and draped it over the heated rail, straightening it so it was perfectly aligned with the one beside it. She remembered the newspapers covering the floor downstairs, then imagined the state her kitchen would be in by the time he had made lunch. She stopped dead.

What was she doing? By letting Don share so much of her life, wasn't she on the brink of giving away her freedom, her independence, the things that had always mattered so much to her? Until now, she had let their renewed affair dictate its own pace, so caught up was she in the delirium of finding Don again, of being able to share her life in ways that had not been possible before. Yet again she was struck by how much they had still to find out about one another.

When she eventually returned downstairs, her hair damp at the ends from the shower, Don was taking roast pine nuts from the oven and sprinkling them over a chicken salad. Thank God he hadn't been any more ambitious than that. The potential chaos had been contained.

'Let me make the dressing.' She crossed

the living area and began to get the ingredients from the cupboard, watching as he went up the spiral staircase.

She began to tidy the kitchen, putting things back in the fridge and the cupboard so that when he came down again, he'd be reminded how she liked the place to be. Sighing, she crossed the room to pick up the newspaper, ordering its pages and folding it in half before putting it in the magazine rack.

When Don returned, he appeared oblivious to the fact that anything had been moved.

20

Lou clasped her coat to her as the wind screamed off the sea. Halyards on the beached tarpaulin-covered yachts chinked wildly in the gale. Sanjeev tightened his scarf with gloved hands as his gaze followed hers towards a gaggle of seagulls loudly squabbling over something invisible at the water's foamy edge. Dark wooden groynes pointed across the sandy-coloured stones towards a sea the colour of well-brewed tea. White horses raced across the choppy surface all the way from the Isle of Sheppey. Further along the promenade a couple walked, bent against the wind, hands in pockets, trailed and circled by three unmistakable black Labradors. Otherwise, Lou and Sanjeev were alone with the elements. Above their heads, a bruised-looking bank of cloud was moving across the sky from the west, simultaneously gathering mass and momentum.

'So this is your English seaside?' Sanjeev sounded puzzled.

'I'm afraid so.' Lou felt almost guilty, as if its failure to meet his expectations was her fault.

'But the sand!'

They both looked down at the patchy grass and smooth stones under their feet. Lou could almost feel their cold penetrating the soles of her completely unsuitable townie's shoes and beginning to work its way up her legs. How far they were from the white sands, the palms and the turquoise Indian Ocean that belonged to the fabled beaches of Goa and Kerala over which he'd rhapsodised when they met. She began to laugh.

'One day I'll show you a real beach where the sun shines, the sand's warm and the sea welcomes you.' He put his arm around her shoulder, pulling her towards him, then lessened the pressure as if worried he was being presumptuous.

She didn't move away.

Would he really show her? Lou hadn't imagined their relationship becoming so close. But then who knew what fate had in store. She huddled into him. Perhaps she would go to southern India one day — and perhaps it would be with him. She glanced up to see that he was half smiling as if his

Indian dream was replacing the grim reality of the Kent coast out of season.

Lunch had been the best part of her plan. No romantic connotations. After all, she didn't want to give the impression that she was coming on too strong after one kiss and besides, wasn't her life complicated enough? And of limited length — unless it went really well. But then she had hit on the English seaside: Whitstable, only an hour and a bit's train ride from London. There was nothing like a brisk spring day to revive the spirits. She had promised Sanjeev something quintessentially English (why?) and that's what she would deliver, however inconvenient it proved to be. But now she was wondering if Fiona had been right. Perhaps the outing had been a mistake from the word go.

'Whitstable?! Are you out of your mind?' Her friend had spoken hers without hesitation. 'In April! On a date!' Her disbelief and despair at Lou's plan had been blindingly obvious. 'What's wrong with London? And anyway, you hardly know the man.'

'I've already told you it's not a date.' Lou had been patient with her oldest friend who was being perversely obtuse. 'I want to show him a bit of English life. That's all.'

Fiona snorted her derision at such an unnecessary idea. But Lou held firm.

Ali had been similarly perplexed. 'Where's the romance in a blustery English beach?' she'd asked. 'Why not a restaurant? Much easier.'

'I'm not after romance. I'm after the real England. That's it. Just an enjoyable day out,' Lou had insisted, although by then the idea was already beginning to lose its initial sparkle. But she was cursed with a streak of stubbornness that came into its own when crossed by opposition.

'And what about the shop?'

'Ah, yes. I was wondering if you'd mind . . .'

The next problem had been to find a day when she could easily skive off for four or five hours that coincided both with Ali's availability and with Sanjeev's hectic working schedule. While he was in London, LBF Electronics demanded as many waking hours as they could legitimately claim. They'd had to wait until he was granted a Thursday off.

When the day finally arrived, it couldn't have been less spring-like or less convenient and Lou was full of second thoughts. Once, she had imagined herself as a boutique owner able to close the shop whenever she wanted, but in fact the business needed her total commitment if it was to work. A big spender could turn up at any time, and she needed to net as many of those as she could. Besides that, she was behind on the orders for the three fifties blouses that had so far resulted from the patterns she and Ali had found in the trunk. The sooner they were done, the sooner more orders would come in. What she longed for more than anything was a rainy Thursday hunched over her sewing machine. Not this.

Inhaling the freezing ozone blown fresh off the sea, she wondered how Ali was coping at the shop. What if Hooker walked in looking for her? But that wasn't going to happen (why would it, except in her wildest dreams?) because today he was going to pick up Shona and Rory at King's Cross. Although she would be back in London long before the evening, Lou hadn't been invited to accompany Jamie, Nic and Tom to meet their half-brother. Hooker had insisted that her presence was both unnecessary and inappropriate under the circumstances, particularly since Shona would be staying with him for the night. Lou wondered what Emma felt about that. Now his secret was out, Hooker was busy wresting back control of the situation, making sure Rory's visit was orchestrated exactly as he wanted it. Lou might have outed him but she was no longer in charge of the show — just as it had always been.

For the last few days, she'd been able to think of little else besides Rory's visit. She wasn't worried about the child himself but about the impact the visit might have on Nic who was still refusing to speak to her father. The only reason she was going with the boys was because Lou had coaxed and persuaded her, hoping against hope that meeting Rory might soften Nic's attitude. Lou felt responsible for the rift between father and daughter, and while not expecting them to kiss and make up — Nic was far too stubborn for that — she hoped that the tension between them might be eased.

As for Lou, she was going to meet Rory after his mother had left for a city break somewhere in Europe. Ali had agreed to stand in for her yet again on Saturday morning, despite muttering darkly about having her own business to look after, while Lou went with Nic and Rory to the zoo. To Hooker's distress, Nic had been adamant that she wanted nothing to do with her father but would only take Rory out with her if Lou came too. Lou didn't have it in her to refuse. Family still came first. Staring dismally into the distance, she became aware of the first drops of rain splatting onto the stones around them. Digging into her bag, she realised she'd left her umbrella at home.

'Let's get back before it tips down,' she yelled above the wind, turning towards the back of the beach where a forlorn row of painted beach huts faced towards the elements. They sat behind a characterless concrete wall, the colours drab in the dull light, the doors and windows boarded up and padlocked shut.

Running over the beach was near impossible when, with each step, the stones rolled away underfoot. Eventually, stumbling onto the walkway, now slippery with rain, Lou stopped to get her bearings so she could take them the shortest route back towards the harbour and lunch. Sanjeev stood beside her, his dark hair sleek as an otter's in the wet, a broad grin on his face.

'What's so funny?' Lou asked, turning to their left.

'You,' he said. 'The weather. England. Everything.'

'None of them seems that funny to me,' she smarted, quickening her pace as the heavens finally opened in earnest. They ran past a weather-boarded block of flats, then a terrace of houses decorated with painted stucco crabs, fish and shells, and on by the empty tennis courts. She glanced over at him, but his coat, now pulled up over his head, hid his face. She concentrated on running back towards the harbour as quickly as she could without further conversation.

They burst into the pub–restaurant and stood on the mat, panting and laughing, water dripping off them. Sanjeev shook his coat down onto his shoulders, leaving his hair standing on end while Lou pushed the wet strands of hers from her face, not wanting to think of the uncontrolled frizz they'd make when they dried. On either side of the door, the sash windows ran with condensation. At the unadorned square bar, backed by bottles shelved in front of a huge mirror, the few drinkers turned to see what had blown in and then, having immediately lost interest, turned back to their drinks.

Shown to a table in the small dining room upstairs, Lou was alarmed by how empty the place was, given its enthusiastic online write-up. She took off her mac, shaking off the worst of the wet, and hung it on a hat stand with Sanjeev's coat. The worn pine table and chairs, the floorboards and small fire in the brick chimney-breast gave the place an unpretentious, homey feel that she liked. But would he? If the meal was as grim as the weather, she doubted that she'd be seeing him again. And that would be a shame. The train journey alone had reminded her of how entertaining he was, and how attractive. Which was more than could be said for the bleak countryside they passed through. She needn't have worried. Half an hour later and the world looked a better place. The tables were filling up, the background hum of voices getting louder. The cooking smells emanating from the open kitchen took over from the tang of wet clothes. Outside, the tide ran to the east, spray flying into the air as the waves smacked against the nearest jetty. They ordered native oysters, followed by fish and chips, following Lou's claim that they were the most 'English' things on the menu and Sanjeev must have them, never having tried either.

'Really, never?'

'No. You promised me something English and that's what I'm getting.' He looked around at the menu chalked on a blackboard, the glasses of lager and wine on other tables, the activity behind the bar. Meanwhile, outside, the rain kept falling.

'I should have left it until the summer. I didn't think.'

'But then I wouldn't have seen it at its

most English. No?'

She thought she detected a definite gleam in his eye although his face remained quite serious. Unsure how to react to the steadiness of his gaze, she forced herself to look out at the lowering sky and the pub sign being buffeted back and forth by the wind. 'Even then, I couldn't have relied on the weather. But that's the thing about this country. You never know what to expect.'

'That's what I like about you too.'

What? He was staring at her so intently now that she felt uncomfortable, wishing her red cardigan with its beautiful black bugle-beaded flowers wasn't quite so figure hugging.

'I thought you were working so hard at your business that you couldn't take a second away from it.' This time, he was definitely teasing her.

'I know I said that and, truthfully, I did worry about taking today off.'

'Then you should have cancelled,' he interrupted, suddenly concerned.

'But I didn't, and now I'm glad I didn't. Not even I can work every second of every day. I went in early this morning to make sure everything was set up for Ali and, if we get the three thirty or four o'clock train, then I should finish at least one order when

I get home. Anyway, to be honest, I'm glad to have the distraction. My three kids are meeting their half-brother for the first time today, so it's good to have something else to think about.'

He looked interested. 'I don't think you've told me about this?'

'Haven't I? I probably didn't want to bore you with my dysfunctional family dramas.' Her two black and red resin bangles clashed together as she raised her glass.

'I wouldn't be bored. Think of it as fair exchange for everything I've told you about my family and my country.'

'But they're not like . . . well, this.'

The waiter leaned forward to put their plates in front of them. On two beds of crushed ice sat six oysters each, their uneven brownish shells in sharp contrast with the pale meat glistening against the pearly inner shell. Sanjeev looked uncertain. Lou took one, squeezed the muslin-bound lemon, sprinkled on a few chopped chives and a dash of Tabasco and tossed the oyster down her throat, feeling the rush of sea and flesh.

'Heaven,' she pronounced, and waited for Sanjeev to follow suit. 'They grow on you,' she added as his face contorted. 'Sometimes.'

His eyes unscrewed and he took a quick

mouthful of brown bread and butter. 'Mmm. Maybe.'

Despite trying another couple, he remained unconvinced so Lou finished off his last three as well as her own. Calorie-free aphrodisiac, as Hooker used to call them — what more could a girl want? Except she didn't want an aphrodisiac at all, she reminded herself. She wasn't quite ready to fan the spark between them into a blaze. When the plates of golden-battered cod and chips arrived, along with a bowl of minted peas, Sanjeev looked relieved but curious. With the first mouthful, his face relaxed. 'Now this is more my thing.' He ordered them both a second glass of wine. 'But go back to your dysfunctional family. Tell me what's happened.'

Lou began to explain how she had found Hooker's will and what had happened since. Sanjeev was as good a listener as he was a talker: he didn't comment, just heard her out. The wine emboldening her, Lou told her story without leaving out any detail. 'The point is, I feel so betrayed by him,' she concluded, in an attempt to explain why the rewritten will mattered so much to her: just as much as the existence of Rory. 'Even now. Isn't that stupid?'

'It's not stupid because it's a fundamental

betrayal. But you do still care for him?' His disappointment was plain.

'No!' she rushed to assure him. 'No, it's not that. I stopped caring for Hooker ages ago. Really did. But I do sometimes get hijacked by emotions that I don't think I have any more. It's hard to explain.'

'Try,' he urged quietly. 'I want to understand.'

She groped for the right words. 'To do with the children, I suppose. I don't know, but those feelings one has for them, wanting to make everything right, to protect them, never go away. It's just as bad now as when they were tiny. Worse in some ways, because they make their own decisions and not always the ones I'd choose for them. As they should, of course,' she added, noticing he was about to object. 'I thought it would get so much easier as they grew up. I thought I was doing the right thing, bringing the family together, but it looks like I've driven us even further apart.'

He looked thoughtful as he took another mouthful. When he'd finished eating, he spoke again. 'Perhaps men and women experience this differently. My two daughters are married now and look after themselves, so maybe I've just forgotten. But for me, it changed once they had husbands and families of their own. Then they really didn't need me any more, and I could let go. And Gita my wife had died, so I'll never know how she would have felt.'

Lou immediately thought of Nic, so protective of her independence, about to have her baby but without a partner to give her the sort of family Sanjeev was talking about. What would happen to her daughter then? And what would happen to Jamie and Rose when they married? She couldn't imagine switching off her feelings for her older son. Or, when the time came, those she had for Tom. Yet she was constantly aware that all three of them were moving away from her, her role as a mother becoming increasingly redundant. But she didn't feel ready to let go just yet.

'What you must do is forge a new life of your own to take their place in your mind.'

'But that's just what I'm doing with the shop and by moving into Jenny's house,' she protested, irritated that he hadn't understood that.

'I mean emotionally,' he said, looking straight at her as he touched her hand across the table. 'That side of you must be nurtured too, you know.'

'Are you saying what I think you're saying?' she asked slightly too loudly, nervous that the conversation had changed a gear without warning. The blood rushed to her face. The three women on the next table suddenly fell silent as if they were waiting for Sanjeev's reply. Their coiffeured grey heads were still, the nearest cocked just enough to show she was listening, her pearl drop earring quivering.

'Maybe.' He lowered his voice and took his hand away. 'What do you think I'm saying?'

The increased tremor of her neighbouring diner's earring betrayed her eagerness to catch Lou's answer. Refusing to give her the satisfaction, Lou leaned forward as far as she could and whispered, 'You're suggesting that we should have an affair.' The wine must be stronger than she thought.

'Only if you want to.' By this time he was leaning forward too, their noses only centimetres apart. She felt his breath on her face. His eyes were dark and wanting.

She sat back abruptly, the women on the next table having resumed their conversation. 'I don't know, I . . .' she began, wondering if she should have thought before she said the word 'affair'.

One of the neighbouring women caught her eye and nodded womanly encouragement. Lou glared back at her, then murmured, 'It's difficult.'

'Look, I know you're still raw. I understand that. But maybe this would . . .' He stopped.

'Help?' she offered, at the same time aware that something was happening between them, shifting their relationship onto another level. 'Well, maybe it would.' Why was she hedging? Where was that woman she had vowed to become, the one who'd kicked over the traces? She felt Ali and Fiona at her shoulder, egging her on. But, when it came to it, nothing was that simple. She might be able to fall into bed with her own ex, but with someone new . . . The memory of what she saw in the mirror every day made the idea of sharing it with a near stranger unthinkable. And sex. She couldn't imagine what it would be like with someone else. Would she even know what to do?

' "Help" wasn't what I was going to say, but I can see that I've said enough, I'm sorry.'

She tried to reassure him but they lapsed into an uneasy silence as they finished the meal in a hurry, Lou unable to eat all hers, both of them embarrassed that too much and yet not enough had been said. Neither of them knew quite where to go next.

On the train home, Lou stared out of the

window at the passing countryside that was lit by a watery sun, her head swimming slightly. She didn't think she'd drunk too much. Two glasses though? She could usually manage two or three without much damage. In the window, she caught her reflection: a woman of a certain age, hair out of control, make-up not quite doing the job she would like.

Sanjeev had leaned his head against his seat back and closed his eyes, so she allowed herself to think about what was happening between them. She was attracted to him. Of that, she had no doubt. And he really did seem to be attracted to her. All she had to do was banish her inhibitions and say yes. That's all it would take. Surely not *so* hard? She looked across at his long fingers resting on the table. She imagined them touching her, touching her breast, her stomach . . . His lips were slightly apart. She remembered their first kiss. Not so bad either. As he shifted position, his foot came into contact with hers. Despite feeling less than her best, her mind snapped into place. Out with the mobile and a quick call to Ali, asking her to lock up. Just this once. When Sanjeev woke, she would ask him to come home with her. The blouses and the shop could wait one day — just one. She looked across the table at him. One of his eyes was half open, studying her. Then he shut it again.

They took a bus home from the station. The swimming sensation she'd felt on the train had been joined by a nausea that was becoming almost overwhelming. Lou rested her hot forehead on the window, trying to will herself better, taking deep breaths that made no difference. By the time the bus reached the end of her street, she felt dreadful as well as furious that this should happen just when she had decided to advance her love life in a major way. Instead of tripping seductively up the road, all she could do was concentrate on the journey, occasionally stopping to close her eyes, hold a railing and breathe.

Sanjeev took her arm without saying anything. Having imagined — no, desired — his touch on the train, now it was the last thing on earth she wanted. She gently shook him off, wanting nothing more than to be alone. His concern was too much to cope with. All she could think about was getting home and to bed. Alone. She felt his presence beside her but her attention was entirely fixed on the tiny landmarks that made up her street and marked her progress home: the overflowing dustbins at number 6, the ginger cat asleep on the doorstep of

14, the bicycles chained to the railings of 22, the quince and wisteria hedge of 30, the stretch of graffitied railway bridge, the squeak of her front gate, the rose bushes she'd failed to prune.

At last she was at her front door, fumbling for her keys, unable to get them out fast enough. She was aware of taking several great choking breaths as she stabbed the key towards the keyhole and missed. Her vision narrowed as she concentrated on getting the door open and herself inside. Then, a hand took the key from her, slid it into the lock and pushed open the door. She was about to dash inside when instinct took over, refusing to obey her brain's strict instruction to rush to the bathroom. Instead, as the enormity of what was about to happen dawned on her, she sank to her knees, her hand on the door jamb. She tried to get to her feet, but too late. Half standing, with a terrible coughing and puking sound, she vomited her entire lunch all over the doormat.

She was dimly, humiliatingly aware of Sanjeev witnessing every ghastly, technicoloured moment. Eventually, when she'd finished, she struggled upright, her head still spinning, only to catch sight of the strands of saliva that had tagged onto her jumper, the sick on her right shoe. Her eyes burned and one tear spilled over to run down her cheek, swiftly followed by a second. She pulled a grubby holed tissue from her mac pocket and blew her nose, despairing when the snot oozed through onto her hand. As she raised one foot to step over the puddle of vomit, she was all too aware of what a hideous sight she must look.

Just when she'd made up her mind to add some romance into the muddle of her life (cue cheers of approval from her friends), the calorie-free aphrodisiac had proved to be the complete opposite (cue despair). A kettledrum beat a tattoo inside her head as she felt herself shepherded into the house and upstairs to the bathroom, where she was left alone (thank God) with the door tactfully left just ajar. In the distance, she heard a phone ringing, then Sanjeev's voice, but she was too preoccupied to listen. At last, when her stomach had completed the evacuation of everything she had so enjoyed putting in it, she felt her way down the corridor into her bedroom. The last thing she remembered was the touch of cold pillow on her cheek.

21

The chimp swung up to the glass, rolling back his lips into a gummy, yellow-toothed grin. Rory and Nic laughed as he clapped his hands at them, but Lou was miles away. Since they'd left home, she'd been functioning on autopilot, saying the right things, asking the right questions but otherwise in her own world, leaving Nic to bond with Rory. She felt guilty about not having made more effort with him but something had held her back. To all appearances, he was a perfectly pleasant child, wiry and earnest, neatly turned out in the obligatory uniform of a boy his age: jeans, sweatshirt, jacket, trainers. He had that slightly unsettling self-confidence of an only child who spent much of his time in adult company. He certainly seemed at ease with Nic who, despite her continuing feud with Hooker, was obviously quite taken with him.

Fully recovered from her 'turn', Lou kept

harking back to the morning after her day out with Sanjeev. Fiona had once been laid up for days after eating a dodgy mussel but Lou had got off lightly. She remembered making her way to the bathroom in the middle of the night, half registering the shut spare bedroom door but with other, more pressing things to attend to, thought no more of it. The following morning, she almost had a seizure when woken by the sound of someone coming into her room. She flicked on the bedside light. She still marvelled at her bravery, or foolishness perhaps. Not that it mattered because Sanjeev was standing there with his shirt untucked, sleeves rolled up and his feet bare. In one hand, he held a full glass of water, in the other a cup of tea.

'Water or bed tea? I didn't know how which you'd prefer,' he said, putting them both down beside her.

Astounded, she wiggled backwards to make room for him to sit on the bed within the curve of her body. She couldn't remember the last time anyone had brought her 'bed tea', apart from the children on the odd birthday. As she moved, she registered with relief how much clearer her head felt, how much steadier her stomach. The explanation for the closed spare room door was obvious. 'You stayed the night?' she asked unnecessarily, for the first time noticing the washing-up bowl by the side of the bed, the towel at the end. He must have put them there.

'I couldn't leave you like that,' he said, evidently surprised that she would think him capable of such a thing. He stroked the hair off her forehead, just as she might her children's, except not like that at all. 'How are you feeling now?'

'Better. Thank you for looking after me.' She took his hand and kissed his fingers, unsure which of them was more surprised. 'Much better.' She remembered exactly what she'd been thinking before she'd been taken ill. Thank God she'd changed her sheets and her pyjamas the day before. Those men's stripy ones might be comfortable but they had to be sure-fire passion killers.

A heartbeat later, they were kissing and she was lifting the side of the duvet so he could climb in beside her.

He raised his eyebrows in question. 'Are you sure?'

'Oh, definitely,' she murmured, thankful that she'd cleaned her teeth on her last visit to the bathroom.

His clothes hit the floor in seconds. As he

swung his legs into the bed, she snapped off the light, ignoring his murmured protest. After all, with the formidable blackout blinds, and her dodgy stomach giving her the ideal excuse to remain horizontal, he'd hardly notice the sad demise of her younger body until it was too late.

As it turned out, he hadn't seemed to mind at all. Quite the reverse, in fact. His lovemaking had been considerate but enthusiastic without being of the wham-bam-thank-you-ma'am variety that she'd known Hooker to employ after a few drinks. She had even got sufficiently carried away to find herself sitting astride him, her initial reserve having been thoroughly abandoned. Now she tightened her grip on Rory's shoulder, remembering the more intimate details.

'Ouch! That hurts.'

'I'm sorry, Rory. I was miles away.'

He scuffed his trainers along the base of the enclosure wall as she let go. His dark head lifted to reveal a face that was spilt by a grin containing teeth of tombstone proportions. For a moment, she saw Tom at that age. They both had that slight Cupid's bow and the thicker lower lip, reminiscent of Hooker. This was the first time she'd seen a resemblance.

'Now can we go to the reptiles?' he asked. Then added as an afterthought, 'Please.'

Over his head, Nic and Lou exchanged a look.

'They're over there. I saw the sign when we came in.' His enthusiasm was hard to resist.

'Of course, it's just that your . . . er, sister . . .' It was surprisingly hard for her to say the word when, in this context, it still felt quite wrong in her mouth. '. . . hates snakes.'

'Well, she can always stay outside. Please.' Sharp blue eyes raised in appeal.

She glimpsed Tom in him again.

'OK. Let's go.' Lou led the way. She was sure her daughter was resilient enough to face her fears if they were safely behind glass.

Once they were in the dim corridor of the reptile house, Rory's nose was pressed to one window after another in search of Harry Potter's Burmese python while Nic trailed behind, looking tense. Lou let herself drift back to the previous day. Sanjeev had finally left as she was running a bath. Work called. When she ventured downstairs, only a slight queasiness to remind her of the previous day's debacle, she found the front doormat thoroughly cleaned and back in its place.

The two men couldn't be more different. Hooker would have left the clearing up to her, irritated by the change in the evening's plans, but not Sanjeev. Hooker's feminine side remained a decided stranger to the world, whereas Sanjeev's was clearly alive and out there. She didn't have to think hard about which she preferred.

There was a muffled shriek from Nic as a green mamba dropped from a tangle of branches high in its vivarium. The snake slithered towards a nearby stone, reared up, then posed motionless, its round yellow eyes watching, pupils wide, its forked black tongue flickering. Small, venomous and deadly.

'Wow!' breathed Rory.

Nic grabbed her mother's shoulder as Lou bent her knees to be on a level with the boy. 'Is this the one that talked to Harry Potter?'

'No! This isn't a python.' He explained with all the patience of a missionary talking to the unconverted and pointed to the label. 'See. A python isn't poisonous like this one. A python's brown and much bigger and crushes its prey to death.' His obvious relish in the idea was accompanied by a small moan from Nic. Lou took pity on her daughter.

'Darling, why don't you go to the café?

You must be tired.'

'Yes, I am a bit.' Nic immediately grabbed at the excuse. 'I'll meet you there. Coke for you, Rory?'

With Nic safely dispatched, Lou concentrated on being with the boy. She'd forgotten how absorbing and funny an eleven-year-old's company could be. They made their way around the exhibits until they found a python. Lou's stomach turned as a dead white rat slowly disappeared head first through the snake's dislocated jaws, but Rory remained transfixed for the full five minutes and she hadn't the heart to move him on. Then, after a brief pit stop with Nic, the three of them set off again together, determined to see as much as they could before they met Tom.

When they finally left the zoo, Rory clutching a book about snakes and other reptiles from the obligatory visit to the gift shop, Tom was waiting for them at the main gate, red-and-white scarf around his neck. 'All right, mate?' He high-fived his young half-brother. 'What've you got there?'

Rory passed him the book.

'Wicked. Nic must have *loved* seeing them.' He winked as he put his hand on the boy's shoulder. 'Come on then. We're going to the Emirates for the Arsenal — Bolton match with Dad. Kick-off's at three. So we'd better run.'

Rory nodded, his eyes wide with excitement. 'Now? Are we going on the Tube? Camden Town to King's Cross, change onto the Piccadilly line to Holloway.'

'Blimey, you know your stuff. That's seriously impressive. Think you can get me there?'

Rory glowed with the unsought-for praise and nodded, rendered speechless as Tom removed the scarf and wrapped it round the boy's neck. 'You have this one. I've got another.' And he magicked it out of his jumper with a flourish.

Watching Rory half running to keep up with Tom's loping stride, Lou felt such maternal pride as Tom looked down at the younger boy, chatting away and joke-cuffing his head. As she watched them, Nic linked arms with her. She had been more attentive to Rory than Lou had expected. When it came to it, the outing had been much more than mere duty.

'Thanks for coming, Mum. Do you think it went OK?' She sounded anxious. 'I'm exhausted.'

'Completely.' Lou touched Nic's arm as they made their way to the car park. 'He's a sweet kid. And you know what? You're going to be a great mum.'

'Only if it swears off reptiles and football. I want one that dresses in pink and likes hair slides and fairies.'

'What? Even if it's a boy?'

'You know what I mean!' Nic laughed. 'I liked him, although knowing him hasn't changed what I think about Dad.'

'Don't you think you should forgive and forget?' Whatever her own feelings, Lou didn't want a permanent estrangement between Hooker and their daughter. Nor did she want to end up as their go-between again.

'No way! After what he did to you, to us?'

Lou knew that look well. The shutters were still down. There was no point continuing the discussion. She would have to keep hoping that Nic would come round in her own good time.

'But do you think Rory liked *me*?' So that was what was worrying her.

'Of course he did. Not sharing his interests isn't what's important. You're just as much a natural with kids as Tom.' Indeed, once the snakes were out of the way, Nic had found plenty to entertain them in the B.U.G.S. house, leaving Lou to cringe at the spiders and maggots before they moved on to the children's zoo.

'Really?'

She sounded so anxious for reassurance that Lou wanted to hug her, but knew how such a public gesture of affection would be received. Instead she contented herself with 'Yes, really.'

By the time they'd reached Nic's car, the usual Nic was back: confident and in charge. 'Can I give you a lift anywhere?'

'Don't worry. I'm going to the shop.' And the sooner she got there the better, otherwise it wouldn't be just her business on the line, but her friendship with Ali as well. She was horribly conscious of how much she'd taken advantage of her during the last few days.

'That's OK, I'll take you. I'm not doing anything much.' Nic opened the passenger door and gestured her inside.

As they pulled up outside Puttin' on the Ritz, Nic leaned over and peered towards the window where there were two of Lou's floral crêpe silk tea dresses. 'It's looking really good, Mum. Who's been looking after it?'

'Just a friend. The one who's making the jewellery you liked.'

'Must be a good one.' Nic sat back in her seat, changed into first gear and glanced in her rear-view mirror, suddenly keen to get on with the rest of her day.

'Mmm. She is. Very good. But I can't keep relying on her. In fact, I think I'm going to look for someone to help out officially for a couple of days a week.' She wasn't sure why she hadn't done that from the beginning. How much easier life would be. Lou got out, slammed the door and gave a little wave, jumping backwards onto the pavement as Nic roared off, oblivious.

She found Ali behind the counter, deep in a paperback with something classical going at full throttle in the background. 'Busy morning?'

Ali looked up, yawning. 'Almost got killed in the rush. Not.' She closed her book. 'Coffee?'

'I'd murder for one. But haven't you got to go?' Lou was already exchanging Ali's CD for the smoky tones of Ella Fitzgerald singing her way through the Cole Porter songbook. As the first notes of 'All Through the Night' sounded through the shop, she felt the contentment that went with being where she belonged, despite Ali's disappointed tut. But it was Lou's shop, so her mood, and this was definitely more the thing.

'Yes, but I haven't been able to get out for a coffee all day. Anyway, I want to catch up on your news before I head off to the studio. Won't be a sec.' She disappeared out of the door to return five minutes later with two of Stefano's triple espressi. 'This should get the old heart ticking.'

'Less of the old, thanks.' Lou was walking the length of the clothes rails, mentally checking the stock. 'Haven't you sold anything?'

'Not a thing. Had a few browsers but no takers. And before you ask, yes, I did try. One of them said they might come back. Best I could do, I'm afraid. Someone did buy a set of stacking rings though.'

'That's right. Look after number one,' teased Lou. She adjusted a couple of bags and belts on the shelf. 'What about these damn frocks? I've got to move them to make way for the rest of the summer stock cluttering up my sitting room.'

They both sat behind the counter, Lou by the sewing machine. Its proximity made her feel as if she was working, or was about to: a good feeling that compensated for the inquisition that Ali would have been preparing all morning. And here it came.

'So? What's he like? Rory?'

'You mean, does he have horns and a tail? Oddly, not. Hooker dropped him off, then Nic picked us up. She still won't have anything to do with her father. I don't know how to fix things between them. Although it's not really my responsibility. But I feel that it is. Anyway, we bonded over the snakes and the stuff in the gift shop. Easiest way to a kid's heart? Spend some money on them! In fact, we had a great time. I'm knackered though. I'd forgotten how tiring kids could be.' She immediately remembered Ali's yearning for them and regretted her thoughtlessness. 'Sorry. Not thinking.'

'Don't be. I'm immune.' Ali brightened. 'And who knows, things could still change for me.'

Lou tried to interrupt, to ask her about Don, but Ali refused to take the bait. 'We're not talking about me. I need to know more about Sanjeev, too. Has he broken down your defences yet?'

They had not talked properly since the oysters and their aftermath.

'You make me sound like a crusaders' castle.' Lou swigged the last of her coffee. 'But before you ask any more, there's not much to tell. Don't look so sceptical. I won't be seeing him until he's next in town, and that may not be for weeks. I enjoyed being with him, and . . . yes, if you must know, we did.'

'Result!' Ali clapped her hands. 'I knew

that smile on your face said something.'

'Despite everything,' Lou continued, pulling a face as she remembered herself vomiting on the doormat. 'But I haven't changed my mind. I still don't want full-on commitment.' She hadn't foreseen how hard it would be to detach herself emotionally from Hooker. However badly he behaved and however hard she fought it, theirs was still unfinished business, particularly since Nic had taken her stand.

'Don't knock it. You just haven't got the *right* relationship yet. Then it'll all change.'

Lou shook her head, wishing she'd worn Ali's more discreet stud bee earrings as her Indian hoops tugged at her lobes. 'It won't. Been there, done that, got the T-shirt. Exciting, orgasm-inducing, no-strings affairs — bring 'em on. That's where I am and that's as far as I'm going.' She was already promising herself that from now on she would devote herself one hundred per cent to drumming up more custom for the shop.

Ali pulled a face. 'Well, I'm meeting a couple this afternoon who want an anniversary ring made. So fingers crossed my luck's on the turn.' She stood up and put on the fitted dogtooth blazer that Lou had insisted she bought because, on her shoulders, it was a great advertisement for the business, and grabbed her coat.

Left alone at last, Lou set about tackling her backlog of orders. To the continuing mellowed-out tones of Ella Fitzgerald and the whirr of the machine, she began to sew. Watching the sprigged primrose cotton as she guided it under the needle, she couldn't help but notice her hands: workmanlike and square nailed with several small but definite age spots. She stopped the machine and ran a finger over her left one so the loose skin gathered near her knuckles, the wrinkles momentarily smoothed out. She stroked the scar on her thumb where she'd sliced it when trying to open a wine box that was on its last dregs, then returned her attention to the blouse, this time trying to focus on her work. But then the Saturday after-lunchers provided a steady stream of distractions. By the end of the afternoon, she had managed to sell a fifties polished floral cotton skirt with one of her own full-net petticoats, a mock-croc handbag and one of Ali's bee necklaces, and to take orders for a custom-made dress and a jacket. Flushed with success, she finally pulled down the shutters and got out the vacuum cleaner so the place would be ready for the morning. She was busy straightening the stock when her mobile rang. She recognised the number.

'Lou? Hooker here.'

As if she didn't know. She walked behind the counter and sat down.

'Who answered your phone the other day? He said you were ill.'

He obviously hadn't liked that, she thought, pleased but non-committal. 'Just a friend.'

'A friend? Already?' He sounded quite taken aback. 'Are you all right?'

'Hooker! Why have you called?' She was impatient to get this over and wasn't going to give him the satisfaction of answering.

'How was Nic?'

A bit of her was surprised that he hadn't called her sooner to talk about their daughter's reaction to Rory's existence.

'You know she's still not speaking to me?'

'It'll blow over. You know Nic. Give her time.'

He sighed. 'Couldn't you tell her I'm sorry?'

Sorry? This wasn't a word that existed in Hooker's vocabulary in her experience, but she could hear how hurt he was. But be a go-between again? No way. 'I think you'll have to tell her yourself.'

'How can I? She's avoiding me. Lou, please!'

She knew what it was to be at the receiving end of Nic's displeasure. Despite herself, she felt a tug of sympathy. He might have brought his daughter's anger on himself but Lou had to shoulder some of the blame. Without her interference, they'd all have continued in happy ignorance. Would that have been better? Reluctantly, she conceded. 'I'll try. But no promises.'

He had to be satisfied with that.

'You got on all right with Rory?' The pride in his voice made Lou want to say 'No' just for the hell of it but that wouldn't be fair on Rory. Nor would it be true.

'He's a credit to you, Hooker.' She hoped that he would detect the irony in her compliment.

But no. He was rushing on. 'Thing is, Lou, I've unexpectedly got to go to the office on Tuesday. Something I can't get out of.'

So this was why he had called. She waited, knowing what was coming. Despite their separation, despite Emma, he still relied on her support. She fumed with resentment. He paused for a second, giving her the chance to step in with an offer of childcare. She said nothing.

'Ah. Well, I was wondering . . . that is, Rory . . . I would have asked Nic but now . . . Well, I thought . . .'

Stand firm, she told herself, pleased to hear his struggle to justify his request. 'The answer's no, I'm afraid. I have to be here.'

'But you weren't there this morning,' he protested. 'And Jamie mentioned you took the day off on Thursday.'

'And that's precisely why I can't take another day. I'm sorry.' She ordered the pins she'd been using in a neat line on the table in front of her.

'Couldn't you just shut shop for the day?' He sounded as though nothing could be more reasonable.

'This is my business, Hooker. It's not a game. I only took this morning off because Nic needed me there.' That's right, remind him. 'And because I needed to meet Rory.' She emphasised every syllable. 'I've got too much on to do it again. I'm sorry.' She stuck a pin upright into the wood with a little jab.

His breathing deepened: the sure sign of impending rage. She gripped the phone more tightly, ready for battle, jabbed in another pin.

'It's only a shop,' he began. 'You're the last person I'd expect to put that before a child's well-being. If you won't, I'll have to leave him home alone.' Years of living with her had taught him just which buttons to press.

'Can't one of the boys step in?' Immediately she knew her tone had given away that she was caving in despite herself.

And in he sprang. 'No, they're working.'

'Unlike me,' she snapped, her resolve stiffening again as she marshalled her thoughts. 'Can't you take him into your office? Hasn't he got a Nintendo DS or whatever they're called? A book? He'll be fine.'

'All day?' His temper was only just under control. 'Even I know that won't work. I've got clients flying in for a meeting that will take most of it, plus lunch. I won't be able to see him at all and I can't expect Sally to double up on childcare. After all, you're the one who insisted he came to stay.'

'Why not? If you can ask me, why not her? And why not Emma?' She would not offer to help him.

'Because she's at work.' The repeated inference that she was not made her boil.

'If you'd come clean years ago, then we wouldn't be in this position at all.' Lou could hear his breathing at the other end of the phone.

'Why can't he come to the shop?' Hooker would counter whatever objection she made until she was worn down. She considered arguing back but thought of Rory. This wasn't his fault, poor kid. She didn't like the idea of any child being left to his own devices for a day. Surely she could find enough ways of entertaining him.

'All right then,' she agreed but with little grace. 'Drop him off at ten and you can collect him before I shut at seven.'

'Thanks, Lou. I knew I could rely on you.' Honey was never sweeter. 'I'll do my best. Time we had another drink so that I can say thank you properly.'

'No need.' Another pin in place. Definitely time to cut this conversation short.

'I haven't forgotten the last time. I do miss you, you know.'

'Hooker, stop.' She remembered Emma on the stairs, her things in Lou's old bedroom.

She cut him off abruptly, angry with herself for giving in to him again, but delighted that at least Sanjeev's existence had registered on his radar.

22

The great joys of driving north late at night were empty roads and the knowledge that there would be little time for small talk when they arrived. Eric liked to be tucked up on the stroke of eleven. Not even the arrival of his daughter and the first, indeed only, boyfriend he'd been allowed to meet would get in the way of his habit.

Ali had left work at seven, having begun some designs for the anniversary ring. After two years of marriage, the husband was giving his wife a mixed diamond ring. The challenge of creating a setting that would allow the brilliance of the different shades of champagne, olive, mink and gold to be shown off was what Ali loved. The success of the meeting had given her an energy that propelled her home in time for the journey that she still worried might not be the best idea.

Don had insisted on driving so, in theory,

all Ali had to do was sit back and relax. However, she couldn't help the intake of breath whenever she thought they were in danger of hitting something or when Don was driving too fast or too slow or too close to the kerb.

'Ali! Will you calm down,' he eventually demanded. 'I've been driving for years and have a completely clean licence. You're quite safe.'

'Sorry, it's just that I —'

'I know. You're used to being the one in the driving seat. Well, not tonight.' He laid a hand on her thigh. 'You've got me now.'

She felt heady with excitement, with anticipation for their future together although she still baulked at the idea of giving up her habitual control, even to him. On the other hand, she loved being loved. Being in charge was one thing but, more recently, even when Hooker was on the scene, she had felt lonely too and that wasn't what she wanted for the rest of her life. Now she had found him again, Don was someone who she didn't want to lose.

She turned and studied his profile sporadically illuminated by the lights of the oncoming traffic: short thick grey hair, long nose, face still lean. He felt her watching him, turned his head briefly and smiled. 'Let's have some music.'

They listened as they covered miles of the M1. They didn't need to fill every silence between them with talk.

As they neared their destination, Ali felt a growing undertow of anxiety. The purpose of the trip loomed large as she worried about what Don was going to say. For all his memories, he didn't know Eric at all. Suppose he shattered the fragile peace that existed between her father and her. She interrupted his slightly off-key humming.

'I'm not sure you should talk to Dad about my mum, you know. He's looking forward to seeing you, so I don't want you to spoil things. Perhaps leave it till next time.'

The humming stopped, though his hand kept up the beat on the steering wheel. 'I know what I'm doing, Al. You've got to trust me and then you'll be able to put this to rest once and for all.'

'I'm not sure.' The final chords swept around them.

'Be sure. Please.' He reached out and upped the volume, signalling an end to the conversation. 'I won't say anything about her without you being there.'

Ali stared out of the window into the dark, aware only of the motorway signs that flashed in and out of the periphery of her vision. If this relationship was to work, then she had to trust him, but giving herself up completely was a whole lot harder than she'd envisaged. Remember, she told herself for the umpteenth time, Don is only doing this for you and you do want to know where your mother went.

They arrived just after eleven. Her father greeted them, tapping Sergeant with his stick to stop the terrier's throaty growl, exclaiming over how well Don looked, asking about his work, offering them a nightcap. Ali coughed as the cheap blended whisky burned the back of her throat.

'Never good with whisky.' Eric raised an eyebrow at Don, signalling Ali's exclusion from their shared world of masculine pleasures. Ali bit back a retort. Within minutes, he was obviously itching to excuse himself and get to bed.

'Let's talk in the morning, Eric,' said Don. 'It's late now, and we'll have plenty of time then.'

Clearly relieved to be given the all-clear, Eric said his goodnights and disappeared upstairs, having allowed Sergeant a brief tour of the jungle that passed for the back garden before he accompanied his master to bed. By the time Ali and Don went up,

Eric's door was shut, a sliver of light coming from under the door. At the top of the stairs, Ali automatically turned towards her bedroom, then stopped. Her tiny single bed wouldn't hold two. 'There's plenty of room between you and the ceiling,' went the old college joke, but that wasn't the solution when her father was only a paper-thin wall away. Neither she nor Eric had mentioned the sleeping arrangements. Feeling like a rebellious teenager, deliberately flouting parental rules, she took Don's hand and led him to the spare room at the back of the house. The musty smell reminded her of the sitting room downstairs while the central light cast an unwelcoming glare over proceedings. She pulled back the balding pink candlewick bedspread. At least the bed was made up. She saw Don eyeing the faded print of West's *Death of General Wolfe* on the wall opposite the bed.

He limited himself to 'Mmm. Nice,' before unpacking his sponge bag and tiptoeing to the bathroom, leaving Ali to gaze at the dying general.

In the chilly, unwelcoming atmosphere of the little-used room, the night was not one that they would remember for its romance.

Eric stomped downstairs in the morning, muttering something about having been kept awake by their 'comings and goings' but no more was said. After breakfast, he invited Don to join him and Sergeant on their morning 'trot along the towpath'.

They departed together, leaving Ali to worry about what might be said in her absence. When they returned, they were chatting easily about the Premier Division and the merits of a new player just signed to Liverpool. Once he had a cup of coffee and a couple of plain digestives in his hand, Eric excused himself almost immediately. Something about a battle plan he had to effect. 'I'll be back down for opening time. You'll remember the Swan, Don?'

'Actually, Dad, I brought some food with me. A roast. Remember?' She tried to sound encouraging. 'I thought it would be nicer to eat here.'

Put out by this change of plan, Eric hesitated, looking towards Don for support.

'Why don't we go for a pint first?' Don suggested. 'Get out of Ali's hair. Then come back for lunch?'

'Strategic thinking,' barked Eric, approving. 'I like that.'

Compromise, thought Ali, relieved that disagreement had been averted. I like that.

By the time the two men left, Sergeant at Eric's heel, Don and Ali had almost finished off clearing the attic. Don moved the heavier items to be thrown away under Eric's supervision. Ali had also retrieved a pile of clothes that she remembered Lou hovering over on her last visit. Nothing special — at least she thought not — but all in reasonably good nick. With Eric's approval, she would take them to the shop. As far as she was concerned now, they were merely shadows of her mother and grandmother and, if left languishing in a trunk, were no use to anyone. Better to find them new homes where they might be given a new lease of life. With the joint in the oven, Ali enjoyed the next hour or so on her own, listening to the radio, pottering in the kitchen as she prepared the rest of the lunch, making sure she washed up as she went along so everything was in perfect order when they got back. Just as Eric liked it.

Eventually, they sat down together at one thirty sharp, Eric glancing at his watch before dispatching Sergeant to his 'barracks!', pointing at a cushioned wicker basket in a corner of the dining room. On the wall, the dragoons of Stubbs's Tenth Regiment stared unblinking over their heads.

'Wine!' he remarked, picking up the bottle

of Beaujolais Don had chosen to warm up the old boy for the kill. 'Thought you were driving.'

'But you're not,' pointed out Don. 'And I know Ali would like a glass.' He did the honours.

Damn right, she would. Anything to dissipate the knot in her stomach. Eric sharpened the carving knife on the steel, the sound returning Ali to the many childhood lunches they'd had at this table, before she and her father were left to fend for themselves. Then they had usually sat in silence, plates of ready-made supermarket meals on knees in front of the TV. She dutifully dished out the vegetables as he passed one plate of roast beef to her after another, doing exactly as her mother had done before her. Don kept the conversation going through the meal, drawing Eric out, asking about his army background, his teaching work at the local school, about his military research and soldiering upstairs. Ali sat back, enjoying watching her father warm to Don all over again, trying to be more interested in his replies.

By the time they had finished the treacle tart and custard, her father's favourite, Eric was the most relaxed Ali had seen him for years, primed and ready. For a moment, she saw him in a new light, no longer the authoritarian figure of her memory but an increasingly vulnerable old man who was quite unprepared for what was coming. She felt unexpectedly sympathetic. Shouldn't they leave his version of past events untouched if that's what got him by? Did it matter if she didn't know the whole truth? Wasn't ignorance supposed to be bliss? Plagued with sudden doubt, she kicked at Don under the table, trying to signal her change of heart. He smiled at her, mistaking her message for something more affectionate.

'The thing is, Eric . . .' he began.

Ali kicked harder but he had moved his leg out of reach. 'Can we have a word?' she asked, pushing back her chair and half standing. But he apparently didn't hear — or didn't want to. She stood frozen, part of her wanting to shut him up but the other part desperate for him to continue. She wanted and didn't want to hear what Eric had to say.

'There's a reason behind our visit. We want to ask you something.'

'Marriage?' barked Eric, beaming. 'Of course, old boy. Decent of you to ask.' He held out his hand for Don to shake.

'No, not marriage, Dad,' said Ali quickly,

her stomach somersaulting wildly as she sat down again.

'No?' He pulled back his hand and reached for his glass. 'What then?'

'Ali's happiness,' said Don, recovering quickly.

Eric looked puzzled as he swallowed loudly. He drummed the fingers of his free hand on the faded checked oilcloth that had been brought out for best for as long as Ali could remember.

'There's no easy way of putting this, Eric, but I won't keep you in suspense.'

Eric's fingers beat a second drum roll as he held Don's gaze, challenging him to continue. Ali's stomach somersaulted again as she concentrated on making patterns with her spoon in the remaining crumbs and custard on her plate, wishing and not wishing that this conversation wasn't about to happen.

Don continued, undeterred, his voice calm and reasonable. 'Something's been troubling Ali all her adult life and I want to help her resolve it.'

Eric pretended puzzlement. 'What *are* you talking about?' He stared at his glass, swirling the wine round and round.

'I think you know.'

Eric looked at Ali, who looked at the

tablecloth, then shook his head.

'Come on, Eric.' Don sounded as if he was talking to a recalcitrant child in a primary school classroom, urging him into something he didn't want to do. He leaned towards him, encouraging his confidence. 'She needs to know the full story of what happened to her mother, to Moira.'

Eric coughed as his wine went down the wrong way. His face flushed as his grip tightened on his glass. His other hand was perfectly still. Ali galvanised herself enough to pour her father and herself a little more to drink. At least the words had been said. There was no going back.

'I realise you may think that, after so long, I've no right to come here and talk to you like this —'

'Damn right, I do,' growled Eric.

'— but I'm doing it for Ali. I know how much she loves you and that's why she won't press you herself but, having talked to her, I'm sure it's something that should be cleared up for her sake, for her future.' A diplomatic note had entered his voice.

To Ali's dismay, Eric reached for his stick and then, with its support, rose from his chair. 'You've got a bloody cheek.' He banged the stick on the ground for emphasis. 'Talking to me like that. What's wrong with you, Al? Didn't you tell him about the last time we talked about this?'

'Dad, calm down.' Ali reached for his hand, but he snatched it away from her. 'He's only doing it for me.' She didn't look at Don, not wanting to give Eric the impression that they were ganging up any more than they were. This was a matter for her father and her now. Don had done his bit. 'I know it's difficult, especially since we've never really talked about Mum. But since our last chat, I've thought about her a lot. I need to know where she is. I think I'd like to contact her.'

Eric collapsed back into his seat, visibly exhausted. 'I've said all there is to say. Enough!'

This was the moment in which she could back off, as usual frightened of going too far. But this time, Don's silent presence gave her the strength she needed and she spoke quietly. 'But why did she leave so much behind? Did she leave very suddenly? Did she really never try to be in touch? Was it me that drove her away? She was my mother as well as your wife. Don's right. I do need to know.'

Eric's face was rigid. The only movement came from a small involuntary tic working by his left eye. He didn't notice that Sergeant, sensing attack, had left the 'barracks' and placed himself by his master's feet, looking up, awaiting instruction.

'You owe it to her to tell her the truth, Eric.' Don spoke quietly. 'This is as good a time as any.'

'Dad, please,' Ali pleaded, as Eric opened, then snapped shut his mouth. 'Don't be angry. Don's only trying to help me.'

'Help you?' Eric put a hand on Sergeant's head as his expression changed to one of sadness, as his faded blue eyes blinked once, twice. 'Al, you shouldn't need help to talk to me.'

'I know, Dad. And I don't about anything else. But this is the one subject that we always skirt around, frightened of hurting each other's feelings. I'm not going to think the worse of you or of her now, whatever happened. I just need to know the truth.'

'Sometimes the truth is best kept hidden.' He spoke so quietly that they could hardly hear him.

Ali thought of Hooker, of the lies and deceptions that had surrounded their relationship and of all the relationships she'd had before him. She thought of Lou. 'I don't agree. It must be better to have things in the open.'

Eric looked at Don in appeal. 'Do you

really agree with that? Do you agree that it's better, no matter who's hurt? That's what you're asking for.'

Ali didn't wait for Don to reply. 'Dad, we should clear the air at last. For both our sakes.'

'I never thought I'd hear you talk to me like that.' He shook his head.

Ali didn't move. She just sat, nervous, waiting for whatever came next. Eric stood up and paced the length of the room. Sergeant retreated to 'barracks', his button black eyes fixed on his master.

'All right,' Eric said at last. 'All right.' He hooked his stick on the back of his chair.

'I think I should leave you to it now. I'll be outside if you need me.' As Don passed behind her, he put his hand on Ali's shoulder and squeezed. The gesture gave her courage.

Eric watched him leave the room. Ali could see the approval in her father's eyes. He sat down, then pushed the pudding plates out of the way so he could lean on his elbows. He steepled his fingers as he deliberated. Eventually he began to speak in the same tone he had used when they last talked about her mother. 'I haven't been honest with you. You're right. Perhaps I should have explained everything when it all happened but I thought you were too young to understand. Then, when you were older, you seemed to be getting on with your own life and I didn't want to spoil things. There was never a right time.'

'But I never forgot her,' Ali protested, alarmed by what Eric was saying. 'I never accepted that she could just leave without a goodbye, without coming back.'

'I know you didn't. But I did everything I could to protect you. No one round here knew the truth.'

'Dad, please.' She couldn't imagine where this was all leading.

'Your mother was ill.'

'What do you mean, ill?' She hadn't expected this.

He sighed. 'She was a manic depressive, bipolar they call it now. I didn't want you to know because I didn't want you any more upset than you already were or to think that there was any risk that you might have inherited the same problem.'

Ali sat looking at him, dumbstruck. She twisted her mother's rings around and around her finger while she waited for him to go on.

'The medicine they gave her meant she hadn't had an attack for years, but she stopped taking her pills. I tried to dissuade her but she wouldn't listen. Not long after-wards, all the signs began again. You won't remember them, but she couldn't get out of bed, couldn't stop crying. She couldn't sleep, couldn't eat. I didn't know what to do.' He looked up at Ali as if pleading for her understanding. 'In the end the doctors sent her to Udlington psychiatric hospital. We told you she'd gone to stay with her Aunt Annie in Scotland.' He paused.

Ali couldn't believe what she was hearing. She watched the tremor in his right hand that had worsened as he spoke. 'And then?' she murmured.

'And then . . .' He stopped again. 'And then, when they thought she was better she was allowed home. Sometimes the danger-ous stage, they told me afterwards. As the pills they prescribed took over and the depression began to lift, she felt in control again. Then, just when I thought we had our Moira back with us, she went off with-out telling me where she was going. All she left was the note that you've read and her rings.'

'But where did she go to?' Ali felt like screaming at him to finish the story, despite the obvious difficulty he was having telling her everything.

'She caught a train to Galloway and

turned up on her Aunt Annie's doorstep. This time, that really was where she went. Annie was in her eighties then, still living on her own, though she went into the home soon afterwards.'

There was a long silence.

'Dad, please go on!' Ali sat, twisting and untwisting her paper napkin until it began to disintegrate. Eric looked up at her with an expression that made her dread what he was about to say.

He bowed his head, patting the air with his hand to tell her to be patient. 'She phoned me to let me know Moira was there. She said if I could drive up first thing in the morning to collect her, she would calm her down that night. But . . .' He sniffed loudly. 'When she went in to wake her in the morning, Moira was dead.'

Ali gasped. 'Dead!'

He carried on as if she hadn't spoken. 'She'd taken all her antidepressants and downed them with a bottle of whisky. She'd planned the whole thing. The doctors told me there was nothing we could have done.' He separated his palms, buried his head in his hands and gave a muffled sob.

'And you said nothing to me?' She felt as if she was deep underwater, her lungs straining for breath, her heart pounding, head throbbing.

'I didn't tell anyone,' he went on. 'We buried her up there, and soon afterwards Annie went into the home where she died a year later. No one else needed to know. You least of all. As far as anyone was concerned, she had run away to a new life.'

'Me least of all?' Ali heard herself shouting. 'I can't believe you said that. I was the one person you should have told. I've spent my life wondering if she'd come back, where she was, why she left, whether I was to blame.'

Of all the things she might have expected, this was not it. Never once, over all this time, had she imagined her mother dead. She had accepted her disappearance by inventing a fiction in which she had gone off with another man, or in search of her independence. Over time, her initial puzzlement and devastation became an unforgiving anger. Hope that her mother might return gradually disappeared. Instead she built a shell around herself to protect her from further hurt.

But not suicide. Not that.

Eric looked up. 'I couldn't bear the idea of anyone knowing. I thought you'd blame me.' He pulled a folded white handkerchief from his breast pocket and loudly blew his nose before stuffing it back. His military bearing had deserted him.

'Of course I blame you.'

He flinched as if she had hit him.

'Who else is there to blame?' Knowing what had really happened to her mother felt as if a physical burden had been removed from her, but it had been replaced by a terrible sadness mixed with a fierce anger. There was to be no rose-tinted reunion, no making up for lost time.

'But, Al, we got through.' He tried to justify himself. 'Then, once you had Don, and seemed so happy, I thought it was better just to forget. And I thought you had.'

'Of course I didn't forget. She was my mother. My mother,' she repeated more quietly as she began to cry.

Eric reached out to her. 'I'm so sorry. I did what I thought was best for you.'

She swatted his hand away, pushing her chair back from the table. 'Best? You stupid man. You had no idea.'

There was a tap at the door, before Don put his head round with a tentative 'Everything all right?'

'No.' Ali got to her feet. 'It's not all right at all. We're leaving.'

'Ali. Please.' Her father struggled to his feet, looking the old man he was.

'Are you sure?' asked Don, looking worried as he came into the room. 'Wouldn't it be better to calm down and sort things out?'

'I don't want to talk to either of you,' Ali said, her jaw clenched. 'I'm leaving.'

'But you'll come again?' The hope in Eric's voice was painful to hear.

'I don't know. Maybe. Probably. I can't think.' Ali left the room, the two men staring after her, and ran upstairs to collect her overnight bag.

Within fifteen minutes, she and Don were on the road home.

23

Hooker took a tangerine taffeta dress off the rail, held it up against himself and gave a twirl in front of the mirror, pulling a face. 'What do you think, Rory?' He sucked in his cheeks, put his hand on his hip, and strutted across the shop trying to get a laugh from the boy who half-heartedly obliged but then looked away, embarrassed. Lou looked on, not allowing herself more than the briefest smile.

'And here's just the thing for you, birdbrain.' Hooker picked a wide-brimmed hat decorated with pheasant feathers and flipped it onto Rory's head where it sat at an angle, obscuring his eyes.

'Careful!' Lou lunged for the hat as Rory's fingers reached upwards. She removed it from his head before any harm could be done. 'I don't want it damaged.'

'Can't think who'd want to wear that dead duck anyway,' said Hooker, hanging up the dress, checking his devoted audience of one was still amused. He wasn't.

'Pheasant,' corrected Lou. 'And it's beautiful.' Balancing the hat with her hand in the crown, she stroked the brim along the lie of the feathers.

'To you maybe,' said Hooker, continuing to explore the rest of the rail, but without really looking at what he touched. 'Not to us, though. Eh, Rory?'

But Rory had lost interest in Hooker's games and was beginning to unpack his rucksack on the floor: an iPod Touch, a well-thumbed copy of a Harry Potter paperback, a map of the London Underground, a pack of cards and the obligatory Nintendo DS. On his hands and knees, he corralled them into a pile. Lou couldn't help but notice that the easy-going lad of Saturday had transformed into a different, less outgoing child, apparently unhappy about today's arrangement. They were at least at one on that.

'Perhaps not right in the middle of the shop, Rory. You'll be interrupted.' She gestured to a space behind the counter. 'Why don't you take them to the cutting table at the back?'

'Come on, Lou. You can't make him disappear,' Hooker mocked her.

'I'm not trying to.' She was not going to let him under her skin. 'I'm just trying to find somewhere he'll be undisturbed and to make room for the customers at the same time. How many times do I have to tell you, Hooker? This is my business, and I want it to work.'

'Depends on your definition of business.' He tapped the end of his nose with his index finger before squatting by his young son who had already ensconced himself beneath the table.

She refused to rise to the bait. How she loathed his superiority, the smug self-satisfaction that oozed from him sometimes. But as he bent over the computer game, a snapshot memory of him doing the same with Jamie and Tom when they were on holiday in Wales momentarily took her breath away. There had been good times. These were only qualities that emerged when he needed to cover up how ill at ease he was.

He straightened up, mussing the boy's hair. 'Now, don't give Lou any trouble. And I'm expecting to see this finished by the time Tom and I see you this evening. Tomorrow we'll do something together to make up. Right?'

But Rory's attention was already involved

in a fast-moving shoot-'em-up, thumbs moving swiftly over the console, iPod Touch on, earphones in. He didn't look up.

Hooker shrugged his shoulders and gave Lou a look that conveyed both indulgence and pride in the fruit of his loins. 'I owe you a thank-you, you know. He and I would never have had the chance to get to know each other like this, if it weren't for your insisting. Having him around has taken me back to the old days. You and I were quite a team.'

'Quite a lopsided one, as it turned out,' Lou snapped, acid tongued, at the same time registering that Rory's enjoyment of this new relationship wasn't quite as obvious as Hooker's. Why should he get away with rewriting history in his favour? 'Being good with the children is only part of being a decent parent. I've told you that before.'

'Oh, loosen up, Lou. We were. And there's no reason why we shouldn't be again. Did you have a chance to speak to Nic?' The question was almost throwaway but Lou heard how much her answer mattered. She decided to ignore what he'd said before that.

'Not yet.'

His face fell. He traced a pattern on the counter with his finger. His disappointment was obvious. However, he quickly recovered himself. 'Having Rory here has really made me think about us.' He picked up his briefcase, smart in his navy blue cashmere coat, and directed one of his most winning smiles at her. 'I want you to think again too. Seriously. About us getting back together.' He mouthed the last words so Rory wouldn't hear. Without giving her a chance to reply, he left the shop, turning just to say, 'Back at seven. See you then.'

She stared after him in disbelief, wanting to laugh at the preposterousness of his suggestion and the extraordinary degree of self-belief that it betrayed. Were they provoked by his knowledge that she had another man somewhere in her life? Was the idea that she might have found someone to replace him too hard for his ego to accept? Or was there something more genuine there? She returned to the table and switched on the iron. 'Well, Rory, this may not be the most exciting day ever, but we'll just have to make the best of it.' Her words fell on deaf ears. His mood communicated itself through the deafening silence punctuated only by the odd tinny snatch of music that escaped his headphones. To lighten the mood, she put on her old Fred and Ginger collection. Humming to the soundtrack of *Top Hat,* she unfolded the dress that she'd completed at home the previous day and laid it on the ironing board. This was a new style inspired by something she had seen online: a floral cotton lawn short-sleeved wrapover dress with pockets on the bodice.

The day stretched grimly ahead of them. Her normal pleasure in being at the shop was disturbed by having Rory at the other end of the table. She hadn't the first idea how she would entertain him when he got bored, as he inevitably would. The iron hissed steam and she began to work it over the fabric.

'Morning!' Ali burst through the door, armed with carrier bags that she dropped in front of the counter. 'I've got some stuff for you.'

Lou looked up, surprised by the earliness of the visit. 'God, narrow escape. You've just missed Hooker.'

'Shit!' Ali noticed Rory and put her hand over her mouth.

'Don't worry, he can't hear a thing. How did the weekend go? Tell me while I finish this off, then we can have a proper look at what you've got.' As she ironed into the bodice, carefully arranging the fabric as she went, inhaling the comforting smell of hot damp new fabric, Lou heard out the story of Ali and Don's visit to Eric.

By the time she'd finished, Ali's earlier sunniness had vanished. 'Why wasn't I enough for her? I'll never be able to find out now. And my bloody father won't be able to tell me. I'll never forgive him.'

'But you must.' The firmness in Lou's voice made Ali glance at her.

'You're joking? After what he's done? When I think of the teasing I went through at school 'cause my mum had run away. I cut myself off from my friends, stopped asking them round to the house, just so I wouldn't have to listen to it. I couldn't look for her because I knew that if she'd wanted me, she would have stayed, but there was always the smallest chance that she'd come back, that she'd discover that whatever she'd gone to wasn't as good as what she'd left behind. If he'd told me . . .'

'He's your only family though. That's important. Try and put yourself in his shoes.' Lou ignored Ali's defiant expression. 'He made those decisions for your sake, however wrong-headed they were.' She stuck a pin into the pincushion on the back of her wrist, trying but unable to imagine the dark place in which Ali's mother must have found herself. As a mother, the idea of abandoning a child was unthinkable. Lou's children were what had always kept her going, even when at their most unspeakable. In between the teenage strops and tantrums, there were periods — albeit they were sometimes very short indeed — of unalloyed happiness, worth every moment.

'He was thinking of himself too.' Ali went on the defensive. 'He said as much.'

'Maybe. But times were different then. Mental illness and suicide carried a stigma they don't have today. The letter said that she'd tried before, didn't it?'

Ali nodded.

'Think what it must have been like for him, then. How difficult it must have been as well as trying to keep his family together. He must have been desperate. And then having to look after his daughter on his own — and you weren't exactly easy, you told me yourself. It must have been incredibly difficult.'

'Well, if he hadn't shut everyone else out . . .' muttered Ali.

'He is who he is. You can't change that. But why don't you at least go back and talk to him again. Find out more about her, her illness. Then you might understand a little better and feel less angry.'

'Why are you so damn sensible? You sound just like Don.' However, Ali sounded as if she might be beginning to come round.

'Years of children and being a parent. And years of hearing other parents' chat. We all do what we think is best and more often than not, it isn't. God, listen to me! I'll get off the soapbox.' Hanging up the dress, Lou stood back to consider her handiwork. The quality was as good as anything on the high street, but the style and fabric were much more interesting. 'Just think about it anyway.'

'OK. I'll do that. But I'm not promising anything else. End of.'

With the discussion closed, Lou changed the subject. 'Now, if you're really sure you want to offload her stuff, let's have a look.'

Still looking thoughtful, Ali bent down to pick up her bag. 'There's nothing designer, but some nice retro-cool stuff.' She took out a jewellery roll and lay it on the counter. 'But what I really wanted to show you first were these. A couple of new pieces from me, but more importantly . . .' She pulled out a sketchpad and opened it. 'In silver.'

Lou studied the drawings. At the top of each page was the sketch of a flower — sweet pea, iris, violet, orchid — in precise detail. Beneath each one were sketches to illustrate the development into a necklace, earrings or a bracelet from the original. 'These are exquisite. But they're not your style. Who made them?'

'Rick, the guy I share my studio with. I was thinking that you needed a bigger selection here and some people do prefer silver. His work's fantastic. He's started working on a technique that makes the silver curve into the shapes he wants. It's . . .' She stopped. Lou wasn't listening but was studying the drawings. 'He hasn't had much luck recently, so I thought he could do a few drawings for you to see. The workmanship will be fantastic, I guarantee.'

'But I couldn't commission them.' Her budget was stretched enough as it was.

'No, no. Same deal as we have. He makes, you sell and cream off a percentage.'

'We . . . ell.' Lou hesitated.

'Come on, Lou. You know you want to. I didn't suggest it before because I wanted to see how my own stuff went. But this makes sense. I tell you what: I'll take Rory to get a coffee and some of those Italian biscuit things that Stefano does. You have a rummage and a think. We'll come back and I'll take away what you don't want, including the drawings.'

Lou agreed. The scent of the chase was in her nostrils, and she was grateful to have Rory taken care of by someone else even if only for a few minutes.

By the time the two of them returned, she had been through everything. A neat pile of four jumpers and a couple of blouses sat on the counter next to several dresses and a couple of fitted jackets. She was studying Rick's designs again when the door clicked open. 'OK,' she said, looking up. 'Let's give him a try. I've marked the ones that I think will go best — to start with anyway. What did you get, Rory?'

'Lemonade and chocolate cake,' he muttered as he slid by her, back to the table. She looked questioningly at Ali.

'No harm in spoiling him,' Ali justified herself. 'It must be difficult. Anyway, Rick . . .' She threw her arms around Lou. 'I knew you'd like them. And you don't want these?' She indicated the few items Lou had put back in the bags.

'It's not that I don't like them, but they're not in as good nick as this lot. I'll have to put the jumpers in the freezer just in case of moths but otherwise everything's perfect. Stitching good, linings undamaged, buttons all there. I'm photographing some stuff for the website tomorrow so I'll include them.'

'Excellent. My work is done, then.' Ali gathered everything up and headed for the door. 'I'll give you a call to let you know when Rick can deliver. Let's catch up later.'

The rest of the morning passed slowly. Eventually Rory got bored and emerged from under the table. Then the talking began. He wanted to know which station came after Bounds Green on the Piccadilly line, then to be tested on all the stations on the Central line, then the Bakerloo line. Playing along meant she couldn't fully concentrate on her sewing. Then he went into a long explanation about the Transport for London rolling stock, how it had been transferred from one line to another and how the sizes of the tunnels change depending on the line. Just as she was beginning to lose the ability to pretend interest not to mention the will to live, her prayers were answered and a customer appeared. For about an hour, the woman tried on almost everything from the vintage-inspired rail, turning in front of the mirror, asking Lou's opinion. Lou watched as the dresses she made were put under intense scrutiny, one after another. Her role was simply to comment or offer a brooch, a belt or a bag. Eventually, just as she was beginning to think the time totally wasted and to wonder whether she should order a pizza for Rory, a decision was made: one dress sold and one commissioned in a size up from the display sample.

As the door shut behind the satisfied customer, Lou started to return the rejected dresses to the rail. 'Just let me do this, Rory, and I'll be with you. I'm sorry. Sometimes they're like that. Take ages.'

There was no reply. Rory must have plugged himself back into his iPod Touch. When she'd hung up and straightened the stock, Lou went behind the counter to find him. But he wasn't there.

'Rory?'

No reply. Bloody child, bloody iPod Touch.

'Rory!' This time much louder.

Still no reply. And in fact, now she looked, she couldn't see him anywhere.

There must be a simple explanation. She knocked on the toilet door before opening it. Empty. She opened the door to the outside back and put her head into the tiny yard, recently decked out with pots and a large mirror on the side wall that made the space seem much bigger. But not big enough to hide an eleven-year-old.

'Rory!' She'd forgotten she could be so stern. 'Where are you? I want to order you pizza. This isn't funny.'

As she pulled the grey curtains back from the empty changing cubicles, she tried to quell the rising tide of concern. No one.

Squatting down, she looked underneath the rails of clothes, hoping to see a pair of boy's legs as he hid behind something. Nothing. She walked briskly (running would be to acknowledge her growing panic) to the door despite knowing that, if Rory had left the shop, he'd be far away by now. There was no sign of him in the street. She ran to the main road and stared up and down it, willing Rory to materialise. Nothing. She ran back to Stefano's. Inside, the smells of coffee, cheese and salamis greeted her.

'Have you seen a young boy?' she panted. 'Fair hair, jeans, checked shirt, jacket.' Had he taken his rucksack? She hadn't noticed.

'The one who came in earlier with Ali?' Stefano stopped pouring a tin of garlicky black olives into a pottery bowl.

She nodded, hope gathering in her chest.

'No, not since. Is a problem?'

'I can't find him.' She stopped herself. She must have made a mistake. 'Don't worry. He must still be in the shop.' She rushed back to find two women puzzled by the shop being unstaffed, but no Rory. And no rucksack. The only sign of him having been there at all was a couple of playing cards that sat ignored on the floor by the door. How had he managed to slip out without her noticing?

'I'm so sorry, but I'm going to have to close the shop now.' Her heart was racing as she explained briefly to her customers what had happened. 'I'm sure it'll be business as usual tomorrow.'

Once they'd left, she went out again to check the other shops in the street. But no one had seen a boy on his own. Back at the Ritz, she shut the door and leaned against it, organising her thoughts. Who should she call first? Hooker? She felt sick anticipating his reaction. But perhaps Rory had a mobile she could try. Hooker would have the number. She wiped her damp palms on her skirt before she dialled.

Put through to his office, she asked to speak to him.

'I'm sorry but Mr Sherwood's in a meeting,' came his PA's automaton-like tones.

'This is an emergency, Sally. Can't you ask him to come out for a moment? Please.' Lou tried to control the edge in her voice. Becoming hysterical would not help.

'He asked not to be disturbed under any circumstances.' A note of steely authority had entered the woman's voice.

'I need to speak to him, urgently. This is a personal matter that he needs to know about now.' Keep calm.

'I'm sorry but I've got my instructions.'

'Fine. But when he hears you refused to let me speak to him, you might regret following them. I hope so.' She cut their connection with an angry satisfaction at having had the last word until she thought of how incandescent Hooker would be when he realised she hadn't been more insistent about speaking to him. To hell with him.

Who next? Nic? Jamie? Tom?

Interrupted at work, Nic was abrupt but agreed to go round Hooker's house in her lunch break to see if Rory had made his way back there. Jamie was unobtainable, wrapped up on the film set.

Lou sank into the chair by the changing cubicles, catching sight of herself in the mirror. An escapee from Bedlam might have looked more competent. She'd raised three children of her own without mishap but, given the brief responsibility of looking after someone else's, she'd failed miserably. She thought of Rory's mother, somewhere in Europe. She should be told her son was missing. She put herself in the other woman's place, imagining the panic, the powerlessness she would feel. They had to find Rory before they found her. Perhaps one of her own children might have an idea where he had gone. After all, they already knew him far better than Lou did. About to call Tom, she saw Ali's name come up on the screen.

'Lou? I'm at the studio. Rick's good to go. Made up that his work might have an outlet at last.'

'Great, but can we talk about this later? I'm sorry, but I've lost Rory.'

'What? How?'

'He must have done a runner while I was busy with a customer. I was so involved, I didn't notice. I've looked everywhere.' She brushed the tears from her cheek.

'He can't have gone far. He's only eleven, for God's sake.'

Ali's voice of reason made Lou feel momentarily better until the panic crowded in again. 'But he's got this encyclopaedic knowledge of the Tube. If he's found a station, he could be anywhere. Anything could happen to him. But he couldn't have, could he?' She tried to reassure herself.

'Ah . . . well.' Ali sounded embarrassed.

That wasn't the answer Lou had wanted. 'What?' she asked urgently. 'What do you know?'

'When I took him to get the coffees, he insisted we walk up to the High Street and round the block. I didn't see that it could do any harm, just give you a bit longer with

Mum's clothes. But of course we walked past the bus stop. He wanted to know where all the buses went to and if there was one that went to King's Cross.'

'King's Cross!' Lou's heart was thumping. 'Why King's Cross?'

'God knows. I didn't ask him. Perhaps I should have, but I didn't think anything about it at the time.'

The horrifying possibility of them never setting eyes on Rory again presented itself. Nightmares of runaway children being picked up at railway stations by paedophiles and child traffickers danced through her mind. This was entirely her fault. She went over to her work table where she slipped on her thimble and tapped it on the table, as if the rhythm would calm her.

'I'm coming over,' said Ali immediately. 'There must be something we can do.'

How close their friendship had already become over the past months. Ali hadn't thought twice about offering to help. Lou hadn't needed to ask. They hung up, Lou impatient for her to arrive.

Finally, Lou called Tom, who was stranded in a greasy spoon somewhere in Buckinghamshire, staking out an MP's house for a story, but at least he came up with a theory. 'The kid's gutted he's missing his football camp this week. Didn't he tell you? He goes every school vac and all his mates'll be there. Why would he want to be down here with Dad and a load of oldsters he won't see again for months? I wouldn't blame him if he did try to get home. And King's Cross is the station for Edinburgh.'

'But he's only eleven,' protested Lou weakly. Why hadn't she engaged with him better and found this out for herself? 'And his mother's not even there.'

'Yeah, but he's old for his age, and quite sensible. He's probably got something worked out. I'd come back to help look, but I'm stuck here. Keep calm.'

A phrase guaranteed to make her do exactly the opposite. She took her mobile from the table and dialled 999. The calm, reassuring tones of the emergency switchboard made her feel better. Yes, she would stay where she was until the police arrived. As she hung up, she noticed Stefano outside, signalling that she should open up. Relieved to have a couple of seconds in which she could delay calling Hooker again, in which Rory might magically reappear, she opened the door. The Italian pressed a large coffee into her hands.

'Maybe you need this? And this?' He gave her a small chocolate panforte. 'Sugar is good in crisis.'

What a man. She thanked him, taking his gifts, then retreated into the shop. She felt too sick to eat but tried passing the time by looking at one of the new magazines she'd brought in with her that morning. But the words slid past her eyes making no sense. Her fears over what might be happening to Rory made it impossible to concentrate.

The next fifteen minutes seemed like an eternity until a police car pulled up outside, its blue light flashing. A couple of passers-by stopped and stared.

Noticeably less than half her age, the two policemen were thorough and efficient. They noted her description and the little she could tell them about Rory's disappearance, asking where she thought he might have gone. She groaned. Despite telling them what she knew, she felt helpless, responsible, terrified. She described Rory's encyclopaedic knowledge of the Tube. He'd be happy riding around on it all day, making connections, changing lines. She relayed Tom's theory about Rory heading for Edinburgh. Eventually they left, assuring her that everything possible would be done, that they would contact Hooker, alert the Underground staff, and giving her a contact number should she think of anything useful or if Rory turned up. She should stay put, in case he did.

There was little else she could do bar pray that they found the boy long before Hooker came out of his meeting. But that was too much to hope for.

24

The moment Lou dreaded had arrived.

A black cab had pulled up by the kerb, its engine still running. The driver took out one of the tabloids and propped it against the wheel while Hooker leaped out and whirled into the shop like a tornado. The police had obviously reached him and he had come immediately. He dived straight in, just as she had known he would. No sharing and caring here, quite some transformation from the Hooker of a few hours earlier. No 'Hallo'. No 'Are you all right?' Just 'Where the hell is he? He's not answering his mobile. How could you have let this happen?'

'Don't speak to me like that, Hooker.' She clasped her hands firmly together. Never had she felt more like lighting up a cigarette even though she'd given up years ago when the children were small. 'He slipped out while I was busy with a customer.'

'How could you not have seen him? This place isn't big enough to get lost in. Have you even been out there looking?' With both hands planted firmly on the counter, he leaned towards her. He tapped his signet ring against the counter as he stared at her, accusing.

Thanking God she was on the other side, out of reach, she took a breath and began to count. One, two, three . . . all the way to ten if necessary. She knew from past experience that the only way to diffuse one of Hooker's rages was to remain super calm however rattled she was feeling. With his hair pushed back on end, his receding hairline was more pronounced than she'd realised. So he wasn't immune to the ageing process, after all. She watched two beads of sweat disengage from his temple and run down the right side of his face. When they were exactly level with the top of his ear, she spoke. 'Of course I have, but the police advised me to stay here in case he comes back. They've gone to King's Cross and Nic's gone to the house.'

'What about Tom and Jamie? What are they doing?' He looked around him as if expecting them to spring fully formed from the walls.

'They're working but coming over as soon

as they can. They're super confident Rory will turn up. Tom reckons he knows his way around.'

'He's got a good head on his shoulders, that's true.' A note of pride inched back into his voice, then vanished as his anger reasserted itself. His signet ring kept up its relentless, and now irritating, beat.

'I've got the CEO of Luther Matthews & King and his lawyer waiting for me to continue our meeting back at the office. Fortunately they were extremely understanding about my coming here. But I've got to get back.' He gestured at the taxi. Seeing his short but neatly manicured fingers, Lou thought briefly of Sanjeev's elegant tapered hands.

But this was a first. Putting family before work wasn't something that had ever come naturally to Hooker. His fathering abilities were at the opposite end of the scale to his attendance rate. She remembered the time fourteen-year-old Nic bunked off school only to be found as night was falling with her friend Caitlin on the roundabout at the local playground, surrounded by an incriminating packet of cigarettes and some empty alcopop bottles. By then, Lou had worked herself into a frenzy, certain her daughter had been abducted or worse. Hooker rolled home later that night oblivious to the panic and fear that Lou had suffered as she exhausted all the possibilities of where their daughter might be. What came back to her most clearly about that day, whenever she thought about it, was the awful feeling of being alone in a crisis. She would have given anything to have had him at home, sharing the load. This time, however, she felt quite different. In control. Just.

'You could have phoned me.' She picked up her mobile. 'Have you been in touch with Shona?'

'No.' Anxiety flickered across his face. 'I don't want to worry her until we know we have to. There's nothing she can do from Prague. Isn't there something *we* should be doing?' He began to pace up and down, his hands in his trouser pockets, staring at the floor.

'The police are doing everything they can.' Though looking for an eleven-year-old somewhere around King's Cross on the Tube system had to be as hard as finding a needle in a haystack. She couldn't bear to think about it.

'Don't be ridiculous, Lou. The police don't even know what he looks like. I had to send Sally to the house to pick up a photo for them. They'll only just have got it.'

She had the fleeting thought that if he'd had the presence of mind to send his PA to pick up his passport copies instead of relying on Lou, they wouldn't be in this God-awful mess in the first place. However, instead, she said, 'I'm sure they'll find him.' She wished she was even half as confident as she sounded.

'You can't say that. You haven't a clue.' Hooker's voice rose up the decibel register. 'My God! How on earth didn't you notice him leave?'

She just managed to control herself. 'I was working, Hooker.' Said through gritted teeth. 'Keeping my business —'

She was interrupted by the sound of the doorbell. A customer? She turned away to compose herself. She had never shouted at Hooker before. Although she was shaking with rage, she was also feeling incredibly proud of herself. She was no longer the Lou who allowed herself to be treated like a doormat because it made life easier. She would no longer take any of his nonsense. She took a deep breath, readying herself, calm again. Or, at least, calm enough to ask the customer to come back tomorrow.

But Hooker's explosive 'What the fuck?'

made her spin round.

She had no idea who was the most surprised. Hooker's face had turned such a rich shade of puce, he looked as if he had forgotten to breathe. She could feel her own mouth open in surprise, her eyes widen. Standing in the doorway was none other than Ali, pale as a winter's sky, her eyes going from one of them to the other, her hand on the shoulder of a very sheepish looking Rory.

'What the hell are *you* doing here?' Hooker's look of bafflement and alarm was priceless. If Lou and Ali had planned the confrontation, they couldn't have done it better.

The two women ignored him as they took account of the situation. Lou was the first to move. She rushed across to Rory, bending down to wrap him in a hug, ignoring his wriggle of resistance.

Ali was the first to break the silence, talking directly to Lou as if Hooker wasn't there. 'I thought I'd come via the station, just on the off chance. The place was packed but then I remembered what we'd been talking about in the street. Harry Potter. All I had to do was go and find that wall where they've stuck the disappearing trolley. He wasn't trying to get on a train, he was looking for platform nine and three-quarters!

He was planning to come back to the shop when he'd found it. Says he left a note.' She looked down at the top of Rory's head, still refusing to acknowledge Hooker's presence.

There was a small convulsive snort from the corner, where Hooker had collapsed into the chair.

Lou was fighting a sudden overpowering urge to laugh as she returned to the back of the shop, bending to see under the table, then straightening. She lifted a bolt of fabric she remembered putting on the table when the last customer was looking at samples, and a scrap of paper fluttered to the ground. She bent to pick it up, looking at the scrawled words on the note. 'I'm bored. Gone to explore. Back soon. Rory.' She smiled. This was just the sort of thing Tom and Jamie might have got up to when her back was turned. The only difference was that their back door opened onto the garden, not the mean streets of London.

'You went to find the platform for the train to Hogwarts?' she asked. 'Harry Potter's school,' she added, as an explanation for Hooker who was looking like a goldfish out of water, gasping for air. 'Oh, Hooker, I think you know my friend, Ali.' She couldn't resist. Ali looked up and the two women exchanged a glance loaded with meaning.

Unaware of the real drama unfolding above his head, Rory swung his backpack onto the floor. 'I'm sorry.' He looked back at Ali who gave him an encouraging nod. 'You were busy and I did try to say something but you didn't hear. So I left you a note.' He hung his head as if waiting for the dressing down. But Lou didn't want to give him one. He wasn't her child. The panic was over.

As for Hooker? For the first time that Lou could remember, he seemed to have lost the power of speech.

'Perhaps I do get a bit carried away when the customers come in,' she agreed with Rory. 'But I didn't see the note. And if I had, perhaps you should have said where you were going exploring.' He looked so contrite that she felt sorry for him. 'I'm just saying that for next time — if there is one. And if there is — don't do it with me. Anyway, it's over now.'

'Over?' said Hooker, straightening in the chair. 'It's hardly over. What's *she* doing here? How does she know Rory?' Every word said as if it was a bad taste in his mouth.

At last both women looked at him together: Ali icy cold; Lou with feigned nonchalance.

438

'Ali?' Lou asked as if she'd almost forgotten Ali was there. 'Oh, we met in India. We've been friends since then. In fact, she designed the jewellery in this case, so we're colleagues too. Quite a coincidence, isn't it?' As she spoke, she realised she was beginning to enjoy herself.

'Dad, I'm sorry.' Rory went over to his father, obviously worried that he was the cause of his anger. 'Ali took me to get a piece of cake earlier on.'

Hooker's right eye narrowed as he reached out a hand to his son. 'It's OK. But why didn't you answer your mobile?'

Rory shifted from one foot to the other. 'I left it at home.'

'For God's sake, Rory. What did I tell you about making sure you have it whenever you're in London?' Hooker was shouting, then he remembered himself. 'All right. No harm done this time, but don't ever take off again.' He almost sounded normal. 'Why don't you go and sort yourself out at the table again. I've a few things I need to talk about with Lou and Ali.' At last, having recovered enough to stand, he crossed the shop to face them.

'Cake?!' he hissed. 'Cake? How dare you let him go anywhere with a stranger, Lou.'

'Ali's hardly a stranger,' she objected. 'We

439

both know her very well. Wouldn't you say?'

'What the hell do you mean by that?'

Both women smiled, giving away how much they both knew.

'I don't really think this is the moment, do you? Not while Rory's here.' Lou picked up her phone. 'Besides, one of us had better tell the police that he's been found.'

'You've known Ali all this time and you never said anything?' Hooker was incredulous as the reality of his situation dawned.

'I didn't know you two knew each other until Ali and I met for tea at the Regis and we both saw you leaving with the gorgeous Emma.' Lou's voice was tight beneath its superficial brightness. 'But you and I have had so much else to talk about instead. What with one thing and another, it never seemed quite the right moment. . . . A bit like you not telling me about Shona, I guess.'

The colour was returning to Ali's cheeks as she spoke at last. 'I expect I might have said something if you'd given me a chance. But of course, as soon as I was back from India, you were off with Emma.'

'But Lou,' he objected, looking as if she were being quite unreasonable. 'I'd have explained . . .'

'Really?' She adopted a breezy incredulity. 'And what exactly would you have said? I

440

don't think even you could have talked your way out of this one.'

Hooker looked like a trapped rat. He glanced at his watch. 'Christ! My meeting. I have to get back to the office.' His recovery was as abrupt as his collapse. He readjusted his tie, before pulling at both lapels of his jacket. Turning to Ali, he said, 'We need to talk too.'

'That's hardly appropriate, under the circumstances,' Ali replied, lowering her voice so Rory wouldn't hear.

'But you owe me some sort of explanation,' Hooker blustered, then realising he was getting nowhere, looked at Lou. 'I'll be back for Rory later.'

'Neither of us owes you anything, Hooker. Not any more,' said Lou. 'Please don't be late.'

They watched him slam the door of the cab, lean forward and issue an instruction to the driver, before sitting back against the seat and taking out his BlackBerry. He didn't look in the direction of the shop once. If he had, he'd have seen the two women clap their hands together in delight and then burst out laughing.

Ali went shortly afterwards, leaving Lou to get on with telling everyone that Rory had been found. She had to endure a short lecture from the police about being more vigilant when in charge of a minor, but enjoyed Jamie and Tom's whoops and cheers. She caught Nic on her way back to her office. Lou could hear from the clipped tones that Nic was sure the whole incident had been engineered to cause her the greatest possible inconvenience. Lou's apology and thanks eased things a little. But that was Nic. She'd get over it, and Lou could hear how relieved she was that Rory had been found unharmed.

By seven o'clock, Rory and Lou were packing up, ready for home. Lou had got through the afternoon on a cloud of suppressed hysteria at the thought of Hooker's face when Ali and Rory had arrived together. Pure gold. The roar of the car engine outside announced his third arrival of the day, exactly on time and in his own car. He looked a different man: cool and composed. He had obviously made the decision not to say any more about Lou and Ali's friendship, not in front of his son and perhaps not at all. His 'Thank you for looking after him' was the most clipped and polite that Lou had heard him. He shepherded Rory out almost without a backward glance, but as he closed the door, he said, 'I'll be calling you later.'

Lou wasn't sure whether to take his words as a promise or a threat. To her surprised delight, she found that neither bothered her. There was only one person to whom she really wanted to talk: the one person, apart from Ali, who she felt would listen and understand what it meant to have taken control when she had felt so frightened and responsible for whatever happened. Sanjeev. They had spoken several times on the phone since the Whitstable trip. Now she called up his number again, her finger hovering over the Call symbol. Then she pressed.

'Sanjeev Gupta. I'm sorry but I can't come to the phone at the moment. Please leave a message and I'll get back to you when I can.'

She disconnected without leaving a message, suddenly relieved he hadn't answered. The ability to reinvent herself within their relationship was something precious she didn't want to give up. With him, she could be whoever she wanted. 'Needy' and 'reliant' were not the qualities by which she wanted him to remember her. Nor did she want him to think she was rushing him into a relationship where she depended on him — or he on her, for that matter. That wasn't what she needed any more. Keep it casual. She'd said it before but she'd say it to herself

443

again: she did not want another all-involving relationship with a man. Definitely not. She'd done with all that high-maintenance support work. Her energies needed to be directed into the business and making it work. She'd show Hooker what she was made of.

Two hours later, she was back home and just settling into an episode of *Mad Men* — useful resource for sixties fashion and, incidentally, pure pleasure — her supper of salmon and leek quiche, new potatoes and salad on her knee, when there was a sharp knock at the door. Surprised, she balanced her plate on the top of the bookcase and went to answer it. Looking through the peephole, she saw her visitor was Hooker. Four times in one day was definitely too much, she thought, an awful weariness settling over her. He was shifting uneasily from one foot to another, looking away down the path, scratching his jaw.

She considered not answering. Any kind of confrontation was not her idea of a fun evening. The smell of the quiche that she had only taken out of the oven minutes ago was tempting her back to the sitting room where she could hear the seductive opening bars of the *Mad Men* theme tune repeating itself, calling her to press Play. No, she would have the evening she wanted. The day had been bad enough. Responding to the siren calls of the TV and her cooking, she began to tiptoe back towards them.

Behind her, the letterbox snapped. 'Lou!' Hooker's voice travelled after her like the hiss of a snake. 'Lou! I know you're there. I can see you, for God's sake. Open the door.'

She stopped in her tracks. Then took another couple of steps in the direction of the sitting room.

'Please.'

The desperation in his voice made her stop. She went back to the door and crouched down, feeling the pain in her right knee, hearing its signature crunching sound, just like a crisp packet. 'Debris' the doctor had diagnosed, unencouragingly she thought. Through the held-open letterbox, she had a close-up view of Hooker's mouth. He must be crouching too. 'Please,' he repeated. 'I need to talk to you.' His teeth looked unfamiliarly straight and white. Chasing after the orthodontic perfection of his youth — sad, Hooker, very sad. This close, she could make out the beginnings of his stubble.

'This is not the time,' she said, her mouth only separated from his by the thickness of her front door. Giving in to the discomfort in her knee, she sat down on the floor, her back to the door. Too late, she remembered that she was sitting exactly on the spot she had bathed in vomit. Too bad. She felt too tired to move.

'No, Lou. Please listen to me. God knows what Ali's told you but I've got a fair idea of what you must think of me. But I can change. I have to talk to you.'

What on earth was he talking about? Change? She didn't know anyone less capable of self-knowledge or with less ability to change. The plaintive *Mad Men* theme tune floated down the corridor, calling her. She winched herself into a standing position, her knee crackling again. 'No, Hooker. It's late. I'm having supper. I don't want to talk to you any more. We've done enough for one day.'

'But you've got to give me a chance. You've got to.' She'd never heard him plead like this before.

'Can't we do this tomorrow when we've slept on things? I'm exhausted after today.' As she spoke, she became aware of a headache forming above her eyes, of the fact that her face felt like melting jelly, that every limb was a dull ache. 'Where's Rory? Shouldn't you be with him?' Lou had a vision of the boy's face pressed against the window of the car watching his father abase himself on her front doorstep.

'Tom's at home with him. They know I'm here. I must talk to you about Ali. Explain. She meant nothing.'

Here we go. Lou paused. For the first time that she could remember, she had the upper hand over him. She didn't have to open the door. But if she didn't, she would only be putting off the inevitable. They had to come to some sort of working arrangement for the children's sake, for Rory's sake too. What she wanted to do was to set them all straight about her. She didn't want them to see their mother as someone lacking the guts to run her own life the way she wanted. But neither did she want to be locked in an unending row. She and Hooker should be able to show that it was possible to end their relationship in a civilised way, however much blood had flowed under the bridge. She should lead the way. She reached out tentatively and put her hand on the security chain.

Hooker must have heard its slight rattle. 'Lou, I'm begging you to let me in. It's beginning to rain out here.'

But not right now. Lou slid the chain firmly into place. 'I'm sorry, Hooker. I'm too tired to discuss anything. You can't come round and expect me to fall in with whatever you've decided any more. We've both got a lot to think about, so I suggest that's what we do.' She turned the key in the mortise lock and put it in Jenny's key box. 'We should talk. You're right about that. But not now. I'm sorry. I'll call you tomorrow.'

The bolt banged into place. She heard Hooker's tetchy sigh.

'I think you're being quite unreasonable. I've come here especially. I want you to think about us, about how we belong together. This has all been a terrible mistake. We'll talk.'

With that the letterbox snapped shut and, once again, she heard his footsteps on the path. Belong together. Had he really said that? She shook her head in wonder. What planet was he on? The self-confidence she'd once so envied and admired was shameless and still there, or was he merely exercising some misguided sense of what was his? How furious the idea made her.

He would have forgotten his words by the weekend or at least by the time someone else took his fancy. Put him in front of a woman and on flicked the automatic charm switch. For years, she had watched him at parties with their women friends, dispensing a wink, a fleeting touch, a sympathetic ear and even occasionally a shoulder. She saw them laughing at his jokes, leaning forward to catch every word, letting their eyes meet his before they glanced away, blushing ever so slightly. She'd lost count of the times she'd been told how lucky she was to have found a husband so interesting, so interested, a man who remembered a telling detail from the last conversation he'd held with any one of them, even a year or more later. She used to take pleasure in the attention he attracted, believing it to be a harmless game. She was the one he came home to. If only those women knew the half of it. He was like a fisherman casting a line. Most of the fish circled the bait and then swam away, but now and then one bit and he reeled her in.

She returned to the TV, bending to pick up the remote that she'd left on the floor. As she straightened up, she took a step back, catching her precariously balanced plate of supper with her elbow. The slice of quiche slid quietly, uncomplainingly, down the back of the bookcase. As she tried to rescue the rest of her food, she tipped the plate the other way so, despite her attempt to catch it, it landed upside down on the floor, potatoes rolling under the sofa, salad flattened, oil and balsamic soaking into the carpet. The *Mad Men* tune played on.

25

Gardening was not Lou's natural forte. When she and Hooker were finally blessed with a large town garden, they'd employed a gardener to impose order on the ever-encroaching forces of nature, much to the amazement and amusement of their friends and neighbours who all managed perfectly well without. But Hooker hadn't the time, and Lou hadn't the inclination: attitudes that probably summed up their future together. Enjoying a garden was one thing, getting down and dirty with it was quite another. Having expended a fortune on landscaping and replanting, Lou had then spent much of her marriage staring glumly at the muddy recreation pitch that was their lawn, the surrounding plants usually flattened and broken by footballs, tennis balls and rugby balls, wondering whether Astro-Turf and netting was the sensible answer. Why pretend? Where the boys saw a space

for a kick-about, Nic had shown little interest, preferring an indoor existence with
books and dolls. Her specially chosen patch
ended up choked with weeds instead of the
profusion of brilliant wildflowers promised
on the seed packet. No dedicated gardener
had been able to tolerate the routine devastation of their work so one after another,
they'd melted away. Eventually the children
grew up and order was restored but Lou
restricted herself religiously to the sort of
gardening that could be done in the early
evening with a glass of wine in one hand.

However, since she'd moved, she felt duty
bound to look after Jenny's garden herself.
Her sister wouldn't have liked a stranger
interfering with her careful plans and plant-
ing. Unlike Lou, Jenny had found real
pleasure in pottering about outside. Her
garden had been a perennial source of
relaxation and pride. Lou was hoping some
of that might rub off on her. So far, there'd
been no sign.

She was kneeling on the ground, surrounded by several black plastic pots containing a selection of bedding plants to fill
the gaps made by those that hadn't made it
through the winter. She picked one up,
holding it at arm's length and squinting at
the label, her right eye shut. The words

remained a frustrating blur.

'Here,' said Ali, from the comfort of her garden chair. She held out the green reading glasses that were balanced on the open RHS encyclopaedia. 'These any good?'

Lou winced as she straightened up, then put her hands on her hips and bent forward to ease the pain. 'My back's killing me after all this bending, I can't see without my reading glasses and I haven't a bloody clue what I'm doing. If Jenny's watching, she must be cracking up. I'm like a bloody geriatric. And look at my hands.' She splayed her earth-covered fingers and stared at them in despair before taking the glasses.

Ali pushed back her large sun specs on her nose and sipped her freshly made lemonade, then shivered as a sharp gust of wind took the edge off the sunshine. 'Gloves?'

'Couldn't find them. Besides, it's too late. The damage is done. I stopped looking after them when I stopped work. Don't know why. Some sort of perverse rejection, I suppose. Stupid really.' She picked up the pot again to check it was the blood red *nicotiana* that she hoped would give a splash of colour in Jenny's typically understated design. She was determined to make her own mark here, just as she had inside the house.

'A few manicures and you'd be amazed at the difference.' Ali examined her own nails, cut short but manicured to perfection, then returned the hand to her lap, satisfied. 'Perhaps I could help?'

'With those hands? You've got to be joking. Anyway, what do you know about gardening?'

'I'll have you know these are the hands of an artisan — in use every day. And I've got a window box,' Ali protested, stretching her arms out in the sunshine so the shell pink nail varnish caught the sun.

'Exactly. Look, I'll just get these in and then I'll stop. So what if I muddle them up? Monty Don isn't going to be checking up on me.' She arranged three of the pots in a triangle on the earth, then moved one to the side. Standing up with another groan, she took the spade and started digging, ignoring Ali's unhelpful directions until Ali took the hint, opened the paper and shut up. Lou soon had the plants in. She finally straightened up, screwing up her eyes against the stiffness in her objecting muscles. Her lower back was like a rusty hinge. She vowed to look up those Pilates classes at the local gym again, even though, deep down, she admitted she'd never go. But knowing they were there was the next best thing to actually doing them.

When she opened her eyes, she saw Ali pouring another glass of lemonade and holding it out to her. 'Get this down you. You deserve it.'

Lou flapped her large smock to cool herself down as a hot flush took over. As she accepted the glass, she sat in the other wrought-iron chair. 'I can't think why Jen ever got these.' She adjusted herself until she was as comfortable as she was ever going to get, feeling the imprint of the metal on her bum, then gazed at her handiwork. 'Perhaps I could get used to gardening after all. Perhaps this is my moment.' She subsided into silence, considering how much had happened since she had moved here, how much she had changed.

After a second, Ali spoke. 'Lou?'

'Mmm.'

'Don's asked me to live with him.'

Lou's head whipped round. 'He has? But that's great. Isn't that what you wanted?'

'Yes and no.' Ali stared into her lemonade as if the key to her future was floating there. 'Part of me feels it's all been so quick. Too quick.'

'So, what's the problem? There obviously

is one.' Lou kicked off her salmon pink Croc and scratched the top of her noticeably unpedicured foot.

'His being away on his executive think-tank thing last week really drove home how much I value my own space. I do want to live with him but, at the same time, I hate that my place isn't my own any more. Oh, God, that sounds awful.'

'No, it doesn't,' said Lou, identifying wholeheartedly with her sentiment. Since moving to Jenny's, she had enjoyed not having the pressure of having to tidy up for anyone else. Nic might raise her eyebrows at the chaos with which she sometimes surrounded herself but living that way came naturally.

Ali's face brightened for a second, obviously relieved to hear the sentiment was shared. Then she frowned, removing her dark glasses so she could look at Lou, as if that would make her understand more clearly. 'I'd just got everything back to the way I like it and now he's back messing it up again. He's even bought me a new potato peeler because he thinks it's better than mine!'

Lou couldn't help laughing. 'Listen to yourself. If it bothers you so much, why don't you talk to him about it?'

'I'm scared.' She picked at a cuticle, pushing the skin back from the nail. 'We get on so perfectly. He's everything I could want: a straightforward, loving guy who really seems to care about me. I do so love him, Lou, but I'm petrified that I'm going to drive him away.'

'Don't be ridiculous.' Lou was horrified to hear herself using Hooker's well-used phrase, and rushed to justify herself. 'At least if you both acknowledge the problem then you can do something about it. God knows, plenty of couples compromise. Separate beds, separate holidays, different houses: whatever makes it work. "Unconventional" doesn't equal "wrong".' She put the inverted commas round the words in the air. 'Just sort it out. Much the best thing.' She stacked up the empty flowerpots and turned on the hose to water in the new plants. 'Bread and soup OK?' she asked as she went inside. 'Oh, by the way,' she threw over her shoulder as she reached the door. 'Hooker's suggesting we get back together too.'

Ali's shriek accompanied her inside. As she put lunch on a tray, Lou wondered what Ali's reaction would be when she told her about her last conversation with Hooker. She had called him as she'd promised and had arranged that he would come round that evening to have the discussion he was so anxious for.

The rest of the afternoon passed quickly with the two women sitting, warmed by the sun, putting the world to rights, remembering with gales of laughter the moment Ali walked into the shop with Rory — how more perfect could her timing have been? — and discussing the preposterousness of Hooker's suggestion, dreaming up ways to house-train Don, wondering when Lou would next hear from Sanjeev, talking about business. The one subject they didn't touch on was Ali's parents. She made it quite clear that was a no-go area and no decisions had been made. However, they had enough easily to pass away the afternoon, thoroughly enjoying one another's company and opinions until the breeze became too sharp to ignore and clouds crowded the sky.

Hooker made himself at home rather more quickly than Lou might have liked. He was lounging on her sofa, his arm extended in a slightly too proprietorial fashion along its back. One leg was stretched out in front of him, the other bent, allowing Lou a glimpse of the striped designer socks she had bought him the previous Christmas. The bottle of wine was by his right foot, which is where Lou intended to keep it, even though there was absolutely no chance of a repeat of the last time Hooker, alcohol and she got involved. He was already halfway down his second glass.

After Ali had left, Lou had just enough time to throw on a pair of jeans and a loose floaty top that hid everything that needed to be hidden. 'Mutton dressed as?' she wondered as she turned in front of the mirror. Then, banishing the thought as unworthy, she applied the minimum of make-up, wanting at least to look presentable.

Now, they were in her sitting room and he had barely drawn breath since they'd sat down. He was behaving as if nothing had happened, as if Ali didn't exist. The situation had already taken on a slightly surreal quality. Lou had listened to how well he and Rory had got on, how he couldn't wait to have him to stay again, how relaxed Shona had been about the whole thing. Lou was eyeing with some frustration the *Bleak House* boxed set that Fiona had lent her and that was beckoning her from just beside the TV. 'Play me,' it whispered. She picked up her knitting so she had something to do that meant she didn't have to look at Hooker.

'The thing is, Lou, having Rory here has really brought home to me what matters.'

The pause that followed seemed increasingly ominous as the seconds ticked by. Hooker rearranged himself on the sofa so he was sitting forward, legs akimbo, arms buttressed on his knees, poised to share his conclusion. Lou waited.

'Family. That's what.' He paused again as if waiting for Lou to fall on him with delight now that he'd come to acknowledge what she had always known. She didn't move.

'You did say that, the other night,' she reminded him.

'You used to think that too. I know you did.' He gazed at her, clearly puzzled by her lack of reaction.

She knew how he hated her knitting, as if it meant she wasn't giving her full attention to whatever it was he was saying. This time, he couldn't have been more wrong.

'But Rory isn't part of my family,' she pointed out. 'He's yours.'

'You don't mean you didn't like him.' Hooker was astonished.

'Of course I don't mean that. He's a child. But he's not *my* child. Surely I don't have to spell it out for you?' How could they have been married without her realising how emotionally unintelligent he could sometimes be? Their wedding photos had shown a couple so confident in their future together: she pretty in a long, lacy cream dress and fine veil with flowers woven into her hair; he a good-looking man, hair touching the collar of his plum velvet suit. In fact, they had hardly skimmed the surface when it came to their knowledge of one another. These days, Hooker shone with worldly success that was reflected in his neatly arranged hair and his expensively casual jeans and striped shirt. His jacket had been carefully hung on the only hanger in the hall.

'You mean Shona?' His lips tightened as he sat straighter, carefully arranging his features into something designed to express his need to be understood. 'But that was a long time ago.'

'A long time, yes. But it happened. If you can't understand why it matters to me, then you don't understand me at all.'

'I know I haven't been everything you might have wanted in a husband, but most men slide from grace at some time or other during a marriage.' He let a small smile cross his lips as if inviting her agreement and therefore vindication. But he was disappointed.

'We're not talking about everyone, Hooker. I don't give a damn about what other people do. We're talking about you and me. And it's not as if Shona was a one-off. There's Ali too.'

The words hung between them in the silence that followed. Lou reached for the bottle, momentarily forgetting her resolve. She filled her glass, then put it on the coffee table. No, she was going to withstand temptation.

Hooker was the first to speak, his eyes dark with anger. 'If you knew, why didn't you say anything?'

'Because I didn't know. I only suspected. With the children living with us, I didn't want anything to spoil their growing up. If I'd said something, if I'd questioned you, then everything might have been different. If we'd split up, what would that have done to them?'

'But we wouldn't have split up.' Hooker sounded incredulous. 'I'd never have left you. Never. That's not what it was about.'

'But I might have wanted to leave you,' Lou said, exasperated at his lack of empathy and by the fact that she had to spell it out. 'But now it doesn't matter.'

'Because you've found someone else?' There was something in his voice that she didn't recognise. Regret?

'No. It's not that.' She wasn't going to

share anything of her relationship with San-jeev with him. That was something she was going to enjoy on her terms without its being spoilt by Hooker's interference or derogatory comments.

'If I wasn't the perfect husband, I'm sorry. But it's not too late for us.'

So here they were, at the point, at last. Lou said nothing, unable to trust herself. Instead she ran her eye along the clothes rail behind him, reminding herself of what she had hanging there, mentally tagging the items she needed to take to the shop.

Hooker put down his empty glass and clasped his hands in appeal. 'I've never stopped loving you, you know, whatever's been going on.'

'Oh, please,' Lou implored under her breath, picking up her knitting again.

'I was horrified when I realised you knew about the other women.'

'Other women,' she repeated. 'How many were there exactly?'

'I'm going to be honest with you. You deserve that.' He looked at his hands, his thumb nudging at his signet ring. 'There were others, but Shona and Ali were the only long-term relationships. Really. And none of them meant anything next to you. If only you'd just said something, asked me straight out, I'd have confessed. I'd have told you everything and made it all right.'

'So it's my fault?' Lou was bewildered by his logic.

'That's not what I'm saying. I want you to understand how it was, though. I want Nic to understand. I know she's furious and has lost all respect for me.'

'She's not alone.' Lou couldn't resist. She introduced a blue and a yellow wool into the pattern of the jumper.

'I know, I know. Do you know how that makes me feel?'

'Bad, I hope.' *Five stitches blue. Two stitches yellow. Repeat till the end of the row.*

'Yes, it does. Very bad indeed. I want to make things better, to have them the way they were before. That's why I've asked Emma to leave.'

Lou looked up, surprised that Hooker had taken action. When she returned her attention to her knitting, she'd dropped three stitches. She began the work of hooking them back up.

He smoothed his hair. 'I knew she and I didn't have a future together. She was upset, of course, but I need you, Lou. Just like you need me.' He sounded as if he was expecting her agreement. 'Nothing's changed.'

She put down her handiwork. This conversation needed her full attention. Perhaps he really did believe that there was hope for them; that they could pick up where they'd left off. God knows, she'd hung onto that same belief until she'd had to let it go. She looked out of the window into the night. Her reflection returned her stare: grave and considered. She pulled her hair back off her face and then let it go so it sprang back into place.

She heard the glug of more wine being poured. When she looked at him again, Hooker had another drink in his hand. 'All I'm asking is for you to give it one more go. You can't like living here. Not really.' He looked around him, taking in the clothes rail, the few hats and bags on the top shelf of the bookcase, the TV almost obscured by her favourite tailor's dummy that she'd used when her last private customer came. The sitting room was so much more comfortable for a fitting — better than squeezing into her workroom where her table and fabrics took up so much of the space. Suddenly she saw it through his eyes, the general disarray, the coloured threads on the carpet that she hadn't got round to vacuuming, the balls of wool escaping from her knitting bag, the fashion prints and samplers not quite aligned on the walls, the

465

posy of garden flowers that spilled au naturel (for want of a better way of describing the lack of arrangement) from the little white jug. She hurriedly straightened her back numbers of *Vogue* into a pile, immediately cross with herself that she let him still provoke her into tidiness. She touched the top copy so that it half slid off onto the tabletop.

'I love it here,' she said.

'But if you came home, we could rent this place — the income would be useful for your business, I bet — and turn the old playroom into a workroom, and Jamie's or Tom's room into storage.' His pleasure in the scheme was apparent in his face. He had it all planned and was confident she wasn't going to say no.

Lou could imagine how badly Nic would take any transformation of her room, which had stayed a shrine to her teenage years since she moved out. There was little hope for he who dared violate it. Very occasionally, Nic would return home and shut herself in, rearrange the soft toys on the duvet, pull out the boxes from the bottom of her wardrobe, then stretch herself out on the bed and pore over her old notebooks and photos, with her favourite old bands at full volume, none of them names that Lou could remember, if she'd ever heard of them.

Being lost in the image for a second was enough to provoke memories of all those occasions that she would love to have back — family lunches, birthday celebrations, long chats in front of the fire, drinks in the garden, watching a film together on TV, Tom at the fridge door, Jamie making lumpy gravy with the zeal of a seasoned chef, the Christmas when the lights fused when Tom attempted to put up outdoor tree lights. These were the times that had fortified her and kept her going.

As long as she was living at Jenny's, they would never happen again. Perhaps she should reconsider . . . She stopped herself. She didn't need any extra income to keep the business ticking over, not yet at least, and as for transforming the playroom to a workroom — that said it all. A playroom was all it ever would be in Hooker's eyes. The only difference was that it would be Lou at play, rather than the kids. How could he possibly imagine that she would ever agree? There was so much that prevented them from loving one another again. And yet . . . She was about to voice all her objections when she realised Hooker was on his feet.

'I've changed and I know we could make it work.'

These were the silken tones that had insinuated him into so many other women's beds, she thought.

'Just think about it, Lou,' he said softly. 'Don't say anything now. I'll wait till you're ready. Think how pleased the children will be.' With the deftness of a magician, he had offered her control over the decision, then whisked it away again.

Mesmerised by his manipulation of the conversation, by his ability to manoeuvre her to where he wanted despite her resistance, by the residue of feeling she still had for him — despite everything — she let him go with a murmured agreement to think about it. She took a neat step back, unable to avoid his kiss goodbye but making sure it was only her cheek that was on offer. 'Grandparents together,' he whispered, but quite loud enough for her to hear. Then he was gone.

From behind the front door, she heard his car door slam, then the revving of the engine before he drove off. She returned to her so far untouched glass of wine and made swift work of it. She remembered how, for one brief moment, she had been tempted to agree to his proposal. He had spotted that and immediately turned it to his advantage, leaving at precisely the right moment on the right note. She thought of their children, of Nic. If she went back to Hooker, Nic would have to readjust her opinion of her father. If Lou could forgive and forget then perhaps Nic could too. That had to be an important consideration, one that definitely swayed her. And, even if her business wasn't insolvent, it would be good to have some extra money to play with. At least, living with Hooker, she wouldn't have to deal with Jenny's garden any longer. Perhaps there were reasons why she should consider moving home. She would lead her own life, just as she had done before she left but on her terms. She would pick up her friendships that had been dropped since her departure. But was there any possibility that she could love Hooker again? That they could be happy grandparents together? Could she exorcise her anger and distrust towards the man who had so betrayed her?

And then she thought about Sanjeev.

26

Ali was getting dressed when she heard the sound of Don's doorbell. She applied some tinted moisturiser, then concentrated on her eyes, smudging the eye pencil and lashing on the mascara, before smearing a pale balm on her lips. The smell of coffee and breakfast wafted under the bedroom door. The standard of catering had gone up a notch since she'd been granted her wish and had been allowed to put his kitchen to rights.

A week had passed since her conversation with Lou about not wanting to give up her independence or to share her living space: a week of self-criticism and deliberation. In the end, she had decided to follow her friend's advice. She couldn't pretend to Don to be somebody other than she was. If their relationship was to stand a chance, it had to be based on the same absolute honesty that they themselves had demanded of Eric just a few weeks earlier.

470

Ready, she checked herself in the mirror and went to join him. In the dark inner hallway that linked the four rooms of the riverside apartment, she was surprised to hear a woman's voice coming from the living room. She hesitated for a second, then opened the door. She saw Don turn quickly, like a man grabbing for a lifeline. Her earlier good mood was overtaken by a premonition that something bad was about to happen.

The visitor was smaller than Ali, slightly older and plumper, with a generous deeply tanned cleavage on show between the lapels of her open coat. Fading blondish hair like spun sugar was arranged around a face in which the features had already blurred with age, the flesh sliding south to settle on her jawline, and a pair of beady eyes clearly summing up what she saw in Ali. On the floor beside her was a large suitcase.

Ali was sure the woman's look of surprise at her entrance reflected her own. The fact that Don still made no move to introduce them made her the more uneasy. However, the other woman jumped to her feet and offered her hand. Ali shook it.

'Hiya,' the woman said, immediately identifying herself as Australian as well as revealing the stain of lipstick on her left front tooth. 'I'm Susie, Donny's wife. Just

471

arrived.' Ali didn't miss the confrontation in her voice as she stared at her, unable to speak.

And nor, judging by the speed of his response, did Don, stung into life at last. '*Ex*-wife, Susie,' he corrected her. 'Remember?' He was about to introduce Ali but Susie didn't let him get a word in.

'Come on, Don. That's just a technicality,' she wheedled. 'I haven't signed the divorce papers yet. Remember? And now, maybe I won't have to.'

Ali felt her legs weaken. 'But I thought . . .' she began, as she took a seat. 'You never said.' She caught Susie's short but triumphant smile.

Don crossed the room to put his arm round her shoulders, to reassure her. 'I'm as surprised as you are by this. I promise you.'

Susie joined them, pulling out a chair for herself. She was clearly not a woman who was easily deterred. 'And you are?'

'This is Ali Macintyre, my girlfriend.'

'Mmm, interesting.' This time the smile stayed for longer. 'Don and I need to sort out a few things, so —'

'For God's sake, Susie,' Don interrupted her, visibly shaken. 'This is crazy. What're you doing here? Where's Mike?'

'Back in Melbourne where I left him.' Said with another of those smiles.

'What? You mean you've broken up?' This was obviously news to Don.

'We've decided to go our separate ways, yes.' Susie gave a small smile. 'So I decided to have a few weeks in Europe and while in the UK, I thought I should look you up and see if we can't mend our fences.'

'I think I'd better go,' interrupted Ali, anxious to get out of there before she showed her upset. She avoided catching Susie's eye although she was conscious that the other woman was making herself comfortable, kicking off her shoes and tucking one plump leg beneath her sizeable behind.

'No, Ali, we've got the day planned,' Don protested. 'If anyone's leaving, it's Susie.' But Susie was evidently going nowhere. He followed Ali into the hall, shutting the door behind him to muffle Susie's querulous protest, and pulling her into the bedroom. 'Sit down. Please. You can't leave without hearing me out. I had no idea she was going to turn up, or that she was even in the country. I promise. As far as I'm concerned we're as good as divorced. Our relationship was over long ago. Obviously something's gone wrong with Mike, the guy she left me for, but if she thinks we're going to make another go of it, she's quite wrong. Why do you think I left the country? Ali, listen to me. Give me time to explain the situation to her so that she leaves.'

His words tumbled around her as she sat on the edge of the bed, frozen, unable to take in what he was saying. All that was running through her head was the fact that he had let her down, just like Hooker. He had lied, just like Hooker. She'd believed he was different but he was just the same as the others after all. Just like Hooker. Except that this time, with his wife in another country, she'd been fooled into believing that what they had was really different. But, no. Another woman had a prior claim on him after all. She felt as if her trust, everything she believed, had been tossed in the air. If Don had told her he was still married then at least she would have known where she stood. She knew how to play the mistress. The one thing she could do well. Her priority was to get out of his apartment. She put a hand on his arm that he immediately covered with his own.

'Don, stop! Please! I don't know what to think. You've obviously got to deal with this. Call me when you're done and we'll talk.' She had a feeling that Susie might not be as easy to shift as he was anticipating.

She had to make herself walk away from the flat and from him, when all she wanted to do was run back inside and turn back the clock half an hour and wipe out what had just happened. Instead she pressed the button for the lift, and when it came she watched him through the closing doors as he went back inside his flat to his wife.

She made her way to the studio almost without thinking. Rick had taken his daughter to see his parents for the weekend so Ali knew that she would be undisturbed there. As she walked, she felt at one remove from the rest of the world. Everybody else's lives were carrying on as normal, when everything had changed for her.

She took her blue overall off the back of the door and slipped it on. As she crossed to the workbench, she kicked the metal bin out of her way, the clatter breaking the silence. She removed her Converse and massaged her big toe. What was she to do? Perhaps Don's still being married was punishment for all the affairs she'd had with other women's husbands. The wives who had always been in the background, the women whose feelings she had never considered while she was enjoying herself with their partners, rose up to avenge themselves:

a battalion of wronged women determined to make her pay.

For the first time, she knew the sort of pain she must have inflicted on all those women whose relationships and whose future she'd threatened.

Ali reached across for her portfolio that she'd left on the table and began leafing through the pages where all the engagement and wedding rings that she had made for other women mocked her. She closed it and went over to the bench, then stopped. She was too preoccupied to embark on any detailed work.

Back on the sofa, she picked up her sketchpad and began to draw, only half concentrating as her thoughts took her back to Don. This time she was not going to let go without a fight. When Hooker had dumped her, she had accepted the situation for what it was however much she disliked it. Both men had lied to her, but her different reactions only underlined the difference in her feelings for them both. And theirs for her. Don wanted her. She was as sure as she could be of that although mystified and angry as to why he hadn't confessed to still being married. Something as significant can hardly have slipped his mind. Then again, they never had talked about marriage.

Perhaps he really hadn't wanted to upset her if, as he said, divorce was just a formality.

But he had kept the truth from her. Just as her father had. It had been in their interests to let her believe what she wanted to, without correcting her. Time and again she came back to this same point. After all that they had said about the necessity of truth. Then she pulled herself up short. She hadn't been entirely truthful with Don either. They had both chosen not to discuss the areas of their lives which might cause difficulties between them. All she wanted now was for him to get rid of Susie as soon as possible so they could straighten everything out once and for all. Cards on the table. She was going to do everything she could towards achieving that goal. Making up with her father could wait.

She looked at what she'd been doodling. Her page was covered with broken hearts cracked in zigzags or speared by daggers and arrows. She stared at them for a moment. She took her pencil and was about to put a line through them, when she visualised the jottings made up into brooches and earrings: gold that glittered with rubies, rose quartz or coral. She had a feeling Lou would love them. She made some brief notes before returning to the problem of Susie. What she needed was a plan. Seated at the bench she took her soldering torch and began to anneal a piece of gold she would eventually shape into a brooch. As she hammered, she began to feel better.

They walked briskly, Ali setting the pace, Lou trying not to lag behind. Exercising the body was a good thing, Lou told herself. She could feel the sting of a blister on the back of her heel, her T-shirt sticking to her back, her fingers beginning to tighten and swell. Why had she let herself be persuaded into this? Ali's and her ideas of a 'stroll' clearly couldn't be more different. When Ali had suggested it, she'd imagined them ambling around Kenwood, chatting, then after a decent interval heading for the café. Instead, she'd been dragged out on a gruelling route march that covered the entire Heath. Ali seemed to know the place intimately as she cut through undergrowth on barely visible paths, ducked under branches to enter woods, then routed back onto the more frequented tarmac paths where joggers and dog walkers dodged the couples and families who moved at a more leisurely pace. Lou stared after them, envious of their lack of speed. Further up the hill, a yellow plastic octopus hovered high in the sky while a couple of stunt kites whirred and twisted in the wind threatening the strings of the simple coloured diamonds being launched by a couple of fathers and their less than enthusiastic kids. She was reminded of their own family trips up here armed with the boys' kites. That craze had lasted for two or three summers in a row and then was abandoned once Hooker lost interest, Tom and Jamie relieved to be able to follow suit. The kites were probably still rolled up somewhere in the garden shed, now long forgotten.

At last she crested the hill to find Ali standing by a bench stretching her quads and hamstrings, looking enviably athletic in body-hugging Lycra. Lou had said nothing when her friend stripped off her tracksuit top and jeans in the car park, too anxious about the seriousness with which Ali seemed to be taking the walk to be able to speak. Lou joined her and immediately sat down. Her throat was burning and her calves zinging. She undid her left trainer and rolled down her sock to examine her heel. The surrounding skin of the soft creamy blister was red and tender. She winced as she rolled the sock back and returned her foot into her shoe.

'Sorry, but I can't walk, think and talk all at once. Not at that speed anyway.' Ahead of them the city spread out into the far distance like a vast architectural patchwork. Beyond the immediate trees, Lou located the familiar landmarks: the Shard, the Gherkin, St Paul's, the Millennium Wheel, the BT Tower. Under a blue sky criss-crossed by the cloudy vapour trails marking the flight paths of innumerable passenger jets, this was London at its best. She felt the sun on her face and shut her eyes, wishing away the insistent pain of her heel.

'I'm sorry.' Ali sat beside her. 'If I push myself, it clears my mind, helps me think.'

The faint citrusy scent of her perfume reached Lou. She squeezed her arms against her sides, aware that her own smell was less than fresh after her exertions. 'So what have you decided?' she asked, turning her head slightly so she could see Ali out of the corner of her eye.

'I'm angry. We've talked on the phone and he says he loves me, but she's still there! I'm angry with him for not having the balls to tell me the truth about her. And I'm angry with her for thinking she can just muscle her way back in and take over. And I'm angry with myself.' Her face was set, more determined than Lou remembered having seen it before.

'She's hardly taking over. She is his wife.' Lou pointed out that small consideration that Ali seemed to have forgotten, taking the Twix she'd brought for this moment out of her pocket. She offered to share the melting fingers of chocolate.

Ali shook her head. '*Was* his wife. There's a big difference. You, of all people, should know that.'

Lou said nothing.

'I've got to do something,' Ali insisted.

'Mmm,' mused Lou, pointing out an unwelcome truth as she took a mouthful of biscuit. 'I've always wondered: didn't you ever stop once to think about the wives of the men you were seeing, what they might be going through because of you?'

'But this isn't the same at all. I really wasn't a threat to them,' Ali protested, brushing away an insistent fly. 'That was the whole point. I told you. I knew nothing about them. I didn't want to take their men from them. I didn't think about them like that. Until Hooker broke the rules.'

'Quite,' said Lou quietly. 'But those women weren't to know that.'

'I suppose. And you do know how bad I feel about Hooker.' She reached across to link her arm through Lou's.

'Only in retrospect, because we're friends. I'd have made you feel a lot worse if I'd ever found you living with him! Believe me. Anyway, you're not about to lose Don. You said he was as stunned by her appearance as you were. He's not going to put up with her staying, is he?'

Ali was staring into the middle distance. 'He says not but, you know what?' She turned her gaze to Lou. 'I'm not going to hang around to find out. I'm going over there to have a full and frank conversation with the woman. I'm going to make her realise Don and I are serious and that she's not wanted.'

'Shouldn't he be the one doing that?' There was something slightly unhinged about Ali's proposed plan that made Lou uneasy.

'Of course. But it's taking him so long.'

'I thought he was good at confrontation. Look at the way he handled Eric.'

'But that wasn't his problem. That was between Dad and me. He just made the resolution possible.' She picked a small white daisy and tore the petals off one after another, tossing them into the breeze. 'You see, he does love me.'

'I don't really see the difference. The point is he got you both to the point where you could talk.'

'I know, I know. But I feel I've got to do something, say something, or I'll go mad.' Ali kicked at a half-buried stone.

'You really think that'll work?' she asked. 'Why would she take any notice of you? I wouldn't. In fact, having you turn up would make me even more determined to stick around.'

'Yes.' Ali scuffed patterns in the dust with her feet. 'Perhaps you're right.' She kicked at a stone that remained wedged in the earth. 'I know! You'll have to go instead.'

'Me? Don't be daft. She's not going to listen to me.' She wasn't entirely sure whether Ali was joking or not.

'But she might if you were telling her something about Don that she wouldn't want to hear.'

'No, no and no. What do want me to say — that I'm having his baby?' She stuck out her stomach and stroked it. They both laughed, although Ali less enthusiastically. Lou stood up, the pressure on her blister making it smart. But Ali didn't move, except to look up at her.

'Look, all you have to do, is go there and pretend that he owes you money, say. A lot of money. Perhaps knowing he isn't worth what she thinks would put her off. Perhaps that's what she's after.'

'She's never going to believe that. No.' Lou began to limp away, still laughing.

Ali rose and caught her up. 'What if you said you were his mistress, then? Three's a crowd, right?'

'Look . . .' Lou stopped so abruptly that two girls behind them almost walked into her. She stepped to one side with an apology as they walked past, tottering on their stacked espadrilles. 'This is stupid. I might as well tell her he's a cross-dresser with an opium habit. She's not going to believe anything I say. Would you?'

'Nooo.' Ali sounded uncertain, all the same. 'But I can't risk her getting her claws in. The longer she's here . . .'

'But, Al,' Lou objected. 'Don't you trust him? If you don't, then what are you fighting for?'

'I do, really. It's just her. Our history might not stack up to much against theirs, but her getting involved has made me real-ise how much I love him . . .' She broke off as her voice choked. 'I haven't seen him for five days. He's worried about seeing me because he doesn't "want to get her back up because then she'll be even harder to shift".' She mimicked Don's excuse in a high-pitched sing-song, but a tear sploshed onto her top and her chin wobbled as she struggled to control herself.

Until that moment, Lou hadn't really appreciated how badly Susie's appearance had rattled Ali. The tough, self-sufficient facade that she was used to had cracked open to reveal a new, more vulnerable side to her friend.

'Look. Either he wants you or he doesn't. You can't go on like this, so perhaps you *should* go round there. Not to confront *her* — that would be madness — but to talk to both of them. It won't be easy and I wouldn't want to do it, but that way at least you'll know.'

Ali shook her head. 'But this isn't how I wanted it to be. This is our second chance. God, I know I sound like someone out of a bad romantic novel, but I couldn't bear it if I lost him again.' She put her hands to her face, her fingers rubbing along the lines of her eye sockets.

'Then you must make sure you don't. Come on, let's get that coffee.'

Following the tarmacked path, Lou made sure she was the one who set the pace, and to something a little less gruelling than before. As they walked, she listened as Ali continued to thrash out her dilemma, retreading the same ground as she convinced herself that insisting on seeing Don and Susie was the right thing to do. But however much she empathised, Lou knew that only one of them could take responsibility for Ali's final decision, and that was Ali herself. She was pleased to be her sounding board, and to offer an opinion when needed, but she couldn't help letting her mind drift to Sanjeev, grateful that their relationship was so much less complicated and intense. The better she had got to know him, the more she felt there was a chance they might reach a happy and relaxed arrangement that would suit them both. Beyond that, she was looking forward to a long bath and a night in when she could confirm to herself the rightness of her decisions about her future. She hadn't mentioned Hooker's attempt to get back into her life to anyone else, simply because she didn't want her decision to be influenced by anyone else's opinions. After all, she was the one who was going to have to live with her choice.

27

The nearer she got to Don's apartment block, the more nervous Ali became. With every step, the idea of any kind of confrontation with him and Susie grew less appealing. He had sounded doubtful when she'd called to say that she was coming over but he hadn't tried to stop her. Now she rather wished he had. She had kept their conversation to a minimum. Everything that needed to be said should be said face to face. With or without Lou's help, she was determined to put her relationship with him back on track. She accepted that she was as guilty as he was of not telling the whole story, so whatever his reasons, she would accept them. How much she had changed in such a short time. After Hooker had shown his true colours and she had met Don again, everything had fallen into place. Between them, the two men had made her focus on what she wanted from the rest of her life and where her priorities lay. She finally felt a clarity of purpose that had been missing from most of her adult life.

Arriving at the base of the sinuously curved, largely glass tower block in which he lived, she pressed the entrance buzzer. After a few moments, she heard Don's voice, distorted over the intercom. 'Hallo?'

'It's Ali,' she said, keeping her voice steadier than she felt.

'Come up.' Then he had gone. A click alerted to her to the door opening. She pushed it wide, wished the doorman a good afternoon and walked to the lift. Before pressing the button, she quickly removed her trainers, swapped them with the heels in her bag and rolled down the legs of her bootcuts. As the lift shuddered into movement, she checked her reflection in its mirrored walls. She had dressed to look seductive but formidable — jeans and the vintage check jacket. Her fingers fiddled with her fringe, pushing its weight to one side. She leaned forward to examine her face more closely, rubbing her cheeks in case she'd overdone the blusher. At that moment, the lift stopped with a judder and the doors opened.

The corridor was empty. The blank white walls looked hygienic and character free, just as she imagined those in a Swiss sanatorium. The only splash of colour was the psychedelic coloured doormat marking Don's front door. As she raised her hand to press the bell, she was seized again by doubt. Was this the most sensible way for a grown woman to behave? There was still time for her to beat a retreat and insist on meeting Don alone. That would be more sensible. What had she been thinking? She turned back towards the lift. At that moment, the door opened.

'Ali?'

She swung round. Seeing him again, everything she was going to say, all that she'd carefully rehearsed aloud the night before, flew from her head.

'Leaving already?'

At that slightly quizzical smile, her stomach turned over. She reminded herself that she was not a lovesick teenager but a woman on a mission to get what she wanted. Him.

'Er, no. Just thought I must have dropped my gloves in the lift.'

'The ones that are hanging out of your bag?' He pulled the door wide. Behind him, the door to his living room was shut. Behind it lurked the monster she had come to vanquish.

'Oh, yes! Of course.' With a forced laugh,

she folded them and stashed them safely before zipping her bag, catching the lining so it wouldn't completely close. She pretended nothing was wrong.

'Come in.'

If she wasn't mistaken the small bow he made mocked her.

'Thanks.' Ali gathered the last of her wits and went inside. With him behind her, unable to see her face, she closed her eyes, took a deep breath and pushed open the living-room door with a flourish.

The room was empty. Her first impression was of the drifts of paper that covered the dining table and spread from there across the floor to the bright red sofa facing towards the Thames. On the kitchen counter, a half loaf of bread was upended by a bread knife, two unwashed mugs and an open tub of reduced fat spread. She could see the crumbs in it from where she was standing. A plastic supermarket bag sat unpacked by the hob. The dining table looked like the office desk of an inveterate hoarder: opened envelopes and plastic files were piled higgledy-piggledy around an open laptop. Susie was obviously nowhere near as pernickety as herself. But of course that probably suited Don far better than her own obsessive tidiness, she thought with a pang of regret. However, there was no evidence of a female presence in the room. All Susie's stuff must be stashed in the bedroom, despite the shortage of storage space. Ali experienced a tiny pang of anguish as she remembered the last time she was in there herself.

'Where's Susie? I was hoping to see you both?' Yes, she sounded appropriately commanding. Too commanding, perhaps.

Don had followed her into the room and was wrestling to impose some sort of order on the paper trail, gathering the pages and heaping them onto a dining chair. 'Not here.'

'But didn't I say . . .' Her voice tailed off as she realised this wasn't going to be her moment after all. The battle would have to be deferred. Deflated didn't come close to summing up what she felt.

'Yes, but she couldn't hang around.' Don looked up for a second before he carried on sorting out a space where they could sit, hardly bothering to hide his smile.

Ali tried again. 'Didn't you tell her I was coming? I need to talk to her.' She despaired of besting her rival now. Don's smile of pleasure at the mention of her name had said it all.

'Sorry.' This time he could barely contain

his amusement. The bastard was laughing at her!

Feeling about two feet tall and wishing she was anywhere but there, she turned for the door. There was no point arranging a rematch if she had already lost him.

'She had a plane to catch.'

It took a moment for the words to register. Then, before she'd had time to face him, his arms were wrapped about her. He was kissing the back of her neck, below her ear, her cheek. She inched herself round until at last she was facing him and could see his grin. Never had anyone looked so pleased with themselves. She pulled back from his embrace. 'You're squeezing me to death! What do you mean?'

'Susie's gone back to Australia.' His grin threatened to split his face. 'I took her to the airport myself at lunchtime, just to make sure. I didn't want to say anything until she'd gone but then you were so damn pushy about coming over, I couldn't stop you.'

'What happened?' She was beginning to feel faint but quite definite stirrings of euphoria.

'Two things.' Don took her hand and led her to the sofa where they sat, knee to knee. Over his shoulder, she could see a police helicopter flying parallel to the river like a giant gnat. 'I told her that she couldn't stay, that there was no future for us under any circumstances. I won't bore you with the tears and tantrums but she eventually accepted that I meant what I said. But then, a miracle happened. As she was packing, Mike called to plead with her to return home. Poor sod. But the combination did the job. She's gone back to him, after all.'

'She agreed to the divorce?' Ali was having trouble taking the information in. She had built herself up to say her piece, and now the ground had been whipped from under her.

'Of course.' He placed both his hands on her knees and gave them a reassuring squeeze. 'She's a determined woman but not a bad one. What I needed was time to persuade her. I told you in the park that I wasn't going to let you go again. You should have trusted me.'

'I'd even prepared a speech.'

'You could always try it out on me anyway.' Don lay back against the sofa, crossing his arms over his chest, looking expectant.

'No way.'

'Shame to waste a good speech. Give me the gist then.'

Self-conscious, Ali looked down at her knees, wishing his hands were still there. As if he'd read her mind, he changed position and grasped both her hands. How stupid she had been to think that she could ever influence him or, more particularly, his ex-wife. Working out their own agenda was something only they could do. He was right. She should have trusted him. And she should have listened to Lou.

'Oh, you don't want to hear it. I was so crazy to have you back that I'd have sounded like a madwoman. You'd probably have begged her to stay after that.'

'No,' he said quietly, reaching out to stroke Ali's cheek, the teasing gone from his voice. 'No, I wouldn't. It's you and me from now on. For better for worse. All that stuff.'

'Is that a proposal?' she half joked in an embarrassed attempt to lighten the mood, but seeing how serious Don looked, wished she hadn't.

'Perhaps it's a bit indecent to be asking you quite so soon after Susie's departure but, yes. If that's what you want then it's a proposal.' His thumb ran up and down her ring finger.

The breath stopped in her throat. She looked around her, calming herself by looking at her surroundings, his way of being.

She took in all his clutter, the paper, the chaotic kitchen, the disordered shelves, the dining table. She remembered his bedroom, the clothes that had missed the laundry basket, the disordered wardrobe. Then she remembered the mess in which he left her bathroom and the stubble in her basin along with his jumbled drawers, his enormous shoes lying in wait to trip her up, the pristine apartment that she loved, the conversation she'd had with Lou. 'But I can't,' she moaned.

His thumb stopped moving. His expression changed from one of dreamy optimism to confusion. His eyes clouded. 'Why ever not? I thought that was what you wanted.'

'It is. I do. But . . .' She stopped, knowing how trite and self-obsessed she was about to sound. The bewilderment on his face made her hesitate. How much easier it would be to say nothing. Yet this relationship had to be based on honesty. If she didn't admit to her feelings now, there'd only be trouble later. And in due course, she'd have to tell him about Hooker and the others as well. But not this minute.

'But what? There's nothing to stop us now. Or is there something you haven't told me?' He sounded suddenly wary.

'Yes, there is. Just one thing. I want to be

with you, marry you even, but I *can't* live with you.' There, she'd said it. She didn't dare look at him, not wanting to see his disappointment or even his anger. All she could hear was the ticking of the clock on the bookshelf, a distant shout from somewhere outside. The longer Don was silent, the more tense the moment felt. Ali concentrated on dropping her shoulders, which were in danger of eclipsing her ears. She closed her eyes and tried to explain. 'I'm so sorry. I don't really expect you to understand — why should you? — but I've lived on my own ever since you left and I guess I'm just a bit, well . . .' How to describe herself best so that he would understand?

'Independent? Set in your ways? Obstinate?' He filled the gap for her. But he didn't sound angry. She opened her eyes, expecting to see him tight-lipped and unforgiving. To her astonishment, he was smiling.

'Yes, I suppose so,' she said uncertainly, not at all sure where they were going with this.

'That's fine.' Don leaned towards her and kissed the tip of her nose.

'It is?' This time it was Ali's turn to stare in bewilderment.

'Of course. We're both too set in our ways to change them at the drop of a hat. I've seen how much you value your own space and how much you love that apartment. And I know how untidy I am and how irritated it makes you.' He gave a rueful smile. 'I'm not saying, never the twain shall meet. Who knows? But how about keeping our own places and extending each other copious conjugal visitation rights? Wouldn't that work?'

Another pinch-me moment. After so many years of being on her own, establishing her independence, she had found a man who understood her. Or at least, understood her better than anyone else ever had. And, more than that, who wanted to commit himself to her one hundred per cent. 'You really mean that? You'd do that?'

'Of course I do, you idiot. Just one thing?'

'Mmm?' There had to be a hitch and here it came, galloping towards her. She waited, tense.

'What would you think about my moving nearer to you?'

Shared evenings, morning runs and weekends coursed through Ali's mind as she envisaged them getting the most out of each other's company and yet being able to retreat home alone when necessary. His work and his dirty washing could clutter his own flat. He could go there to listen to

Genesis, Dylan, whatever, at full volume, or watch football till he was blue in the face. She could continue to enjoy her home as she knew it. Surely the perfect solution. At least for the time being. She kissed him, feeling him relax and respond in kind, before she disengaged herself and said, 'I can't think of anything I'd like better.'

'I can think of one thing *I*'d like better, right now,' he added, the twinkle back in his eye.

'What?' She didn't think she could take another surprise.

'Follow me.' He stood and pulled Ali to her feet. Finding no resistance, he led her from the room across the hall and into the bedroom.

A couple of hours later, they emerged, flushed but booted and suited to face the rest of the day. Ali was reluctant to leave but had promised to meet Rick at the studio to go through his first collection for Lou. As she left the flat, Don folded up the edge of his doormat to hold the door while he walked her to the lift. As she reached the ground floor, she took out her phone to find two texts and a missed call. One was from Don sent half a minute earlier:

Luv u. This is def the rt thing. D xx

She smiled and ran her finger over the

words before scrolling to the next text. This announced a missed call from none other than Mrs Orlov. She immediately switched to the voicemail to hear her customer's excuse of being out of the country for reasons she couldn't explain, and about which Ali didn't care, then punched the air in the knowledge that the jewellery was going to be collected and paid for after all. And the last from Hooker:

Call me, please

She pressed the Delete button without a thought.

She hardly noticed her journey to the studio. Don had made good his words of all those years ago, and had come back. Susie was part of his past. As importantly, they had settled on a modus vivendi that would suit them both — for the time being at least. Perhaps one day she would feel differently but not having that pressure to change was the best gift he could have given her.

As soon as she walked into the studio, Rick looked, not very subtly, at his watch. 'What kept you? You're never usually late. I've got to get off in a minute.'

'Relax. We won't take long. Call her to say you'll be half an hour late, that it's your business partner's fault.' Ali wasn't going to let anything spoil her mood.

'How do you know it's a her?' He took a tray from the bench and brought it to the table.

'I know you!' She took off her jacket and hung it on the back of the door before joining him on the sofa. Since Rick had paid off his debt to her (she hadn't asked how he'd found the money), the awkwardness between them had vanished and their friendship was back on track. And now, Ali was delighted if her connection with Lou could mean a break for him too. She picked up one of three open-ended bangles loosely modelled on the outer petals of an iris and turned it in her hand. She slipped the bracelet over her hand and twisted her arm to examine it from different angles. 'Rick, this is wonderful.'

He looked pleased. 'I'm glad you like them. That means a lot. I had to experiment a bit but I think I've got it now.' He stared at her. 'Has something happened? You've been grinning like a lunatic ever since you came in.'

She picked up one of his sweet-pea earrings between her thumb and forefinger and held it so it hung against the black velvet pad they kept for display. Again, he'd managed to catch the fragility of the flower through the undulating silver. 'I'm sure these will sell.'

'Hope so, I could do with a change in fortune. So . . . Are you going to tell me or not?'

Unable to keep her own good fortune to herself for another minute, as she examined the rest of his work, Ali began to tell him everything.

28

At the sound of the door opening, Lou looked up from her work table, pleased to have an excuse to stop working on the set of accounts that lay in front of her. On the other side of the counter, the shop was exactly as she'd once imagined it with her own designs complementing the mint-condition vintage stock. Her careful selection was paying off. She had built up the accessories, modern and retro, until the shelves were crowded with hats, bags and belts competing for space. The only line was drawn at shoes and underwear. Vintage shoes always looked like cast-offs, however unworn they were — it was one thing on which she agreed with Nic — and were invariably bloody uncomfortable. As for underwear? No need for a justification there. The business had started to tick, albeit slowly, and her reputation for custom-made clothes was beginning to spread. At this early stage, she could ask for little more. The day so far had been spent sorting out her accounts, one of the least appealing chores that underpinned all the stuff she did enjoy: buying, designing, making, selling. From now on, she vowed, she would be more organised and would fill in her accountant's spreadsheet as she spent and sold. Anything to avoid this disorienting chaos of numbers. She put down her pencil as Ali crossed the shop, lifting the flap of her satchel.

'What's happened?' It was impossible not to notice the transformation from the last time they had met. All signs of Ali's previous anger and disappointment had vanished.

'Why?' Ali was pulling something out of her bag, untangling it from her white earphones cable.

'You're glowing. I take it you saw off Susie then?' Lou had been imagining the confrontation between the two women and what she would say should Ali emerge the loser. Hard though she found that to imagine.

Finally, with a flourish, Ali produced a jewellery roll and closed her bag, dumping it on the floor. 'You know what? All that fuss was a complete waste of time. When I arrived, she was already at the airport on

503

her way back to Melbourne. And, when the divorce comes through, which it will . . .' She paused for maximum effect. '. . . we're getting married!' She looked up, beaming, giving Lou time to rehinge her jaw and come out from the back of the shop to hug her.

Lou remembered their other Don-centred conversation. 'So when does the house-training start?' she ventured cautiously, wanting Ali's happiness to be complete.

Ali looked as if she was about to explode with pleasure. 'No need. Not yet anyway. We're going to keep our own places. I did what you said and told him how I felt and that's what he suggested.'

If anyone ever admitted to having followed her advice, Lou was always fearful. She didn't want the responsibility of someone else's decisions. Being in charge of her own was quite enough. That was the downside of having an opinion. Why didn't she just keep her mouth shut and her views to herself? She watched Ali untie the jewellery roll and unfurl it on the counter.

'And you're confident that'll work?' she said, trying not to sound too doubtful.

'Completely.'

She'd never heard Ali sound so sure.

'He's going to move nearer me. In fact,

the caretaker told me that one of the flats in my building's coming up. How spookily serendipitous would that be? It's going to be a thoroughly modern marriage. An apartment each. None of that old-fashioned stuff. Now take a look at these. I told you he'd do a good job.' Ali had started taking out several plastic packets and then arranged Rick's jewellery on the counter.

Lou picked up a small hand mirror and held an ivy-leaf-shaped earring to her ear, the tiny white price tag dangling by her hand. She looked at it. 'Mmm. Pretty reasonable. These'll gallop out of here. Look at this bangle. It's beautiful.' She slid on the unfolded circle of silver, the light dancing off the hammer marks. 'The word-of-mouth on your jewellery is definitely spreading, you know.'

'That interview in *City Life* must have helped a bit, too. The photos anyway. As well as those recommendations in *Stylish* and *Chic to Chic.*' Ali took the key to the jewellery cabinet and began to rearrange her own pieces to make space for Rick's. 'Mix them up — gold and silver on the same shelf — do you think?'

'Whatever you like.' Lou was happy for Ali to display their work the way she thought best. In the past couple of weeks, several customers had come hunting out Ali's jewellery. Sometimes, they dickered over price, but she had made three sales — not a bad hit rate at all. There was no doubt their arrangement was beginning to pay off.

'What I'd like is . . .'

Lou froze, aware from Ali's pause that she was about to broach something she thought was a sensitive subject.

'. . . to know how you're getting on with Sanjeev. You've been very quiet about him lately. Your starter for ten.' Said casually but Lou noticed how she concentrated her attention a little too exaggeratedly on the task in hand as she waited for Lou's reply.

'I'm seeing him tonight,' she said, preparing herself for Ali's reaction. 'Happy?'

'More than,' said Ali, this time looking up, her eyes alight. 'What are you doing?'

'I think he's got tickets for a concert. Not really my thing, but still.' Lou turned to straighten up the two piles of advertising postcards.

'Shame. I was going to suggest we all met up.'

'Really?' Things between Don and Ali must really have changed for Ali to suggest a foursome. But however curious she was to meet Don, Lou wasn't ready to introduce Sanjeev into the mix. She didn't want him to be a given in her life, to have the official sanction of her friends. More exciting was having him to herself, being in a relation-ship that didn't impinge on the rest of her life. As long as he was happy with the ar-rangement too, she had no plans for chang-ing it. She was beginning to understand the value of keeping one's private life to one's self.

Still irked by her last conversation with Hooker, she had since thought a lot about what he had said: 'I need you, Lou. Just like you need me.' His continued attempts to undermine her decision to leave him had finally succeeded in unsettling her. 'Don't say anything now. I'll wait until you're ready.' Since they'd last spoken she had envisaged them being grandparents to-gether, helping with Nic's baby and even sharing the care of Rory on his visits to London. 'Together' being the operative word. In some ways he was right, they had been a good team. Once. Long ago. Perhaps they could be again. Was she being unrea-sonable? Selfish? However, then she had reminded herself how conveniently selective his memory was. For the argument against, she weighed up everything she had worked so hard to achieve: her shop; her indepen-dence; her house; her visibility. Being a loving and involved grandmother did not mean she had to give them up. She and Hooker did not have to be a unit for her to achieve that. Eventually light had dawned. What Hooker really wanted was not her so much as Nic, his precious only daughter, who still refused to speak to him, taking the side of her wronged mother. He might not have realised that at a conscious level, but Lou understood him. Her returning home would make his life easier, true, but in fact she was only a means to an end. She was ready to say something, at last.

Ali had finished her arrangement and locked the case before standing back to assess the display. 'What do you think?'

'Actually, you're going to think this is a bit . . . but I was thinking about Hooker,' Lou confessed, only half hearing the question. 'He's been badgering me about getting back together. The answer's no, of course.'

'But you did stop to consider it? Lou, no!' Ali was shocked.

'I'm worried about Nic and her baby. I'm worried about her not speaking to her father. So yes, I did wonder whether giving her back some sort of family stability would help her. Help them.'

'Lou, she's twenty-six, not twelve,' objected Ali. 'And anyway, that's no grounds for a reunion.'

'Of course I know that. Though sometimes it's hard to accept that your children have grown up and don't need you in the same way any more. But in the end, even though I was dithering, I admit it . . . Hooker made the decision for me. He told me that he'd asked Emma to move out — proof of how serious he was about wanting the two of us to get back together. A bit of me even fell for it. But then Tom told me that he went to the house to pick something up and found her packing. The truth was that she had dumped Hooker, having fallen head-over-heels for a guy her own age. Hooker simply couldn't admit it to himself, and lied to save face and to convince me.' This new piece of information had come when she needed it, confirming to her that the Hooker she knew was never going to change. She had doubted the wisdom of her actions for the last time. 'Maybe he's worried about being alone, but he only has himself to blame. I can't let that be my problem.'

'I'm sure he won't be alone for long,' said Ali wryly. 'Have you told him?'

'Not yet. Waiting won't do him any harm.' Lou took a couple of dresses from the changing rooms and replaced them on the rail. 'No harm at all.'

■ ■ ■ ■

Brahms' 2nd symphony was not the sort of music Lou would have chosen for herself. She was a self-confessed unreconstructed shlock chick. Cheesy pop and songs from the shows were more her thing but there was no way she'd admit her secret shame to Sanjeev. So far this evening, she hadn't had a chance to admit much thanks to her late arrival at his hotel. Not late because she'd been so busy at the shop but because she'd had a major wardrobe crisis. Her thoughts drifting with the music, she pictured her bedroom as she had left it, shrouded in clothes, all of them tried and discarded. Nothing had seemed quite the thing for the evening ahead. She wanted to wow him without embarrassing him, look edgy with-out looking as if she'd tried too hard. But the task she'd set herself was impossible. In the end, time had dictated her decision by simply running out. If she hadn't left at that minute, she would have been not just late, but unforgivably late. So she had arrived wearing a deep raspberry jacket that, with the right outfit, looked pretty damn sharp. However, that evening, teamed with a peacock blue skirt, the look she'd put together in her panic was a disaster.

Sanjeev had seemed not to notice. If anything he appeared preoccupied, not keen to communicate. He showed no signs of wanting to share whatever was bothering him and as they rushed to the Festival Hall, it seemed the wrong moment to ask.

She shifted in her seat, glancing sideways at her companion. His head was tilted back, eyes half shut, lips slightly moving as if he was following the music. In his lap, the fingers of one hand spelled out the rhythm on the other, but so surreptitiously that the movement was hardly visible. His silver bracelet had slipped down his wrist. His hair was brushed back from his forehead, inter- mittent white hairs showing through above his ears. His skin was smooth, hardly touched by time. She studied his profile. A distinguished-looking man, she thought, before turning away, closing her own eyes. But instead of losing herself in the music, joining him there, she found she just couldn't let go.

Her mind kept returning to Hooker as she once again pushed herself to come to terms with the man he had turned out to be. She wasn't angry with him any longer. If any- thing, she was bemused, marvelling at the way they both had grown apart and changed without the other noticing. How little either of them seemed to know or understand each other now. They'd been so happy in the early years when she was still sure that, despite not being one of the last great romantics, he had felt the same way. Her memories returned, faded around the edges like old colour photos: the time they'd walked the Kerry Way from Killarney to Kenmare, and came on a red deer in the mist; the Tuscan farmhouse where they spent the first night of their honeymoon; moving into the small terraced house in Highbury; the birth of Jamie, their first precious child; and many more. But then those early years together gave way to a blur of bringing up children and holding down jobs, succeeding not failing.

The demands of family life and their separate professions had ground away at them. She saw that now. Unlike other couples, they hadn't been enough for each other in the end. An old age staring across the fireplace at each other or fighting over the TV remote was not for them. They had been so busy keeping their heads above water, grabbing at whatever kept them afloat, that they had forgotten to put out a hand to help the other. She didn't blame Hooker for that. She had played her part in their game, obsessed as she had been with her work at *Chic to Chic,* then resentful at having to stay at home with the teenage children, however much she loved them. No wonder Hooker had looked for distraction elsewhere. All *that* she could accept, indeed had accepted. Her astonishment came from the fact that, after all they had recently been through, he was still lying to her. How little he must think of her now. Or how desperate he must be.

As the music drew to a close, Sanjeev emerged from his trance and gently touched her arm. They exchanged smiles. When the applause died down and the orchestra had left the stage, she followed him up the stairs of the auditorium to the exit. When they reached the street, he flagged down a cab, stood back while she climbed in, then clambered in beside her. To her surprise, he gave the cabbie the name of his hotel.

'No curry?' So far, their dates had always included a curry house where they had eaten well and he had continued to entertain her with his stories of home. Afterwards they would go to her place, she enchanted and wanting more, he as charming and loving as she could want.

'Not tonight. There's something I need to say to you and I thought we could eat at my hotel or order room service. If you don't think that's too presumptuous of me. It's just that it's more private.' He tilted his head like a bird, eyebrow arched, asking for her approval.

'Could you be planning on seducing me, Mr Gupta?' If only she felt anything like as coquettish as her words sounded.

A slow smile crossed his face. 'That could be arranged.'

'I can't think of anything I'd like more.' She tucked her arm in his. The idea of them making love in a hotel bedroom smacked of something shameless, exotic. Not at all what she was used to. Playing the role of femme fatale hadn't been part of her repertoire for years. If only she'd been more successful in the wardrobe department that evening, she might be more confident in her potential licence to thrill.

The taxi pulled up outside the hotel and in they swept, Lou still on Sanjeev's arm. They only stopped to pick up his key from reception. In the lift, they stood side by side, staring ahead, lost in thought, almost as if they didn't know each other. Lou was beginning to feel faintly embarrassed, but the brush of his hand against hers was charged.

He turned the key and the door swung

open on a room dominated by a neatly made, rather clinical-looking double bed. A couple of jaunty sketches of Parisian street life hung on the cream vinyl wallpaper. On a table holding a bowl with a tired-looking apple and a browning banana, a couple of tumblers wrapped in plastic stood next to a vase of white silk peonies, the inner curves of the petals finely filmed with dust. All Sanjeev's possessions were hidden apart from a pair of shiny black shoes lined up side by side near the door. None of this tallied with the scene Lou had conjured up for a hotel seduction. There the bed was inviting, the flowers fresh, the atmosphere . . . well, at least there was an atmosphere instead of the faintly antiseptic smell that emanated from the bathroom.

'Welcome,' said Sanjeev, helping her off with her coat and hanging it with his on the back of the door. 'It may not look much, but for now, it's mine. A drink?' He crouched over the minibar and held it open. 'Or I could order us a bottle of wine.'

Plumping for a vodka and tonic on the basis that she would get it sooner than any bottle of wine brought by room service, Lou was suddenly aware that the mood had changed. As he passed her the drink, Sanjeev looked uneasy.

'Perhaps this wasn't such a good idea. We could go downstairs or to the restaurant round the corner,' he suggested.

'It's a fine idea,' said Lou firmly. 'I'm not hungry anyway.' Not quite true but, as long as her stomach rumbling didn't embarrass them, what did it matter? Even if the reality of a sandwich didn't match her vision of a small vase of roses on a white-tableclothed trolley with a waiter whipping silver domes from dishes of steaming food — too many black-and-white movies, Lou — she liked the intimacy and privacy of his room. She lay back on the bed in what she hoped was a reasonably seductive pose. In her head, she saw Manet's *Olympia.* In the strategically placed mirror, she saw a middle-aged woman whose skirt had rucked up to emphasise her stomach. Undeterred, she patted the bed beside her. A relative newcomer to the ways of seduction, she'd had to rely on what she had seen in films. She shifted herself so she couldn't see her reflection in full any more. Nothing could be done about what she was wearing, bar taking it off, and it was definitely too soon for that.

He sat beside her, stretching his legs in front of him. 'Shall we order food?'

'And wine?' she suggested, sounding more desperate than she'd intended, focusing on

his left big toe where his sock was danger-
ously thin.

After he'd rung down for their Welsh
rarebits and Australian Merlot, they waited
for a moment. Sanjeev was sitting ramrod
straight. Lou adjusted her position again to
avoid her arm cramping, unsure how to
proceed. Side by side, they sat rigid, like
two strangers. She was reminded of the
poster for *The War of the Roses* starring
Kathleen Turner and Michael Douglas: a
couple at war. Surely seduction wasn't
meant to be as difficult as this? Especially
not for two consenting adults — even if they
were both a bit rusty. After all, it wasn't as
if this was their first time.

'Lou?' He sounded cautious, unsure.

'Mmm.' She didn't dare speak in case she
gave way to a sudden urge to laugh.

'I need to tell you something.'

In the mirror, she could see how anxious
he looked. He was clutching his whisky in
both hands as if it was a life raft. She took
pity on him. 'Of course. Whatever you like.
I'm listening.' She stilled her nerves with
her vodka.

'I'm going back to Delhi.' So this was what
had been troubling him. His relief at getting
the news off his chest was obvious. 'We've
got the Birmingham plant of LBF Electron-

ics running smoothly now, so I've been recalled to head office.'

'Oh.' Lou wasn't sure how she was meant to react. What did this mean for them?

'They only told me a couple of days ago. I'm leaving in three weeks.'

So they still had a little more time together. She gazed at his reflection. 'Won't you be coming back?' She was surprised by how sad she felt, not heartbroken but deeply regretful. At the same time, the recognition that there was going to be no pressure on her to conform to a conventional relationship was nothing but a relief.

'Yes, maybe every three or four months, maybe a little more often than that. They'll still need me to ensure that everything's running smoothly. And you can't do that from a distance without visiting.' At last he turned towards her, his face concerned.

'But we can see each other when you do?' She heard herself sounding like a heart-sick teenager and abruptly cleared her throat. 'I mean, it doesn't have to make any difference to us, does it?' This time she sounded too brutally matter-of-fact. She tried again. 'What I'm trying to say is that it sounds like a workable arrangement.' A workable arrangement? Where had she plucked that from? 'We're adults. We can make it work if we want to.'

Sanjeev was staring at her, uncertain. 'Really?'

'Why not? I'd rather we took things as they come. If we can't see each other all the time — well, I think it's probably a good thing.' Sanjeev's expression told her she'd gone too far again. 'Seriously. I'm not ready for full-on, bells-and-whistles commitment. You know that. Apart from making the shop work, I just want to have fun, and we can have that whenever you're here.'

Whatever had come over her? What had happened to the Lou who had never looked at another man apart from Hooker for the last God knew how many years? The Lou who had never thought beyond a full-time, committed partnership. Until now.

'And when I'm not?'

'I don't know,' she answered honestly. At least she owed him that. Maybe she would meet someone else. Who knew? 'But can't we just make the most of the time you are here?'

To her astonishment, Sanjeev had started to smile. He took her hand and raised it his mouth, kissing her palm. 'You are a remarkable woman, Lou Sherwood.'

'I am?' Lou was thrown by this unexpected turning of the tide in their relationship, but she reminded herself of Ali's description of her life as a mistress. A no-strings relationship, she'd said. And she'd agreed that came with no boredom factor, no irritating habits, no being taken for granted. That was what Lou had envied and that was what she was being offered. This was something to celebrate.

'Yes, you are.'

They had both slid down the bed without noticing and were half lying on their sides facing each other, just a few inches of freshly laundered bedlinen between them. They moved together to close the gap.

When the knock from room service eventually came, neither of them heard it. Or if they did, they chose to ignore it. The Welsh rarebit, when they rescued it sometime later from outside the door, was stone cold.

29

Lou was watching the kitchen clock. Never had the second hand seemed to move so slowly, inching around, giving a little shake every time it reached the next Roman numeral. Her coffee sat undrunk in front of her, the plate of four biscuits untouched. She had tidied the ground floor of the house with uncharacteristic care so that there was no room for criticism.

Hooker was due at seven. Tick. Tock.

She ran her eye around the room. Everything was in order, including her collection of teapots, old and new, that she had finally unpacked from their box and lined along the top of the units. In the sitting room, all the coloured threads had been vacuumed up, her knitting and patchwork had been stowed in her workroom along with the tailor's dummy, and she had covered the single rail of clothes with one of the mirrored bedspreads she had shipped back from India. How long ago that seemed now. She glanced at the photo of herself sitting on Diana's bench, sweaty and cross but exhilarated inside, at the Taj Mahal. She picked up the wooden frame, wiping the dust from it by rubbing it on her hip, then looked at it more closely. Despite her doubts at the time, the shot was special after all. As she had self-consciously marked the end of her marriage with a photo to show her on her own at last, so she had struck up her friendship with Ali. How strange to think back to that day when they had no idea what close friends they'd become.

When she heard the bell, she replaced the photo on the table by the jug of pink and white gypsophila, beside the two she had framed of the children. At the doorway, she turned to check everything was in place, cushions plumped, pictures in line. She quickly straightened the framed sampler that she'd picked up recently at a vintage fair, imagining nine-year-old Rebecca Spilsbury, back in 1837, earnestly cross-stitching the birds and dogs and blossoming trees under the alphabet and religious verse. She nudged the ottoman with her knee so it moved closer to its chair. Only when she was absolutely satisfied, did she answer the door.

Lou led the way into the sitting room.

Hooker looked around him, noticing the order that had been imposed since his last visit. 'This looks different.'

Lou didn't want to discuss her resolution to be tidier, to keep her home more the way Jenny would have liked. She just wanted to get everything said that needed to be. She sat down while Hooker picked up her Taj Mahal photo. He didn't comment but put it back at a slightly different angle.

'Ali took that,' she said, unable to resist.

He didn't rise to the bait, but turned, expectant. 'Aren't you going to offer me a drink?' The musky scent of his cologne rolled across the space between them.

She went into the kitchen to pour him a whisky. For herself, nothing.

'Have you seen Nic?' he asked when she returned. 'How much longer to go now?' His face was pathetically eager for news.

The least Lou could do was keep this civilised. 'About six weeks. She's doing well, working like a maniac of course despite my trying to persuade her to take it easy. I hardly see her. But you should talk to her yourself. Do sort this out, Hooker. Call her.'

'Do you think I haven't tried? She at least talks to me when I ring, which is better than it was, but she obviously can't wait to get me off the line. I don't get it. Shona was over so long ago.'

'Oh, Hooker.' His lack of understanding made Lou almost sorry for him. 'Don't you see that you've made her question all she thought she knew about our family? Her childhood wasn't what she thought it was — at least that's how she sees it. She feels betrayed by you.'

A glimmer of irritation was swiftly replaced by something more confident. 'But it's going to be different now, isn't it?' He came over to perch on the arm of the sofa. She slid sideways to the other end so that contact would be difficult, if not impossible. He looked surprised but stayed where he was. 'When you come home. Then, it'll be different. If you've forgiven me, then she will too.'

He was still in denial, believing that everything would fall into place around him, just as it always did. Always. This time would be no different.

'I'm not coming home.' She spoke as gently as she could, not knowing whether he'd be angry or sad.

'I don't mean now,' he said bluffly. 'Of course not. We've got a few things to work out, the playroom to adapt. But soon. You're coming soon.'

She was reminded of the children when they were young and had wanted her reassurance and encouragement over something. There was no way of letting him down gently. The fairest thing was to be straight with him.

'No. Not now. Not any time. I'm going to live here alone.'

'But you can't,' he blustered. 'Not after everything I've said. I'm a changed man. You're all I want, all I've ever wanted.' He dropped down onto the sofa, next to her. 'We could be happy together again, I'm sure.'

She got up and took a few steps to the centre of the room where she stood looking down at him. 'I've thought so hard about what you said, about being grandparents together, but the way you've behaved has made me see our marriage quite differently. I'm not that woman any more. And you're not a changed man really, Hooker, are you? You couldn't even bring yourself to tell me the truth about Emma leaving you.'

He seemed to shrink as he closed his eyes and let out his breath in a long sigh. 'I meant to but I thought —'

'You thought you could twist the facts to convince me of your sincerity. But then Tom bumped into her and she told him the truth.'

'Tom?' He sat up, alert.

'He thought that it was far better I know. And it is. But that's not the only reason I'm not coming back. We're better apart. We may miss out on some of the big family gatherings but I'm sure we can be civil towards each other, at least in front of the children. As for Nic? She'll get over all this eventually, I'm sure. And so will you. You'll just have to wait.'

He stood there, the proud, self-possessed man she had always known, looking at her as if disappointed by the change in her and the wrong-headedness of her decision, then he shook his head. The whisky glass hit the table with a thud. 'There's no point in prolonging this. You've obviously made up your mind. I'd better go.'

Lou wanted one last stab at trying to make him see things from her point of view. Later he might remember her words and mull them over. 'Hooker, listen. We're at an age where we've got time to change our lives, meet other people. You must see that. If we leave it much later, those opportunities might not be there.'

'I don't want to meet *other* people. I want the mother of my children. I've been stupid, I know. But I don't believe that our marriage is irretrievable. I won't believe it. I never have.' He got to his feet. He looked for a moment as if he would break down, then recovered himself. 'I'd better go.'

'I think that's for the best.' Their marriage was over. At last. She saw him to the door, feeling nothing but relief that he had accepted her decision at last.

Ali lay on the sofa, eyes shut, groaning as Don's knuckles dug into a spot near the instep of her right foot.

'Is reflexology meant to be this painful?' she asked, squinting at him.

'Maybe I am a bit rusty.' He moved his attention to the other foot.

'Ouch!' She winced. 'I'll say you are. Tell you what. Let's stop and I'll make a start on supper. Lou will be here in a minute.'

He removed her feet from his lap. 'I'm looking forward to meeting her at last.'

Ali went over to the kitchen, talking as she went. 'Not as much as she is to meeting you.' This was the first time she had ever entertained as a couple and she was keen nothing should go wrong.

'Can't I do something to help?'

Thinking of the mess that would engulf the kitchen if he did, she replied, 'No, thanks. It's all under control.' She angled her hand to look at her engagement ring.

Originally she had wanted to make it herself, but then realised the ring should be something they shared equally, so together they had chosen the violet sapphire and its plain platinum setting.

When the bell rang, Ali didn't hear it above the noise of the blender whizzing up the olive tapenade to go with the cod. Don answered barefoot, introducing himself as he let Lou in.

'I love this room.' Lou stood for a second, just looking round her, taking in the space, the light, the careful arrangement of everything, disturbed only by Don's cast-off shoes and the couple of mugs on the table. 'It's everything I'd like, but can't quite achieve. Or at least not for more than about five minutes.'

Ali rushed from the kitchen area, amused to find Don trying not to be transfixed by Lou's get-up, her uncontrolled frizz of red hair and bright lipstick. She'd obviously come straight from the shop, cutting a somewhat colourful figure in her fuschia lace gloves and matching tights. 'I didn't even get to introduce you!'

Drinks were soon poured, seats were taken and talk began to flow, Don and Lou discovering they had a shared interest in classic movies when she mentioned a coming retrospective on femmes fatales of Hollywood. Within seconds they were debating the merits of Barbara Stanwyck, Rita Hayworth and Lauren Bacall and the various films in which they'd starred. As the conversation carried on, Ali was delighted that the two of them were hitting it off better than she could have hoped.

Eventually she broke in with an invitation to the table where the good-humoured discussion continued, Ali weighing in with an argument for Dietrich and then Hepburn in *The African Queen*.

'You couldn't call her a femme fatale in that, surely. If ever,' Lou challenged while Ali hit back with a spirited defence. After they'd eaten, Lou turned the conversation to Ali and Don, their plans for the future.

'As soon as Don gets time off, we're going to Scotland.' Ali looked sideways at him.

'In her car, with her driving,' teased Don. 'Ali doth not a good passenger make.'

She punched his arm affectionately, then looked more serious as she turned back to Lou. 'I took both your and Don's advice and went back to see Dad.' She waited to see the effect on Lou who failed to hide her surprise.

'You never said.' A piece of cod fell from Lou's fork.

'Some things you have to keep to yourself until they're resolved. I know you understand that. It took a bit of time, but I did listen to you both and I reckoned that however furious I feel with him, I should try and paper over the cracks. He's an old man and has done his bit for me after all.'

'And?' Lou leaned forward, glass of wine in hand.

'And he told me that Mum had been diagnosed bipolar, not that they called it that then, after I was born. She had another bout when I was tiny — she tried to kill herself when I was at a friend's but Dad found her in time. After that she was medicated up to the hilt and after seven years of living in grey, the years I remember her, she took herself off the pills. The rest you know.'

'Are things better between you?'

'I can't pretend it's easy. I still feel he could have done everything differently and I keep thinking I might have saved her, if only I'd known, though the rational bit of me knows I couldn't have done anything. We were both powerless, really.' Her voice faded away as Don took her hand.

'But look.' She recovered herself and crossed the room to the sofa. From the shelf beneath the coffee table she pulled a brown envelope. She held it upside down and out slipped several loose album pages stuck with tiny Box Brownie prints along with a couple of other larger photos. Lou picked up the pages that were stuck with small black-and-white images captioned in careful loopy handwriting. In them a man and woman were photographed in different holiday poses, against their Austin Cambridge, having a picnic, by a hotel, in front of a municipal statue. Smiling. Always smiling.

'It's Mum and Dad on their honeymoon in Buxton. He hid them because he couldn't bear to look at them again, but he dug them out for me along with this.' She passed over the larger photo. 'And this is us.'

In it a young woman sat smiling into the camera, her eyes distant, a young girl holding a teddy bear standing by her. She was unmistakably Ali, scrubbed and dressed up for the photograph. The similarities between her now and her mother were marked: same smile, same reserve that Ali showed when Lou first met her.

'I couldn't stop crying when I first saw us together,' Ali said quietly. 'I'm just glad Don was here to pick up the pieces. Again.' She turned to smile at him, then looked back to Lou. 'I remember seeing these when I was a kid, in fact I think I even remember this one being taken, but I'd forgotten all about them.'

Lou was turning things over in her carpet-bag and eventually retrieved her pair of smudged reading glasses. With them on the end of her nose, she studied the photographs one after another.

'It's as if Dad closed down after her death, and admitting what really happened has opened him up again. He wants to share all this with me at last. He even sent me a cheque for two grand — that's a huge amount for him. Here's the letter. You can see for yourself.'

Ali waited while Lou read the letter. It was written in the same hand as the captions, but now betraying the tremor of old age. She had read it so many times herself that she knew snippets of it off by heart.

Thinking about you . . . I hope the photos prove to you that she was happy once with me and with you . . . I've tried to be the best father . . . perhaps that wasn't good enough . . . Maybe I can make up for it now. You mentioned that business was tough . . . Would this contribution help?

'This is so unlike him.' She couldn't wait

for Lou to get to the end. 'I wish I could remember what he was like when Mum was alive or at least when they were happy together. He must have been so different then. But I can't. Not really. Of course, I'm going to send the money back.'

'You're going to do nothing of the sort,' objected Don.

'Of course I am.' She heard how stubborn she sounded and tried to justify herself. 'Besides, he's always said I must stand on my own two feet and get out of my difficulties on my own.'

'He's a proud man.' Don gazed at one of the tiny photographs in which Eric was on a picnic rug, squinting into the sun, laughing at the photographer. Unrecognisable from the man he had become. 'It will have taken a lot for him to dig out these and send you the cash. The least you can do is accept graciously. He's trying to make it up to you.'

'Don's got a point.' Lou was still looking at the photographs. 'Let him make his peace in his own way.'

Ali looked at them both and, seeing they meant what they said, grasped Don's hand and squeezed. 'I guess you're right. As usual.'

'This must be a mistake.' In Lou's hand was a picture of a graveyard. Beyond a rusted wrought-iron gate set in a high stone wall stood a modest but nonetheless forbidding Presbyterian church surrounded by ranks of unadorned granite gravestones. The sky was clouded, the trees angled sharply by the wind. 'What's this doing here?'

'That's where she's buried,' said Ali, taking the picture and staring at it.

'That's why we're going to Scotland,' added Don as he put his arm round her.

Ali moved into the security of his embrace. 'Yes, Don suggested that we go there to see her grave for ourselves. To begin with I thought it was a terrible idea but now I kind of want to. I hope it'll be some sort of resolution for us. I can't hope for more than that.'

'It's near a small village on the south coast of Scotland,' Don explained. 'We'll be going up for a week to explore.'

'I don't know what happened in her childhood,' added Ali. 'I don't even think I ever met my grandparents. But I want to see where Mum grew up, some of what made her the person she was and where she died. And then when we next visit Dad, I'm going to ask him more. I want to understand her better. To really understand what happened, if I can. I hope he'll tell me everything he can now.'

'Does he know you're going?' Lou slid the photographs back into the envelope.

'We're going with his blessing. I even asked him if he wanted to come too, but he said he didn't feel up to it.' Ali still held on to the photograph of her with her mother.

'This is the best we can do, under the circumstances, to bring them a little closer,' said Don, and kissed the side of Ali's head.

Later, as Lou sat on the bus, she could only think about the change in her friend since they'd first met. Gone was the reserve that had characterised Ali on the Indian trip. Seeing her with Don made Lou see how happy they were together, relaxed, content and loving. How instrumental Don had been in getting Ali to start mending fences with her father. While happy for her, Lou was also quite clear that what her friend had achieved was no longer what she wanted for herself. It was almost as if she and Ali had reversed roles, finding in each other's lives what they now wanted for themselves. She leaned her head against the window and gave a small private smile.

30

A month later, an ear-splitting din interrupted Lou's dream, checking her pursuit
along a beach by a black panther wearing
one of her floral cocktail dresses, and
returning her rudely to the real world. She
knocked her mobile onto the floor as she
switched on the light, then groped for her
reading glasses. She reached down the side
of the bed, guided by the Take That ringtone at full deafening volume. Since her sad
and secret passion for Mark Owen had
waned a little, she'd been meaning to switch
the tone to Louis Armstrong for weeks.
Years of anxious waiting up until the small
hours for their teenage children to return
home meant her alarm bells were primed
— even now. A phone call in the middle of
the night could only mean one thing — the
police. What every parent dreaded. Something terrible had happened to one of them.
With adrenalin pumping, she checked the

caller ID — Nic.

'Mum! Where are you?' Nic's voice wobbled.

'Nic? Are you all right?' She was propping herself up, still struggling through the fog of sleep.

'Of course I'm not! They've started the induction. I thought you were going to be here.'

'I'll be with you in half an hour.' She didn't point out they had agreed with the midwife that she didn't need to be there till ten. Nothing would happen straight away. Already half standing, Lou was organising her thoughts as she gathered the random clothes within her reach. This was not the time for sartorial considerations. Not even for Nic. Anything would do.

This was such bad luck. Nic had made a birth plan of military precision, which covered every single procedure: the drug-free labour, the water birth, Lou as her birthing partner. How thrilled and deeply flattered she had been to be asked. The invitation was proof that, despite the occasional glitches in their relationship, deep down Nic did love her. Their relationship did matter to her, even if it wasn't quite the one of which Lou had once dreamed. Over this year, they had become so much closer thanks to the pregnancy, thanks to Hooker. However, neither of them had chosen to imagine any complications. Nic's blood pressure had risen a couple of days earlier and showed no signs of lowering, so she'd been admitted to hospital the previous afternoon to be induced this morning. She had insisted Lou went home to sleep but of course Lou had lain awake worrying, only dropping off in the small hours. She dressed quickly and dashed to the bathroom where she splashed her face with cold water to bring her round before she got behind the wheel of her car.

Switching on the ignition, she then waited a moment, opening the windows, letting the early morning breeze finish the job the water had started. By the time she pulled up at the hospital, she was wide awake. The breeze had dropped already. It was going to be another hot day that would suck the air from the city. She rushed to the labour ward, to be shown to a delivery suite where Nic, her face pinched and anxious, was propped up on a bed with a midwife examining her. Electrodes were planted on her stomach and paper showing a graph of the baby's heart rate spewed from the monitor beside it. Around her was the paraphernalia of equipment associated with assisted births.

'Mum. Oh, thank God, you're here.' Nic reached an arm out towards her. 'I'm so scared.'

Lou took her hand and went to the head of the bed where a plastic chair held Nic's overnight bag. At least she'd had the foresight to pack it a week earlier although at the time, her over-preparedness had made Lou laugh. 'Everything's going to be fine,' she soothed, brushing Nic's hair back from her face. 'You're in the best place.'

That day would be one of the longest Lou could remember. Watching her daughter suffer without being able to relieve her discomfort was like a slow torture. Just before lunchtime, the midwife broke Nic's waters to speed up the process, and her contractions began in earnest.

'Jeeesus!' she yelled. Then groaned, 'Why didn't anyone warn me it would be this bad?'

Lou busied herself in Nic's bag, digging out a flannel that she wet at the basin before wiping away the sweat on Nic's forehead. Her daughter brushed her away.

'You've got to call Max, Mum. I tried earlier but he didn't answer.'

'But I thought . . .' Hadn't Nic told her months ago that he didn't want anything to do with the baby?

'Don't think. I didn't tell you we'd been seeing each other again, because I knew exactly what you'd say. My mobile's in my bag.' She waved a hand towards the small cupboard by the bed, before another wave of pain took her over.

What should Lou say? Should she be encouraging and hopeful, or hostile towards the young man who had absented himself at the first hurdle? She poured a glass of water for her daughter, then went outside to make the call. Leaving the building to get some air. She stood at the back entrance by a huge concrete urn filled with sand and a million cigarette butts, staring up at the sky, waiting for Max to pick up.

A wasted-looking man in a wheelchair with a drip attached to his arm watched her, puffing away as if his life depended on it.

When Max eventually answered, he sounded distant although he was polite enough, thanking Lou for letting him know what was happening. He made no offer to come and she thought it not her place to insist. Presumably he was at work where it would be difficult to talk. After he'd hung up, she stared at the phone. Nic had definitely given her the impression that the news of the pregnancy had blasted a crater-sized hole through their relationship. Perhaps the situation was retrievable after all and the baby would have a father to play a part in its life. She hoped so for Nic's sake.

She braced herself for her return to the delivery suite, when she remembered Hooker. She had spoken to him the previous evening and briefly this morning but had promised to keep him updated. Whatever difficulties lay between the three of them, he was Nic's father, and he deserved to know what was happening.

Unlike Max, Hooker was immediately full of concern. 'But it's too early.'

'We know that, Hooker,' she said, summoning every ounce of patience. 'But only a couple of weeks. We talked about this last night. Sometimes other circumstances dictate when babies come into the world.'

'Isn't there a danger? What if something goes wrong?' Hooker's distrust of hospitals had been ingrained ever since the time when his arm, which he'd broken in a rugby game, was set badly enough to have to be rebroken and reset. After that, he would rather eat nails than place one foot in another.

'Nothing's going to go wrong. She's in the best possible place.' Lou was calm but insistent. Again. If she could make herself believe that, then she could make him believe it too. 'I'll call you as soon as there's some news.'

'I'm coming over now. I must see her.'

She couldn't remember him ever volunteering to visit anyone in hospital. But of course his urgency stemmed from his desperate desire to repair the rift that still existed between him and Nic, to put his broken family back together.

'No, you're not. Nic's better on her own right now. There's nothing you could do.' The distance that existed between them now made it easier for her to be assertive without being aggressive. 'I'll let you know when to come. For now, just keep the boys in the loop for me.' As she moved a cigarette butt off the path with her foot, she noticed for the first time that in her hurry to get here she'd put on odd shoes: a black quilted pump and a red one.

'But shouldn't I be there too?' He hesitated as the inappropriateness of his suggestion dawned on him. 'I could wait outside.'

Eventually Lou convinced him that any reunion with his daughter was unlikely to take place while she was pushing a baby into the world. 'And don't call me, Hooker. I'm switching my phone off now.'

The afternoon passed with, at one point, Nic making the reluctant decision to abandon the remnants of her birth plan and agree to the offer of an epidural.

'Oh, Mum,' she wailed, shaken by another contraction. 'This wasn't meant to happen.'

'Darling, they know what they're doing. It'll be all right.' She stepped out of the anaesthetist's way as he gave Nic a consent form. Wishing there was a way of alleviating her daughter's panic, she gripped onto her hand and listened. Nic was talked through the procedure and signed the form, tears streaming down her face.

'But this isn't what I planned,' she moaned. 'I want it to stop. Now.'

Lou remembered how Nic, rather like her grandchild, had been in no hurry to be born at all, taking a long thirty-two hours of labour, running the show her way right from the start. Lou had screamed at Hooker to take her home, she couldn't stand the pain any longer. At that point, it was too late for an epidural. 'Darling, you're going to have to take their advice. You don't want anything to happen to the baby.'

Another couple of hours passed, interrupted by the midwife regularly returning at half-hourly intervals to monitor Nic's blood pressure. The baby was staying firmly put. At six thirty, Lou left the room to get a sandwich and to call Hooker and the boys.

When she returned, she found Nic surrounded by gowned medical staff.

Her daughter's face was bewildered as she listened to one of the midwives explaining something.

Lou rushed to her bedside. 'What's happened?'

'Her blood pressure's up and so's her temperature,' the midwife explained. 'We're going to prep her for an emergency Caesarian. Are you going to come into theatre with her?'

Nic answered for her. 'Of course she will. She's my mum. I need her there.'

Lou squeezed her hand and stayed by her side as she was transferred onto a trolley and wheeled to the operating theatre. While Nic was readied for the operation, Lou was given a blue gown and cap to wear. By the time she entered the theatre, a screen had been hung in front of Nic's stomach to shield her from the procedure. Lou took a seat by Nic's shoulder.

'Is there anything you want?' she asked quietly, feeling powerless as well as intimidated by the amount of activity on the other side of the screen.

'God, Mum. I feel sick.'

'Shhhh.' She stroked the damp strands of hair from Nic's forehead.

On the other side of the bed, a midwife talked Nic through what was happening. 'Deep breaths in and out. You'll feel the pressure as they help baby come out . . .'

Nic shut her eyes, concentrating on her breathing while Lou tried to calm her own nerves, not daring to think of what she would do if something happened to Nic or her baby. She swallowed hard as the obstetrician explained what he was doing while he cut into her daughter's belly. She wiped the sweat from Nic's forehead.

The minutes crawled by, Lou praying there would be no complications, forcing herself to remain calm so that she could help Nic to relax. 'Shhh. Everything's going to be fine,' she whispered, stroking her cheek.

Nic's eyelids fluttered, her face pale.

'You might feel a bit more tugging in your tummy.' Beyond the screen, the obstetrician was bent over the bed with his colleagues. 'Come on, little one. Come and meet your mum. A little more manoeuvring . . .'

The wait seemed an eternity.

Then: 'There you go, a baby girl.'

Nic's eyes flew open.

'Congratulations.' The words were immediately followed by the unmistakable sound of a baby's first cry: lusty and insistent, outraged at being dragged from her comfortable home.

Lou felt an overwhelming rush of relief and excitement, comparable only to her feelings at the birth of her own children.

Nic smiled. 'Thank God. No football then.'

Lou couldn't help but laugh, so relieved that everything was going to be all right. A tear ran down her cheek.

Within moments, the baby was weighed, wrapped up and placed in Lou's arms. Mother and daughter looked in wonder at this bloodied scrap of humanity. Lou felt her eyes brim as she held her granddaughter towards Nic. Her first grandchild. The expression on Nic's face was beatific. Lou couldn't remember ever having seen her look so radiant.

'Hallo, you,' she said and kissed her baby. 'Oh, Mum, she's beautiful.'

A little later, Nic had been stitched and given a side room off the post-natal ward. Lou sat by her bed still enjoying the extraordinary post-birth delirium, far too excited to feel tired. There was a tap at the door and a bouquet of flowers was carried into the room, hiding the bearer. They were moved to one side to reveal an anxious Hooker. Lou saw how nervous he was about

Nic's reaction to him being there and hoped her daughter would be generous. She looked at her.

'I called him,' she explained. 'I had to. He should be here too.'

For a moment, she thought the blinds were going to come down, shutting Hooker out. She stared at her odd shoes, tensed, waiting for him to be dismissed.

But when it came, Nic's voice was pleased. 'Dad! I'm so glad you've come.'

'Are you OK?' He moved towards her.

'Bit sore but fine really. Mum was with me all the way.' She exchanged a smile with Lou.

'Where's the baby?' Hooker looked around the room in alarm.

'She's in the baby unit being monitored. But it's all routine. She's a bit underweight but she's breathing on her own and they say she's going to be fine.'

'We've got a granddaughter, Hooker,' Lou said. 'Violet,' added Nic proudly.

'Violet.' For a moment, Lou thought he was going to object to the name. But then his face filled with pleasure and pride. 'My little girl. I can't believe it.' He sat on the other side of the bed from Lou, leaning forward to kiss Nic's forehead. She clasped his hand.

'I'll see if I can scout out a vase or three for those flowers.' Lou exited the room, leaving Hooker and Nic to talk alone. Perhaps Violet's birth would be enough to make them build the necessary bridges. As she turned towards the nurses' station, a familiar-looking young man in a white T-shirt, black jeans and jacket walked past her, his concentration miles away. She looked back at the spiderlike figure making off down the corridor.

'Max?' Had she made a mistake? She'd only met him a couple of times in the last year, before she left Hooker, but remembered his look.

He turned back, peering through his dark-framed glasses, obviously without a clue who she was.

'Nic's mum,' she added by way of explanation.

His features cleared. 'I'm sorry, of course. I was too busy thinking about Nic. I phoned. They told me she'd had the baby.'

Poor thing. He sounded terrified. 'She's had a little girl.'

'A baby girl?' His face lit up.

He seemed only a boy himself. The same age as Nic. To Lou, they were both so young to be taking on the mantle of parenthood. Even though she hadn't been much older herself when Jamie was born. Perhaps she shouldn't really be surprised that he'd opted to duck out of any responsibility. But to have him turn up here unannounced was not at all what she'd expected.

'Yes, her father's with her now.'

'Oh?' He looked uncertain, scratching the side of his nose. 'She's forgiven him then?'

So they'd talked about what had happened, about Nic's refusal to speak to Hooker. Knowing Max knew about the family's business made Lou faintly uncomfortable. He was obviously much closer to Nic than she had realised.

'I'd give them a couple of minutes. I think there are a few things they need to say to each other. Perhaps I could take you to see the baby first — your daughter?' Surely Max wouldn't refuse her? And once he'd seen Violet, he'd want to be involved.

He hesitated. Then at a gesture of encouragement from her, he walked beside her along the corridor.

When they returned to Nic's room, armed with three vases, Max's demeanour had changed. Instead of the uncertain, scared-looking individual Lou had met half an hour earlier, he seemed to have grown in confidence. She had watched him as he let his daughter wrap her tiny fingers round one of his and refuse to let go. She could almost see him melt as he gazed at Violet's perfect features, her tiny fingernails and smooth little feet.

Lou put her head around the door, praying that things between Hooker and Nic would still be, at the very least, cordial. In fact, he was sitting with his head thrown back, laughing, while Nic tried to keep a straight face. 'Dad, don't make me laugh, please. My stitches . . .' She looked up as the door opened. 'Mum, where have you been?'

'I thought you two could do with some time together so I went to check on Violet. I met someone else on the way.'

Nic looked puzzled. 'Who? No one else knows we're here except . . .' Her eyes widened in disbelief, then pleasure, as Lou stood aside to let Max into the room. Her hand flew to her hair. 'Oh, God, I look awful. Mum, could you pass me the comb?'

But Max was quite unperturbed. He didn't gasp with horror at the sight of his unmade-up girlfriend in her non-designer hospital gown. Instead, he went to the other side of the bed from Hooker, leaned over and kissed her. 'I don't care what you look like. I've seen the baby, Nic. She's amazing.'

Hooker was staring at him as if he'd just

landed from outer space, and then at Nic who was gazing back at her boyfriend.

Lou beckoned to her ex. 'We'll leave you for a bit. I need to go home and catch up with what's been happening in the shop. But I'll be back tomorrow with some bits and pieces for you, Nic. Come on, Hooker.'

Looking as if his nose had been slightly put out of joint by this second reunion that promised considerably more than anything he could offer his daughter, Hooker joined Lou at the door.

When they reached the main exit of the hospital, he tried to take Lou's arm but she gently removed his hand. 'Shouldn't we celebrate?' he asked.

'I'm afraid I can't, Hooker. Business awaits.' Despite his evident disappointment, Lou took out her mobile and was checking her missed calls when it rang. Shrugging an apology, she answered the phone. It was Sanjeev.

'Sanjeev, you're here. That's fantastic. Nic's just had her baby, a little girl called Violet. I know, sweet, isn't it. Friday? Yes, of course. Yes. I'll be there. See you then.'

Hooker was looking almost bereft. 'Not even a small celebratory something?' he urged, hope lifting his voice. 'If not now, tomorrow.'

'I'm sorry, Hooker. But you should celebrate with the boys. I'll see you soon, I'm sure.' She turned and headed for the car park.

But where was her car? In her haste that morning, she hadn't registered where exactly she'd left it. She would have liked a more stylish exit but instead she was forced to walk up and down the rows, hunting, with Hooker keeping a couple of footsteps behind her.

Just as she spotted the car, he spoke. 'But Lou, I need you. I'm lost without you. Nothing's the same if you're not there to come home to.'

She aimed the key so the car flashed its lights in welcome, then turned to him. 'I'm sorry, Hooker, I know it must be hard to get used to, but you've really got to find your own way now.'

Squeezing herself between her car and its neighbour, she opened the door the little she could and manoeuvred herself clumsily into the driving seat. Unhooking her jacket from where it caught on the lock and thanking God that the engine started without a hitch, she inched out of the narrow parking space. Giving Hooker a little wave that he responded to with a rueful smile and a raise of his hand, she followed the signs to the exit. Glancing briefly into her rear-view mirror, she saw him standing where she'd left him, arms by his sides, staring after her. As the car in front of her moved forward, Lou returned her attention to the road ahead and began her drive home.

ACKNOWLEDGEMENTS

Many thanks are due to Clare Alexander, agent and friend, who I couldn't do without; to my publisher Patrick Janson-Smith, my editor Laura Deacon and my copy-editor Mary Chamberlain. A special thank-you to Liz Dawson and the crack HarperCollins publicity, marketing and sales teams. I'm indebted too to goldsmith Esther Eyre and vintage clothes expert Caroline Turner of Frillseekers Vintage who both took me behind the scenes of their businesses (any mistakes are mine). I must also thank all my friends who have helped me in different ways, in particular Richard Barber, Lizy Buchan, Lisa Comfort, Emma Draude, Angela Kennedy, Sally O'Sullivan, Julie Sharman, Fleur Smithwick Louise Tucker . . . and my sister, Sarah.

ABOUT THE AUTHOR

Fanny Blake was a publisher for many years, editing both fiction and nonfiction before becoming a freelance journalist and writer. She is the author of *What Women Want*. She lives in London.

The employees of Thorndike Press hope you have enjoyed this Large Print book. All our Thorndike, Wheeler, and Kennebec Large Print titles are designed for easy reading, and all our books are made to last. Other Thorndike Press Large Print books are available at your library, through selected bookstores, or directly from us.

For information about titles, please call:
  (800) 223-1244

or visit our Web site at:
  http://gale.cengage.com/thorndike

To share your comments, please write:
Publisher
Thorndike Press
10 Water St., Suite 310
Waterville, ME 04901